Open To C

Mexic

Johnny Proctor

A Paninaro Imprint

www.paninaropublishing.co.uk
info@paninaropublishing.co.uk

Contact - info@paninaropublishing.co.uk

A catalogue record for this book :
Library.

ISBN - 13: 978-1-0683859-0-2

CW01465588

Socials;

Twitter @johnnyroc73

Instagram @johnnyproctor90

Blue Sky @johnnyproctor

Acknowledgments

Thank you to Graham Cawsey, a man forever on hand to give the once over to your finished masterpiece. Respect, amigo.

To Toby Muse - author of the phenomenal 'Kilo' and, in my opinion, the best piece of literature written on the cocaine industry - for being good enough to help me out when it came to providing me with some inside information on the subject of 'combo culture,' inside the barrios of the cities of Colombia.

Also to my undoubted better half Rachel for possessing the abilities to put up with living with someone who decides that they're going to bring Zico back but to mark the occasion instead of writing one novel, they'd write *three*. Thanks to her, despite this ambitious project in bringing the character, who I launched my writing career with, back for the first time. I've still found the time to see what's going on away from the screen and keyboard in real life.

And finally, with this novel feeling almost like a case of me coming full circle with the return of the main man in my debut, I'd like to reiterate my unwavering thanks to everyone who have been on this journey over the past seven years as much as I have for those who are currently dipping their toes in all of these years later through word of mouth. Without the knowledge that you're out there reading my work I would *never* have been still here by book - checks notes - eleven.

All love x

Dedicated to

Mum.

Who knew that as a result of my childhood some of that Spanish would come in handy years down the line?!

Love you always, JP xx

Chapter 1

Myles Lomas

No, not now. Why now? My initial reaction on seeing the name *Daniel Garnier-Colston* showing up on my phone. This had not been the first time inside the past twenty four hours that this name had flashed up on my screen through phone calls, text message, email *and* WhatsApp. Far from it. Each time I had seen it - in whichever form he was contacting me - I'd decided against answering or offering a written response but knew that, regardless of my own personal disposition, the longer I delayed in offering him some confirmation pointing to proof of life, the *more* he would end up severely pissed off with me. And whatever your job, if you can go about your business without ending up with your manager on your case - *especially* when your 'case' is in the most fragile of conditions, ironically due to your line of work - then it is a road that you should always look to be travelling down.

'Myles, where the bloody hell have you been?'

Daniel exploded in that way someone tends to do after making multiple phone calls to someone without even one hint of a reply or acknowledgment from the other person.

'Danny Boy,'

I said, digging deep and finding a bit of life about me after the truly woeful 'hello' that I had - reluctantly - answered the call with. Already knowing that having ignored all of his previous attempts to reach out to me, he was now going to pull me up about it.

'I'll Danny Boy you. I've been trying to get hold of you since yesterday. Where the fuck have you been?'

Like I alluded to. It wasn't a phone call I had wanted to take. Not then, with the state of mind I was currently dealing with. Should've taken his call the previous day but didn't think it wise to be speaking to el gaffer when I was two hours into the mystery 'LSD drink' that I had gubbed while sitting on a Indian beach, talking to a Swedish couple - from Malmo - as part of my job. There, reporting on a yearly summer festival that had began to gain some prominence on the South West Indian coast amongst backpackers and general party people.

Years ago, I'd have just answered the call. No doubt telling my man in charge about how I was concerned about the alien mothership that had been hovering above the festival site for the past few hours and how if I didn't report back in twenty four hours to consider me missing, and most likely anally probed. But that was a years ago Myles Lomas. And it was *because* of me and years ago that I could no longer answer phone calls during these more delicate moments. Despite having been reporting on the industry for more than two decades, it had been difficult to shake off the reputation of what I had been like while getting a free pass to any club or event that I was asked to cover, and how I had 'embraced' such privileges in life. You get older and wiser, though.

You don't stop embracing the privileges of being a House Music/clubland journalist. You just stop *broadcasting* to those - who you don't wish to know - that you're embracing it every bit as you always did. Which, obviously, means avoiding talking to people of importance - career wise - during those messiest of moments when you're on the other side of the world in the pursuit of those four thousand words to send back to London.

'I'm in Goa, India. Am I tripping here or didn't you specifically sign off on me going?'

I laughed, trying to take the sting out of things while not being able to resist from inserting a little inside joke. One that Daniel was not in on.

'Yes, Myles. I'm perfectly aware that you're in Goa. Believe me, I was fifty fifty about even *sending* you there, especially after your recent trip to Thailand and that whole sorry business involving the U.K consulate but, for your *many* sins you're still my best journalist.'

I was sat there glowing at the high praise from our editor, especially since he wasn't one for such sweeping examples of accolades. Not that this lasted long, you understand.

'But that's not the point. If I call you, email you, text you, fucking pigeon and smoke signal you, *multiple* times. You should know that it's not because I'm bored and could do with talking to someone. **SO, and I repeat, WHERE THE FUCK HAVE YOU BEEN?'**

You know? I was starting to think that the whole me being his best writer was only to butter me up for the maximum impact of when he completely let rip at me.

Despite the seriousness of having your boss on the warpath and - clearly - in the mood for taking several strips off you, I couldn't help but be distracted by the constant - almost repetitive - thud of something that I was hearing over top of Daniel when he was speaking. I fell silent as much as to listen out for the thud again as it was to buy me time before I could give him a response. Because it went without saying that I could no longer try to explain away simply not answering his calls or returning them. And I *definitely* wasn't going to be telling him the truth.

And there was the thud again, then again.

'What's that noise in the background, Dan? I've heard it a few times now since you called. Maybe a bad line, perhaps? Not like I'm next door, eh?'

'It's a squash ball and don't you try to change the subject'

What do you mean? You tell someone that you're calling to berate them and you're playing squash, and then think that they'll not have thoughts on further questions and to change the subject?

'I'm not trying to change the subject.'

I lied.

'But, where are you right now?'

'I'm in the office. I've had one of its walls swapped with a mini squash front wall since you were last in,'

he said it as if it was the most natural thing in the world even if it was, in reality, quite demented.

Dan could never have known that he was speaking to me - still on the beach after the party, which had ended at nine in the morning with the magical and, admittedly, quite wonderful journey that American Seth Troxler had taken everyone on to close things down with - having not long come down from the colourful, exotic and wonderful cocktail of narcotics that I'd consumed across the night where I had began writing my article - sitting there with the beats still playing to the side of me as the festival entered its final stage - as the sun had begun to come up for the morning. The aforementioned Troxler playing a sunrise set to one side of me while across the beach to my left a siege of herons - looking like they'd been plucked out of some Attenborough documentary - had started to congregate on the beach to soak up the light that was creeping out ahead of them. Feasting on worms from the wet sand they were stood on. The rays of the sun enjoyed by not just the sea birds but also myself and others who had moved from festival stage to beach and everyone still facing the DJ while going for it until the final track had been spun. Ahead of me, with the sun coming up for the day - fuck, that golden glow - over the horizon, the shadowy figures of fishing boats already sailing out for the morning, trying to get ahead of the game before the sun had officially surfaced. The whole scene - from left to right - in no way tracked with each other. The conflation of the sound of the electronic beats from the speakers, the grating noise from the sea birds and the puttering sounds coming from the small boat's engines was the kind of mix that you didn't feel that you'd ever hear - collectively - again in your life. Which made it all the more the beautiful sensory assault that it was to me in that moment.

(Fuck, I do love my job at times)

Whether it came across as natural or someone who was truly twisted after his night out or not, the thought of Daniel running around a small part of his office - as extravagantly large for a semi successful music magazine as it was - playing squash just ended me and, despite being in the middle of an apparent haranguing, just burst out laughing. There really was no need, but Daniel went right on the defensive over this, telling me that squash was one of his passions but due to the hours he - along with the rest of us - had to continually put in on the magazine and website, he virtually lived in the office - or was on the road - at times. So, he thought if he couldn't get to the squash court, he'd bring it to him. Fair play.

It had been enough to buy me enough time to conjure up some kind of lie to explain away me having gone AWOL while out in the field. Patch anyone else when you're out reporting. Other half, kid, mum and dad or mates? Fine. Not the editor, of the music magazine which employs you, though. Not that this had stopped me but now I was going to have to explain it, and diverting the conversation to him and his squash court in the office was never going to be enough to fully do the trick.

Sure enough, he got back on track.

'So, where have you been? Are we back to the old Lomas days again, yeah?'

He asked. Accused, really.

'Not at all, Dan,'

I tried to assure him before launching into the biggest pack of lies I could muster in this moment. The kind of lies that you don't even have pre prepared and just kind of wing it until you're left standing back completely feeling yourself in an approving way, wondering just *where the fuck* you dug them all out from in such a cohesive way and in the short space of time provided to you to put it all together.

'It's been a bit of a nightmare, mate but I guess the only thing that matters is that I got the story. I'll be able to email it over when I can get some Wi-Fi. As I'm sure you'll already know - I was sure that he *wouldn't* have known when saying this - this festival was practically a twenty four hour affair, but it's down by some remote beach, so there's been no Wi-Fi to speak of. I mean, there's stickers around the bar telling you what the Wi-Fi is along with the password but it hasn't worked since I've been here. And, yeah I have to admit in a 'my bad' way here. It probably hasn't helped that, ironically, while also, weirdly, there's been a pretty good 4G reception that hasn't been helped by me dropping my phone into the sea inside the first half hour of me arriving. I've had some hippie bury my phone in a bag of rice for the past eighteen hours and it's only recently started to show signs of recovery with only the smallest of water marks now under the screen, so what's happening? Have I missed something with all of these so called missed calls, that I wouldn't have even *known* I'd missed if you hadn't just told me about them.'

I threw so much at him, without providing any chance of response that it left him not knowing which attitude he should now take with me. No doubt he'd have more than loved to have learned that not only had I been ignoring him while up to my eyeballs in drugs but that I was now entering 'the fear' territory and without having written a single word as part of my assignment. But I was a professional. Professional at not being caught.

If it wasn't for the constant thud of the squash ball there would have been nothing at all coming from Dan's side. With this being the case and me already assured that I'd defused things through the lies told, I pressed on.

'So I have my flight back later tonight. I'll probably be back in the office at some point on Tuesday, give or take jet lag, you know?'

Jet lag, for me, wasn't really a thing. Comedowns, however, almost certainly *were*.

'You know what, Myles. Since I got the top job, there's times where I forget what it can be like, out there reporting on clubs and festivals, thousand of miles away. How unpredictable things can be, and *that* being the beauty of it all. I'm sat here giving you grief because of perceiving you to be ignoring me, even though I'm your boss and the very *last* person to be blanking, while not thinking of your own personal surroundings.'

'Don't worry about it,'

I offered. I was a touch concerned about how quickly he had climbed down, in such a way though. It would've been considered a result to have just taken the sting out of him when he was calling you, intent on giving you his own special eccentric - yet volatile - version of Alex Ferguson's 'hair dryer' treatment. But something close to an *apology*? I'd had to engage in the exercise in biting one's tongue at the pure revisionism - as well as gaslighting - that was coming from him. He's standing there giving mention to the things he'd forgotten about being out in the field when he'd hardly been someone that we'd have looked upon as a hardened warrior from the House Music scene. Still at school - primary? - during the halcyon days of Sunrise, Raindance, Biology and Back to the Future, when House Music had gatecrashed the British Isles and caught the attention of the bored British youth and not someone who had been tasked with making their bones across the U.K as an electronic music journalist while visiting some of the more sketchy venues that were to pop up before either being closed down by law enforcement within weeks or forced to close down through their own self inflicted mis-management.

For some - see Garnier-Colston - all that was required was for 'daddy' to buy a media company and throw him the job of his choice from the various magazines and companies that made up said media company. We *easily* had half a dozen experienced people on the team that could've - and should've - taken up the position of editor when the much loved Tony Bowman had been forced out as part of the company takeover - but when it came down to it. If you want to keep your job, you can't beat nepotism. Not that I'd have ever wanted the job in the chair, anyway. To have taken on that role would have meant an end to my globetrotting days and if you'd asked me to swap them for an almost unbroken five days of being in the office, stuck there in London each week, you'd have been as well asking me for my resignation. But just because I hadn't wanted the position of editor, that didn't mean to say that I had wanted to be taking orders from a nepo appointment in the form of daddy's son. A person who I'd forgotten more about electronic music and its culture than he'd gathered in his time as editor.

As is the way in life, however. Sometimes you just have to play the game, to make life easier for everyone concerned.

Just because you're not a fan of someone there's no point in making life more difficult for you by *informing* them of this. Keep your opinions to yourself while saying the correct things with Garnier-Colston, however, and the trips to places like Goa would continue. Make waves with the so called Kingmaker, though, and you can just as easily find yourself in a stinking and filthy Rotterdam warehouse, surrounded by the chaos of scores of skinheads, out their nuts on speed paste, all pushing each other around a mosh pit to Gabber House instead of sitting on a warm Indian beach, enjoying the tranquility of the sun coming up for the day while casually puffing on an early morning joint and sipping on some kind of an elaborate and exotic alcoholic drink that has been poured into a hollowed out pineapple, as you sit writing your article.

Despite how broken the best part of twenty four hours spent at a festival in India had left me. A veteran of the House music scene from eighty nine right up to present day - two thousand and fourteen - I was someone who had been able to retain the ability to keep my motor skills, no matter how much I had caned it the night and morning before. I was still sharp enough to see that there was clearly something behind all of these attempts from Dan to get in touch with me and how he was now being so understanding to me having went missing in action, and the eyes of suspicion that this would have brought.

'So anyway, Myles. Just you take some time and recover for the next couple of days, there in Goa. The changes to your schedule have already been arranged.'

Red flag. My flight was taking me back in the direction of home that very same night. And my gaffer is telling me to what? Just kick back and enjoy recovering from what was, admittedly, a bit of an extended session when it came to covering a story.

'But I'm heading back home tonight, am I not? I need to be out of the hotel by eleven.'

All I could say, even though I knew that certain decisions affecting me had, apparently, already been made. Ones that I could already see that would involve myself, even if it had been felt that I hadn't been required in them being taken.

I was looking forward to getting home to see my girlfriend and kid. It's not all gardens of roses, reporting events that are mainly talking place at some point over a weekend, if not the *whole* of it. Because with that you then automatically miss out on time with your kid, doing the stuff that you want to be doing as a dad. Making memories, bonding in ways with your kid that will come back in spades when they're older. All of that stuff. After a weekend away in India, the *only* thing I would want to do would be the simple things like walking my son to school, taking him to the park to kick a ball around and to visit some rank fast food place of his choosing for tea, generally whoever is offering the most attractive toy to go with the food.

'Well, yeah, Myles. That was the *original* plan. But here's the thing, we've had an opportunity open up for us. It's big and it's a world exclusive for us, if we have someone up to the task. And you already know that you're my guy for the top tier of assignments and, trust me, this is the kind of top tier that no one in electronic music media has ever been handed. And I'm giving it to *you* to cover.'

Ok, *now* he had my attention. Even the squash ball had stopped battering off one side of his office. I thought of who had won? Daniel or the wall, but kept that one to myself.

He'd said that is was big and without telling me any details I could already see that it must've been something to get excited about purely on the basis that he was fronting me some time off - paid with expenses - from work until the next assignment began. Because this was not normal behaviour from Garnier-Colston by any means. Us - the journalists and photographers from the magazine and website - would be more likely to be on the rough end of the stick when it came to flights and accommodation, when it came to covering an event with the intention of writing about it. Flights with about four connections instead of paying a few extra hundred pounds for a direct one and the standard of hotels that we'd find ourselves staying in while, ironically, covering deejays who were found in five star accommodation, sometimes yards from our own hotels. That one time where I was only travelling to Milan for the opening of a new super club and yet found myself having to fly from Stansted to Dublin then Dublin to Brussels before actually setting foot on a plane headed to Italy. And even then it was to the further out - from the city centre - airport of Milan Bergamo instead of the much more central Malpensa.

'So what do you have for me then? Jane's expecting me back tomorrow morning so if I'm now *not* heading back she's going to be the first person I'm going to have to call after this.'

Without even knowing what Daniel had in mind for me I was already not exactly looking forward to breaking the news to my better half that I was now no longer heading back to her and little Jackson. My occupation hadn't ever been a problem to Jane - when we'd first met - as she had literally met me *at* a rave and, as a result of how she'd liked spending her time recreationally, she'd had no issues at all with me working at the weekends both domestically and abroad. Not when she would just travel with me and enjoy all of the trappings that an accredited journalist would have open to them by the event organisers who would wisely look to 'take care' of a visitor like myself in the hope that it would help when it came to how I would portray their club or event in print. When Jackson came along, however, her chances to travel the world with me were then drastically reduced, as was her understanding when it came to having to hold things down at home all on her own.

'Well, Myles. What would you say if I was to tell you that we, at One's and Two's Magazine, have been granted fly on the wall access to, drum rollllllll, DJ Selecao's tour of Mexico and South America?'

You could tell how pleased Daniel was about this. I mean, I couldn't see him as he'd said this but I could still see the massive smile on his face nonetheless.

DJ Selecao, I was aware of. There was barely a DJ on the circuit that I *wasn't*. It *was* my job after all. I had been up for almost two full days, though, and in this time had plied myself with numerous drugs and kinds of alcohol so maybe I wasn't as sharp as I could have been. Had I been so, I would not have required Daniel to explain to me just *why* this was a big deal. I was thankful for him doing so, however, as all I had been able to absorb had been the words 'Mexico and South American tour' which I had not been ready for, not when prior to the phone call I'd just about managed to accept that I was going to have to travel thousands of miles before I could get myself home and finally recover. Instead, I was now seeing that this was going to be a potential couple of weeks - plus - before I could return back to London, and what kind of a state would I have been in by this time? And on the surface of it. I'd have much rather have avoided this extended stay away from home and - as added context - would have *gladly* attended a four day Gabber festival in The Netherlands than spend a couple of weeks travelling across Latin America.

Sensing how underwhelmed, - more from what I was wasn't saying than what I had - Garnier-Colston offered me some reminders over just how much of a coup this was for the magazine.

'Now I'm not going to insult your intelligence by asking if you know who Selecao is,'

he said before - feeling like I needed to prove myself - I let him know that I most certainly *did*.

'Scottish but based in Amsterdam, a Grammy nominated DJ and producer who's been on the circuit since the early Nineties. An Ibiza veteran with various residencies and who has played at most of the big clubs in Europe. If I didn't know who he was I wouldn't even deserve to work for you, Dan.'

I butted in before leaving it at that, feeling that I'd told him enough when it came to a general description of the artist that it was appearing that I would be covering on the road. If he'd wanted me to expand, then I would've been happy to do so. Daniel, though, offered some expansion of his own.

'Yes, Stevie Duncan, as his non performing name goes, is all of the above. But that's not why I'm asking you to spend a couple of weeks following him on tour. It's because of the *baggage* that comes with him that I want you there. Were it just left at his deejaying and production skills alongside his CV of clubs that he's played over the past twenty years then he'd been looked upon as one of the respected set of players in the game. Someone who has kept the head down, learned his craft and reached the higher echelons of the House Music industry. But we both know that no matter what he does, he will never shake off the *additional* baggage of what can often happen to him when he's *away* from the decks. And that's before we even get to the chequered history of his father. Yes, many know DJ Selecao in relation to him as a performer but there are just as many who know him because of the well published story of him being the son of a narco for a South American cartel. Over the years the guy has tended to be box office, without even trying. And *you* have just been granted bloody AAA - Access All Areas - to the man.'

The penny started to drop for me. I had initially taken things too literally and had seen the assignment as simply following a DJ around on tour while writing up each city and venue visited on from tour date to tour date. In reality, with the colourful character who at times in his career had seemed like a magnet to chaos I'd be shadowing, there would be a high chance that half to most of what I would end up writing in the field would be well away from the DJ booth or the venue.

'Tour consists of dates in Mexico, Colombia, Argentina, Peru and finishing in Brazil.'

He continued, pretty much spelling out a dream assignment for me, had I not been awake for two days and was now in a heightened state of confusion and requiring several days in bed to recover.

'Given the guy's history when it comes to South America I would be astonished if this tour doesn't pass without some form of incident taking place and when it does you're going to be there to capture it. I'm thinking that we'll have you do a brief update on what's going on in each country for the website and our socials and then once the tour is over you can write up a big summary for next month's print run.'

Daniel had, apparently, worked it all out. This included the photographer that he was going to have accompany me to capture things for posterity. Luke Clifton. I winced when Daniel said his name as while we had previously worked together both abroad and domestically and him being a decent guy, god was he a liability. I think part of this came from him being strictly freelance so was not bound by any fears of upsetting any 'bosses' in the way that us salaried journalists and photographers were.

I'd managed to go a few years without working with him so this would mark a return of the band getting back together again. The previous time had been the pair of us off to Berlin to cover a secretive club that did not quite care - or *need* to - for music journalists there to promote their club. This was proven when it actually took the pair of us three attempts across forty eight hours - of the club which simply did not close from Friday night to Monday morning - before we were even let in by the bouncers. By the third attempt we'd already learned that Luke was wasting his time by bringing his camera with him as that alone was one of the reasons we'd been refused entry previously. This, though, did not stop him from going while I - mentally - took in enough over the night and morning to come up with something in the way of words. This *also* did not stop him from consuming so much ketamine over the night that by morning had slumped into the most brutal of k- holes where he could not see and required babysitting by myself until leaving to go back to the hotel around ten in the morning.

'So, Luke will be meeting you in Guadalajara for the start of the tour but meanwhile just chill there in Goa for a few days until heading to Mexico. If this trip goes anywhere near I believe it will, you're going to need a few days of rest,'

he laughed while leaving me questioning what kind of antics he was imagining up that he was hoping to see being broken by One's and Two's Magazine. Telling me that I'd already been emailed my new itinerary - along with the contact details of Lee Isaac, Selecao's agent slash manager and the man who had green lit me for tagging along on the tour, - to enjoy the rest of my time in India and for me to check in with him once I got to Guadalajara, he was saying his goodbyes and hanging up again, leaving me trying to get my head around this more than slight adjustment to my plans.

Having his editor's hat on? Yeah, I couldn't really blame Daniel for snatching at the chance to have one of his journalist's following a - colourful caning party animal of a character - DJ around South America, a DJ who - in the past - had been jokingly referred to as a 'junior narco' due to his father's well publicised links to the region. The raw components of someone with a history as DJ Selecao visiting *that* part of the world would surely produce some 'tea' for the public to consume but as far as my part was concerned. It all felt a little tabloidy and not the kind of writing assignment that I'd ever went on before, despite my many years in the industry.

Sitting there on the beach - no longer in a position where I felt like I'd need to get myself going to pack and be ready for vacating the hotel that I now no longer needed to - I managed to find some solace in the knowledge that, unlike the very worst of the journalists who write for red tops, I would, at least, be writing what I saw and not trying to instigate matters, to give me the story to write about. Now recalling all of the mini pieces of data involving DJ Selecao from over the years that I had stored away, I was quite comfortable with the fact that with Stevie Duncan, *no one* needed to instigate anything and that he was quite capable of finding things for me to write about all on his own.

What I didn't, couldn't have known as I sat there on the - now - sun drenched beach with numerous 'casualties' lying around post rave was that while I had absolutely zero desire to - or the requirement - create a narrative that could then be exploited by me as a journalist. This, though, would not be enough to stop myself and Luke Clifton from - through our own idiotic actions - *creating* a story that would place a dark cloud over the DJ Selecao open to close tour of Mexico and South America.

For once, at least, the Scottish DJ would be entirely innocent in proceedings and left with no fault on his part. Unfortunately for him, this would matter not a jot with regards to how his life would be placed in danger, by proxy. The *exact* kind of danger that the two out of their depth music journalist and photographer from the United Kingdom in myself and Clifton would, indeed, find themselves in.

Unlike the Scottish DJ, however. At least us two - and without coming across as self preserving, *specifically* Luke Clifton - had done something to actually *deserve* to be left fearing for our lives.

Chapter 2

Zico

I genuinely don't even know why I bother flying Business Class, like? What really is the point when you bang a couple of valium down you, a few glasses of wine in the airport and then two more to follow, once you're on the plane, and then it's goodnight Wien. Normally I only wake because of the massive fucking bump you experience when the plane touches the tarmac. Proper gives you a fright, that. For a wee second you don't even know you're *on* a plane for one thing and then your next thought is that the fucking thing has *crashed*. This, then followed up by the realisation that, instead, you've touched down safely and that, *once again*, you've missed the majority of the flight, and paid a stupid amount for the privilege.

Just like that afternoon, touching down in Newark, Noo Joysie.

It's not like I'm scared of flying as such so don't be going classing me as equivalent to the boy Dennis Bergkamp. I was on a flight from Amsterdam to the east coast of America, that boy would be on a fucking *fishing trawler* for that journey! It's more a case of me really not being remotely arsed about travelling, so try to just blank as much out of it as I possibly can. And for all of its faults, Diazepam *will* blank things out.

On the American side of things I was soon regretting the mix of sleeping pills and chilled Sauvignon Blanc, once the exchange with the TSA agent at passport control had started to go a little sideways. Maybe it was *because* of the potion I'd concocted to eat into the eight hour flight over from Amsterdam that had caused the whole unfortunate chain of events? I don't know but what should have been nothing other than a procedural entry into the United States from a European who was only *in* the country due to connecting to another flight to Guadalajara from inside the same terminal, ended up being anything but.

I'd travelled alone, with Flo - not so - politely passing on the opportunity to see five countries inside just over a couple of weeks. Over the years she'd not been shy when it came to travelling the world with me - when on business - but this had always been done on a trip by trip basis. Aye, we had her part time work with the homeless charity she had helped form back in the Dutch capital but it was the kind of gig that allowed her a bit of freedom and room for manoeuvre, when it came to organising her private life. I always preferred it when she came with me. Helped keep me out of trouble for one thing and I don't mean that from a riding point of view with groupies and that, either. Almost touching twenty years together and still the love of my life and woman of my dreams and I'd always assumed that if you could go that length of time and still feel the same way about your other half then I couldn't have seen it ever changing. Nah, there was no issues on that score but just having her around - to be the voice of reason when I needed to hear it from someone that I was actually willing to listen to - would always tend to keep me on the straight and narrow and help keep the radgeness at arms length when it was ready to surface.

This time, however? I was going to have to go it alone. Flo not exactly sitting on the fence about going or not going when she heard that Colombia was marked down for two dates of the tour - Medellin and Bogota - when telling me.

'There's as much chance of you catching me in Colombia as there is all the jungle cocaine labs being turned into kids' soft play areas by the FARC paramilitaries.'

It had been as far back as ninety six - on the island of Ibiza - when Flo had suffered from the harrowing, and apparently never ending PTSD supplying, treatment from those Bogota cartel sicarios but even then, years later, in twenty fourteen she was still suffering from the emotional and mental scars over it. I wasn't surprised to see her knock back the chance to come away with me for a couple of weeks but I had to at least ask the question. When the tour was in the process of being arranged by Lee she had already pretty much told me that she wouldn't be coming - but that had been in the way where someone hasn't even been *invited* to something, and was just giving their opinion in advance - while also raising a few concerns with me over whether it would be completely safe for *me* to be cutting around that neck of the woods, given my own links to the country.

It hadn't been my first time playing in that part of the world though and I had enjoyed playing some dates there as the warm up for the American - now - superstar DJ, Citizen Caner. The previous time had passed off without any kind of grave incidents, cartel related or otherwise. Obviously, it would be preposterous to think that you could tour some of the more exciting and edgy cities in South America *without* them passing without any kind of incident or, more realistic, incidents, plural.

But there hadn't been anything serious or cartel related in the way which Flo was concerned about. Caner had been an absolute diamond of a boy, if a little bit on the unhinged side of things. He'd made me think of those American college boys and girls who just want to party all the time while screaming 'SPRRRING BRRRREAKKK' into every cunt's ears. The boy was on a right riding fest on every date of the tour while taking advantage of the fact that on the occasions where he even needed to pay for his own gear, we were talking about a fucking blue spot for a gram of sniff.

Five British pounds for a packet of the most pure ching you'll ever find and the kind of purity that when you *did* find, it wouldn't be inside the British fucking Isles, that was for fucking sure.

After being in the game for so long it had felt a wee bit strange me being a simple warm up act and for someone who had only really been on the scene for a couple of years but had enjoyed an almost overnight success with his debut song 'To The Moon' - when still unsigned - which had led to a bidding war from all of the majors and since that moment he'd been on a stratospheric trajectory, career wise. Lee had advised me that the one mini tour opening for Caner would open me up to a whole new world of fans. Both through the American market and the *Latin* America one.

My agent wasn't far wrong with this estimation as by the end of the tour my followers count on my socials had increased by thousands while Lee was starting to see the knock on effect of my dates alongside Caner in the form of enquiries for booking me to appear in American clubs and festivals at a later date. And it would also not exactly be classed as a stretch to suggest that had it not been for Citizen Caner - and the tour I supported him on - there would have been no stand alone Mexico and South America tour, that I was now standing in a New Jersey airport waiting to connect flights to, taking me back out of the United States again after a 'planned' two hour stay.

But to land up in Mexico - ahead of my first tour date in Guadalajara - I, first of all, needed to *leave* America. Which was to prove not an easy thing to do. Not when I didn't' exactly find it a breeze in fucking *entering* the country to kick things off. Which, in itself, made no sense to me on what was a mere procedure and something that I had done more times in my career than I could have even barely remembered.

Newark passport control was as rammed as always. An airport where I have never seen a swift arrival, show of your passport and off you go. There's always that snaking queue for as far as the eye can see which feels like fucking thirty planes have all arrived at once, with all the passengers thrown together. Aye, there's the entrance for American passport holders which would, you'd assume, help speed things up but not when there's about one percent of travellers who actually fucking go *through* the thing.

Stuck in the long queue which was snaking up and down, up and down, and taking up most of the space in the large arrivals hall, I tried to have a check of my emails, WhatsApp messages and my social media notifications and lasted all of two minutes before being informed by a jobsworth TSA agent that mobile phone use - he said 'cell' - was not permitted in the passport control hall. Pointing to one of the pillars behind me where, underneath a TV screen that was playing live coverage of CNN with the sound down, there was a list of do's and don'ts on a sign fixed to the pillar for my assistance. Actually, come to think of it. It was pretty much a list of what you *weren't* allowed to do, as opposed to what you could do.

Letting him know that I was just checking my emails did not cut any ice with the boy and I knew that to push things any further would in all probability see me risking having my phone taken off me. You never know with the Shermans, like. They're an extreme type of people and, as a consequence, prone to extreme behaviour to match. The kind of cunts that wouldn't bat an eyelid if you strolled down the street with an M16 around your shoulder but would send a SWAT team to execute you if you played a game of Tiger Woods on your iPhone in a restricted area or hit you with a felony charge if you had a quick reek while standing in a no smoking area.

He'd interrupted me right when I was in the middle of reading a disturbing email from Lee where - and I never got a chance to reach the middle of the email, never mind the end - it looked like he was telling me that he had granted access to a couple of people from a music magazine - one which I'd read on occasion so was at least familiar with, even if this did not in any way leave me thrilled over the arrangements that had been made - and how they'd be meeting up with us all in Guadalajara. I wasn't much chuffed about what it was looking like but agreed to not let my imagination run away with itself while I wasn't in a position to read the rest of the email and then have the inevitable phone call with Lee, moments after reaching the end of the email.

Even before having any phone call with him I already knew what he'd have said.

'*Good for business, Stevie. You can't buy that kind of exposure, Geezer. Better to be talked about than not talked about at all. And so on and so on.*'

Maybe all of this was so but that did not take away the fact that I was heading off on a three week tour of some of the most exciting cities in the world, and I intended to enjoy myself as much as I could. Because you've got to love what you do, don't you? And that would have been a *lot* more difficult when you've got snooping journalist's hanging around you taking notes.

I put the phone away back into my jacket pocket and just stood there praying for the line to start moving a bit faster than it had been up until then. Because of the wine and the Diazepam, standing up was a bit of an issue. Well, standing straight, to be exact. At times I was swaying like one of those inflatable boxing training aids that everyone used to get as kids. The ones where you gave it a bit of a dig and it went flying backwards before coming back up and towards you again. What I'd have given for a seat, even though in a situation like waiting to go through passport control the very last thing that you want to be doing is to stick out as *different* to any of the agents who may be giving you the once over, ahead of you entering their country.

When it came to 'looking different' though, I had some *competition* stood directly behind me who would've ensured that I'd have had to seriously go some distance before I stuck out to the authorities next to them.

I'd actually heard them arguing first of all before I turned round to fully notice the two of them.

'I can't believe you'd do that to me, Gregg. Actually, *who* does that to anyone, never mind their fiancé?'

'Awww, come on, babe. Do you not think that you're overreacting a little, here?'

Their decibel levels were pretty high, for the environment that they were in, but the girl wasn't too concerned about any of this due to how raging she was with her man by the sounds of her. When I turned around to have a look - without trying to make it obvious I was looking at the arguing couple while in reality was unable to do anything *other* than make it obvious I'd turned around to look at them - *nothing* could have prepared me for the two of them, visually speaking, like.

Each half of the couple were out and out goths. Which took me a bit by surprise. Hey, live and let live is my motto and you'll meet a *lot* more weird or dangerous people in life than a goth but, I don't know? Seeing the pair of them going at it with each other - which from what I could pick up from the two of them, this was all in relation to the relatively minor matter of the man having eaten his other half's bread roll during the in-flight meal - I was left with the realisation that despite the hundreds - thousands? - of times I had flown across Europe or beyond. I had *never* seen a single goth on a plane or even in an airport, until there in Newark. It was something that I had never considered in my life before but, now that I was, I couldn't fucking *stop* thinking of. Have *you* ever seen a goth, when on your holidays? Case closed. Imagine one with a fucking *tan*? That would just be plain weird, like.

The girl - who I couldn't help but judge over if that was how she reacted over some cunt eating her roll then what would she have been like if you'd shagged her mate or smoked her last gram of green - had her hair gelled and shaped into sharp points that would've had a good chance of taking an eye out if she caught you at the wrong angle. Coupon decked out in ghostly white make up like it was Halloween and with jet black lipstick and eyeshadow to offset the whiteness. A spiked collar round her neck that wouldn't have looked out of place around a Rotty. Pair of ripped fishnet tights that looked like she'd been assaulted by someone during the flight and a pair of big chunky black shoes that you wouldn't have wished on your own worst enemy to receive a boot in the balls from while her man was looking like he'd come straight from the set of The fucking Matrix. Dark sunglasses wrapped around him. Multiple skull rings - with sparkly jewelled eyes - on his fingers. Tattoo across the front of his neck that looked like some kind of occult symbol. Leather jacket that stopped around a couple of centimetres from the floor, partially hiding the massive boots that seemed to hold about twenty buckles and - unnecessary - zips on each side. Pair of black baggy jeans that looked so oversized I reckoned that there must've been approximately twenty wrinkles between the bottom of his knee and the sole of his boots.

'Well, this is a great start to the trip, eh?'

The boy said but appeared to be saying it for the benefit of those watching on than for any kind of a response from his girl, whose face was absolutely tripping her and had now fallen silent, possibly realising that she'd maybe went a bit far, especially in public.

The jobsworth who had got me told over the phone had been loitering about and I'd expected them to have got involved and told the couple that there was no shouting in the passport control hall but they'd stopped short of getting in between the pair of them. Which I couldn't have blamed them, to be fair. Normally I wouldn't have been against passing a wee bit of judgment with the both of them. Maybe a wee joke to try and lift the mood. Possibly a wideo comment to inflame things even more but, being honest, the girl scared me a wee bit and when some cunt is losing their minds over something as innocuous as a complimentary bread roll then you're best not getting yourself involved as things could tend to be a wee bit on the unpredictable and irrational side.

I thought it wise to just keep my head down and, if anything, enjoy the fact that I was right beside the kind of passengers who would stick out like a sore thumb to the agents of the Customs & Border Patrol and, in doing so, help smooth my passageway into the United States because with the combo of how the wine and vallies had hit me, I was looking for a straightforward and hassle free entry to the US of A.

Well, that was the plan, anyway.

The moment I saw the look on the face of 'Agent Vieira' of the US Customs and Borders Protection Agency, I knew this wasn't going to be the most standard of entries into the United States through Newark airport. Being a frequent flyer to the States, I'd experienced the post 9/11 'joys' of passing through Newark passport control - where they *always* came across as cunts acting like they were trying to close the stable door while the horse was galloping over the horizon - numerous times before, but the whole vibe this time around struck me instantly as different. I'm not saying that any of the previous times I'd ever been showered with a twenty one gun salute ticker tape style reception. Fuck, even a smile & welcome to the USA had always seemed beyond the call of duty for most of the previous agents processing my entry but this time around my spidey sense picked up on the feeling that *this* particular agent had a problem with me even before I'd opened my mouth.

For those who haven't entered the United States via Newark airport before I can sum it up as best as I can by saying that you're made to feel as welcome as NWA turning up as the after dinner entertainment at a Klan convention. No mobile phones, no cameras, no electronics, full stop. The no 'cell phone' rule already brought to my attention by that surly officer who, for my heinous crime of checking my emails, had me fearing that my connecting flight to Guadalajara was going to be making a detour via Guantanamo Bay on my account.

This is all fairly standard stuff in terms of your first moments setting foot in New Jersey from the moment you get off the plane until you pass through immigration after answering a few set questions, providing your fingerprints and posing for a mugshot but - in my experience anyway - what *isn't* standard is finding yourself being grilled for half an hour, asked every question under the sun stopping short at what my inside leg size is then carted off to a side office to be detained beside what seems like an all-star team of apparent Al Qaeda prospects. And once detained there, having a *second* interview - one that while much more detailed *also* wastes everyone's time by going over the same fucking questions that were already asked back at the passport control booth and *following* that, a gruelling wait while Homeland Security make their final decision on whether they will let you into the country and send you on your way, or put you back on the next plane out of there, returning in the direction you'd came from.

Relations with my designated agent started off frosty and got even colder as we started our downhill descent. Having seen the couple in front of me appearing to have their entry rubber stamped and let through, I waited to be called. This apparently was my first mistake as it turned out that I was actually required to be in possession of not only my passport - and my pre filled out CBP declaration form when entering the country - but *also* the power to read minds, which was evident by the look on Agent Vieira's coupon when he motioned to me to step forward to the booth in the trans international language way that screamed 'well what are you fucking waiting on, cunto?'

Was my face red at that moment, with me actually stood there thinking I was following the rules that were set out in front of me in writing on the sign fixed to the booth he was sat in which stated in big fuck off letters.

WAIT BEHIND THE WHITE LINE UNTIL CALLED.

The fact that I'd put this particular agent out so much by actually having to make him go to the trouble of *looking* through the glass at me and *then* lift his arm to wave me towards him sitting in his booth was confirmed by his reaction when I handed him my passport.

With a look that suggested that I was the one responsible for assassinating Abraham Lincoln and JFK as well as masterminding the attacks on the twin towers he asked me where my customs declaration form was. Alerting me to the fact that I'd neglected to hand it over along with my passport. I quickly - but semi drowsily - apologised to him before fishing it out of my pocket for him.

Too late, however. As far as he was concerned, the tone for this exchange had now been set and he spitefully announced to me that since I didn't appear to be in any hurry - through the ridiculously insignificant issue of me not handing him both required documents in one go - then *he* was going to take his time too. Never mind the fact that him and his colleagues were obviously busy as fuck, trying to process the entry of hundreds of passengers who were still waiting in line from the numerous international planes that had landed all around the same time.

He evidently had a point to prove here and this appeared to be the most important thing to him in this moment so, as I waited there questioning if he'd actually said what I'd heard, he sat there deliberately doing nothing. Blatantly so. Leaving my passport on the counter while he sat in silence doing nothing in particular. Then making a show of reaching round to lift his bottle of Snapple, taking a slow sip of that then even more slowly screwing the cap on and placing it back on his desk. I wanted to tell him to grow up, like.

I remember standing there looking at him with the inner thought of what an absolute immature fanny he was being while wanting to share this with him but sensible enough to know that to do so would probably mean a swift return back to Amsterdam for me before the day was over.

It was actually quite remarkable how petty and childish the boy was being. Acting this way, however, while safe in the knowledge that I couldn't say a single thing about it for fear that he would knock me back from entering the country. Something I was already aware that he could've done without any hope of an appeal from myself.

Eventually he picked up my documents and decided to actually drop his act and finally begin to do his fucking job. This started with the standard questions that are normally asked when passing through immigration. Purpose of visit? How long is the visit? Where will I be staying? All of these questions something that should have been fuck all other than moot, considering I was scheduled to be *in* his country for no more than two hours. Purpose of visit ... To connect with a flight to get me to Mexico. How long is the visit? Two hours tops, subject to United Airlines keeping to their flight timetable. Where will I be staying? Well, not in America for one thing.

After answering multiple questions from him. He eventually asked me.

'Have you taken any narcotics today, Mr Duncan?'

With faux surprise at such an accusation - not wanting to disclose the Diazepam aspect of things, not while they weren't exactly prescribed in my own name and knowing how seriously they treated that stuff in America - I answered back something along the lines of me having had a few of the free drinks in business class along with a sleep and me needing to do a bit of sobering and waking up.

He eyed this answer with suspicion in the form of an extra long look at me while looking for any signs of me lying before appearing to deem this response from me as plausible.

He then moved on to my occupation - which he had eyed with a bit of scepticism, almost as if he hadn't considered it as a *real* job - which had left me having to try and explain that the last time I had played in America it had been in front of fifteen thousand people at Ultra in Miami, something that he hadn't seemed to be remotely impressed over. Already by this point a general standard five minute entry through immigration was now at the thirty minute mark and with no sign that it was coming to end. So I decided to ask him if there was a problem here, which predictably brought on the response of.

'I don't know, Mr Duncan. Do we have a problem? Maybe you can tell me?'

I followed this up by asking why I was still there being questioned at this point - the arguing goths both already well processed and let into the country - and got a simple answer of.

'Because you're wanting to enter my country and, also, because I can.'

I wanted to respond but, wisely, I could see where this was going and I was in one of those positions where you know someone wants to draw you in for their own ends, so I just bit my tongue and didn't give him the satisfaction that he was so obviously looking for. Eventually, he advised me that he had enough suspicion to detain me for further questioning and told me to wait while a colleague came to collect me.

Suspicion, for what? I wasn't even going to be leaving the fucking airport before I'd be gone from his country again. Something that I tried to remind him of only to receive fuck all but sarcasm back in return.

'This may surprise you but just because you have a connection to leave Newark in two hours time, this does not mean that you will *actually* get on the flight, and that your plan all along was simply to enter the United States, using a cover story, when, in fact, you have no plans to leave once here.'

That left me shaking my head. The high estimation that American's had for their own country always left me confused as - well, in my opinion, anyway - it was not the country that they all believed it to be. I genuinely would not have lived there had you fucking paid me but had this customs agent eyeing me with an accusatory glance while thinking that I was a potential illegal alien in the waiting.

'Listen, pal. I don't mean any disrespect here.'

I launched into a spiel while, inevitably setting myself up to do *exactly* that, cause disrespect. Because never in the history of mankind has anyone ever uttered the words 'I mean no disrespect' without actually then saying a combination of words which would then go on to contradict what was said originally.

'Your country isn't as great as yous all crack it up to be, ken? American dream and all that stuff, eh? It's a proper myth but you all have managed to convince yourselves it's the greatest country on earth and *everyone* is just dying to live there. I just want to get to Mexico, like, and, being honest, if United hadn't cancelled my flight from Amsterdam to Mexico City and then onto Guadalajara, earlier today, I wouldn't even *be* standing in front of you right now. America wasn't even part of my plans when I woke this morning, never mind throw away my life and career by trying to sneak in by the back door to make a life here. Trust me, it's not that deep, pal.'

I was reminded by him that I wasn't his 'pal' just as one of his colleagues - fully strapped with a sub machine gun around his neck - appeared, to lead me off to some kind of a passengers holding area where I was instructed to take a seat and await being called for further questioning by the HSI agent assigned to take my case.

At this point sitting there alongside an assortment of Arabs and Africans who on first look had been so clearly detained on racially profiled principles. This only serving to highlight just how much of a fish out of water *I* must've looked like, sat there. Sat beside my fellow detainees, however, only served to show me how serious things had become as I watched each one come and go after being called for questioning. The majority of them reappearing under armed guard and visibly none too chuffed with the news they'd been given. Assumed to be that they weren't being granted entry into the country and were now heading back home on the next plane out of there.

There were more tears and raised voices in that one area of the airport than you'd find in an Eastenders Christmas Day double bill although due to the different amounts of foreign languages that were filling the air I had no idea what *exactly* was being said. Sometimes you don't need to know the finer details like that to know what's going on, though. Seeing things like an Iraqi throwing his shoe at an agent sat behind a desk is something that does not require subtitles.

One agonising wait later my designated agent finally called out my name from behind his desk and off I went for round two of questioning. Things had taken so long up to this point that I was now inside the second hour of the two allocated to me for transferring to the second flight and I, by this point, was now feeling that unless things started to take a dramatic turn for the better then I was going to be facing a struggle to be on that connecting Guadalajara flight. Which, considering my Amsterdam to Mexico City flight had already been cancelled that day, I shouldn't have been surprised about. Before we even got down to things, I was disturbed by an Arab lady accompanied by three screaming kids who had decided to stage a sit in protest, right there beside where I sat at the interview desk. No doubt, this brought on by receiving a crushing knock back from one of the other agents. Screaming

'ASYLUM ASYLUM'

to the rooftops as three border patrol officers rushed her out of the holding area and away to Allah knows where although I'm guessing probably not Disneyland. Once we finally got the peace to sit and get down with the interrogation it was a case of more of the same for me from what Agent Vieira had treated me to. By this point, however, I was approaching the stage where I'd already decided that my entry to the country was going to be knocked back - and that I was going to have to return back across the Atlantic to Schipol and get on *another* plane that would take me directly to Mexico - and I'd decided that if this was going to be the case then I was going to make sure that my dignity was going to stay intact, and I was going to go down with a fight.

Unlike my answers to the questions posed to me by the previous agent, this time around I had decided to go with curt, hostile and quite simply what would be described back in Scotland as *wide as fuck* answers to everything he asked. Almost taunting him to send me back. Reverse psychology at its finest, or so I'd hoped. A big problem for this next agent was my three month stay - which wasn't actually going to *be* a three months stay but due to the terms of my visa, my trip was down as being open ended *up to* the three month period - and something he kept coming back to. Funny but me reminding him that

'It's your government that made the rules allowing my Visa to last three months so what's your fucking problem with me being inside the States for that allocated time?'

didn't go down too well with him but *did* go down extremely good with two Ghanians sat both wearing their country's World Cup shirts from back in the summer, looking on and laughing behind me further back in the room. Due to my colourful language I was given my first and last warning that it would not be acceptable and for all my bravado, I sensibly heeded said warning.

The questions continued at such a rate I felt like I was on The fucking Chase, with that Bradley Walsh looking on as they got fired at me, waiting to see if he was going to be writing a big cheque at the end of it. Next I had to pull up my bank details and show how much money I had in my account to prove to the agent that I could subsidise myself during my stay. Yes, for all of less than - by then - one hours. I can't deny, though. I took a wee bit enjoyment out of the face that the agent had when he had got himself access to looking at my bank account, and how much was sitting inside of it. Clearly, he had misjudged this groggy and scruffy looking Scot.

It was an absolute fucking nonsense and the longer it went on for the more wound up I became. This coming crashing against the fact that my glasses of wine and vallies had started to wear off. It was a horrible mix to contend with. I'm sure that each day these agents just decide that x amount of passengers passing through will be picked to have their day made worse by them and I guess it was just my time? They had issues with how many times I had visited America, looking through all of the stamps on my passport. Trying to tell them that these stamps were all in relation to my work, which lead to them speculating that I had possibly worked when there under a visa - like the one I was using that day - that did not allow for any work being undertaken. Explaining to them that if they wanted to check they would find details of my previous visas, which would show them that they had been verified as working visas and how the only reason I was not flying in on a working visa - that day - was due to the fact that I was not going to be *doing* any fucking work on American soil. It didn't matter. They had taken the decision to be cunts with me from beginning to end and it was a decision comfortably taken while knowing that they had the law on their side.

After perusing my bank details. Officer Placente was then finished with his questioning and asked me to take a seat back over where I had initially waited, and advised that he would now think things over and make his final decision and call me back to speak some more with him, after he'd reached his conclusion. By then it was clear to me that when I next spoke to him I would be told that I was either being sent back on the next available flight to AMS or I would be granted entry to the country, but by this point I was past the point of caring.

Some time later I was called back to speak to him and with no explanation - or apology for any inconvenience caused since my arrival - over what had happened from the moment I had attempted to pass through immigration control to now, I was handed my passport back and advised that I could go on my way with the obligatory

'Have a nice day.'

Unable to help myself, I had to get one last word in and decided to feed back to him that if this is how someone like me had been treated who came from the UK and, traditionally, the undoubted biggest ally that America has ever had, I was only glad that I hadn't flown in from an Al Qaeda hotbed such as Somalia or Yemen. His reply to this involved a *friendly* reminder that him and his colleagues had plenty stocks of latex gloves ready to be used and that they would happily go fetch them - if I had wanted to push my luck any further - which I'll readily admit was enough to have me on my not so merry way.

Grabbing my belongings, including my suitcase and flight box containing CDs and vinyl, which I'll be honest in saying that when I saw that they had been retrieved and brought to me at the detainment centre, I had taken as a *sure* sign that I was being sent back to The Netherlands, I was escorted from the detainment centre and let out through a door which brought me out at the right side of the passport control booths. Taking a quick look at my watch, all I could do was shrug my shoulders over seeing that my Guadalajara flight had been scheduled to take off twenty minutes ago, although I'd already taken that as part of the service from the CBP. If my flight hadn't been due to take off for another couple of hours then, without question, I'd have still been sat inside the detainment centre.

Half hoping that the flight had been delayed, I made for the flight information monitors purely on the off chance that the flight was still up there but no joy. All information relating to the 3.25pm United Airlines Guadalajara flight had been wiped from the screen. *Of course* it had.

With a sigh that only someone who had travelled across the Atlantic in a eight hour commute only to be welcomed by the obnoxious and arrogant best of the American Customs and Border Patrol - leading them to miss their connecting flight - would have been justified in sighing, I went looking for the

United Airlines customer services desk to see about them getting me on some kind of an alternative flight south of the border, down Mexico way.

While I done so, I tried Lee to get to the bottom - in other words, to have a good old moan at him - of this whole fly on the wall access pish involving this journalist and photographer but my two attempts calling him both went straight to his voicemail. Me leaving a half hearted recording for him on the second call. Telling him that I'd encountered problems in Newark and that I wouldn't be getting into Guadalajara at the previously planned time, and that I would let him know my new scheduled arrival as and when it had been arranged.

Lee, himself, should have already been there in Guadalajara, with him having the relatively quicker journey down from Fort Worth, where he had been for the previous couple of days on business at some music seminar. Lee had agreed to accompany me on the majority of the tour, something I had not asked for but got all the same so with him on duties to make sure I was collected at the airport, it was felt that the least I could do would be to let him know that I wasn't going to *be* there at the expected time.

Lee - the complete liability that he was and absolutely ride all like the role model which he liked to make himself out to be as my agent and manager - at times in my career had tended to be a hindrance when in tow with me than the help that you'd expect from someone playing the roll that he does and when he'd informed me that he was going to come on the tour I'd tried my best at persuading him otherwise as, already knowing how intensely messy it could get on the road in the kind of countries like we were heading to, I'd been of the opinion that he'd only have made things *worse* for all concerned. Even though I had extremely sugar coated this when trying to change Lee's mind about coming.

Nonsense, he'd replied to this. Advising that I would *need* him and his experience and guidance over those three weeks. I was of the opinion that it would be the exact opposite of this - which it would turn out to prove me correct - but sometimes there's no telling people.

One of the main reasons for me hoping to keep distance between Lee and South America - and in turn, distance between him and me - was the cocaine side of things. It didn't take a genius to work out that he was going to hit the powder hard. The man would be the kid for the candy store that every one of these cities would offer up. And it went without saying that the more of it he would end up taking the more stupid shit he would do. And who would be the cunt having to put up with two plus weeks of that caper? Aye, muggins, here.

Obviously, I did not ever possess any kind of fantasy where I, myself, was going to go through the tour like I was an alter boy or someone out of Coldplay on tour, eating kale salads and visiting local museums and cathedrals. But at least I'd be looking after *myself*. It's when you find yourself having to look after - or be affected by the decisions and actions of others - someone else that it gets to be a problem. To be fair to Lee, though. When it came to the fears that I had of having him cutting around all of these cities with all the temptations that they can bring, he never let me down in any way and showed at *every turn* that I'd had every right to be worried about the maniac that would be unleashed, once he entered Latin America.

Spying the sign for the United Airlines help-desk - still a good walk down the terminal, mind - I headed off in its direction, hoping that the day was going to start taking a turn for the better. I didn't really care how I got there - or if now, I would need to take a connection *on top* of my original connection. I just wanted to be there in Guadalajara, in my hotel room. The first date of the tour wasn't for another couple of days and, until then, my plans consisted of doing as little as humanly possible.

The tour, once started, was never likely to dip at any point and there would be days where sleep would be a commodity found in short supply, substituted for partying.

Until then, though. I planned to stock up on as much rest and relaxation as there was going once I arrived.

With the mini adventures that were there waiting to be embarked on in the kind of exciting and illuminating cities such as Guadalajara, Mexico City, Bogota, Medellin, Buenos Aires, Lima and Rio de Janeiro ... I was going to fucking *need* as much in the tank as possible.

Chapter 3

Lee

World travel, yeah? I'd always seen it as an opportunity to broaden the old horizons, while making new friends along the way. Didn't much feel like any of that energy, however, to the inside of 'Cantina La Oliveira' in the centre of Guadalajara, where I'd found myself only a couple of hours into my first morning, after arriving in the Mexican state of Jalisco.

My now - very much - ex wife, Suzy, who had never been the most sympathetic of partners had always said - when things went a little breasts up - that I always brought things upon myself. Never an alternative view, there. Maybe she was right? Who knows, though? She *was* unsympathetic, after all. And very possibly a little bit biased, and not in my favour either.

Maybe it was an attitude problem? Confidence, maybe even arrogance? Obviously, cocaine that comes by the gram cheaper than a double espresso? Well, yeah, that probably wouldn't have helped either but in my honest defence, I wouldn't have survived all of the years that I'd managed in the harsh and unforgiving environment of the arena that is House Music DJ and artist management without any of those advantages. Of course, though. There *is* a difference in surviving the electronic music industry and managing to keep yourself safe and sound in Guadalajara.

Whoever's fault that it may or may not have been - spoiler; it was *definitely* mine - the one thing that was not up for debate was that I hadn't wasted any time, whatsoever, in losing friends I hadn't even afforded myself the chance to *make* on arriving in Jalisco, ahead of my deejay's tour opening a few days later. By my standards it would've been almost impressive, were it not so fucking gravely serious.

I'd arrived - from a flight out of Fort Worth - in the middle of the night and had managed a couple of hours sleep before surfacing and leaving the hotel mid morning. Barely making it out onto the street before one of the street urchins - hanging around the street level's hotel entrance - had sidled up to me and whispered the magical words.

'Coc-ay-een, señor?'

I'd already seen him moving in my direction and had assumed that he was going to be with his hand out for a few pesos from what he'd taken as a tourist. His offer, though, was enough to make me do a double take. It hadn't been the first time I'd procured some sniff from someone in Latin America who looked like he wasn't even age for leaving primary school, so this was not that unfamiliar from me. In an ethical sense, it certainly was not a transaction that left me looking too clever but to offset this, the cocaine had been at a level that no adult had *ever* sold me. And *that* really is the most important thing of all and if you feel differently to this then you may want to re-examine how you go about trying to score drugs, wherever you are in the world.

Stood there in a filthy and battered pair of Reeboks and - not old enough to be classed as vintage and nowhere near new enough to be looked upon as recent - a fake Barcelona shirt with Lionel Messi's name and number embedded on the back, the kind that you'd always find in Spanish tourist resort shops where not one single piece of the shirt is not of the same material as the main body of it. I assumed that he had a pair of shorts on, even if the oversized shirt travelled so far down his torso that you could not see for certain.

Already taking it that a kid of this age who, technically, should've been at school instead of hanging around the street trying to sell drugs to tourists, would not have been exactly too fluent in English. I kept things as simple as possible by talking to him in Spanish. I was never what you'd have looked on as speaking it as some kind of a second language or anything but knew more than enough to get by. I'd - semi - learned the lingo, decades before when I'd figured out that Ibiza was going to play a big - and important - part in my career. With the way the music industry was, when dealing with club owners and promoters etc, I'd felt it in my best interests to learn Spanish, just so I would know for certain if some of the more unscrupulous out there was trying to con me. And there are plenty of that type, *especially* on the island of Ibiza.

'Cuanto por dos?'

I asked the little man, trying to establish how much the asking price was, while knowing it was - as that mahogany coloured chap from BBC 1 would've called things - already going to be cheap as chips.

Surprised at the 'gringo' replying to him in Spanish he smiled back before telling me that, for two and I assumed, correctly, for this to mean grams, it would cost two hundred and sixty pesos, which worked out at the, frankly, stupid amount of just under nine squid. On hearing this, the animal inside of me thought that there wasn't much difference between two grams or three so, instead of asking for two from him I put my hand up with three fingers showing. Fishing the money out of my wallet while thinking about that actor in Inglorious Basterds and how much bother he landed up in through doing the same hand signal but instead of ending up shot in a bar's basement I was heading to a bar to get myself fucking lit.

Taking pity on the boy, and how this was his life, instead of handing him the three hundred and ninety pesos, I handed him five hundred while saying.

'Ciento diez pesos para ti.'

Telling him that the extra pesos were for him. Pointing at the notes and then to him for good measure. I guessed that this didn't happen too often for the kid going by his reaction. Telling me *gracias gracias gracias* while making the international prayer slash thank you signal to me.

A couple, who looked local to me, walked past the two of us during this exchange and the man flashed me a look that if it could've killed I would not have even managed to get myself to line number one. Line number *none*, more like. His other half electing to shake her head before launching into what looked like a rant which the paranoid in me was seeing as her talking about me buying drugs from a kid. While my Spanish was decent, I struggled with people when they were animated and talking fast paced, like her. That she mentioned cocaine and a gringo was enough confirmation I required to know she was talking about me, the rest of it? Right over my head.

Before heading on my way I went to say one last thing to the mini Messi only to realise that I wasn't exactly sure of the words I needed and with this not the time for standing around in broad daylight completely baiting myself up by talking to an underage drug dealer. Well, if there's such a thing as an 'underage dealer' that is?

Without having to resort to too much Spanish, I was able to get it over to him that if the sniff that I'd just popped into my wallet was as good as I was hoping it to be, then the kid should come back to the hotel again tomorrow. I figured the three grams I'd just bought would've been more than enough to see me through the rest of the day - although you never, ever know these things - but sure as shit, I'd be looking for more by the next day.

Pointing at my wallet with the gear in it and telling him that if the 'coc-ay-een' was *muy bien* then - pointing at him, and then the hotel - I simply said mañana. He nodded excitedly, seeming to understand, before looking up at me and offering an enthusiastic fist bump before the two of us went off in completely different directions.

I found Cantina La Oliveira not by any kind of desire and more out of need. I just wanted somewhere that I could sit for a few hours and get 'freshened up' for the day by the way of some strong Mexican coffee and some even stronger - origin unknown but an educated guess would've been Colombian due to the ties between the Colombian growers and Mexican smugglers over the years - cocaine.

Due to the seminar that I'd been to in Texas, I had neglected all other parts of running the Ragamuffin Agency and things were at risk of getting out of control. The amount of emails sitting in my inbox as *unread* was enough to give anyone the fear. All of those missed calls - with accompanying voicemails left - which would need to be listened to and returned. It was the *last* thing I wanted to be doing on the first day in Mexico but knew that now was the time, because once our esteemed DJ Selecao arrived, things would most likely take over from then.

It was felt that before even attempting to boot up my MacBook and start making various calls, that I should have went nowhere near any of it until I had got a couple of cups of coffee inside me, along with a few Patsy Clines up my hooter. Once I'd met that objective, everything else would all fall into place.

I'd thought at first that the bar wasn't even open when I'd walked in purely due to the fact that there wasn't a single person - other than the barman - inside the place. The polar opposite of the bright morning sunshine, the boozer was dimly lit with a long bar running down the middle and booths to either side of it. It looked like the place was set up for serving food as well as drink although there was no sign - or smell - to confirm it.

Looking at the booths, though, it wasn't hard to imagine families sitting down inside them, tucking into enchiladas and burritos for their dinner. The barman - an old guy with a white T Shirt on and matching white apron, like an old school bartender - appeared pleased to see me. Greeting me with a 'buenos dias, señor' as I approached the bar. Nodding back at him I asked what strong coffee he could recommend.

The reply back from him being that a cup of Oaxacan - Mexican - coffee was just what I was looking for. I just about managed to pick up that it was traditionally served without any sugar or milk. An already strong coffee made stronger just through this alone. Of course, with what I was about to go and do in this establishment's men's in a few minutes time really all rendered the subject of how strong the coffee well and truly moot.

While he began preparing the coffee my initial move had been to pick a booth to sit in and get my laptop booted up there on the table. The protected common sense that you try to carry when out and about in a strange city, however, was enough to stop me and take it directly towards the men's, complete with my rucksack still around me. If I would be sceptical about returning to my table - from the toilet - in a London pub and still finding my MacBook there on the table then, no offence Guadalajara, why would I have expected any different in Mexico? Even if the pub *did* have only the one patron inside of it, me.

Taking the only cubicle that was inside there, it wasn't hard to notice that it wasn't the cleanest of spaces and no question about it, the *last* place that you would pour out some sniff and get stuck into it.

As a plan B. I covered the seat in toilet roll and - still with my chinos on while there was paper also strategically placed on the floor to ensure that my Gucci loafers did not come into contact with any of the *fluids* that were there on the floor and took out my phone and tipped some of gram numero uno out onto its screen. To fuck with all this chopping into lines caper, I thought to myself. Placing the phone on top of my knees and pushing myself forward enough for me to trace my right nostril along the screen. Pretty much managing to take the whole lot in one go, except for a few particles of dust that had escaped the human vacuum cleaner that had just ran over top.

Jesus fucking Christ and all his apostles. What *was* this that the kid was walking around punting for almost pennies. Yeah I'd done cocaine over the years. Lots of it, if I can be honest. And I'd had some *unbelievable* gear sold to me in doing so but *this?* Yeah it bore all the resemblances of what you'd expect from a dunt of powder, and then some! Bloody hell, I thought as I made my way back from the bathroom - absolutely fucking *flying* - whistling that Bette Middler song *Wind Beneath My Wings* and not having the first fucking clue *why.* Throw some strong coffee into the mix and I'll get through these emails and phone calls in no time.

And who knows? Maybe I *would've* done. If things, inside there, hadn't turned out the way that they did.

The barman - Miguel from the El Salto part of the city which was about the only thing I found out about him in between the time I walked into his bar and when I opened my MacBook and got on the phone to make my first phone call - was just serving up my coffee for me as I returned so, paying for it and telling him to have a drink on me, grabbing the cup and saucer I hopped into a booth nearer to the back, figuring it would be the perfect spot for some peace to sit and work while already trying to estimate if it would be secluded enough a spot for a cheeky bump every now and again to save me the pain of having to go back into the men's. That was blown when I realised that despite it being further back from the entrance it was still within view of the bar.

Taking it anyway, I got started on my things to do.

I know that there would've been some who would've looked on me dropping everything to be there for Stevie on his tour as selfish on my part and, actually, quite unnecessary. DJ Selecao being a big enough boy - the eighteen year old raw Scottish DJ that I took under my wing back in the day in the early nineties had only recently turned *forty*, fuck how time flies when you're having fun, and fun we most certainly had - to be able to handle himself across a mini tour of Mexico and South America. But I guess they just didn't know enough about Stevie 'Zico' Duncan. The chances of him going through the tour - without me monitoring things - without some form of international incident happening were in the slim to zero category. Yeah yeah, but look at all the partying and cheap cocaine, they'd surely say.

Well I pity them and their cynicism, I say. Like I had three weeks spare that I could dedicate to just the one of my vast stable of artists, both sides of the pond. But like the guy who puts himself last as always, I decided that I wanted to be there for the duration. Hell or high water.

With him presently on his way to Mexico from Schipol - via a connection in New Jersey - the plan was to collect him at the airport and have a meal, few drinks and catch up for the first time in a while and as for the next day? Well that really was all going to be about keeping him out of trouble ahead of his tour opener, the following night. But again, you make these plans without ever really bargaining for *other* things to get in their way.

I'd made three calls to three different people in different time zones with scant regard of if I was calling them too early or too late. I'll admit, pop a little bit of *absolute fucking fire* gear into me and you'll have to deal with me on *my* terms. The coffee was good too, strong but tasty and probably not helping when it came to how fast I found myself talking. It wasn't an issue with who was on the other end of the line so I made no attempts to rein myself in a bit.

I wasn't even finished the first cup when I asked for Miguel to make me another. I never got a chance to receive it from him.

While in the middle of my fourth call, which wasn't on my original list of call backs but had spawned from an email I'd opened - from Europe's biggest electronic music festival, in Belgium, where they were inviting Selecao to curate his own stage for their 2015 summer bash - which, on reading, I'd felt deserved an instant response over. It was a pretty big deal to have one of my deejays get the chance to choose the day's entertainment over the stage of theirs and, obviously, I would be able to see to it that it wouldn't *just* be Selecao who would be representing Ragamuffin on that specific stage.

Claude, one of the staff at Eurotopia who I'd enjoyed a friendly business relationship with since first having some of my deejays booked for their festival, and who had sent me the email in relation to the offer for next summer, sat explaining what their company had planned for next year - and ambitious as ever from them, it was - when I saw the front door to the bar open, and this little guy walk in. I kept it inwards but smiled at the sight of him as the big cowboy hat that he had on looked like it was too large for the rest of his body. It was maybe a distance thing but from where I was it looked like - if it rained - he would be able to keep himself dry by standing with his arms and legs tight against him and remain motionless underneath the hat.

Claude was talking away about the numbers they were looking to bring in for the next summer, due to the expansion they'd had done to what was already a festival site the size of a large fucking town and I watched the little guy - around fifty-ish with a full moustache which did a good job of obscuring part of his face - walk in and greeting Manuel. It was clear that the pair already knew each other but, I don't know? While Manuel was friendly with the man, there seemed an anxiousness behind it, if you were to look hard enough. Me, on the other hand, didn't have to look hard enough for *anything*. I was as switched on as I was ever going to be, right there. Combining speaking to a Belgian festival promoter - with broken English and weird accent - while surveying scenes taking place across the bar I'm in, while the people are talking in Spanish.

The little man placed an order for a coffee himself but the moment Manuel nodded with a 'si señor' the man then turned and made his way in my direction. Until then, I'd been sat over my MacBook with phone to my ear and doing a good job of not showing that I'd been watching the two of them. But now I literally couldn't *not* look at him. Now that he was closer to me, I could see the fancy suit he had on. One of those that has lot of the stitching left outside, down the front and edge of the collars. He also, instead of a traditional tie, to go with his cowboy hat and suit had one of those *bolo ties* that you see cowboys wear. The centrepiece of *his* bolo tie, though, was not the head of some form of cattle but, instead, a menacing looking silver skull, pulled right up to the collar of his white shirt.

Assuming that he was on his way to the bathrooms I continued speaking with Claude. Only once he reached my booth, he stopped, and despite clearly being able to see that I was having a conversation with someone, started to speak to me in Spanish.

Regardless of what he was trying to say to me. The fact that I was talking to someone and he felt that he could just butt in, didn't go down too well with me. And if that hadn't went down well with me, once I'd managed to understand what it was that he was saying. I was finding myself acting on pure instinct, sitting there telling the guy to stop being an ignorant cunt and for him to fuck right off.

Out of what was an empty boozer, with *plenty* of room for everyone, he was saying to me that I was to move, because this was *his* booth. These cunts, eh? You find them everywhere. People who think that the space outside of their house belongs to them, even though anyone who has paid their road tax are cool as a cucumber for parking there. Those who lay claim to a certain sun bed down by the pool and get all arsey if they get there and find someone has already taken it. Where does the entitlement come from, I ask you?

I mean, I reckon that I'd have reacted in the very same way as I had with him, even if I hadn't had a drop of coffee or ching. But *with* the coffee and the sniff? Well, it was all delivered with that little bit more oomph, you know? Fuck, though. This coc-ay-een was *propahhhh*, and I was already looking forward to my next wee top up, something that was very much in my not too distant future.

He's trying to - gently - pull at my arm to get me to move while I'm pushing him off and pointing at the other booths, telling him to not be so ignorant.

His reaction showed that he wasn't planning for A. Someone to resist him and B. For them to lambast him in English.

'Ingles?'

He said, taking his hand back from off my arm.

'Si,'

I replied, hoping this moment of weirdness had now passed.

He just smiled this sarcastic smile, all cocky and sure of himself - which I'm sure would've been like looking in a mirror for him, when it came to me - before doing some kind of an exaggerated

'HUH,'

as if to say, ok then, and then turned around and instead of taking one of the other booths - if he'd wanted one so much? - he took a seat at the bar, and started to have a chat with the bartender. Whatever they were talking about it was too low for me to hear but it would've been a decent bet that I may have been the topic of conversation. Even when the man had been over at the booth and I'd became a bit animated. I had looked over to Manuel behind the bar and he'd looked a little worried by the exchange that was taking place but I had put that down to someone hoping there's not going to be any trouble in their bar in case lots of shit gets broken.

During all of this, Claude had remained on the line. At first, thinking that I had called *him* an ignorant cunt which had led to the farcical situation where I was apologising to him while giving it straight to the little man at the same time. Once he was back at the bar, I was able to get the peace to wrap up the call with Claude, while apologising to him over what was going on, this side in Guadalajara. We'd shared a bender together in Ibiza ten years before so both had each other's number. Before hanging up, him laughing about the fact that there I was - winning friends with the locals - with *it* already having begun, and my DJ hadn't even arrived yet.

He may well have joked about it. But neither of us could've known what was about to follow.

Ending the call with him, I thought it wise to not go calling anyone else. Not for a while and definitely not until I knew that things were going to be cool. As it would play out. Things were going to be the fucking polar *opposite* of cool.

With one eye very much on the man in the suit and the other trying to clear my inbox as much as possible in that environment, I noticed him - following the brief chat with Manuel - making a call. Once again, he was too far away for me to make much of what he'd said. I heard a Jorge - who I'd taken to be the person he'd called - I heard a Luis mentioned and I also picked up him mentioning the name of the cantina.

Sometimes as sharp and switched on you are with illegal substances, you can be too busy congratulating yourself over how 'on' you are, only to miss something completely fucking obvious. Had I realised the significance of this call and the sheer basics of it. Two people connected to someone that I'd just had a problem with, and the name of the bar that we were sitting in being mentioned, I'd have had that MacBook inside my rucksack and out of there as fast as my loafers could take me.

But I *didn't* spot what was going down, and by the time I did, then it was all too late.

It also didn't help me, when it came to a distraction, that once he'd ended the call, the man with the bolo tie left the bar and headed back in my direction. Already proving to myself that I'd been correct to hang off on undertaking any further email or phone call duties. This time, however, there was no attempts to move me on. Instead, as brazen as you like, he slid into the booth and took one of the two seats that was facing me. And with a smile that was not at odds with the eyes fixed on me, he began speaking. Despite previously having a few choice words for him - exclusively in English and, indeed *confirming* that I was English - he started speaking in Spanish.

Even though I would've been able to understand the majority of what he was saying - and going by his opening gambit, was coming across as a vent over tourists and disrespect - I judged it wise to plead ignorance and actually play *up* to the fact I wasn't from around the area and or country. This, being a waste of time as the moment that he sensed that his words would've been lost on me, he switched to near flawless English.

'You, Eeenglish.'

He shook his head in what looked like some serious exaggerated exasperation.

'Do you *really* feel the need to play up to the reputation that you have when travelling the world?'

'What reputation would that be?'

I asked, but already knew what he was getting at and I felt a little shame over being categorised as some of the ambassadors England has representing, when visiting tourist resorts across the world.

'Disrespect. The feeling that people should bow down to you because of where you come from. Your sense of entitlement. You *do* realise that the days of sailing the world and colonising wherever the hell you found are past, amigo? That your stupid little island doesn't mean sheet?' Let me tell you. You come to somewhere like Jalisco. Do you think that the British navy will come to save you when you get into trouble?'

'I didn't know I was *in* trouble.'

I kept it short and sweet. But there was something about the confidence that this man oozed that troubled me. When we'd spoken moments before it had been a completely different situation. I was flying on the ching and, to me, this little man wasn't going to cause me any problems and telling him that I was busy working and for him to fuck off and sit at another booth was something that I'd done on autopilot.

Now that we were face to face. He was giving off heavy gangster vibes. Fuck, I'd dealt with enough of those types in Ibiza and back in London.

'Amigo? You were in trouble from the moment you did not give me the one thing that I asked you for,'

he replied, completely emotionless.

'Now where was I again? Yes, you people, thinking that you can come to this part of the world and act like you own it?'

'Look, mate. I didn't mean no offence. I was in the middle of an important phone call and if you still want the booth then …'

'Amigo? Can you please pay me the respect of not interrupting when I'm speaking?'

He cut me off straight and, in doing so, put down a marker for who was in control of this meeting of minds.

'If you had done your homework before visiting, you'd have already been aware of the statistics for gringos who visit

Mexico, and *specifically* Guadalajara and Sinaloa, but never leave again. And I do not mean through having such an enjoyable visit that they decide to stay.'

Not liking where this was going, I flipped my laptop down and, before attempting to put it back into my rucksack, had a quick scan of the table for any valuables. I felt it best all round if I was to head off somewhere else to continue my day as there was now a menacing atmosphere that hadn't been there until the man had sat down with me.

In fairness, even if I'd got the laptop into my bag, I wasn't going to be leaving. The bell of the front door going again and Manuel, myself and the man beside me all looking in that direction. It would've been nice for it to have been a couple of cops, coming in for a coffee on their beat, but it wasn't and even if it was, who's to know which side they'd have been on in any case. It was the opposite of law enforcement. Two 'goonish' looking characters entered. The first, a thin rakish looking guy with an early nineties style raving style long middle parting and facial hair that looked more a case of having not shaved from a few days than any planned growth, - about mid twenties - wearing a green classic style Lacoste polo shirt, jeans and pair of dirty looking khaki Timberland boots. Following him was a much scarier looking chap with a shaved head and tattoos on his face, neck and - muscular - arms, exposed by a white wife beaters vest.

The one with the face tats - once in the door - turned around and flipped the sign on the door from *abierto* to *cerrado*. Manuel looking over at our booth - to the little man - as if to confirm that this should have happened and him nodding back at Manuel to confirm that, yes, his establishment had now been taken over.

Fuck, this was *not* good, at all. The two men walked towards the booth and took a seat each. The nineties raver taking a seat beside the little guy and the face tattooed one - a snake travelling down his left side face and a tear drop coming from his right eye - took the one beside me, blocking me in.

The man in the cowboy hat shouted across to the apprehensive looking Manuel to go over and lock the front door, or words to that effect as, without any kind of a question from who I had assumed owned the place, he obediently walked across with his keys in his hand and locked the door.

There was no doubt that these two worked for the man facing me. Which, in itself, kind of confirmed that the little man was *someone*. I'd already began to think that way - although far too late to do anything about it, behaviour wise - from the way he carried himself, but to have goons that he can just call who'll appear a few minutes? There's only really a certain type who fits that kind of a bill.

He looked to the side of him and then across at the one beside me and - in Spanish - said that him and me had been sitting talking about all of the tourists who simply disappear in Jalisco. The one beside me - Luis, apparently - cracking the funnies, saying, sarcastically, how that didn't sound like people from Guadalajara and Sinaloa. Not that I was supposed to understand this, of course.

It wasn't easy to understand it all but from what I *had* picked it up. This little man was telling his boys that I had shown him disrespect. The two of them both pulling faces that were close to the one you get from a tradesman when you ask him how much the job is going to cost, on hearing this from him.

'I have spoken to my associates about our little problem, and .. oh I am sorry, where are my manners? I don't even know your name?'

I was more interested in hearing the end of what he'd *meant* to say before getting sidetracked. What difference did my name make? I told him all the same. Even if I kept it to just my first name. Figuring that there could be no advantage in him knowing what my surname was.

'Lee,'

I replied, noticing that as good as the sniff had been, this man - and his goons - had managed to sit down with the ability to completely *wipe it* from my system. I was on my fucking own, here, with no assistance.

'Well, Lee. My name is Enrique Emilano Garcia Flores but you may have heard of me as 'El Hombrecito?'

I hadn't heard of him in my life but the fact that he was sitting there already holding the assumption that I *would've* heard of him in some capacity told me that I should at least pretend to, so as not to disrespect him any further. I sat there nodding my head and saying that, yeah, I'd heard of him and that had I known what he'd looked like then we'd have had a completely different experience. They absolutely fucking nailed his nickname though as I was positive that this translated to something of 'the little man' or 'the small one.'

He wasn't looking to hear any of my apologies. It was too late for that shit with him. But, at least, he seemed quietly pleased that this gringo had heard of him. Hey, as long as he was happy enough not to ask me *where* I'd heard of him - or what I knew of him - I'd have been more than accommodating when it came to massaging his ego.

I kept trying to build bridges as we sat there but, in fairness, I should've picked up on things at the start and just not bothered. I'm sat there offering to buy the three of them drinks and - to highlight how off I was with the situation - the bar man who would've been *getting* the drinks is standing talking back and forward with 'El Hombrecito' and preparing himself for leaving the gaff, and the three of us to it. His only request that he had for little man Flores was, chillingly.

'Not inside the bar.'

His last words before he unlocked the front door - to allow for his exit - and then locking it again, to stop anyone from coming in and disturbing us.

But disturbing us from *what?* And what was it that Miguel did not want taking place inside his bar? These were both questions that didn't need to be asked out loud. I was going to find out soon enough, but not sat there at the booth. The door had only been locked for a matter of moments when the guy in the Lacoste polo pulled out his gun and put it on the table in front of him.

I sat frozen, just looking at it. There had been no need for it and it was hardly as if I was going to be able to take the three of them out. I was hardly the type for that caper. But the message was felt strongly all the same when I saw it sat there.

'Ok, it's time we took this elsewhere. Get up.'

Flores said as, first, he stood up, then followed by his two men. The sicario (?) opposite me picked up his gun from the table and motioned for me to get up by pointing it at me and gently raising the muzzle upwards.

With Flores and his tattooed faced 'employee' leading from the front and the feel of the end of the gun being pushed into my back from the younger one, we left the main bar and moved into what I thought was going to be a back room but, in fact, turned out to be a kitchen. With my sole intentions - on entering the cantina - being cocaine and coffee, I'd noticed that the place done food also. And when I saw some of the 'instruments' lying around the kitchen's worktops, I was fucking wishing that it *hadn't*.

With one chair available, I was told by Flores to take a seat. Once again, the feel of that hard steel prodding into my back, I did as told. The young one - Jorge - moving to the side but keeping the gun pointed at me while Luis stood to the other side of me. Their gaffer, meanwhile, was not looking at me. Instead, he appeared to be deciding on which bladed implement he was going to pick up.

Well I just went into sheer panic mode. Trying to tell him that had I known who he was there would've been no question of me giving upon the booth to him, while asking what would *he* have done in a similar situation. Also not ideal during this moment was sweat that I was covered in through the combination of the sniff, the searing Jalisco heat … and beginning to take on board that I was about to be done some *serious* harm. I *looked* a mess, and had I been able to smell better through my 'cocaine nose' who knows, probably smelling just as bad .. and my actions weren't much better.

61

'You *do* realise that I cannot just let you walk? It is a matter of principle. You need to take away a memory of Guadalajara. Something that you will not forget, should you ever wish to come back again.'

Flores, picking up a small cleaver, said it so cold, so 'as standard' that it made it even more menacing as a result. When you've got someone ranting and raving at you while holding a weapon, you can sometimes attribute it to them acting irrationally and that they'll possibly pull back and come to their senses. But when it's the same situation, only someone speaking calmly and softly?

'You know how it works, Lee, don't you? If one tourist can come here and get away with insulting and disrespecting the kind of man who holds the power that I do in the region, then what's to say that the next one tries the same, and the next. And tourists get to go home at the end of their vacation. I have to live here.'

Before I could reply, but really? What could I say that was going to change his mind? He nodded to Luis and, without any words required, this saw him grabbing my right arm and - moving anything in range out of the way, spreading it tight down on the kitchen worktop. Call it muscle memory or fight or flight instinct but when someone is standing looking over you holding a cleaver and they have someone hold your arm against a flat surface, you're going to struggle.

Which, I guess, was a decent chance for me to be issued the reminder of the gun. Feeling it pressed into the side of my head, enough for me to stop resisting.

This is a new low for you, Isaac,

I thought to myself while, fully taking on board the gravity of what an innocuous 'fuck off' can result in. The sweat was trickling - and tickling - down my face. Then the heavy breathing started. Fuck knows how I hadn't pissed myself. Overall, though, I was immensely pissed off with myself because this could've all been avoided.

Even before arriving in Mexico, I'd already known that every country on the tour was one where we would be needing to keep an eye open at all times and while not exactly sticking to our best behaviour - which wasn't ever going to happen with all things considered - at least taking *care*. And here I was, not even making it to day two and looking like I was about to lose a hand at best and an arm at worst. Fuck me, what a choice to have? The heavy breathing was going to take me directly into a panic attack if I didn't contain it but it was hardly the circumstances for me to get a grip on things while not exactly being around those that could've been described as compassionate towards my needs.

He stood there for a moment, holding the cleaver and looking like he couldn't decide if he had any final lines to deliver or if he was just going to get it over with. He'd already grabbed one of the white aprons - that were hanging up on the inside of the door - and had put it around him, so was clearly ready for carrying it out.

When you're in a moment such as this. And every part of your instinct is telling you that this is fucking happening. There's a part of you who wants to just scream all kinds of abuse at the person, in the knowledge that they're going to do it anyway. For example, when he covered up his suit with the apron, I wanted to tell him not to bother as his suit was fucking shit anyway and if he was to wear it in Europe he'd get deported back to Mexico on the grounds of committing a crime against fashion. But I never. Something about the fact that things could actually still become *worse*, had I shown further insolence. What was to say that the cleaver would've just been replaced by the handgun that was currently being pointed at me?

But still, I cannot lie. While you would *clearly* choose to lose a limb than your life. The prospect of losing 'just' a limb *feels* like you're going to lose your life.

In one last throw of the dice, I tried bribery. In that moment, I would've chosen to lose everything I owned, rather than that right arm. Trying to bribe someone who - by this point I'd been left with no choice other than to assume as one - appeared to be some narco with a bit of power behind him?

Stupid, pointless and laughable. But desperate people do desperate things.

Walking over to me while telling Luis to hold my arm straight, I knew it was now or never, as far as being able to find a way to talk the man around.

'Look, Don Flores - which I'd hoped would be a nice touch although what did I know? I was grappling for *something* - I have money, I am a successful businessman from England, Europe and America. I I I I I I work in the music business,'

I said, developing a bit of a stutter, brought on by the sheer stress of it all.

He just laughed off this attempt at turning him. Which left me broken. It was all I had, and he didn't even want to talk numbers. Wouldn't even let me through the door to sit down and negotiate. *Then* I saw why. Taking a step closer to me, he took one arm and, bringing his hand across to lift the sleeve up, gave me a look at his watch.

'This is worth more than what you'll make in a year, and you think you can bribe *me?* And besides, money doesn't mean a thing when you don't have respect.'

As soon as I saw the watch he had on, I knew it was over. Around his wrist was the almost mythical Richard Mille 052 Skull, from a couple of years before. It - possibly on purpose - completely tracked with the skulled emblem bolo tie that he had on and at - approximately - over a million dollars in value, he was quite correct in his estimation that it was worth more than my annual earnings.

And with this confirmation, all I had left was fear, panic and absolute fuck all in the way of hope or positivity. For fear and panic. See my feeble attempts at screaming for help, hoping that somehow someone would hear it all the way on that noisy and busy street that the cantina was sat on. I would fully admit that I was no longer rational. I was trying to bribe multi-millionaires and screaming for help from people who wouldn't have dared dream cross El Hombrecito and his men, even if they *had* heard me, which they could never have done out on that street over top of all the shouting, music and car horns.

My cries for help only seemed to irritate Flores who in no time had instructed Jorge to give me a hefty whack on the side of my head from his gun. Once I felt that cold and hard steel crashing against my skull. Yeah, I wasn't much in the mood for crying out loud anymore. Just crying. It felt like almost a miracle that I hadn't been knocked out by the blow to my head but, instead, I was left with the absolute worst of pains shooting down one side of my head. Acting on instinct, I immediately went to feel my head for blood but my hand movement was enough for me to hear the trigger from the gun being cocked which sent my arm back down again. It was either blood or sweat that was running down the side of my head and hitting my neck, but I was going to have to stay in the dark over that.

'Now that you've had your little moment and got it out of your system, shall we continue? I have *enough* things to do today after this.'

Flores said rhetorically, since I was never going to be part of the decision making process. Surprising me with an apparent act of mercy by picking up a large wooden spoon and tossing it over to Luis, who had momentarily let go of my arm while his colleague was pistol whipping me.

'It would be better for you if you were to bite on that,'

Flores said while his man started to force it sideways into my mouth.

Yeah and it would be better for you if you were to bite on me, wanker. I thought to myself but, obviously, kept to myself. And that was it. Sat there with a wooden spoon in my mouth between my teeth, a gun pointed at me while someone stood holding a cleaver up in the air, ready to bring it down on me. I could not have dreamed of any scenario where things could've been any worse for me.

I don't know who or what was looking over me that morning but instead of things getting any worse, which they definitely could have, with at least one - that I knew of - gun in the room, they, out of absolutely nowhere, got better.

At the exact moment where Flores had measured up and calculated where about he was going to bring the cleaver down on me, and was in the process of now readying himself to accurately swing downwards. And with all of the tension and momentary silence filling the room. The sound of a mobile phone going off cut right through it.

It was one of those old style polyphonic ring tones that you used to get on early phones, before their smart versions came on the scene. It felt surreal as hell but from what I could make out from it, the tune playing was Satisfaction, from the Rolling Stones. Talk about timing. Flores had been standing there, in the zone, ready to do it, but the sound of his phone going off had been enough to pull him back.

I about fell off the chair through relief? Possibly not as I was sure we would resume normal service one he'd taken the call, but it was something, at least. It was possibly more through the exhaustion of it all but when he put down the cleaver - as opposed to what I'd been anticipating seconds before - it felt like it had sucked every ounce of energy out of me. Looking at the phone screen for a second, he let out a little sigh before answering.

I'm sitting there unable to sit straight while nursing the worst headache I'd ever experienced, by then sure that it was blood that was trickling down my head while Flores paced around the kitchen, heavily engaged in the conversation. I didn't know if this was a good thing or bad but whatever he was being told over the phone he looked much, much more irritated by it than he'd done by not getting his favourite booth.

Due to the pain I was experiencing, it was difficult to try and keep up with what little words he was speaking to the other person but through it, I managed to pluck out a few key words that left me, once more, with a little nugget of hope that maybe I might *yet* be able to come out the other side of this with both arms and not one single bullet put into me.

Thank FUCK for those Spanish lessons I'd taken back in the nineties. While they were taken purely on the grounds of preventing anyone from trying to shaft me during business. I'd never have considered that they would've possibly ended up saving me from some medieval style punishment from a narco. Although, in all honesty, in hindsight, I should not have been *that* surprised by it.

What little I'd picked up Flores saying, I had heard him mutter something about *fiesta de cumpleanos* along with *dey jota*, and none too chuffed he was about this, either. He rattled off something else before he angrily hung up but more than half I couldn't quite make out due to the ferocity of his words.

Putting the phone back into his pocket and picking the cleaver back up. He motioned to his men in a kind of 'lets get this done' way, which had them back on point and prepared. I'd thought all along that the best policy would've been to play the dumb non Spanish speaking tourist and hope that my ignorance would be my saviour, but that hadn't worked out too well for me. But *now*, now was the time, I'd felt that I would reveal to them that I could actually speak a bit of the lingo.

'Puedo ayudarte con tu problema.'

I shouted out in desperation. Basically telling - while *hoping* I was correct - Flores that I could help him with his problem. This bombshell, enough to surprise the three of them. Flores breaking out into a laugh while - jumping on my use of the local language but replying in Spanish.

'Well look at that, eh? Our dumb idiot of a tourist is perhaps not so dumb.'

Oh I *am* dumb and truly idiotic, I thought to myself but saw no benefit in correcting him. What then followed - once I had been given the chance to elaborate on my surprise outburst - was more of a 'mature and adult' conversation between people where I no longer had a gun on me or my arm forced down in such a precarious position that it was in danger of being broken, never mind fucking lopped off. Fuck, I was even allowed a cigarette and a couple of bumps of sniff, to try and ease the incredible pain emitting from my throbbing head. All of that an absolute pipe dream from happening, moments before the phone call.

Explaining to Flores that while I'd said that I had worked in the music industry, I was *specifically* a DJ agent slash manager and owned a company back in London that had deejays from all over Europe and America on my roster. And my actual reason for being in Jalisco *wasn't* there as the assumed tourist but, in fact, because one of my deejays - someone quite famous in the circles of house music and clubland - was opening his tour, here in Guadalajara. Flores' face lighting up on hearing this, clearly already sensing *why* I was telling him this, specifically.

'And due to what I heard you say in your call, and how it sounds like your DJ has let you down. I think I might be able to help you fix your problem.'

Unless I had picked it up wrong, I was sure that I'd heard something about Flores wanting the DJ killed which, if true, would've been completely on brand for those type of guys. Look at me for not wanting to give up a simple seat?

And Flores is standing there, puffing enthusiastically on a cigarette of his own, nodding his head like fucking YES! I pulled up the Ragamuffin Talent website to show him I wasn't bullshitting him. Then some pictures of me from Google, confirming who I *was*. Sat there blowing the biggest amount of smoke up Zico's arse, telling Flores that he was one of the world's biggest deejays while showing him a choice selection of YouTube footage from some of the biggest events he'd played.

'And you know what I'm thinking Don Flores? To make up for my rudeness earlier on. I would like to offer you the services of my DJ, free of charge, as a gesture of goodwill to you on your son's special day. Normally the fee is thousands of dollars but not for you.'

My only request - not that I was in a position to be sitting there making any kinds of demands - was that DJ Selecao would be ready for opening his tour the next night. Explaining that I was no stranger to parties that could go on for days but that, on this occasion, I - and my DJ - had a contractural commitment to meet for the opening of the tour, and all the thousands of tickets that had been sold for it.

I appreciated that Zico was most likely somewhere thirty thousand feet in the air during this moment and would no doubt be left with something to say when he arrived and got here to find out that he had been booked to play a junior narco's birthday party - for free - the night before his tour opener but it wasn't like I'd had any other option open to me. And besides, given some of his *own* personal experiences over the years, I'd like to have thought that he would've understood.

Enrique Emilano Garcia Flores - to give him his full name - was in complete agreement with this. Not only had he managed to avert disaster - and headache from his wife, who had called him and left him to find another - but he'd done so and come out of it looking even better, due to *now* having a famous international DJ hired, instead of the - likely - local one that had originally been booked, and a DJ who had now quite possibly played his last set.

Flores took my business card from me along with a note of which hotel myself - and soon to be - Stevie were staying with the agreement that he would call me in the morning ahead of sending transport to take us to his mansion in Mazatlan.

I didn't know where Mazatlan was. And didn't really care, either. Not when there was an arm at stake. If Flores' son's birthday party had been on one of Jupiter's ninety five moons, DJ Selecao would be playing at it.

Snatching victory from the jaws of defeat. I was allowed to gather my belongings and leave. Flores and myself exchanging a strong firm handshake to end what had been a real meeting of minds. When I turned to leave he must've seen enough of the side of my head that had been bashed to cause alarm and called me instantly back. Throwing a dish towel towards me. Saying that it might be a good idea if I was to try and stop the blood that was coming from me. I just wanted out of there before anything happened to change Flores' mind about things.

Thanking him and nodding to the two goons, I left the kitchen to find that Manuel was now back behind the bar, pretending to clean glasses while he stood as close to the kitchen - from the bar area - as he could to listen in.

Strapping the rucksack to my back and checking that I had all of my vitals, being phone, wallet, cigarettes and my gear, I made the international sign for turning a key to Manuel and he was prompt in coming behind the bar to let me go. I could see the relief on his face that I was walking out of there relatively unharmed, save for the pissing blood coming from my head wound. But that was something I'd have *gladly* have taken, once I'd realised the likely consequences of my actions.

I met Manuel's look of relief with a comedy wipe of the brow, which I took him to have seen that this was not me saying that it was a hot one.

As much as I'd liked to have said that I was there on the tour to be the voice of reason and the moment of calm when required, but it was likely bollocks. The trip and tour we were about to go on had *always* come with the high chance of becoming messy and, potentially, dangerous. Having said that, though. Even then, I didn't think the dangerous part would arrive inside the first morning of the first day. And before my DJ had even *arrived*.

Understandably, my introduction to Guadalajara had spooked me, big time. Leaving the cantina, the initial thought of finding somewhere else to sit inside and get back on track was quickly shouted down. Instead, I headed back to the hotel for an afternoon of answering emails and making phone calls while I made a dent in my three wraps of sniff and pestering room service to bring me margaritas approximately every half an hour.

Zico was getting in later on in the evening so I decided to sit tight in the hotel until it was time to get him. Thinking I would take my boy out for dinner when he arrived and break the news to him that he'd now had an extra date added to his tour, and the baggage that it would come with.

Chapter 4

Zico

'You never fucking told me it was a twelve hour round trip, you bastard! And in this fucking heat, as well?'

I wasn't thrilled with my quote unquote *manager*. Not chuffed about the round trip he'd signed us all up for. And just as equally not chuffed about the shit he had put himself - and by extension, *me* - in before I'd even got there to the state of Jalisco. An absolute liability of a man and I don't give one single fuck that he'd most probably say the very same thing about me. Aren't these cunts meant to like, manage, though? And make things better, instead of badly worse? Well, aye. That's the plan but if all managers actually *did* possess the ability to 'manage' then that fucking radge Atletico Madrid owner - Jesus Gil - from years back wouldn't have went through about a trillion of them.

The fact that before I'd even *arrived*, there in Mexico, Lee had almost gotten bits of himself chopped off - inside two hours of hitting the fucking street, mind - was not the best of omens for the weeks that lay ahead, as much as I'd been looking forward to them.

As I pulled up the approximate journey on the maps app and found it to be - at the very least - six hours. Lee's reaction to this had told me that he hadn't even bothered to work out the logistics of where exactly we were being sent to when he'd agreed to supply me for selecting duties, at the birthday party of someone I *still* didn't know their name. Well, I suppose 'agreed' wouldn't have been the exact word. Offered up and said a fucking Hail Mary for it to be accepted would've been more accurate for him in the sticky situation he'd landed himself in.

It had been when he'd let me know that the arranged car was collecting us at 1pm that I had felt something a little off. I'd been told - out of the most vague of details from my agent - that I was playing a birthday party *that night*. So why the fuck were we being picked up at such an abnormal early time? The answer provided by the application on my phone. That we'd be on the road for around three hundred fucking miles to just *get* to the venue.

Earlier on that morning - when, technically, I should've been sleeping but had, regrettably, found sleep in short supply over the night - the two from the music magazine had arrived from off their flight. Lee bringing them to me to do the introductions while I sat in one of the downstairs hotel lounges, having a cup of coffee while attempting to find out something about the man who had threatened to dismember Lee, and who I had now been booked to play for. Never wanting to go into what could be a precarious situation blind mixed with the experiences I'd had to go through in the past. I felt that it wouldn't have hurt to have done a little bit of homework.

What I'd managed to find - in the short space of time awarded to me - was that the boy Flores - known generally as El Hombrecito - seemed to be one of the main Sinaloa Cartel bosses, in the Mazatlan area of the region. I'd only really heard of Culiacan so had been happy to learn that we weren't going as far as that into Sinaloa but - reading up on Mazatlan - I could see why the cartel would've had a heavy presence in that town, with it being a popular Mexican resort, sat overlooking the Pacific shoreline. The town, itself, looked like there was a lot of money behind it with scores of high end hotels and mansions dotted around, although I'd already taken things for granted that I wasn't going to *see* much of the place. Which, funnily enough, wasn't much different to most of the other trips I'd make from week to week on bookings.

Fly to A, the city destined for. Get taxi to B, the hotel booked for me and then, later on same day, get taxi from B to C, the club or event. Perform your set and then repeat every one of those steps, only in reverse.

'Stevie, I want you to meet Myles and Luke, from One's and Two's Magazine,'

Lee said, breaking the peace and quiet that I was sat enjoying while pulling me away from a - badly - translated to English article I was reading online, in connection with Enrique Emilano Garcia Flores, and the attempts that the American D.E.A had made to try to have him arrested and extradited to the States for prosecution. That mob not really bothering with minnows so that, in itself, was evidence that the man was regarded as high up enough the food chain to matter. One of their bosses - Chapo Guzman - had been arrested earlier on in the year and it was telling that while trying to capitalise on this upheaval to the Sinaloa Cartel, that the Shermans would feel it appropriate to try and take Flores out of the game. The article, from what I had managed to read up to before being disturbed, had suggested that the Americans had failed due to how many 'friendly faces' a man like Flores keeps on the payroll on the law enforcement side of things. Aye, Lee couldn't have just pissed off a low level sicario or something and, instead, had to attract the attention of someone sitting at the very top of the cartel's 'family tree.' Never did do things by halves, though. Lee Isaac.

I looked up and saw what appeared to be a couple of men who looked like they'd been travelling for *days*. This confirmed to be the case when the journalist out of the two - Myles - told me later on that he'd travelled from Goa to Guadalajara on what had been chosen as the cheapest route to fly - by his editor - and had involved five different connections between India and Jalisco. They'd both seemed ok enough as far as first impressions went, even if I'd not tried to hide from Lee that I was pissed off that he'd even green lit their presence in the first place.

'The legend, himself,'

Myles Lomas said out loud with his hand out to shake mine, when being introduced to me, before saying how he'd seen one of my earliest gigs back at the long since - now - gone club, The Venue, in Edinburgh. He looked old enough to have been around back in those days - I'd estimated him to be around fifty or so - but to even mention an establishment such as that would let someone know that you weren't some novice and, for some, it was like a badge of honour that they were able to - years later - tell people that they'd visited it when in its pomp. Kind of on the same par as clubs like Manchester's Hacienda or Liverpool's Quadrant Park. Venues that as the years had passed there would've been some serious revisionism done by clubbers with many lying, saying that they'd visited it back in the day, when they, in fact, hadn't.

'Oh *that* was some gaff, wasn't it?'

I replied, unable to stop myself from going all misty eyed at the mention of it for a brief second, while I shook his hand. The other - Luke Clifton - the consummate photographer with camera fixed around his neck and snapping me shaking hands with his colleague. Then asking if we could both turn his way for a photo of us both. Me joking - in that way that some from the Caribbean would describe as 'truth pass as joke' - that *no one* would want to see a picture of two men who both looked like they hadn't slept for days. Not their readers and *definitely* not me and Myles. I then shook Luke's hand, once he let go of his camera to rest back around his neck.

Aye, on the surface of things, the two of them seemed to be decent enough boys but even as frazzled as my head was that morning, I'd known that now was not the time for judging either of them, and that I'd have known after a day or two of their company on how I *really* felt about them. I'd found it funny at the front that my agent had been putting on for them. One of this professional DJ - Mr fixer. While feeling that it had been a waste of effort from him due to the fact that before the day had been done they'd have surely seen the *real* Lee.

While the four of us sat there at the table and the subject of my tour opener - the next night - was brought up, Lee sat and informed them that there had been a hastily arranged 'additional date' confirmed for later on that day. Telling them that with the tour not officially due to start for another day, they were free to acclimatise themselves there at the hotel but, also, if they liked then they were free to come with us to - what he had put across as - the birthday party for a friend. The way he'd delivered all of this, though? This was pure Lee. Aye, he was giving them the choice but while doing this, he was clearly trying to sway them in the direction of coming to Mazatlan with us.

My opinion was that they should've just been here to cover my *official* appearances and should have been let nowhere fucking *near* a party filled with narcos. But Lee - always ready to play up to my links to cartels and shit, as a result of my dad, to make me more marketable - had other ideas and was clearly of the opinion that to report on a story like me playing a private party for known Sinaloa Cartel members would've been box office. Maybe he was right - he often was, despite being a complete liability - with that but it had irked me how he was always ready to go down that road instead of just recognising that I was a good enough - and known enough - DJ to stand or fall on my own talent.

Despite Lee being a bit - aye, a bit - of a caner and someone who was always ready to resort to hyperbole - if he thought it could benefit his DJ agency and generate him and his DJ more money - he was not a stupid man. In no way did he give hint, to the two of them, of what *kind* of party I was playing at later on that night, but knew that it wouldn't have taken long for them to see for themselves when they'd found themselves in and amongst it all.

They both looked at each other, to see if they were both in agreement on whether they would come with us or stay behind, even though I'd already assumed that they would. When Lee added that the car was coming to collect us in around three hours time, there had been a bit of hope from me that this extra piece of information would've been enough to see them just stay behind for the day, because that's *exactly* what I'd have done, had I just got off a plane a few hours before and been given the chance to relax or travel six plus hours in a car in the Mexican heat.

'Would love to go, Lee,'

Myles confirmed. Luke, nodding alongside this.

'Please don't feel the need to come, lads. You don't have to feel obliged or anything,'

I said to them while treading the fine line of trying not to come across as someone who didn't *want* them to come and, instead, someone who was trying to look out for their own interests. Absolutely no offence to the pair of them but the way I was feeling - through a dangerously severe lack of sleep - the fucking *last* thing I needed was to sit in a car for six or so hours making small talk with two strangers.

I could feel Lee's glare at this due to him - having already known my feelings on the two of them having been invited to cover the tour - seeing *exactly* what I was trying to do, which was going against what he'd literally just stood their trying to engineer.

'Aye, it's just a wee set that I've been asked to play on behalf of one of Lee's contacts.'

I left it at that, with the ambiguous term of *contact*. Lee already telling me - in advance of them arriving - that I was to keep it shut, when it came to what had happened with him the day before. That was pure Lee. Aye, perish the thought that anyone should know that he'd been fraternising with cartel members but having no hesitation in hamming up any connection that *I* might have with the same kind of colourful characters.

The pair of them, took my advice on board but said that they'd both like to come. Lomas saying that a journalist normally doesn't get access to a DJ playing more personal sets - away from the clubs and festival big tents - so it was an opportunity that he'd jump at. Clifton, backing his mate up by saying that, as a photographer, he *also* generally never got the chance to take photos in more of an intimate environment.

Not that I said it, but the image of him walking around a junior narco's birthday party snapping photos felt like an absolute fantasy - as I'd already knew a few things about a few things and could not see *any* scenario where people from the Sinaloa fucking Cartel, and who knew who else that would be in attendance, would be complete 'tranquilo' about some gringo walking around talking photos of them - but I decided that I would let him travel all of those miles and hours only to find out that he wouldn't be allowed to. Don't get me wrong, it would've quite possibly been a very easy way to have them change their minds and to not go - if they'd been told that it was the type of bash that their camera and notebook would not be welcome - but to tell them this in advance would've had Lee all biscuit ersed and the thought of him and me travelling so far in the same car while on bad terms was not something I was willing to have to put up with. My day had already been complicated enough already without any of that shite.

There was no change of heart. The two of them agreed to meet up with me and Lee - back in reception - at the pick up time. Departing to go and freshen up and prepare for their trip. Lee saying he was also away to take care of business - whatever that actually meant - which was fine with me as it let me get some peace and quiet on a day where *that* was going to be rare in supply.

'Just make sure you've got all your stuff ready for one o'clock. It might be a long day.'

He said, before leaving me to it. *Might* being his code speak for *will*. He couldn't tell me - as in had been so intent on saving his skin that he hadn't asked much in the way of details - how long we were going to be there in Mazatlan for and even when it was time for us to leave, we'd then have that bastard of a return journey back to Guadalajara. Due to all of these factors combined, had we been arriving back at the hotel twenty four hours after leaving, I wouldn't have been surprised.

When it came to our chariot, to take us to Sinaloa. No expense had been spared and, frankly, the *hospitality* laid out for us by El Hombrecito was something that the club owners and festival companies that were responsible for looking after me when I'd come to town and play, could've learned a lot from.

The four of us were stood there in the lobby when bang on 1pm a chauffeur - dressed in back suit and tie including the obligatory hat - walked into the hotel and asked the lady behind the desk for Lee.

'Señor Isaac,'

she said from the desk towards our group, and pointing the driver in our direction. The man walking across to greet us with an hola while asking us if we'd like to follow him out to the car. Walking outside we were greeted by a stretched black limo. I'd had ride all knowledge of what kind of manufacturer it was, only that it was long as fuck, and looked like it was so new it had just come straight from the factory production line.

Lee looked at me as if it say 'Eh? Impressive or what?' while the two from the magazine looked visibly excited about this development. If any of us were impressed by this - and we were - then we only knew *part* of the story, because we still hadn't seen the *inside* of it yet.

With the chauffeur - who we'd find to be called Carlos and an absolute gentleman who knew the line between talking to his passengers and talking too *much* to his passengers - holding the door open for us, I slipped in first. The inside simply exuding luxury, comfort and literally *begging* to attend to your every need. The plush leather wrap around seats that were deeply cushioned and soft to the touch, the incredible leg room, the air conditioning which made the back of the car feel like the inside of a butcher's freezer and the mirrored ceiling. But that really was just the start.

In the middle was a polished bar with crystal glassware - which I'd taken to be filled with some kind of a scotch - and ice buckets that were filled with either bottles of 'Estrella Jalisco' and soft drinks such as Coca Cola and Sprite or filled with fresh fruit. Then there was a fridge elsewhere, stacked with more alcohol and snacks. And *that* was without even mentioning the amount of fucking *ching* that was sitting in one of the small cupboards that kept most of the glasses in. And then there was the accompaniment to go with the ching in the glass case that was filled with pre rolls. They weren't - by my standards - what you'd have called a fully sized joint and were more the smaller sized ones that you'd see Pablo Escobar puffing on back when he was alive. The kind that Americans would be seen smoking in films and TV shows. But in a case of beggars against choosers. It meant that I wouldn't have to roll any for myself while there was, also, the assumption that they were going to be pure joints. Just as fucking well there was premium grade ching to go with it otherwise you'd be baked after a couple of puffs.

I couldn't have known but if you'd told me there was a quarter of a kilo inside that large wooden tub, I would not have argued with you. Surely that was *way* too much than required? Even accounting for Lee - simply being Lee - or maybe myself, when things started to get out of control? I suppose, when you're in the trade and the 'staff discount' that you enjoy, what can be seen as a 'large' amount of cocaine can be something seen as objective?

It had been a drug that - over the years - I had seen destroy so many of the lives of my fellow deejays so had always shown it the respect that it deserved and was someone that had possessed the ability to take it or leave it but, being honest, when I took it, I fucking *took it*. Always of the opinion that if you're going to get caught for stealing a lamb then you may as well make it a fucking *sheep*!

This had been supposed to be my day of rest and sleep. Instead of this, I'd - finally - arrived in Guadalajara late the night before and after an absolutely fucking stinker of a day travelling, dealing with dickhead TSA agents in New Jersey and then the ripple effects of me missing my original connection to Jalisco and the various hoops that I'd had to jump through to still reach my destination inside the same day that I'd first left my home in Amsterdam. Lee collecting me and taking me for a late dinner - when I'd have been happy enough with a taco truck by the side of the road somewhere - which then, when going to our own rooms in the hotel for the night - slotted right into my jet lag striking. Which had kept me up all night. Fucking kid you not. *Three* wanks I had, trying to put me to sleep. Not that it worked. After the third I said to myself that I could still be sat there pulling the fucking end of it when the alarm clock was going off to get me up for the day. But instead of now being given the chance to recover from all of that, here we were off along the coast of Jalisco on our way to Mazatlan. Fucking *right* I'd be tucking into the free gear that had been laid out for us. Only my consumption would be required in a medicinal sense, rather than as recreational.

As we were getting set for the off, my phone sparked into action. The caller? Well if wasn't my best buddy, Simon Milne. There wasn't many people in the world that I'd have been too interested in speaking to at that point in the day but - alongside my good lady, Flo - Si was one of them.

'Ahoy, hoy,'

I answered, mimicking Mr Burns from The Simpsons during the episode where he learns to use the phone, due to Homer Simpson not being the most helpful of assistants at the power plant.

'*Raddddddgeyyyyyyyy,*'

he replied back, in a deep gruff - rough as fuck and possibly either presently drunk or still a little under the effect after waking up for the day. He was in Vegas - with his girl of only a couple of months from back in Amsterdam - on a week's holiday. Well that's what *I'd* thought, anyway.

'What's happening, lad?'

I asked as the car began to pull away from the entrance to the 'Mayan Mansions' hotel.

'Where are you, Zeek?'

He asked, even though he already *knew* where I was. The two of us exchanging a few messages back and forth across the previous day when I was trying to get to Mexico.

'Guadalajara, mate. Have you forgotten all of yesterday already?'

'No, where are you *right now*?'

'I'm in a car with Lee and the two from the music magazine. Honestly, don't even fucking ask, mate.'

I shot Lee a quick evil eyed stare which had been wasted since he was too busy eyeing up the wooden tub of ching.

'Any chance you can pick me up at the airport then?'

Now this confused the fuck out of me for a moment until he explained that he'd had a big argument with Greta - who I had already warned about going on holiday with someone who was still relatively new in his life - after him suggesting that they extend their trip by ditching Las Vegas and flying down to Mexico to catch me on my opening night, and then beyond. Her, apparently, wanting to stay there in Vegas, and Si having decided differently.

'Aye, in the end I got her telt, like. Told her to enjoy the rest of Vegas and that I had her flight back covered, but I was off.'

'I take it that's the end of the relationship then, Si?'

'Not sure, mate. I'd imagine so, to be honest. She wasn't best pleased about me leaving her there, like.'

He didn't sound too crushed about things. But that was Si. I was glad to hear of this unexpected development as - along with Flo - Si was the *one person* that I'd have wanted along with me for the ride that was going to be Mexico and South America. We'd been through so much over the years and it had felt like a chance missed for me to be on such a tour and him not be there. He'd obviously felt the same and this had not been the first time over the years where he'd - completely out of the blue - dropped everything to fly out and play his part in the 'festivities.'

While Si was still on the phone, I knocked on the see through glass partition - separating passengers from driver - to ask Carlos how long it would take to reach Guadalajara airport. Half an hour to forty minutes, his reply which led to me asking him to make the detour before we got on our way to Sinaloa.

This, enough to get Lee's attention away from the free powder and for him to try and argue the fact that we wouldn't be diverting to the airport to pick him up.

'Tell that Cockney cunt to go and throw shite at the fucking moon.'

Si's opinion on what he was overhearing from Lee. The term 'Cockney cunt' being a - semi - affectionate term that Si had for my manager and agent and had called him to his face on pretty much every occasion they'd been together.

'Listen, pal. There's two choices, here. Either we pick Si up at the airport and then head to Sinaloa or I just get out this car right now and we don't go to Sinaloa at all.'

I chose the nuclear option of calling Lee's bluff. It hadn't been me who had talked their way into the trouble that they had now found themselves in, where they had promised a bit of a serious boy, in Flores, a DJ. But with me being the *actual* DJ, then I clearly held a bit of sway, when it came to what happened next.

'You fucking tell him, Zeek,'

Si laughed before quickly following up with '*Sinaloa? Why the fuck are we going to Sinaloa?* You literally said last week to me that it was probably for the best that you didn't have any dates for there'

I had Si on one side and Lee on the other, both talking at once. Leaving me with the impossible task of trying to take in what was being said.

'Aye, mate. Like I said, don't ask. I don't have a fucking clue where I'm going, who I'm playing for and for how long but when you see the car that they've sorted out for transport, not to mention the goodies that were inside of it, then it'll give you some kind of an indicator.'

I noticed Myles and Luke exchanging a glance at each other on hearing this from me as, for the first time since they'd arrived, they were now hearing that this unscheduled appearance from me in Mazatlan seemed to be something that even I hadn't known much about.

In the end, I'd left Lee with no choice. I know that part of the reason was that he'd have wanted to have kept Si away from the cartel party, for fear of how he might've behaved. But to do so would've been pretty fucking high in its hypocrisy. Since we were only *going* to a fucking cartel party because of *his* behaviour.

'International arrivals, Carlos. Just look for the whitest man standing around outside.'

I instructed our driver who offered nothing other than a compliant

'si, señor'

as he pulled out onto the main street. Me then confirming things with Si to wait around arrivals while assuring him that he'd see us coming.

I don't think Lee was too happy about it all but I hoped that the knowledge that he never had a choice in it would've helped get him over it. I wasn't sure if it was either having two relative strangers sat in the car with us that stopped him from saying his piece or him knowing that I'd have hit him with all kinds of truths which would point towards him not really having been in a position to even start to open his mouth but whichever it was, he never said a word about it, following me ending the call with Si and returning to the room again.

Speaking of Lee, I'd found it highly amusing sat facing him in the back of the limo and knowing that he had wanted to get fired into the ching sitting there from the moment that he'd seen it. But, I'd assumed, he was self aware about the two from the magazine, and had wanted to remain professional. Myself, on the other hand, had been comfortable in the fact that when I wanted to have some, I'd have done so without any issues of having these two from the magazine sat there watching on.

Well known House DJ in taking drugs shock. A headline for an article, one that you would never be likely to ever see. And fair play to him because he managed to remain professional for all of twenty minutes before saying to the rest of us, and almost in that kind of way where someone really wants something but feel like they should put the feelers out for some approval from others, before going on and doing it, regardless.

'Well, it would be rude not to take up our host's hospitality. How's it going to look if we arrive in Sinaloa and he finds that we've not enjoyed his generosity. That stuff can be offensive with some cultures, can't it?'

'Oh for fuck's sake, mate. Just get some up your fucking hooter and have it done with,'

I laughed at him, even if he'd already had the lid from the wooden box off and picked up one of the - apparent - gold mini cocaine spoons that were sat to the side of the box in the cupboard.

'Whoooahhhh, that'll wake you up, Stevie, my son.'

Lee, now a completely new man, smiled back at me. Any hesitancies of how to behave - around company - now evaporated. Straight away, now asking me if I wanted a bump or two. And I say this without any kind of self justification. I was on my arse, and only going to get worse. So I was not against a few medicinal dosages. Which, obviously, would not stop at 'a few,' once started.

Telling the rest of them that I was close to falling asleep while already knowing that Si simply would not have allowed this to happen once he got in the car at the airport, I took the box and spoon and had one bump up each nostril. Fuck was it a heavy knock to the brain. The kind of hard impact on your senses that made you question how your average cocaine dealer would have the red neck to be selling the quality of gear that was generally accepted in the west.

Any thoughts of sleeping, removed within a matter of seconds. I then offered the box and spoon to the journalist and he, along with the photographer, declined the offer although I could see that it was written all over Myles' face that he'd *wanted* to accept the box. If he'd been around in the electronic music business for the years that he was showing - age wise - then there was no question that he wouldn't have been a stranger to drugs, or Luke.

I didn't press it. Still didn't really know them - or if I could trust them - so didn't feel like giving the boy any unnecessary ammunition by presenting him with the chance to - factually - say that I'd been instrumental in him getting fired into any drugs during the tour. Of course, being the kind of double act that we were. For me to offer it once to them and then pass the box back to Lee to store away after them passing up the chance, Si got into the car and did the exact *opposite* of me.

First of all, when we pulled up outside arrivals, I jumped out the car to give him a big hug. I'm not sure if it was due to how thankful I was to have him there or if it was a result of the quality of the gear laid on by the Mexicans, because it definitely hadn't been through some massive gap in when we'd last seen each other. Three weeks prior to Guadalajara to be precise. Back in two thousand he'd came over to Amsterdam to hide out for a bit when his life had turned to shit and he simply never left. Of course, it was easier to do once he'd got his payment for the whole illegal imprisonment that he'd suffered at the hands of the Spanish, and something that only came to light at the end of his sentence. Obviously.

Jumping into the back of the limo beside everyone else he was introduced to Myles and Luke, nodding to Lee while unable to resist sarcastically - but not overly - apologising to him for putting him out in any way. Lee, in his happy place, smiled - genuinely - while telling Si not to be daft.

'Check this fucking gaff out, though, eh?'

Si said, now beginning to fully appreciate the luxurious surroundings that he'd stepped into, and helping himself to a bottle of cold beer.

'You don't know the half of it, fella,'

Lee said, grinning from ear to ear, while reaching back into the cupboard and producing the box with the gear in it, opening. the lid to let Si look into it.

'Oh, **Fuck. Off!**'

He laughed while motioning with his hand for Lee to hand it over, whole placing his beer down onto the table beside of him. While there had been some initial hesitancy for Lee to have cracked open the box and undertaking the inevitable. There wasn't so much resistance from Si.

'JESUS FUCKING CHRIST… What *is* that?!'

He shouted to me, after his second dunt. Pinching at and massaging his nose before going for a secondary sniff to make sure nothing had been left behind.

'Didn't I fucking tell you?'

I laughed, while remembering my one and only previous time in this part of the world, and what I'd told Si about the cocaine.

'Aye but there's telling someone and then there's them being prepared for it. And there's *no* fucking preparing yourself for that shit!'

Si then passed - forced, even - the box into Myles' hand while insisting.

'There you go, pal. Get fired into that. No point handing it to Zeek or his gaffer because neither of them look like they fucking need it, eh?'

He elbowed me in the ribs, while laughing. Combining this with a nod towards Lee. Myles chose to stick to the original script, prior to Si getting in.

'No, I don't ...'

'What do you mean, no?

Si asked in that non negotiable way someone will often be with you when they decide to get inebriated and, as a result, have decided that they don't want to be the only one who does so. Si going on to tell Myles - and Luke - that we didn't want any of an 'us and them' scenario there in the car and that if we were going to make this the party limo then we'd *all* need to do our bit. Telling them that if me, him and Lee were going to end up as insufferable cunts - through the bollocks we'd inevitably end up talking - then that could be combatted by Myles and Luke *also* being just as insufferable.

Si had always been the convincing type and a boy who'd possessed the ability - and talent - to have you agreeing with his suggestion - whether that would be a good or bad thing - simply through a couple of carefully selected words and the smile to go with it. So it wasn't surprising to see, first of all, Myles and then his photographer give in to this one man's peer pressure. Even without Si's persistence, that Myles had looked like he'd been fucking *itching* to get involved in things so at least Si had put the boy out of his misery.

With everyone inside the back now absolutely flying, and us left with everything we could've ever needed. The six hour -

plus - journey had now been given another spin put on it, and the thought of it was nowhere near as bad as I'd imagined, when back at the hotel and being horrified at the journey time, once I'd looked it up.

The hours seemed to fly in, as we drove along the west coast. All five of us not short on conversation. The two from the magazine, while still strangers to us, had found it no problems in opening up to us and fitting in, following them meeting up to every one else's wavelength. Myles - with some of the stories he shared with us - *was* a fucking caner. Something he'd pretty much given away when he'd clocked that box of ching. And Luke was no better. Myles telling us about the previous time the pair of them had worked together and the state Luke had ended up in through too much ketamine. And there really is not many things worse in life than too much ketamine. *This* is widely regarded as fact.

Si had us all pissing ourselves laughing with some of the tales that he'd come away from Vegas with. The farcical scenario where he was almost the cause of a big fight - at one of the blackjack tables - one night due to *how* he was playing. I mean, I thought it was a free country - and I guess so did Si - but when he was sitting on something like an eighteen and was asking for another card. This, apparently, wound up both the dealer and the others there at the table. According to Si, the dealer - knowing what Si was already on - wouldn't give him another card, which then wound Si, in his eyes and the paying customer, right up. This happened again a few rounds later, only one of the other players voiced their displeasure. Accusing Si of not taking the game seriously and to go play on another table and leave things to the pros. Which was always going to wind up my mate.

'Honestly? What did I do wrong? You'd have thought the casino would've *loved* me taking risks like that. Dealer was well annoyed though. Was proper baffling. As for those dickheads there at the table. I told one of these Shermans, someone there for the weekend from Oregon with his breadknife to mind his own cards, and to mind his own fucking business. Even though the obese cunt looked like he'd have suffered from a stroke through getting up too quickly from his chair not to mention about him being a good twenty years older looked like he was wanting it. Dishing out the threats of 'kicking my ass.' Is that with or without using a gun, aye? I told the cunt before saying to sit back down before I put him down. Didn't push my luck, though as you ken what those casinos can be like, eh? Before you know it you're in some back room getting all sorts fucking done on you, eh?'

The fact that while he told this story. He was sat there with a flute of champagne in one hand, a half cut orange in the other while he had one of the pre rolls shoved firmly in his gub, only enhancing the story.

For me, normally, a road trip somewhere I've never been before, seeing what's going on outside is a big part of the journey. But in truth, on that Guadalajara to Mazatlan journey, I doubt any of us barely even clocked it. Free alcohol and drugs, and the impact that can have on the average human being, and the free flowing complete nonsense of a conversation will do that, though.

I *did* manage to clock a bit of the Pacific Ocean when we were running along side of it at our closest point, though, and couldn't deny how stunning it all looked. I'd watched one of those Discovery Channel programmes on it and was sure that the narrator had said something like how it was so large that it covered about thirty percent of the planet, which was one of those things that you struggle to get your head around. The kind of creatures down thirty six thousand feet below - where the light doesn't reach - would be the stuff of nightmares. From a distance, though? Looked well barry.

As far as the journey had been far from ideal, it had also - kind of - worked in your favour. Because it allowed the chance to enter deep into the party spirit for the majority of the journey and *still* provide you with enough time to try and straighten yourself, ahead of arriving at the destination. Because it didn't matter *where* I was playing. Turning up out of your nut was never a good look and not the road to take to pull out a good performance. I'd made all of those mistakes when I was younger, many times.

Due to the dramatic change of the landscape ahead of us, I'd been given the impression that Mazatlan was now close. The buildings that could be seen sprouting up into the sky up ahead - as opposed to what had been our scenery for the majority of the coastal drive - gave off the idea that we were entering proper civilisation again.

Carlos confirming to me - when asked - that we were coming up for what looked like a lively town. Telling me that we weren't too far now from reaching the mansion that belonged to 'Don Flores.'

In anticipation of our imminent arrival, paying more attention to where Carlos was driving. No sooner had we found ourselves entering what was a much more busy area in terms of traffic, buildings outside and members of the public walking around, we had again pulled off this main strip and looked to be heading into a more secluded area. Apart from the odd car travelling in the same direction as us, the road had been practically deserted.

Eventually, after a few more miles, I thought I had now seen the reason for the road being so quiet. Coming into view, up ahead, seemed to be something blocking the road. Closer still and I could now see what looked to be two Toyota Hilux, which unless I was seeing things each had a gun turret on the back. Closer still and I could see that we were heading in the direction of the military, with various soldiers standing around in full camouflage uniform, holding onto some serious pieces of weaponry. And with me having clocked them, this had, of course, went both ways.

Watching us approach, and with Carlos slowing down, the soldier standing at the front of his group was signalling for us to pull up while two others appeared to the side of him - one on either shoulder - and raised their rifles, pointing them towards the limo.

Chapter 5

Zico

'Do not do anything weird, do as I say and everyone should be ok.'

Carlos looked around for a second and told everyone. Don't do anything weird? What the fuck did that even *mean*? Luke the photographer had been chewing the inside of his cheek for the best part of the last couple of hours. That, alone, could've been construed as 'weird.' Did that mean that we were going to be gunned down as a consequence?

Slowing the car down to a complete stop by the side of the road, Carlos put the drivers side window down for the soldier who was walking up to the car. The two of them exchanging words while the five of us in the back looked at each other worried. Despite our best efforts along the journey, we still had a ridiculous amount of ching left in the back with us, along with the majority of the pre rolls which - with Si and me being the only tokers present - we'd barely made a dent in.

This did not seem good. After the briefest of chats - while in the back we sat deathly still as well as mute - Carlos turned around and asked us to get out the car. Trying to assure us that it was fine as Lee opened the door nearest to him and started the procession. No offence to Carlos here, like, but he was just a driver who I'd only met for the first time hours before. His assurances - while I was a stranger, thousands of miles away and deep in cartel country as the military stood outside holding automatic rifles - meant Scottish fucking Fitba Association.

Before getting out of the limo - last of all - I had the fleeting thought of maybe I should try to hide the gear, but really? Where the fuck was I going to put a box as large as that in a car? Besides that, though. There was the *real* possibility that if the soldiers had clocked some suspicious movement going on inside the car, who's to say what their response to this was going to be?

Due to the length of the limo, it had made it relatively easy for the army to line the five of us - only Carlos had not been asked to - against the car while they dealt with things. The soldier - who I was now taking to be the rest's gaffer moved around to look over us. While he hadn't felt the need to raise any of his weapons, he had a couple stood beside him who very much *did*. There rifles up and trained on us while he barked at us in Spanish. The three of them were proper kitted out, like. Even had the helmets on with the Go-Pros slotted snugly into the front. Fuck knows the coupons on all of us that someone would possibly be looking at when the recordings were played back.

When his barked instructions was met with blank looks he took on the appearance of someone now annoyed by this. Muttering 'pinches gringos,' which while I didn't know what this meant, it was clearly not a term of endearment. While continuing to speak Spanish at us he lifted one hand and twirled his index finger around, indicating for us to do a one eighty and face the roof of the limo. Compliantly, we all did as told. It had been my hope that this was asked of us so that we could be contained while searched. But that's all it had been. For all I know, we were being asked to turn our backs to make things easy for them to put a bullet into each of our nappers.

I don't think I could've ever felt such relief at another man laying is hands on me and running them over my body than I did when I felt the hands belonging to one of the soldiers on me. Starting at my ankles and running all the way up my legs. Reaching the top of my leg and then up to the elastic band of my boxers where he ran his thumb inside the elastic and all the way around. Personally, when he got around to the front of me and traced his thumb around - literally running his thumb through the top of my pubes - I felt that this was a wee bit above and beyond, when it came to a frisk, but really, what the fuck was I going to be able to *do* about it? Satisfied with my full search from top to bottom, he moved onto Si.

'The boy's going to get a wee bit fruity with you, Si, but don't react, mate.'

I looked to the side and said to Si. Carrying on my rich and well documented tradition of saying dumb stuff at the worst possible times. The soldier wasn't having any of it. Shouting *'Silencio'* at me while kicking my leg from behind which - not knowing that it was coming - almost buckled both legs and sent me to the ground. It was a mistake I wouldn't be making again.

Still, that didn't appear to put Lee off, when the series of searches reached the end of the line and my manager. While we'd been told to look forward, it had still been possible to see out of the side enough to clock what was going on with the facial expressions of the rest. Si had just sucked it up and stood there while he came close to being sexually assaulted. You could tell that he'd wanted to say something but knew it wouldn't have been wise. That, though, did not stop me from bracing myself for the possibility of him *still* having a word, while saying a prayer inside that he wouldn't. As for Myles and Luke? The pair of them looked like they'd been regretting their choices in coming to cover my tour. They looked shit scared if I'm being honest. Hey, maybe I had too, for all I knew. Because I knew that this was a highly delicate and serious situation.

Had we been back in Britain, it wouldn't have been out the question - when searched outside your car - to have asked the coppers *why?* Shit, the coppers would've *told* you why, before they even started. But this wasn't the United Kingdom and these were not traffic cops, looking to see if they can get you for a wee bit of personal.

When the fifth and final search got around to Lee, rather than just stand there and take it like the rest of us. He thought he'd try a different tact with them. This cunt? I thought to myself. Not happy enough to engineer the situation which saw us even *in* Sinaloa but now that we were there - and now stopped by what had looked like a fucking army unit. He now felt that he would open his mouth and get the lot of us killed.

'Todos estamos aquí como invitados del señor Flores.' Yo soy responsable del entretenimiento para la fiesta de cumpleaños.'

Spanish wasn't close to being something that I was fluent in. And even for as many Ibiza summer seasons I'd played at there hadn't really been any requirement to learn it. Not when enough people spoke English and on the occasions that they never, it generally involved pointing at an object to break through the language barrier. Even so, there was enough words that Lee had said to the soldier for me to see what he was trying to say. Even though - in my opinion - the best policy in this situation was to just keep your fucking mouth shut and hope that everything would be all good at the end of it.

I was sure that the 'invitados del señor Flores' was something along the lines of that we'd been invited here by Mr Flores. The rest had come across something that sounded close to being in relation to him or us being responsible for the entertainment for a birthday party? I'd always known the word 'cumpleanos' to be birthday as had once spent my birthday there in Ibiza and when being presented by my cake, the song playing - the Spanish version of the birthday song - had mentioned cumpleanos quite prominently throughout the song.

If Lee had thought these to be the magic words to get us on our way, he would soon find this to be wide of the mark. The soldier, clearly not impressed with Lee's use of Spanish *or* his attempts at trying to talk our way out of this. You know how cunt's can seriously take umbrage at their authority being questioned? Aye well, Lee evidently fucking *didn't*!

The soldier's voice from behind turning - surprising - to English where Lee was told that had we *not* been invited by Don Flores we wouldn't have even made it as far as this part of the road.

In a mix of emotions I found this chilling but also confusing. Chilling as in who had been stationed along the journey with orders to stop certain vehicles, and what had their instructions been. Confusing as, from what he's said to Lee, did this mean that the military were working in *conjunction* with Flores, and his cartel?

Mexico being that kind of a country where absolutely fuck all was ever off the table when it came to law enforcement and military, and who their alliances *really* sat with. Public or 'paymasters.'

Following this disclosure from the soldier, he carried on and subjected Lee to the same treatment as the other four of us. All of the time that we were being searched outside the car, a mini team of soldiers were going through the limo. In the back where we'd sat, in the boot of the car and even one getting onto the ground and rolling underneath to check it.

Weirdly, though. Through out all of this. Carlos the driver had been allowed to stand to the side of it all, sharing a cigarette while talking away with one of the men in uniform, who had initially been sat inside one of the Toyotas But who had got out at some point and walked over. It all had taken probably less than ten minutes but, fuck me, it had felt like ten hours due to how tense it all felt. This while the unknown of things was playing on your mind, where you started to game out various scenarios of what might end up happening to us by the time the military had been finished with us.

By the time Lee had been searched, it had looked like the others had finished looking through the limo. I couldn't help but notice that at absolutely no point had any of the soldiers reacted to the prize of finding the large quantity of ching and that glass jar filled with pre rolls. Because it wasn't like they were hidden in any kind of secret compartment by any stretch. Had this same situation taken place on a British road, the copper - on discovering the gear in the car - would've reacted as if he'd just busted the entire Turkish Mafia. But here, crickets.

So much so that when Lee's frisk had been completed. I heard a 'bueno' coming from behind us, followed by some Spanish which soon saw Carlos telling us - from the front of the car - that we could now get back into the limo again. The three soldiers that had come over to us looking neither friendly or hostile, which I guess was as good as it was going to get from this mob.

But hey, we were free to go, apparently. No one shot and thrown in a ditch. Or lifted under grounds of being foreigners in possession of a shit load of drugs. Something coppers generally get an erection over the prospect of, when it comes to locals, never mind the much bigger prize of tourists. We all filed into the back of the limo again while wondering just what the fuck had really gone on. The fact they hadn't charged us with the drugs possession *or* simply stolen the gear for themselves - which you could never really rule out when it came to people in authority - was a minor miracle. But that through it all they had been searching us? This had you arriving at the - by default - conclusion that giving someone extensive searches - the kind of search that I reckon only a couple of UK festivals could've come close for the levels of frisk - while turning blind eyes to a not inconsiderate amount of drugs could've only meant that they were looking for weapons, not narcotics.

So did this mean that this army unit had been on Flores' payroll and were acting as some form of security for the party?

The answering to this, provided by Carlos once the two Toyotas reversed off the road enough for our car to pass between the two of them and we were once again on our way.

This army unit that had stopped us from carrying on - until we'd been subject to a thorough search - hadn't even *been* an army unit. It had actually been part of Flores' *own* cartel security detail!

Carlos telling the rest of the car, with us all looking on in wide amazement - Si and me already puffing on one of the pre rolls each and something we had reached for within seconds of the car pulling away - that you can always tell the difference between the actual Mexican army and any cartel operatives due to how superior the cartel's uniforms, weaponry and vehicles were, compared to the army. Wild as fuck that they have more of a budget for kitting them out with their toys than the actual Mexican government can give to their own soldiers.

Our driver explaining that with such a big birthday party taking place at Flores' mansion *no one* would've gotten within fifteen miles of the sprawling grounds of his property without being properly *vetted*.

'I thought we were all destined for a night in some Sinaloan nick, if we were lucky.'

A relieved Si, puffed on his joint as if his life depended on taking in the smoke from it.

'Still glad you came now, aye?'

I looked over at Myles and Luke, wondering if they were questioning their latest assignment that they'd been sent on, because it probably went without saying that as a music journalist and photographer for a *music* magazine. You wouldn't really anticipate scenarios such as what they'd had to just go through. Aye, if you're some world reporter who covers conflicts and wars, then you'd have to make peace with the fact that you might take a wrong turn and end up kidnapped by some freedom fighters. By comparison, the most danger you'll probably find in a club or a festival is if you come across some chinged up squad boys from Clacton who are intent on showing someone in the crowd how they used to cage fight.

Myles appearing a little stunned by what had just happened managed to stammer something about how, possibly, him and Luke hadn't been fully told what kind of a party they'd been invited to.

Me just laughing at this and telling the journalist that he didn't know the fucking half of it.

Aye, our journalist and photographer looked well shook by it all. Maybe I did too, though? It's not like I hadn't been in some dodgy situations before - or Si - so maybe, as concerning it had been, we'd just been able to deal with things more rationally. Lee, sensing this from the two of them, reached for the box - which still had easily more than half of the ching left inside despite how hard it had been hit across those three hundred miles - and passed it to Luke, who looked the more impacted by our unplanned stop.

'Aye, I'll get a wee bit of that after you when you're done,'

Si chipped up, while adding for the rest of the car that he still couldn't quite believe that it had still been left in the car for us.

'Everyone's got a boss, Simon.'

Lee, added to things while elaborating that as scary and menacing as the cartel soldiers had looked - to us - they still had to answer to El Hombrecito and as appealing as it would've possibly been to relieve us of what had to be several thousand dollars worth of gear, what good would that've been when one of us - at the party - inevitably ended up telling others the anecdote of us being stopped on our way up to the Flores mansion.

Carlos, more part of this conversation due to the value that he was able to add to it due to his knowledge of these matters, chimed in that Lee was correct and that with someone like a 'Don Flores' you really only ever stole once from, and not because the boy would give you your cards. Aye, he'd give you your fucking cards, alright. But just not in the way of where you'd get a P45 to hand to your next employer.

With Carlos, telling us all that we were now only ten minutes or so away from Flores' mansion, we got ourselves prepared for arriving. Under any other circumstances, I'd have laid off any more gear between then and now as I hadn't wanted to get there and be giving off 'out your nut' vibes, especially as I had no point of reference for what the fuck I was even going *into*. But with what had just happened back on the road up, I needed something to steady my nerves, and the pure weed pre roll had not been enough to do the trick. I wasn't the only one, either. While we'd agreed that it wouldn't have been a good look for us to arrive there and the back of the car resembling like Tony Montana in his office, we'd all felt that maybe a wee bump or two would've put us back on an even keel.

Carlos taking us down what looked like it may have been a dirt road - due to the surrounding on either side which was pure forestry - at some point but had now been converted with a proper tar surface laid down on it. As we drove along it, you could begin to see the structure of the mansion, up ahead. The large white building looming over the sprawling estate, there on ground level. Not being an aficionado - when it came to architecture - by any stretch of the imagination the mansion itself - as we crept closer and closer to it - seemed to be a mix of modern and colonial styles. I swear that as each second passed and the building - and grounds - became closer and closer, it felt like an extra million was added to the likely market value of the gaff. Balconies seemed to wrap around the upper floors, lined with ornate iron railings and stone sculptures of animals such as jaguars, tigers and massive fucking birds appearing to guard the top level from one corner to the other.

Looking back to ground level and the *outside* of the mansion, you couldn't help but notice the wealth that was on show in the form of the luxury super cars that were lining the driveway. Lambos, Ferraris, Porsches and Bentleys. You name it. There was also quite a few more of those same - now confirmed as *private* - army branded Toyota pick up trucks, with modifications added to the back in the form of automatic rifles.

I'd guessed that through passing the roadblock, the 'security' were not as suspicious about anyone coming up the drive, with no one stopping us from driving all the way up and then Carlos pulling the car to a stop outside of what looked like the grandest of main entrances. This massive stone arch - on either side of the large wall that seemed to stretch all the way around the ridiculously spacious premises - in front with a door that would've rivalled those wooden doors that you see at the front of some of the world's biggest cathedrals. I remember looking at it and wondering how the fuck a human being was even meant to fucking *open* a door as big as that until I then noticed the much smaller door within a door, towards the lower middle.

Because we'd now arrived at the actual mansion though, that didn't mean an end to the scrutiny from the security detail before being allowed inside. Carlos, who by now we'd been able to see was 'known' to those connected with ensuring the safety of Don Flores and his family and friends, walked us up to the entrance - but not before I'd pinched a few of those barely smoked pre rolls from the back, figuring that it would be better to have some on hand J's for when I was playing - and, saying something in Spanish to the two soldiers who appeared to be playing the role of bouncers, told us to form a line and we would be vetted before going in. While doing so, telling us to enjoy our night and that he would maybe see us across it while confirming that when it was time to return back to Guadalajara, he would be ready for us.

One after the other, we filed past the soldiers - who gave us a secondary search although this time around, no hands were placed on us. Instead, we were checked over for any weapons through the use of an airport style metal detector wand accessory - and were let loose inside the place.

I'd seen a lot in my time but this was absolutely surreal. Standing in line to enter someone's private house alongside some of the other party goers there for the night - women in skimpy short cocktail dresses who would've been pulling off the impossible by smuggling in a weapon, subjected to the same treatment as someone like myself or Si - where no one was allowed entry in until they had been checked, double checked and *triple* checked.

Our entry *almost* went flawless and I'm assuming it would've done, had it not been for Luke Clifton. The soldiers taking one look at the professional camera around his neck and simply shaking their heads and telling him a clear and unequivocal 'nada.' Motioning for him to hand it over to them. Something that - possibly fearing for if he'd ever see it again. You could see from the look on his face and general body language that he was hesitant to do so. But really, was he going to try and debate with the men holding Kalashnikovs?

Before even knowing where we were going or the kind of level that this cartel boss was operating at - and now seeing where he called home, that was *all* you needed to see to know he wasn't low level - I'd already had the thought that Luke may have ran into difficulties, when it came to any designs on walking around the party taking photos of every cunt. So was not surprised in the slightest when it appeared to *be* a problem. In fairness to the boy. If someone had been gracious enough to provide him with enough of the backstory of *why* I was playing this hastily arranged additional night. He'd have probably been street smart enough to have left it in the hotel.

Carlos, spying this apparent problem in Luke gaining entry double backed from walking over to go and park the limo and had a brief conversation with the two soldiers. Pointing at us and - no doubt - explaining that he had driven us all from Guadalajara. As he done so, I hoped that for the sake of Myles and Luke, Carlos did not spill that they were both from a magazine. Because I would've assumed that this would not have been too welcome. The press - rightly for some and wrongly for others - can be generally looked upon with suspicion. Fuck, I myself had been - and not fully having worked it out of my system - wary of Myles and Luke for what they may have ended up writing about me, so could never have blamed any concerns that actual top level criminals may have had, on learning of the press walking around the party. My feelings being that while I could tell the difference between one kind of journalist and another. Someone like a Mexican cartel member would not be so discerning and be more ready to just lump them all in with each other.

Whatever Carlos had said had been enough to calm things between everyone, resulting in our driver asking Luke to take his camera from around his neck and hand it to him, where he would store it safely in the limo and how Luke could get it back again on the return journey to Guadalajara. Luke - and still also, Myles - had a bit of a rabbit between the headlights look about him when doing as told. This was not the kind of environment where you would want to get into *any* kind of a confrontation. Being so far off the grid and around the kind of people where you would have absolutely *nothing* in the way of protection from so called public guardians like the police, you really did want to be of the yes sir no sir how many bags would you liked filled full, sir kind of attitude.

With this minor issue all sorted, we walked through and into the grounds of the mansion as the five piece that we had arrived as. I had barely taken two steps inside and had been greeted by a pretty looking woman holding a silver tray with glasses of champagne on top of it.

'Gracias, bonita,'

Si said, winking to the girl - while probably using up the extent of Spanish he knew - as he picked up a glass, leaving her blushing a little. Taking a glass from off her tray too, me and Si clinked glasses while he toasted.

'To good times, good wines and good lines.'

This, making Myles laugh for the first time since we'd come across the road block. The journalist raising his in accordance with Si's salutation. I looked for Lee - who seconds before had been standing right beside me before disappearing - and could see that he had walked off and was stood talking to an older gentleman. Some small boy that Lee - hardly Lebron James - looked to almost tower above. The pair of them stood chatting like they were old mates so I had no choice but to assume that this was Flores himself. Stood to the side of the wee man was a younger boy, head to toe in the most garish of Versace gear. I'd always had no flying fucks to give over how much these Versace shirts cost. The price did not ever protect you from what was nothing other than grievous bodily harm, on your eyes.

As the two of them stood speaking to Lee, I noticed him - while in the middle of talking - turning around to look for where I was and - upon spying me - lifted his arm to point me out for them.

This leading to the three of them walking over towards the four of us who were standing there with our glasses of champagne, taking in the opulent surroundings.

'Zico, meet Don Flores and his son Ovidio,'

Lee said, while standing a few steps to the side.

'Ahhh, Zico, like the Flamenco player, yes?'

Don Flores smiled warmly and said with impeccable English before reaching out to shake my hand, me meeting his while making being conscious that whatever I done here I needed to make sure my handshake was firm but not *too* firm. Knowing the score here and playing the game exactly as should be I told him of the great honour it was to play for him at his mansion on what was such a special occasion. No good could've ever come out of him knowing just how put out I'd been by this all and, especially, since I wasn't even being fucking *paid* for it.

In return, he thanked me for my gesture of offering to travel and take care of the DJ duties for the night. Offering? That was a pretty strange way of putting it that in return for not cutting Lee's arm off I would play some records across the night. But like a lot of things in such an arena, some things best left unsaid and not challenged in any shape or form.

Next he introduced me to his son, the birthday boy.

'Meet, Ovidio. My only son and who, today, becomes a real man.'

With the benefit of this being his father, rather than a potential bogeyman for any of us, should we have ever gotten on his wrong side. Ovidio had felt no issues in flashing his dad an embarrassed - at his father's actions - look. The one we've all done at some point in our lives when it comes to critiquing over something a parent will have said. This was mixed with what appeared to have been genuine excitement at standing there meeting me. Something I could never have expected from a junior narco - and someone who you would've imagined was being groomed for the day that he would play a major part in his dad's organisation - who I had never heard of until that day.

'I am *so* excited to have you play for my birthday party,'

he beamed and while I had thought this had only been said for effect he then went on to tell me that he's been a fan of me since seeing my warm up for Citizen Caner on the Mexico City part of the tour we had been on, the last time I had visited Mexico. Talk about a small world, eh? Still, what a way to get some influential strangers on side.

He joked with me about how - when his girlfriend appeared - his other half, Veronica, was going to be all fan girly with me and how the first thing she would probably do would be to ask for a selfie, for her Insta. Which, to be fair, was *exactly* what she did when she appeared a few moments later, clocking her boyfriend standing talking to the bunch of gringos that must've stood out like a sore thumb in amongst all of the party attendees who were standing around in the large courtyard.

Letting out a loud squeal which had us all laughing, she launched into some excited chatter but with it being all in Spanish I hadn't a scoobie of what she was actually saying. Ovidio only really a quarter of the way translating, by the looks. What he *did* translate was a mix of confirming that she was a fan, that she listened to my mixes on Soundcloud, if she could have a selfie with me and, finally, a couple of requests for some songs that she was hoping for me to play over the night. Obviously, the last part was a *big* no no but, really? Who was going to tell the girlfriend of a Sinaloan narco that she was committing a cardinal sin in telling a DJ what to play and that she could go and shove her requests to hear Gecko, by Oliver Heldens, and Need U, from Duke Dumont? Not fucking moi, *that* was for sure.

After that mini introduction to Veronica, she seemed to spy someone else that she wanted to speak to so after giving me a quick hug and kiss on either side of my cheek, she was off again.

'What a fantastic woman you have there, Ovidio,'

I said to him, hoping that I was sitting on the right side of the fence when it came to complimenting someone on their other half. He smiled and thanked me while laughing, telling me that she was crazy but his *kind* of crazy.

I introduced Si, Myles and Luke to him as my 'friends.' While that had obviously been accurate for Si, not so for the other two. Because just because you've spent a six hour car journey sniffing ching and talking complete pish with someone, that does not mean that they are your friends. For the purposes of making sure there was no issues or suspicion with the two from the magazine, only a fool would've introduced them to the junior narco as 'press.'

Following the situation with Luke and his camera, I'd had the briefest of words with them to advise that where we'd been brought to did not appear to be the kind of place that would be there with open arms extended for journalists and photographers, and that maybe they should keep their cards close to their chest. I hadn't completely spelled it out for them that this was proper cartel business, but trusted that they had enough brain cells and nous to see what was there in front of them. I mean, they should've known the score when a private army with better weaponry than your average small European country had taken over the road and searched us and our vehicle.

Ovidio shook all of their hands and welcomed them to his birthday party. To the side of our group, Lee stood there with Flores and with their body language you would *never* have guessed that just over twenty four hours before Lee had been left in such an uncompromising situation with this same cartel boss. They appeared to be best buddies although I'm not sure how much of that was due to Lee and his deep fear of finding himself on the wrong side of Flores' goodwill that was there for us all to see there on our arrival, knowing what the man could be like in one of his not so good moods.

While Ovidio stood there and told me that the DJ booth - which I hadn't even stopped for a moment, prior to getting there, to consider in terms of what kind of a set up - had all been prepared for me, ahead of my arrival, but if there was anything else I needed then I just needed to say.

The 'DJ booth?' Well, it left three quarters of the booths I'd played in right in the shade. And this was just some rich cunt's mansion. Looking across the large lawn in the direction of where Ovidio had pointed to. This semi raised booth that - while not too high to be out of proportion - looked down on the lawn where I'd have imagined some of the party goers to be stood around. The front of the booth - and below the opening where I'd have been visible from - was some kind of a large

LED screen, flashing hypnotic fractal patterns of which I'd already taken would move in time to the tracks, once my set began. The size of the speakers, too? From the quick look I think I'd managed to spy half a dozen speakers strategically placed around. Each one bigger than any human being inside there, and some of those cunts in the camo gear hadn't been what you'd have looked upon as midgets, either.

As I was about to compliment Ovidio on having a better DJ booth than most clubs in Europe, his father butted in to shake my hand and thank me for coming again before announcing to us that he was now away to Culiacan on business, while playfully digging his son over how regardless of business, he wouldn't have wanted to cramp his son's style.

A small microcosm for us that showed that while your father can be a psychotic killer and with the kind of power that he can have private armies looking out for him, he is *still* a normal father, who understands the needs of their kids.

Telling us all to have a good night before - while thoughtfully, I'd felt - wishing me well for my tour. Don Flores, flanked by a couple of handy looking boys in suits and cowboy hats alongside boots that had silver on the toe tips and, again, on the heels, made his way towards the large mahogany door.

Fair play to Don Flores - and Ovidio - because while I hadn't been fully bricking it about the night ahead at this birthday party, only the deluded or naive would *not* have possessed a hefty dose of apprehension about what lay ahead for the night. But since arriving, I'd felt ride all other than the warmest of welcomes.

This only enhanced further when - now that his father was no longer in ear's shot - Ovidio, completely buzzing, told us that there would be nothing that we would want for over the night.

'We have Cristal, Dom P, Macallan and all the other best alcohol from around the world. We have cocaine that was only processed in the jungles of Medellin yesterday morning. And there are so many girls that your dick will drop off through exhaustion before you run out of girls to fuck.'

Lee could not contain his glee over pretty much every word that Ovidio had just said, and Si wasn't exactly reserved about things either. The other two? I think they were still trying to process what they'd ended up coming along with us to. The majority of Ovidio's *treats*, something that I would not be taking much advantage of. Couldn't get fired into the drink too much, as I had long stopped trying to master the art of deejaying when drunk. Wouldn't be with any of the women that Ovidio mentioned either, for obvious reasons. And even if not for Flo. I could've hardly stood behind the decks - with no other support - taking some strange woman from behind while making sure the mix I was attempting was looking like working out. Aye, maybe a wee bit of that fresh as a daisy Colombian jungle lab ching though, just to keep me alert, like.

Telling me that he would need to go and circulate amongst some of the guests who had now arrived after our group. With a huge vibrant smile, he slapped me on the back while looking around everyone and telling them to *enjoy*. As he started to leave he promised us all that this was going to be a night that we'd never, ever forget.

For good or bad, Ovidio really was not joking about that and even while saying it, I don't believe that even he had known just how accurate he would be.

Chapter 6

Zico

I'd played at - and attended, recreationally - many wide and varied not to mention completely *random* events in my time. That time when I played at an all nighter inside a decommissioned prison in Lancashire. The pedalo - shaped like a swan - on in the sea next to S'Arenal de San Antonio, which almost fucking sank. A Dundee kebab shop, after a social media poll ended up being hijacked by internet wideos. That cool as fuck castle in Dubrovnik, Croatia and - one of my personal favourites, the ice hotel in Sweden.

But *none* of these came close to the birthday party of junior narco, Ovidio Flores, at his father's big bastard mansion in Sinaloa, Mexico.

The venue - for a kick off - was a gaff that made your average Ibiza mansion after party venue look like a bed sit that you'd find sat over a chippy. And the *clientele* were like nothing I had ever seen in front of me while in the booth. Gone were the 'tech bros' in their Burberry shorts, all trying to outdo each other when it came to physique. And so were the girls - in the equivalent of beach wear - with balloon perpetually hanging out of their mouths.

Instead, you had men - half in cowboy hats and elaborate suits - who wouldn't have probably known what the fuck Burberry, Moncler and Balenciaga even *was*. Or cared for that matter. While the women were decked out in high heels and party dresses and - with some of the best and pure cocaine on the planet in plentiful supply - who would've looked at you like you were 'loco' if you'd handed them a balloon and asked them to suck on it.

The sheer size of the area that the mansion was situated in completely boggled the mind. The lawn - that the DJ booth primarily looked over - I swear - was bigger than the fucking terrace at Space. And as spectacular a venue Space was, its terrace did not possess an - almost - Olympic sized swimming pool. The pool itself, which I had been unable *not* to go over and have a wee deek at when walking over to the booth. An absolute work of art and looked almost like it had been the result of an archeological dig. Through the glistening water, you could see what appeared to be mosaic tiles that depicted Aztec warriors, having a bit of a swedge. Soft blue lighting - sitting at the base of the pool - streaming up through the water. The sun loungers and soft furniture that was dotted around this area, also, something you'd have done well to have found in the platinum plus VIP area of any club back on the White Isle.

And while maybe not a factor that one could claim Sinaloa getting one up on Ibiza - or any other party destination, for that matter, - this venue had not been short of security with *visible* weapons. These boys - unlike the outside - were not in full military get up and, instead, were in smart black suits. Kind of like the Secret Service. Despite not being in your face wearing camouflage uniforms, you could still see their weapons, though, which meant that they had hardly managed to take the edge of things with the suits. This, alone, had left me with the impression that the security, there, was not for the reasons of making sure that attendees behaved themselves, like any other club or event security. Without being specifically told - and I hadn't felt it appropriate to ask - I had already taken the leap that no, these bad bastards packing heat were there to protect everyone from any 'gatecrashers.' This, something that I'd felt was best not dwelled on.

The DJ booth itself had been as impressive inside as it had looked from a distance, outside. Looking over everything that had already been put in place for my arrival had me questioning if this was always like this - for any parties that would take place - or if this had all been sourced in the previous twenty four hours, following the development which had seen an 'international DJ' booked to play for Ovidio and guests. I'd been asked to play with much, much worse. When it came to equipment.

I'd felt a huge - but surprising in the moment - surge of relief when entering the booth to find three Pioneer CDJ-20000NXS' all set up on the table. The subject of CDJ's had not even been brought up and had completely slipped my mind to ask Lee about, in advance of us going. Turning up with a MacBook, collection of USB flash drives and a MacBook would have meant absolutely *nada* had I got there and found that they had old school Technics rigged up and the car crash of finding this out at the very last moment was a scenario that didn't bare thinking about. The DJM-9000XS - also from Pioneer - was also a welcome sight, there on the table. They'd even sorted out an elevated and tilted laptop stand for setting up the MacBook. Whoever it was who had been in charge of this had clearly either known what they were doing or had sought assistance. They even had the code for the WI-FI - quite possibly due to the prior knowledge that I would require this for using the Rekordbox software - written out in large letters onto a sheet of A4 and sellotaped to the table for me.

Apart from the technological aspect of things, they had more than looked after me in other ways. This, specifically, through fixing me up with my own private mini fridge which housed everything from alcoholic drinks to soft and energy ones. Apart from the drinks side of things, they - whoever this angel was - had made sure that I had *other* party favours set aside for me taking my place in ten - I counted - pre rolled joints, each in their own individual plastic tube, like how most of the coffee shops back home in Amsterdam would supply you with. The cherry on top came through a medium sized zip locked back with a decent amount of ching sat inside it. Due to it all being in one bag - and not separated into individual wraps - I didn't even know how much they'd put behind the decks for me. It wasn't an inconsequential amount and, in a mark of what kind of party I was playing at and in *which* area of the world. I would go on to play my entire set without even having to *open* the bag of ching.

While I'd only had eyes for all of the equipment set up there in the booth - alongside the 'hospitality' that they had arranged for me - others must've had eyes on me because as I was finalising getting my own gear set up, Ovidio appeared from nowhere into the booth, while I was trying to get the laptop up and running.

'Are we ready to party, hermano?'

Seeing the WI-FI symbol appear in the right hand corner of the screen and the Rekordbox software opening up, I smiled and nodded to him while trying to work out what tune I was going to start off with. Due to everything That had been going on and all of the mitigating circumstances across the day, I hadn't even begun to think of vital things like this. Fuck, I hadn't even really given thought towards what kind of a *set* I would play across the night. Subjects like this are not an easy thing to think of when - unlike one hundred percent of any other bookings - you don't even know what kind of a crowd you're going to be playing for, or what their tastes are going to be.

Just because Veronica had mentioned to me an Oliver Heldens and a Duke Dumont tune, that didn't mean to say that everyone else would've felt the same. To be fair, if there was *anyone* I wanted to please on the night, it was Ovidio, the birthday boy. The rest? Well, that would've been a plus but I'd felt that I should have at least tried to play things a little safe and appeal to all the party attendees, in the most broadest of senses. A *lot* of where you would go in Mexico, you would hear their kind of folk style mariachi band type of music. Didn't matter if it was young, old or in between. They lapped that stuff up big time. Knowing this, I knew that I would have to be selective in what I played and that I couldn't just - on a whim - cue up something like Energy Flash or Dominator, just because I felt like it.

Seeing that I was getting ready to begin. Ovidio told me that he wanted to introduce me to everyone who had arrived.

Telling me what I had already suspected, that most of who had came to the party would not have heard of me. Anything that may have bought me some form of goodwill from the locals, I was fully behind.

Taking the mic and tapping on it to make sure it was working, he set about introducing me to everyone, while I stood there feeling a bit daft, unable to understand what he was saying and, instead, relying on reading peoples faces and body language. Giving everyone a round of applause while doing that heart shaped sign with my hands - and dying inside over having done so - when it had appeared as if they were all acknowledging me. A series of mini claps, raised glasses and whistles greeting what Ovidio had said to them.

'*Ahora todos, gracias por venir. Vamos a tener una noche brillante junto y este hombre que esta a mi lado sera Una gran parte de eso. Por favor, unanse a mi en dar until fuerte aplauso al unico e inigualable DJ Selecao, uno de los DJ mas grandes del mundo, que ha venido aqui para hacerlos bailar a todos!*

I hadn't a clue how long the boy's speech was going to be so had the first track ready to go the moment he finished speaking and to follow the crowd's reaction to this.

Mozalounge, the Louis Vega - Jazz N Groove mix - track kicking in after I'd clapped back at the crowd while expressing love by the heart shape, produced by the medium of my two hands. That and a couple of kisses blown indiscriminately. With the lawn now filled with the beat of the music, I curiously, asked Ovidio what he had said to the crowd.

'Oh, nothing, hermano. I thanked them all for coming and introduced you as one of the world's biggest deejays and said that you had come all the way from Europe to play just for us tonight and for everyone to give you a round of applause.'

He said it as if every single part of it had been complete gospel. While I couldn't have agreed with him, I was happy that *he'd*, at least, considered me one of the world's biggest deejays. Nodding to the beat of the opening track, Ovidio then looked back at me while giving a wee nod of approval. Doing so while tipping some ching onto the turned sideways clenched fist that he'd made. Swiftly making it disappear before replacing it with an equal amount and pulling his fist up towards me. Across my career, willpower had been my undoing but even so, if I didn't want a bump of ching then I had it in me to actually say the N word. But let me tell you, when the son of a Mexican cartel boss offers you a bump, it probably would be for the best that you take it, which I did.

I remember - there - having the thought that with how pure this ching was around these parts - and with Colombia up next on the tour and that hardly likely to be worse - this three week tour was going to be over in a fucking blur. The stuff really was levels above. Giving me a cheeky smile of approval when I took care of all the powder sat on him, he grabbed my shoulder hard and tight - uncomfortably so - and squeezed me and, without saying a further word, made his way out of the booth. I watched him go back onto the lawn where he didn't manage to make it even ten yards before being stopped by a man and woman who had wanted to wish him a happy birthday.

I'm not saying that within a minute of me starting that the whole place dropped everything to all begin dancing, far from it. But the opening tune had appeared to at least draw a few nods to the beat from those standing around in earshot of the speakers. Although, to be fair. The size of the speakers, you'd probably have heard the track all the way up the coast in Culiacan.

Encouraged by this, it gave me a little piece of confidence in my decision to open the night by playing a selection of Latino House. I'd figured that hitting them with some soulful and funky beats which were high on Spanish samples and vocals would've at least have met them half way, when it came to what they would have ordinarily have liked. Even dropping the occasional Latin Disco track in, like Cuba from the Gibson Brothers. Different times require different measures. And *this* was unequivocally 'different.'

It hadn't been immediate by any stretch but by about an hour, several of the head nodders had started to let loose a little, having a wee shimmy on their own or with a partner. I suppose it didn't matter which corner of the planet that you found yourself. If there's music being played, alongside copious amounts of liquor and narcotics, cunts are going to end up dancing. Fish in a barrel. Still, nothing worse than- for a DJ - than standing there playing dance music, and no one partaking, especially in *this* kind of environment. It was with relief more than anything when some of the party goers started to dance. By the time I'd entered into hour two, I'd noticed that the place was well busy, compared to when we'd arrived. The lawn and swimming pool area populated by people stood around chatting and dancing. When the night had began, anytime I'd looked up from the decks it hadn't been too difficult to spy everyone who had travelled in the limo with me. Lee had been stood talking to a couple, him doing the talking and me fearing what pish it actually was that he was saying to them. With him and his sketchy Spanish - which, aye, was infinitely better than mine - he was probably trying to ask them if they were having a good night and, instead, was asking them if they knew somewhere he could have his brogues cleaned.

Myles and Luke - appearing to be invisibly tethered to each other - had been walking around with amazed looks on their faces, pointing at something every now and then. Just don't point at the wrong person at the wrong time, that's all I ask. I thought to myself, while speculating what kind of people were there at the party. The full range of attendees - and where they stood in life was something that I would have explained to me later on in the night.

As for Si? Clearly making himself at home. The last time I saw him - for a while, at least - he had a glass of champagne in one hand and his other, reaching out to a random girl who was standing watching and giggling at him, asking her to dance with him. Her shyly turning him down before finally giving in all of six seconds later after one more 'come on' from my mate. Seeing him so comfortable in his surroundings and the Mexicans seeming to take to him, despite the obvious language barrier because even if they spoke English, they wouldn't have spoken *Dundonian*, it put me at ease with regards to how the boy was going to fare over the night.

By the end of the second hour of my set - and things beginning to very much heat up - I had to start looking after myself rather than my friends and associates. They were adults and I had to just trust them to not embarrass themselves, at the least.

I took it as an indication that things were going well, when this girl came into the booth. Me not noticing due to having my head stuck in my MacBook, cueing up the next tune.

'HOLAAAAA.'

She said, me about jumping out of my skin. I turned to see this dark headed - well, of course - woman with this big smile on her heavily made up face. Standing there in a flowery summer dress and high heels.

'Tu musica esta muy buena,'

which was just about something that I would not have required Lee and his translation skills to fill me in. Her grooving on the spot right beside me as she spoke. I wasn't big on people just gatecrashing the DJ booth - and had gotten into numerous arguments, mid set, with some out of their nut clubber who had bumped into me or tried to put a hat on my head without me knowing. Most of this happening in Ibiza, and specifically the booth at Amnesia - but, also, I didn't know who this woman was and in a situation like I was in, it's always better to be polite first and then - if appropriate - rude later. Some would have said that had Lee went into his day in Guadalajara the day before with such an attitude then I wouldn't have even been standing behind the decks, in this Mazatlan mansion.

Trying to make sure that she didn't distract me, I just offered a friendly *gracias* before looking back at the MacBook screen and then turning my attention to the CDJ's. But this was not a hint that she was willing to take, possibly hadn't *noticed* it. She couldn't have done because she wouldn't have then put one arm around my neck and in an almost neck hold, pulled me upwards and swivelled me around to stand alongside her while she was holding her iPhone out to take a picture of us.

'SELFIE!'

She screamed - over the music - and stood with a big smile that I tried my best to match, if only for those split seconds for the photo. Once she'd taken the photo she placed her hands together to thank me, and then before leaving the booth, repeating the same departure that Ovidio had done. Only this time, instead of tipping out some gear just to sniff up from a hand. She deployed her extra long nails, managing to scoop up enough for a bump as if she had a cocaine spoon fixed to her finger.

One for her and then one for me and this was her cue to leave. Giving me a kiss on the cheek before raising one hand in the air and dancing her way out of the booth onto the lawn, where two other girls were there dancing, ready for her coming back. The three of them whooping while she appeared to show them the selfie she'd just taken. *Then* one of her pals started to show the other two something on her phone, which had them laughing. Something in the extended way that they had looked at the second screen had given me the impression that her friend had taken a video of her up beside me in the booth.

Fucking barry, eh? I thought self depreciatingly. Videos of me sniffing gear beside some Latino hottie - as she kisses me - while I play at a mansion, and a 'date' that was most certainly not on my tour schedule. Flo would fucking *castrate* me with a rusty ice cream scoop if she was to see such a video and not know the context behind it.

And her actions had not been something that was what you'd have classed as isolated. Maybe she'd been the watershed for it but while she'd been the first to do so she certainly wasn't the last. Every now and then I'd find someone just popping their head in - no matter the predicament I was in, when it came to my mixing; I'd already taken it by person two that they did not appreciate the intricacies of a deejay's craft, and had been left with no choice but to accept it - for a wee word, selfie and the inevitable bump of ching.

Words that I'd never thought I would say but the incessant offers of a sniff of powder from each random was starting to get a bit old. Because in this kind of a setting, I just didn't want to offend anyone. Outside of this mansion, I'd have refused the offer by the third bump, but I wasn't outside. This all, inevitably, led to one completely flying 'international DJ' and I started to try and balance it out by hitting the pre rolls hard while having no choice but to swerve the alcohol as that would've tipped me over the edge if I'd got involved there. I had enough battles to fight. Because it went without saying that if I let the ching get on top of me then the careful way that I'd went about choosing my music for this crowd would soon turn to careless.

Speaking of the set, by hour three there were as many people dancing as you'd find back in Europe at any club appearance. The fact that there was still piles of people not dancing and still standing around chatting only served to show just how many people were in attendance.

Finally striking a good balance - which was helped by no one coming into the booth for at least the past half an hour - I was starting to enjoy myself and was now considering moving the needle - figuratively - when it came to the tunes that I was digging out. While doing so I clocked a pile of boys making their way through the crowd, all wearing matching suits - white with this gold embroidery over the jackets and trousers, most of them carrying guitars, making their way towards the front of the booth, where a series of microphone stands had been erected that hadn't been there when I'd arrived to take my place in the booth.

A fucking mariachi band! I was well chuffed to see them for a couple of reasons. Who doesn't love a mariachi band? And, also. Both them and me could not do our thing at the same time so I was already assuming that these boys were due for a wee set, which meant I was probably going to get a break. This confirmed to me from a 'well lit' by then Ovidio. The birthday boy popping into the booth to tell me that the band - Mariachi Solo de Culiacan - who were the most popular mariachi band in the whole of Sinaloa had also been booked to play a gig, so asked me to play a few more tunes while they got ready and then I would be free to enjoy the party for a while when the band played and that once they'd finished I could then resume duties again.

I was happy to oblige and - knowing that my first set was coming to an end, I thought to try them with a wee shift on from the stuff I'd been playing - in what had been an almost four hours of continual build up of the set - by trying a couple of tunes that had been big in Ibiza over the summer.

I only realised that I'd been underestimating a lot of the crowd from the start when half of them danced while singing along to 'House Every Weekend' from David Zowie. Seeing this, I knew that the rest of my night playing for them - even if the *actual* time had still proved to be a sticking point - was going to work out. First time I'd ever have to go on after a mariachi band though, mind.

I finished up with Route 94's 'My Love' and handed things over to the boys from Culiacan. Grabbing a pre roll from the decks, and the bag of ching, just in case it was needed to be 'social.' The crowd who had been invested in my set all clapping me out of the booth and then issuing pats on the backs as I made my way through the crowd.

While I'd - primarily - just been pissed off about going there to play because I'd wanted to prepare for my tour opening. I'd also been nervous about the actual environment and *who* had brought me there to play. Just seemed a bit of a serious business that you'd have been better avoiding if you could. But, fair dues, it was barry as fuck.

Friendly and - mostly - glamorous people who all seemed happy enough to give you a wee nod or say a few words when you were passing. Copious amounts of gear being done but - as far as I could see, anyway - no one behaving like complete dickheads and everyone appearing to be able to handle things without ending up completely buckled.

I stood there to watch the first couple of songs from the band. The crowd's reaction to their opener showed just how known they were. Everyone singing along to the words and, especially, jumping into life when it came to the chorus.

Con astucia y sin temor. Los jefes del cartel van. Al gringo lo enganaron. Y Sinaloa sigue iqual. Del norte hasta la sierra. Siempre burlan al gaban. Con la hey en los bolsillos. Somos duenos de este plan.

At the end of the song, a helpful Samaritan who had been standing beside me belting it out from start to finish explained to me what the chorus translated over to in what I was now realising was that it had been a tune that glorified the Sinaloa Cartel. I suppose if you were from Culiacan, as a band, you'd have been more likely to write songs about the local faces than you'd be writing about the CJNG. Wouldn't be too long a career in the music business to have done otherwise, to be honest.

With cunning and no fear. The cartel bosses go. They fooled the gringo - the DEA - and Sinaloa stands the same. From the north to the mountains. They always outsmart the man. With the law in their pockets. We're the masters of this plan.

Fair play, eh? I stood for the next song before going looking for Si, Lee, anyone. Figuring that as much as I liked mariachi bands, and not being able to talk Spanish, each song had a tendency to sound like the other. Something a mariachi band could *easily* say about house music.

Si was nowhere to be found, but then again, it wasn't exactly as if we were in a two bedroom flat having a party. There was the sprawling lawn filled with people, then the poolside area which with its soft lighting alongside the lights streaming from out of the pool itself, was a cool place to sit, drink and chat. But that was just the *outside*. Up the massive steps that - at the foot - had a row of thirty foot high white Roman style pillars, was the *inside* of the mansion. I had a wee look inside but it was absolutely fucking roasting, and I think it was the heat which made the smell of cigar smoke and leather from the large sofas worse than it should've been.

I was making my way out again when I felt an over enthusiastic tug on my tee shirt, pulling me back like I was an elastic band.

'Here he is. The man of the hour.'

It was Lee and if *I'd* been acting out of politeness to have taken every gratis bump of cocaine over in the booth then I'm not sure what *his* story was. Beaming with pride he started to talk some semi fluent Spanish to this woman. She seemed to understand what Lee had been saying about me and had her hand out to shake mine. For some reason, I grabbed it and gave her a kiss on it, like some fucking Disney prince.

'Check out the gentleman, here,'

Lee looked at me then her and laughed while putting me into a headlock and pulling me in for a kiss on the head. I'd been blessed with a break from deejay duties and - whatever I did to spend the time - I was fucked if I was going to waste it standing beside Lee in that annoying as fuck state. Asked him if he'd seen Si and Lee replying that the past few hours had seemed to fly by but the last he could recall seeing Si was him dripping wet after falling into the pool and being led up to the inside of the house by Ovidio who was going to give him something else to wear, while Si's gear dried up. It was impossible not to laugh on hearing this and my only regret was that I hadn't witnessed it myself.

'Can't take him nowhere, eh?'

I joked while Lee - without skipping a beat - reaffirmed that this had been a long held, and voiced, opinion on the boy.

'After yesterday, you're in a bit of a glass house, when it comes to chucking stones at others and their behaviour, eh?'

I said this in the way it was meant to be. Passive aggressive, to fuck! Telling him that I'd catch him later, I went searching for Si, now with the 'benefit' of knowing that instead of looking for the boy in the distinctive pink Stone Island light overshirt and khaki Paul & Shark cargo shorts, I would now have to look at every single fucking man that was not wearing a cowboy hat. Fuck's sake, again.

After searching several places and coming up with nothing I ended up in this big courtyard, with a fountain in the middle. Once again, no sign of Si and, conscious that I was in danger of using up all of my time away from the decks just wandering around looking for someone who could be up in a bedroom riding for all I know and not wanting to be found, I decided to have a seat around the fountain and have a smoke. Pulling the joint tube from out of my shirt front pocket, I then went to retrieve my lighter from my shorts and had one of those mental flashbacks the second that my hand found an empty pocket. It was there to the left of the very left hand CDJ. Sat there by the fountain, I could fucking *see* where the lighter was.

With the courtyard not exactly being deserted, like any other area of this mansion, by the looks of things, I noticed that on the other side of the fountain sat two men having a chat, and judging by the smell filtering over to me, were having a smoke to themselves. I walked clockwise around the fountain to approach them, holding my joint towards my mouth while asking them if they have a lighter, pretending to spark up my J with my fingers.

Impulsively one of them in a Tommy Vercetti style Hawaiian shirt replied to me by using Spanish while digging his zippo out and throwing it to me. Somehow, in the dimly lit courtyard I'd managed to catch it, saying 'Gracias' and lighting my J up. Thankfully, they had a wee bit of a grasp on English which had been more than enough for us to sit there having a wee blether. The two of them were well interesting, like.

We started off with them both saying how good the music had been and that they were taking a break until I was back on again. Same here, I confirmed. They introduced themselves as Santiago and Jhonny, both of them - from all places - Bogota and friends of Ovidio through Instagram. Ovidio, they'd told me, was one of those junior narcos who would go on social media and flaunt their wealth. Pictures of diamond encrusted pistols sitting beside thousands of dollars. Him posing beside his latest super car, and so on. Due to it being his 21st, Santiago and Jhonny felt that they should make the trek from Colombia to be there. But they were not the only ones who had pulled out the stops to be there that night. Santiago, explaining to an otherwise oblivious me that anyone who was anyone was there at the party. Narcos - obviously - actors, musicians, fitba players, socialites, the lot.

'People want to be here just to have their photo taken with Ovidio and be able to brag that they were here,'

Jhonny said, offering me a smoke of his joint while I took it, and handed him *mine* in return. Jhonny pulling a face which suggested that he'd been happy to get rid of his and did not need one coming back his way.

I understood completely what he was talking about. Even at some of the nights I'd played over the years I'd seen some 'celebs' get into VIP and all they would do was sit there with a clueless look on their face, not even sure *why* they were there but in the knowledge that *being* there was enough for their own agenda.

We shared a laugh over the 'why' a Scottish DJ - based in Amsterdam - had found himself playing for a junior narco in Sinaloa, Mexico. When the laughter stopped, though. Both Santiago and Jhonny were in complete agreement that had Lee not been in the position to offer me up as some kind of a sacrifice then, aye. Ovidio's father would have one hundred percent have chopped off Lee's arm, and apparently that would've been a result. Jhonny letting me in on the rumoured 'numbers' that Don Flores had, when it came to killings over the years.

I asked Jhonny how they knew so much about Ovidio's dad and Santiago, then Jhonny almost bashfully admitted that they were both in a similar kind of occupation, only much lower level than the likes of a Don Flores. They told me that back in Bogota they both had - and ran - their own 'combo,' which they explained was like a designated piece of turf that their gang owned and could deal drugs from. Despite how they were sitting there as friends, Jhonny explained that the two of them had their own combo and whether they were friends or not, if one of their gang entered - never mind sold drugs - the other's territory then they would have a serious problem. But they were cool in the fact that they had always ensured that there was never an issue between both gangs.

It was all fascinating, but then again, *they* were fascinated by my answers to their questions, about the DJ life and, also, what it was like to live in Europe. Amsterdam, for the two of them, something on the bucket list. Me telling them that if they were ever to visit - and if I happened to be in town and not away on spinning business - then I would show them around the place. Jhonny immediately asking me to take him to the red light district. Santiago chipping in *only* after a coffee shop.

Conscious of the fact that the mariachi band appeared to now have stopped playing I knew that I should've been starting to look towards getting myself in the booth, I started to say my goodbyes to the two of them but this didn't take as quickly as I'd visualised. First up, Santiago said that we should all give each other a follow on IG so we took care of that. When Jhonny looked at his screen - and my IG page - he excitedly nudged Santiago, to prompt him to look at the screen too.

'You're coming to Bogota?!?'

Santiago said as he looked up from his mate's phone.

'Aye, pal. Bogota and Medellin, as part of the tour, ken?'

Thrilled that I was coming to their city to play on my tour. They got me to swap numbers with them, promising me that I was going to be treated like absolute royalty in Bogota and that they would catch me once I arrived. With one final series of handshakes and - bring it in - shoulder bumps, I got my Richard Gere back to the booth. The mariachi band were all standing around posing for selfies with fans, smiles all round.

By this point of my second set starting it was around one in the morning and - with the good and happy vibes that were flowing through the party - I decided for set two, I was going to let the handbrake off a bit and just go full house, knowing they'd go for it. Opening up with Gerd's Crooklyn mix of Let Me Show You Love. When the beat started coming out of the large speakers, the crowd in what looked complete muscle memory from the hour before skipped no beat whatsoever by starting to groove to it. A mini cheer going up amongst a fair few on noticing that the tunes were back on.

I was in the middle of bringing the next tune in when I finally noticed him. Stood dancing away with both hands in the air, facing a woman with a massive smile on his coupon. I confirmed that I hadn't seen him when out having a look for him because *no cunt* was missing him, and the get up that he'd been given, while his original clothes were soaking wet.

Dressed in lime green Lacoste polo that was so bright you'd need to stick your shades on to just look at the boy while - below - he had on a pair of full Burberry checked shorts. Colour coordinated, he was not. This woman didn't seem to care a jot, though. She looked like she was having the time of her life with Si dancing facing her head on while occasionally twirling her around to then have her face him again.

Through staring over at Si, I completely neglected the mix that I'd been attempting and with it starting to get a little out of control and the beats no longer matching I needed to leave Si to it and take care of my own business. The next time I looked up, he was gone again. I *did* also finally see the pair from One's and Two's Magazine. Both looking much, much less the rabbits between headlights that they'd appeared to be, post roadblock by the army who turned out not to be the army, which was probably even worse.

Myles, clearly out of his nut but in a nice place by the looks, reached up to give me a quick handshake while Luke took a few pictures of me deejaying from his phone. I wasn't too chuffed about the 'press' taking pictures of me, not that night. It had only been around twelve hours since we'd sat in the limo getting drunk and high, and to an extent, we hadn't really stopped in one way or another and for some, *every* way possible. Having not had the luxury of looking at myself in the mirror since the limo, I had no idea what I must've looked like after such an extended session. But an educated guess would've been that I wouldn't, *couldn't* have looked too clever. I felt fucking *magnificent* but that did not necessarily mean that this would transfer over and align well with the *visual* side to me. I gave Luke a good natured - but fully intended - middle finger from behind the decks, which he lapped up and took another photo. Wanting rid of them, catching Myles' attention again I pointed at the decks as of to say that I should get on and he gave me a thumbs up and led Luke away through the crowd.

What a first twelve hours for them as well. Must've been questioning what the fuck they were doing out here but well, it wasn't me that volunteered to shadow a DJ who has habitually attracted the most radge of situations over the years around places like Mexico and Colombia. That one was on *them*.

The crowd had been just as receptive to the move to general house music from the Latino themed stuff that I'd started the night with, which was just as fucking well considering I was about to run out of options for what to play. During the - second - set I surprised the crowd by pulling off the very special mix that involved me playing some minimal Ricardo Villa Lobos edit which really was nothing more than a repetitive beat, but *perfect* for what I'd wanted to do. During the break, and seeing how radge everyone had went to that first song from the Culiacan mariachi band, I thought that I could maybe enhance that further by running their vocals alongside something minimal enough to match.

And that's *exactly* what I managed to pull off. A great moment made even greater by the fact that a couple of members of Mariachi Sol de Culiacan - who were in touching distance of the booth - quick smart ended up in the booth with me, one to each side of me, both strumming their guitars. The crowd were going off their heads at this. Absolutely fucking surreal, like.

After I finally mixed them back out and continued with matters, Ovidio was then in the booth beside me. Grabbing one of my hands - from right off the mixer slide - and raising it in the air like some boxer being confirmed as the winner in his fight. The crowd cheering while Ovidio pointed at me. Me finally taking a - shy - bow for them.

A few hours passed without the party ever looking like it was for dipping. Like the first time around, I had quite a few randoms - living their best life - entering the booth, with the same steps repeated from earlier on in the night. Selfie, handshake - for a man - or kiss - from a woman - and then the obligatory bump of ching in some shape or form. The first person, this boy with a pencil thin moustache that made me think how you never saw cunts with tashes like that anymore outside an old /New York gangster setting. When he went to tip out some of his ching for him and me - knowing that I hadn't even fucking *opened* the free bag I'd been given, I told him that we could use mine. But in such an environment where it had looked like it had fucking *snowed* ching, I couldn't even *give* it away. While not even getting the chance to take it, either.

I think it was about three or so - my head was starting to begin to depart from reality, due to how sleep deprived I was and, aye, the drugs across the day surely were not helping - when Lee bombed into the booth to join me. Fuck, was he in a blaze. I'd seen him in some states but *never* as let loose and fancy free as this. Not in Ibiza, not in Amsterdam and not at Miami Music Week, when *everyone* gets completely fucking busted.

'I fucking LURVVVE Latino woman, fella,'

he shouted in my ear, way too loud for how close he was to my head and I put this down to his whole spatial awareness being all to fuck. Clearly there was a story behind such a statement from him but I was fucked if I wanted to hear about it there and then. With all the respect in the world to the crowd who were all on the lawn partying, they would have woken up that morning in their own bed after a nights sleep and been all refreshed and ready to party big time at the birthday party that night. I didn't have that luxury, and by then I didn't even now know how many hours I'd been awake for, but knew it was an obscene amount. And there's only so much that drugs can do to help you outrun the brick wall that you are inevitably going to run into. I wasn't interested in hearing about Lee with Latino women. What I *was* interested in was how much longer we were going to be here for.

When I asked him, he replied with some ambiguous nonsense about playing things by ear and when we started to see people start to leave, maybe I should take that as my cue to start to drop the BPMs and wind the night down. Saying that, until them, I shouldn't risk upsetting the locals. Pointing out at them all dancing and having a good time.

'Wait and see what time some people start to leave?'

Was he taking the fucking *piss?*

The vast majority of the crowd has - all night - been sniffing the kind of gear that the general Western World's drug taking community could not even comprehend. As long as they're sniffing that snuff THEY WON'T EVER FUCKING LEAVE. Now I've been awake for so long I no longer know what day of the week it is, what time it is and what my middle name is. Lee, mate. I'm going to crash and burn, and soon.'

Lee just looked back at me as if this was the most minor of problems. Fishing a wrap of ching out of his pocket and forcing it into my hand and saying

'Problem solved.'

The second word barely out of his mouth and he was already on his way out of the booth. Watching him - while asking if there was ever going to be a scenario where I would be able to go half an hour without someone giving me fucking cocaine - he made straight for the direction of this woman - different to the one he'd briefly introduced me to indoors - who held a feather boa out and then - looping it over his head and resting on his neck - pulled him towards her, where the two of them danced at close quarters.

Like any good self respecting DJ, though. As the next hour passed, I could see the tiniest of dips in energy from them, so matched them with what I was lining up. Trying to maintain the feeling of synergy, even as things changed. I'd deliberately managed to avoid having any gear for a while. Settling on the occasional puff of a J while sipping on a cold beer but eventually reached the point where I could barely keep my eyes open so - for the first time - broke open my freebie bag of powder. Tipping some out onto the desk that the decks were sat on this coincided with a voice from behind saying.

'Don't mind if I do, Zeek.'

Turning around, Si was now back in his own clothes and it was only when he was stood there that I remembered that we hadn't spoken once to each other since the start of the night.

'Where the fuck have you been, cunto?'

I joked but still wanted to make my point that I'd had the limo divert to pick him up at the airport so that he could come with me to the party and I never see him until about four in the fucking morning!

'Where have I been? Oh you have no fucking idea, mate!'

He said while stating that 'those narco cunts are all right once you get to know them' this, making me cringe over the possibilities of what might have been the case *before* he had got to know them? Well, he was still alive so things must've been cool, whatever the case. Raving about the free drink and drugs and saying he hadn't seen such riches since him and me had been pulled into that VIP area of the Blackburn rave, back in nineteen ninety.

'Oh and I *have* to tell you about the fucking drug piñata,'

he said before doing anything *other* than tell me about a drug piñata. Instead of this - although I really *did* want to know about it - he went on to tell me about the woman who he had pulled. Someone who he'd said was a TV star in Latin America. He *was* quite out of his bonce when telling me this so I was not sure how accurate this all was from him. TV star or not, he had decided that he was going back to her hotel in Mazatlan and was asking me to just take his case back in the limo to my hotel, and how he'd get it the when he returned to Guadalajara. Saying that she had already agreed to have a car drive them from Mazatlan to Guadalajara in time for my opener.

'I take it you'd be cool to give me a plus one to go with my ticket tomorrow night?'

Tomorrow night? It *wasn't* tomorrow night, it was less than twenty four hours before I'd be taking to the decks in Guadalajara. Nineteen hours or so? Fuck!

'Tell you what though, Si. You better hope that she's a barry fucking ride after giving up a stretch limo full of drugs and drink to get you home after this party,'

I joked while nodding to him about it being a cert for him to get a plus one. Even if I was already questioning whether I would even see the boy for the remainder of my tour, if he didn't come back to Guadalajara with me.

Wishing him all the best for the night ahead and giving each other a wee hug, we said our goodbyes for the night. Fucking wish I was saying my goodbyes to everyone else, I jealously thought, watching Si leaving the booth. I finally got what I was looking for around half four in the morning, kind of.

A clearly 'been through it' and nowhere as near to the fresh party boy that he'd appeared over the night Ovidio came into the booth and asked me if I could slow the music down. Telling me how - under grounds of his father returning back from Culiacan in the morning and going fucking radge if there was still people there partying at his gaff - he was hoping to have everyone gone within the next half hour to an hour. Which would see us leaving around half five, six tops. Brilliant, when you have a six plus hour journey home.

While in the booth - you could see how tired he was - he offered me one last massive thank you for coming to play at his party. Saying how I had his guests dancing in ways that the original DJ could never have done. I joked about hamburger and steak. He got the meaning. He told me that him and Veronica were going to be travelling down to Guadalajara at night - after getting some sleep in between -and going again, at my opener in the city centre. Hearing this I told him that I would have the pair of them added to the guest list and to just say the magic names when they got there. With a big smile he hugged me again, calling me his hermano and telling me that him and me would be friends for life.

I told him that if I did not see him the rest of the night that I'd had a tremendous time and hoped he'd had a riot of a birthday, and that I'd see him down in Guadalajara. I think it was around just gone six when the four of us found ourselves back in the limo and getting on our way, with a clearly more fresh Carlos than his passengers. I pitied the fools that hadn't brought their sunglasses with them, although myself and Lee were not in that category. The two members of the press? I'm not sure a pair of shades could've saved either of them, to be honest. Myles' jaw was swinging like a gate left open in the wind and his photographer was crunching his teeth together like he was at the dentists, going through an x ray.

It was a difficult and draining journey home. Difficult because while I had wanted to try and get some sleep. Lee, for example, did not. And preferred to continue on with the sniff, along with Myles. And with them carrying on carrying on, they were never going to be silent. And draining because, well it *was* three hundred fucking miles of listening to them.

We didn't reach the hotel until one in the afternoon, exactly twenty four hours after leaving. It was almost poetic, in a Shakespearean tragedy kind of way. Because the frightening fact was that I was due to start my set in ten hours time. It was four broken men who slouched their way out of the limo when Carlos pulled up at the hotel entrance.

All I now wanted - fuck wanted, *needed* - was to get some vallies down my neck, ear plugs in and eye mask on and blank out as much as possible of the day. Telling Lee that without being a diva or fuck all that I didn't want contacted until nine pm at the very earliest.

As I lay there on the hotel room bed enjoying the warm buzz that was starting to come from the diazepams, I started to replay some of the moments from over the night - and morning - and how what an unbelievable experience it had been, despite the niggling thought that I couldn't help but feel that I had missed out on *most* of it because I'd been stuck behind the decks. It had still been a pretty special thing to be part of, though.

Helping my agent keep an arm, stretch limos with free drugs ferrying you about, playing alongside mariachi bands, making friends with narcos, Si away with a TV star. And *that* was only day one, and the tour hadn't even *started* yet. If this was some kind of a subconscious raising of a bar then, also, the subconscious me was ready to meet it head on.

Chapter 7

Si

Not a fucking chance that Carlsberg could have even *dreamt* of drafting a script never mind making a commercial that showed someone having the kind of night I had, at that young narco boy's birthday. The public would deem it *too* preposterous. They'd probably say that if Carlsberg would lie in an advert then what else would they lie about? That their beer was semi palatable? Have never actually tried it - out of all the beers I've loved before, Enrique Iglesias, eh? - in my puff, though, like, so maybe I should just swerve any talk of them outside of their famous ad campaign.

Once Zico had departed the group, to go and get himself set up for his 'extended' set, I wasted no time myself in untethering myself from the rest of the team that had travelled up in the limo from Guadalajara. What? You think I was going to be spending my night with that rocket of a manager? If the day before had shown anyone anything, it was that he was the fucking *last* cunt you'd want to be standing beside at a Sinaloan narco party. The man would have you beheaded within an hour of getting there through his inability to read a fucking room.

Being gen, though. Even if he *hadn't* managed to get on the wrong side of the fucking Sinaloa Cartel within a couple of hours of hitting the street - after arriving in Jalisco - I'd have still swerved the cunt, at the party. Lee and moi - over the many years we'd known each other - had always shared a bit of a 'strained' relationship.

Strained, of course, being code speak for us not liking each other very much. But at least we'd been in complete unison, when it came to that page, because that was about the fucking *only* thing that him and me were in agreement over. Due to Lee being in Zico's life since the early Nineties, and me a year or two more. We'd both existed in the same world at times. The world of Stevie 'DJ Selecao' Duncan. And we had found, early doors, that the two of us had a difference of opinion, when it came to what was best for *my* mate, and *his* cash cow. And due to this. Well, we were never going to be the best of buddies.

Let's face it. Which managers - or agents - in the world of entertainment are there - first - for their client and - secondly - for themselves? None. That's who. And Lee Isaac was not any different. The lengths that Zeek had gone to to try and lose the narco reputation that he had - unfairly - gained, due to his dad. While Lee fucking played that shit up at *every* opportunity, knowing how marketable this all made Zico, in the environment that he worked in. Fuck, you really would not have put it past the Cockney cunt to have engineered this situation with the Sinaloa Cartel, just so that he could have exploited it to his own advantage and get some headlines generated for Zeek.

In saying that. To have landed himself in the kind of trouble that he'd done, - the day before - and I'd had no reason to doubt it, *especially* after overhearing a few words exchanged between him and that Flores dad which had referred to the previous day. Well this would've been a commitment towards generating money and exposure that I'm not sure *I'd* have been willing to get behind.

The *one* thing, though, which had wound me up the most about Zeek's manager had been that, get this, he had seen me as a bad influence on his DJ. Me, a fucking bad influence? Give me peace, for fuck's sake. Listen, Zico had proved over the years - time and time again - that he was *perfectly* capable of landing *himself* in trouble, thank you very much. And even if Zico had been whiter than white - no, just suspend reality alongside me just for a moment, here - then what good would that have been when his manager had quite the talent for landing them - or on many occasions, just Zico - in trouble?

But, aye. *I* was the trouble maker. I had never known if Lee had actually *believed* this or if he was purely engaging in protection. But it had never washed with me. Zico hadn't ever admitted it to me but I'd been sure that over the years Lee would've had many cracks at getting Zico to jettison me - overhearing him in the limo at the start of the day telling Zico that the limo wasn't going to pick me up from the airport, an example of his attitude when it came to moi - but, in reality, Lee could *never* have understood our friendship and - with the things we'd both gone through together - how deep it was and how it transcended stuff like *money*.

On the occasions that we were in each other's company. We just did the bare minimum when it came to co-existing in the same room or place. So with that, why the fuck would I have ever wanted to stand around chatting to him at a party? The answer being, I fucking wouldn't have. Which meant - that evening - that I'd been more than happy to take my chances of bumping into randoms that could speak English at the party than be in his company for any length of time.

Of course, for reasons of diplomacy - as well as the fact that, unlike any previous time in each other's company, I'd have been seeing quite a bit of the man over the next couple of weeks - I didn't flat out tell Lee that I was fucked if I was standing around with him all night, watching him do too much ching and then annoy the fuck out of everyone and anyone, as a result. Instead, I chose to go down the other road. Say that I was away for a slash, and just never returning again.

The mansion was absolutely fucking massive with plenty to explore and full of all kinds of colourful characters - and some *very* tidy women - so why the fuck would I want to stand around someone who - when it came to ching - looked like he'd arrived at the Ray Liotta 'helicopters' stage of his Henry Hill story arc?

Grabbing a glass of champagne from off the silver tray that one of the waitresses were holding while circulating the party with. I went off to see what I could find. Casually walking through the crowds that were already there and mingling. Chatting in that Spanish form of - what sounds like to a non Spaniard - breakneck speed and laughing with each other. The smell of cigar and weed smoke seemingly in direct competition with each other to stink the place out. I hoped that I would come across some folk who spoke English, otherwise it was going to be a *long* night.

Luckily, as I took a walk around the swimming pool area, it didn't take long to find someone who could speak my lingo, and who had looked like they'd actively wanted to speak to me. Literally shouting me across to join him and his group.

'Heyyyy, gringo.'

He shouted over to me, beckoning me with one hand. He was standing beside another four men and without any need for clarification, you could tell from the air that he had about him that these other men looked to be 'his boys' and that he was sitting higher up in the food chain. From the expensive looking powder blue cowboy hat on his napper all the way down to the extravagantly designed black cowboy boots, which looked to have more intricate details on them than the inside of your standard European cathedral. Pictures and designs on both of the leather and steel which sat at both the front and back of the boot. Now while for boys like myself and Zeek, where adidas trainers had perennially been the footwear of choice. I had already noticed that these expensive looking boots - that a lot of men had worn - had appeared to be the height of fashion, at least in twenty fourteen, in this part of the world.

This man's cowboy boots had the letters *PG* engraved deeply into the tow caps of each boot. Which I would go on to find stood for Pablo Gomez.

Now I wasn't a *complete* fish out of water, despite where I'd found myself partying for the night. I knew that one of them calling me gringo was an insult. But from the body language that he was standing there with - while calling me one - I could tell that this hadn't been done through any nastiness or hostility. And, anyway. If he'd wanted to *insult* me, he could've called me Jock. An insult or not, though. This was clearly not the kind of place to get on the wrong side of any of the locals. *Especially* someone looking like this who screamed narco.

'Americano?'

He asked with a cadence that suggested that he had already taken this to be fact. Making me think of that old Holly Johnson tune from the the end of the eighties. Shaking my head as I walked the few metres to join him and the rest of the group I replied.

'Nah, señor. I'm Scottish.'

This kind of threw him for a second. It generally always does though, to be fair, when a foreigner hears you - as a Scot - speak. Aye, they *hear* the English words spoken - well, at times, I suppose - but when it's delivered with the accent that we carry then it's never what they're expecting. He took a few seconds before issuing me back with a response.

'Ahhhh, whisky, kilts, castles and golf, yes?'

Well, it beat 'Rangers, Celtic, deep fried pizza and Buckfast' I suppose, when it came to things we were known for by those from elsewhere. Him and his group of men were standing by a Fuss-ball table, with one doing a line of ching right off the wooden panelled edge. The man - Pablo, although he hadn't formally introduced himself yet - pointed at the table beside him and boasted that I was speaking to the best Fuss-ball player in the whole of Mexico. As he did so, the sound of my man, Zeek, starting his set started to flow out of the speakers. I wasn't anywhere near as good as Zico when it came to knowing the names of songs - it *was* his day job, to be fair - but the song sounded like that Louis Vega one that I'd heard doing the rounds in Ibiza over the summer. I wasn't sure how I had been meant to process the information he'd just shared about table football but with the wee smile he had on his face as he'd said it, my inclination had been that he was just fucking about. Not that I wanted to just go on and spell this out to him or his boys because, well, what do I know about table fitba? He continued on, though.

'I called you over *because* you're a gringo. Figuring that if nobody here can give me a competitive match, I'd maybe have to take things international, yes?'

He looked around his group, for any reaction but there was none forthcoming, which would've helped me suss out

135

what was going on. Going with what I thought was the flow of things, though I thought I'd chance things and gauge the temperature of the boy by replying.

'So if I was to *beat* you, would that then make *me* the best player in Mexico? Would be a decent story to go back to Scotland and tell people, eh?'

He smiled at this but did not laugh in the way that I'd expected him to. Me thinking that it hadn't travelled across completely and had been a wee bit lost in translation. First of all. I hadn't played the game since I was in primary school and second, I'm not sure it was much to boast about to anyone. Not like I'd have won the Balon d'Or or fuck all.

'But you *won't* beat me,'

he replied, continuing to look at me while holding his hand out palm upwards. One of the boys with him - straight away - tipping a wee bit of gear out onto his hand and him turning back to face it before bringing his nose down towards his palm and hoovering that shit right up. I think this may have had an assist in what he then followed things up with as he turned back to face me.

'In fact. If you can beat me - first player to five - I will give you my watch.'

As he spoke he started to take off a Rolex that looked like it would choke a fucking horse. I was far from a watch expert - I didn't even *own* one. Who needs a watch anyway when you have a phone that'll tell you the time, eh? The boy was clearly well rich from his whole appearance so it wouldn't have been a stretch to suggest that it was probably worth a fair bit of money and was not something that he'd bought during a two week holiday to Playa de las Americas. All his mates all kind of going 'woooooaaahhhhh' to accompany the gesture of him putting such a beautiful looking watch at risk, although I was pretty sure he knew what he was doing.

'Nah, pal. It's fine. I wouldn't want to be taking your watch off you, eh?'

I tried to pass this off with a wee joke, so as to avoid the whole thing, because it had escalated at a mental speed. But that's cocaine for you, like. Things escalate.

'Oh now we're *definitely* going to be playing, amigo. I like your fighting talk.'

He laughed and patted me on the shoulder while telling me his name - which I reciprocated - and telling me to choose a side. The two teams, looking like they were Barcelona and Real Madrid. Before picking one, I just wanted to make sure that I hadn't missed a step, one where I was meant to match his gesture by putting something of my own up as collateral so said to the boy that I had the square root of fuck all to match a Rolex but he just waved me away - as if to say no worries pal - and once again asked me to pick a side. Barcelona it was. Leaving him to stay at the side he was at and me walking around the table.

Before we started, I felt comfortable enough to joke with him and his group - I didn't know if any of the rest could even speak English or not yet - that Pablo had an unfair advantage as had just had some sniff. Saying that his reaction times would be quicker than mine. This rectified when he signalled for someone to come over and shove a pre filled spoon under my nose. These fucking Mexicans, man? Some boys, like. One of his men - a guy with the most oily of slick back hair with one of those ties you see cowboy's wearing that consists of two pieces of rope and what looks like a tiny animal's skull, up where the knot of a *normal* tie would normally go - walked over to the middle of the table and counted 'uno, dos tres' and dropped the ball down into the centre circle. Game *on.*

With a mixture of the sounds of Zico's Latin infused house set playing from across on the lawn and the additional sound of Pablo's men all cheering him on - some other people had filtered over to watch what the commotion was - I got myself in the zone. Thinking that surely this game was the equivalent of riding a bike. I was *still* trying to think and he'd already made it one scud to him.

'Goooooooolllllll,'

he screamed and laughed, possibly already thinking this was in the bag, after seeing how slow I'd been to react to things. Made him work for his second goal, as I started to get a grip on proceedings. By the *third* goal of the match scored, though, I was fucking zenned up to fuck. Could barely hear Zico or all of the shouts around the table. The furious rate that I was swivelling the rows of players round around - attached to the steel rod - was taking me back to playing Track & Field, when you pushed those buttons as quick as possible for dear life. This was me on that table. Twirling each row of players round and round at the kind of blurred speed you wouldn't have been able to see what strips they were even wearing.

Two one to Pablo Gomez and now we had a match on our hands. Match? It was a fucking classic of the genre by the time it was all done and dusted, in what was an epic see-saw battle. For additional drama, we got to a four four winner takes all scenario. I'd be honest enough to be guilty of getting right into things, but so was he. For example. When I made it four three, he turned around and absolutely *booted* a plastic garden chair right into the pool. But then - moments later - when he equalised to take it to sudden death he went off for a wee run, doing an aeroplane celebration, Careca style.

Prior to playing the decider, and moments before the ball was in play, I'd had the wee thought that this Pablo was obviously a bit of a boy and *really* looked like he loved his table fitba. And I'd thought that maybe it might not have been a bad thing if I was to like, lose. But nah, fuck that. I wanted it every bit as he did - fuck that cocaine, like - but along with that, I knew what I was doing. Wasted no time in scoring the fifth, either. The ball was barely down and one of my defenders had managed an - admittedly - lucky strike that through his sheer desperation to not concede, he panicked. Cue another piece of furniture - this time thrown - going into the pool. I couldn't help but notice that while he was invited to this mansion that no cunt was pulling him up about his outbursts. Turning back to me he - I *think* - sincerely smiled and told me it had been a great game and handed me the Rolex.

'This is yours, amigo.'

I think to everyone's surprise, I grabbed his hand and closed his fingers down onto his watch.

'Nah, Pablo. You keep it, pal. Your friendship is enough.'

Now let me be fucking clear as day. Any other environment, you better believe I'd have had that watch around my wrist before you could've said 'you got the time, mate?' but this was a *different* scene altogether and Pablo was a serious boy, something that it wasn't hard to pick up on over a short course of time.

His reaction to this was something I don't think I'll ever forget. Genuinely thought that cunt was going to start greeting his eyes out in front of me. He just looked at me, kind of glazed eyed and with this proper smile emerging, told me that he didn't think people like me existed in the world - someone telling me that could either be a good thing or a bad thing - and how he could not believe that a man would do and say such a thing.

Hey, it was a touching and special moment, and absolutely fuck all like one's you'd see in films about Latin American narcos. Of course, it was a *whole* lot more touching when he handed the watch *back* to me. Insisting that he wanted me to have it. Telling me that his friendship was already assured. Like I said, it was like the honeymoon period of a fucking bromance. Sacking off any more games of table fitba. We all sat - six of us - around the pool having a blether. Turned out he was the only one who could talk English but he done a bit of translating on behalf of his boys. It was well mental to be sitting swapping stories with guys like that, and have me captivated by some of their stories fighting against the CJNG and those brutal bastards from Los Zetas while *they* were as sucked into my tales from the old casuals days. Well mad, like.

It all came to a bit of a sudden and abrupt end, though, when this boy, flanked by what I thought could've been security or bodyguards. The guy - I thought curiously - had on one of those flappy rimmed army hats that have the drawstring under your chin and a buttoned up short sleeved shirt that was like a faded camo print, same as his hat. When Pablo clocked the boy coming over towards our table and wasted no time in letting me know that maybe it was time for me to 'circulate the party,' I wasted no time in taking him up on his offer. So said my goodbyes - handshakes all round - and left them, one Rolex watch up. The watch, Pablo had told me, was released the year before and was worth around sixty thousand dollars. Something about an Oyster Perpetual Master in the title but half of what he'd told me about it had went in one ear and out the other.

As I walked around the - massive - gaff, I bumped into those two from the magazine. I hadn't been able to make my mind up about the two of them on the journey up in the car. They still had that look of wonder about them, that they'd had when entering the premises. I asked them about what they'd been up since the party started and - even though you could well see that he'd been getting fired into the free bar - the journalist out of the two said something about how he was working and just trying to take everything in. Aye, ok then, Myles.

Telling him how I'd just won Rolex off of a narco in a game of table fitba I issued Myles with a wee friendly word of warning in that he should keep his occupation to himself

'Any cunt finds out that you work for a magazine you'd probably do well to leave Sinaloa again. Best keep that stuff to yourself, lads.'

Luke laughed. I didn't which, in turn, wiped the smile back from off his face. Without any loyalty towards Lee, whatsoever, I then told them the story of *why* we were even there at the party. You could literally see the life drain from that journo's coupon as I told them this.

'Anyway, have a good one, boys. I'm away for a wee walk to see what trouble I can get into.'

I left them there, trying to process some of what I'd just told them. Pissing myself laughing over how much of a state of nam I'd put them in. None of it lies, either. Just putting them straight, eh? Some cunt had to, by the looks of the two of them.

I made my way over to the lawn to get a better listen to Zico's set for a while, grabbing a couple of bottles of beer from one of the ice boxes that seemed to be sitting around whatever direction you looked in, and they seemed to magically be filled anytime you went back to them. Swiping a couple to save me going back for a while, I had a wee dance to my man in the booth. You could see what he was doing. He'd started with a strong Latino vibe but was easing things away from that but in a style where it wasn't blatant. Definitely laying the groundwork for tunes to come, knowing him. It was straight up surreal as fuck, though, watching a crowd full of men in cowboy hats and fancy suits - and their women who were dressed up to the fucking nines - grooving away to Zico. Completely different kind of a crowd to what he'd have ever played to but he was apparently making it work.

When I was having a dance to myself, a girl to the side of me started to catch my eye. Due to my dance movements, every three seconds or so she would come into my line of vision. By the forth time of me seeing her, when turning my head her way, she now had a smile on her face, and unless I was a bit wrecked by this point - which I definitely *shouldn't* have been so relatively early into the party - the smile was in my direction.

She was well tidy as well, mind. Tidy *and* tiny. Could've only been five foot tops. Long black hair almost to her waist. The standard Latino body. But it was the smile. Aye, she had the big arse and the tits to match and absolutely stunning - movie star - looks. But the smile what made me unable to look away at her. I had a wee look around to make sure that she wasn't there with some psychopathic sicario or anything but nah, she was standing there having a wee dance to herself. Plus, unless *she* was a psychopath, she wouldn't have been smiling at the way she was at me if she'd come there to the party with a psycho of a boyfriend.

'Hablo ingles?'

I thought fuck it, if I'm going to try and have any hope here, I need to know if I'm going to be wasting my time from the off. Typical British Isles. Travel the world but still hope that the locals will be able to speak your language, instead of the other way around. She started nodding her head with the smile re-emerging. Telling me that she spoke good English, she introduced herself as Marisol. Which I almost asked her if that was Sol as in Sol Campbell or the beer but didn't think that it was too important. We had a wee dance with each other for around the next hour but - with the volume of the music on the lawn - having an actual conversation wasn't really much of a possibility, so we headed over to - first of all, the living quarters inside the mansions' building but found it almost as noisy through the amount of people that were in there chatting - the swimming pool seating area. It was a lot more deserted than it had been when hours earlier I'd played table fitba. Which was cool, as it gave us a chance to talk. Absolute fucking house on fire as well, the pair of us. She told me how much she loved my accent and seemed to hang on every word that I come out with. Which I'm sure, most of it, was absolute nonsense, but she seemed to lap it up all the same. Gen up, part of me was thinking that maybe she'd been some free prostitute who had been hired for the party, because it didn't seem possible that someone like her would've been interested in me. Talk about fucking punching, eh?

Couldn't have been further from the truth, when it came to her occupation. And when I found out, I was *well* glad that I hadn't went and done something daft by asking her if she'd been laid on as 'entertainment' for the night. Nah, she wasn't a prostitute. She was a *fucking TV star* from Peru!

Fuck right off, eh?!! Which was kind of my reaction when she told me that, my facial features had been enough for her to hear the words said by me but not to take the offence they might cause. I think this was maybe a bit refreshing for her, having someone beside her who didn't know who she was. She told me to look up her name - Marisol Bolivar - into any search engine and I would find her pictures in connection with a show - a telenovela - titled 'Disputa en la Familia,'which was like Family Feud or something along those lines. Looked her up and, aye. There she was. Something like three million followers on Instagram and known by everyone from Mexico and further south. I couldn't have felt any more small by comparison as I told her that *I* dealt in vintage adidas trainers and clothing for a living.

Whether she was some famous star and I was just some radgey who had ended up at the party without being invited, it didn't really matter. The two of us were getting on and, by then, I thought that it was pretty clear that we fancied each other. That tension between the two of us, something that could've been cut with a knife.

We sat for well over an hour, just sharing a bit about ourselves, while coming from thousands of miles away from each other. She laughed a lot, which is always a good sign. She was into her drugs as well, which *also* helps. Her pulling out a cheeky wee pre roll for us to sit and smoke. Eventually we decided to go back over and join the party as she said she wanted to introduce me to some of her friends - from the show - who were also there.

Then I just couldn't help being me. I wasn't to make it away from the pool area without ending up *in* the fucking thing, and pulled her along with me, just for good measure. We'd got up from the table that we'd been sitting at and were making our way around to head towards the lawn. And there's only one part of this journey where you come into close quarters of the pool. But sometimes, that's all you need. Not looking where I was going, I put my foot down and found it half on half off of something, like when you stand on the edge of the kerb by accident and almost break your ankle? Well that was what happened to me, stepping on edge of this raised step or platform - the darkness didn't help - and it sent me toppling to the left, trying to balance myself. This is happening while I'm holding Marisol by the hand, next second she's letting out a loud scream and ... Well, you can guess the rest. And *thank fuck* for that Rolex and it's waterproof properties, as well.

A huge cheer went up around us from those sitting around chatting. The loud splash that two people made not going unnoticed. Fucking *soaked*. I could've dealt with that but she was too, and you have to think of things like someone having hair all done up for a party and now what? And yet she was absolutely sound as a pound about it. I swear, if there had been any priests in attendance that moment I'd have fucking *married* her.

I was mortified, like. I mean, it was a pretty fucking on brand thing to happen to me. Meet a model of a TV show star and within a couple of hours pull her into a swimming pool by accident. But she just giggled about it. Having playful banter - in Spanish - with some people who stood around the side teasing her. You can never discount the impairment of drink and drugs, however, I was fucking smitten with her. If I'd thought that she looked sexy before, now she was dripping wet with her dress hugging her figure ever further.

The boy whose birthday it was? I'm not sure if someone had told him about two people falling into the pool but he came over quite quickly to make sure every cunt was ok. Seeing me - and taking a second to place me before linking things to Zico - and then Marisol. He told us that he'd take us up to his bedroom where we'd be able to borrow something from him and Veronica, while our clothes were drying out.

We walked with him from the pool over to the mansion and then up the stairs. Him and Marisol sharing some jokes in Spanish that neither felt the need to translate for me. As long as you can understand vibes, sometimes language doesn't matter. And when it came to vibes, this party had them. The only exception being from that moody looking man in the army hat, that I'd come across earlier.

Looking out a short loose flowery summer style dress for Marisol, I waited to see what fit Ovidio was going to sort me out with, even if whatever he he gave me to wear was going to be better than my soaking wet gear. My hopes were well up when the first thing he threw me was a pair of classic check Burberry shorts, but then he threw me over a bright florescent lime green Lacoste polo shirt. I thanked the boy gracefully for his help and kept the obvious colour clash concerns strictly to me myself and I, and Marisol. Once Ovidio had left us to get dressed, telling us to hand our wet clothes to one of the staff on the way back down from the upstairs bedrooms.

The level of comfort between me and her was highlighted right there, in Ovidio's room, when she, and then me following her, slipped out of her wet dress, right there in front of me. Knowing exactly what she was doing, her eyes never left mine when she was undressing, and setting me the task of keeping eye contact with her, or finding my eyes straying elsewhere. They strayed elsewhere, which made her smile with a bit of confidence behind it.

Before we got changed, the two of us had a *moment*. Was a bit more than a moment, to be fair. We started kissing - for the first time - and that started to escalate. I was stiff as a fucking board and she could feel it pressing up against her, teasing me by pressing *back* against it, and wiggling her hips.

I was about ready to go. Fuck, *was* ready to go. Grabbed her and threw her onto the bed and was about to follow her before I had the 'what the fuck are you doing, lad?' thought pop in. Aye, this Marisol was hot as fuck but is having sex in the bed of a junior narco who has just been sound enough to let you borrow some of his clothes a good idea? Would he be cool with that? I'm guessing that he definitely *wouldn't* be cool with that. I wouldn't have been? Narco or not. Goes to his bed at the end of the party and finds all of my fucking cum stains over his sheets and in his bed. Nah, man. *No cunt* wants that. But definitely not someone who is in the fucking Sinaloa Cartel.

I pulled back, and then grabbed Marisol's hand and pulled her back of the bed. Her with a confused look on her coupon. When I explained to her, she understood straight away. But I knew that it would only be a matter of time before me and her revisited that situation again. Speaking of sexual encounters. Due to how large this mansion was, I had become a wee bit disoriented with which way we were meant to go, to leave the upper floor. I could remember that we'd went through a door at the top of the big staircase which led us into the bedrooms and bathrooms which lined all the way down this corridor, the one that we were trying to get out of. Marisol when we opened one door, there was a bathroom inside so Marisol, saying she wanted to quickly redo her hair told me to carry on and find our exit.

They could've made it easier for me though by at least making *some* of the doors different to the other, instead of them all being identical to each other. It made me think of that thing you see where someone has to open a door to escape from somewhere but behind some of the doors is tigers that'll kill them, if they choose the wrong one to open. Which was fitting, I suppose, because I'd have fucking *taken* a tiger behind the door that I next tried, instead of what was *actually* behind there.

Turning the handle and hoping to see the top of the staircase, I instead, was confronted by the sight of a fully naked Lee. Mexican girl half his age - easily - lying on the bed behind him giggling while he stands there - fully erect - taking his cock and slapping a picture frame - on a bedroom table - around. I mean? What do you even say to that? Worse still - if possible - while he was sexually abusing this wooden frame he's fucking talking to whoever was in the picture.

'You like that, you old hag, yeah? You like that hard cock in your fucking face. I bet you want to suck it, don't you?'

The girl was fucking ending herself. I wasn't. Lee, who had been well into things didn't look like he'd noticed the door opening at first. So much so that I was on my way to *closing* the door by the time he turned to look at me.

'Hey, pal. I don't want to fucking know.'

And I really didn't. I said, holding a hand in the air before closing the door. Fuck him, I thought to myself once the door was closed. I didn't fucking choose to be left with that as a memory and if he hadn't been such a fucking depraved deviant then I wouldn't have. I know there's always some element of risk when opening a closed door at a party but no cunt would've ever predicted that what I'd seen would've ever been a possibility.

'Are you ok, Seemon? You look like you've seen a ghost,'

Marisol asked, when meeting up with me again. What I had seen was much, much worse than something that the paranormal could throw at you. *That* was fucking para-not-normal, from Lee.

We left the building with intentions of heading over to see what was going on with Zico but were diverted after hearing some people shouting that Ovidio was going to be doing his birthday piñata. I'd never seen anyone over the age of eight using a piñata so was well up for going to watch him, when Marisol suggested we should go over to see. The donkey itself was hanging from a rafter inside some kind of a rustic looking converted barn, I'd clocked the building earlier when I'd been on manoeuvres around the place but had been given the impression that it wasn't a building that was being used for the party. Maybe it was being prepared for later, I thought as we both stood there and watched Ovidio having the blindfold placed over his eyes and a baseball bat put into his hand.

With everyone in the barn counting down to zero - and one of Ovidio's taller friends grabbing the donkey and pushing it back and forward a few times, the birthday boy was let loose on it.

Swinging wildly at it and missing badly. The crowd cheering each swing he took and then mock moaning with every miss. He must've taken a good dozen swings at the thing and the best he'd managed had been to clip the edge of it, as it was swinging past the flight path of Ovidio's bat. Even a stopped clock can be right, though. And such was the case with Ovidio. Eventually hitting the donkey straight in the middle, and the contents coming flying out of its inside. The crowd going mental, and - assuming they knew what was coming, as opposed to me who had been completely in the dark - everyone cheering Ovidio. But it wasn't any fucking 'candy' that was inside.

Different coloured wraps and pre rolled joints fell to the floor and with enough to go round, everybody who wanted something from the floor was able to get what they were looking for.

A fucking *drug* piñata. Honestly, these cunts?! Still swiped a couple of grams of their mad coc-ay-een and some pre rolls while they were going, mind. Marisol picked up some as well. What's the point of having a drug piñata if no cunt is going to take the drugs that come out of it, eh?

Hours behind schedule we finally managed to make our way back over to hear a bit of Zeek playing. I'd actually made my way over with Marisol to introduce her to him but he'd had a few of the locals in his booth and I could see that he was doing that being polite thing he can do with people who can't see that they're doing his head in, so thought I'd leave him for a bit. Us just having a wee boogie to ourselves, with Zico now on full house mode and playing some proper heaters in his second set. I say second set because, apparently, there had been a mariachi band playing a gig, not that I'd seen it. I thought that it had maybe taken place when we were in the house or something. The night, to be fair and quite honest, was a blur in a lot of stages. Which was understandable because you can't be *that* fucking high and not lose a few hours here and there.

Over the course, with it being *that* kind of a bash where you didn't know what was coming next, she never did manage to introduce me to her fellow actors from the show but *did* manage to introduce me to one of her friends - from Michoacan - who was a professional fitba player. A pro who was currently playing in Mexico's Liga MX. Now *this* was fucking CLASS. When she introduced me to him - Rafael Arroyo - I knew the name from somewhere, but looking at him - someone who looked like they had to have been in the twilight of their professional career - I didn't recognise him from anywhere. And then it hit me.

He couldn't speak English but Marisol was happy enough to translate for me.

'Ask him if, earlier in his career, he came to Scotland and the city of Dundee, to sign for Dundee United …or so he thought. And that when he realised that it was actually *Dundee* who was trying to sign him, he got his agent to get him out of Scotland straight away.'

It was asking a lot from Marisol to have translated *all* of that and she even laughed at me when I finally stopped speaking. But she got enough over to the boy to have him standing there and this wee smile forming on his face while looking at me and nodding his head quite enthusiastically, saying,

'Si, Si.'

I think he found it amusing that he was at a party and someone was asking about such a random thing as that to him. That someone even *remembered* it.

Marisol translated something on behalf of the boy, telling me how he knew there was a problem when he arrived at the stadium - Dens Park - and took one look at the place and felt there was something up. Which had us all laughing. Marisol too, even though she'd have had no concept on what a dump the place was, and I think I'm being objective with that statement, not because I happen to support the rivals of this football team.

Telling him that he was a legend amongst thousands of Arabs. I got him to pose for a selfie with me and then took a separate video where - after teaching him to say it, about half a dozen times, the two of us stood for the video and shouted

'Fuck the Dees.'

I'd have asked myself if this night could have gotten any better but was pretty sure that at some point it was going to involve me and Marisol and sexual and intercourse. So, aye? It fucking *was* going to get even better.

The two of us hatched a plan. When telling her that I had to go back to Guadalajara - at the end of the party - and how I was here in Mexico as part of Zico's wee tour he had ahead of us. She said that she had a better idea. That I skipped the ride back with Zico, Lee and the rest and, instead, went back with her to the hotel she had in Mazatlan, and that she would have transport arranged for later on in the day, and we'd *both* go to see Zico on his tour opener.

Well, win win, eh?

By this point of the morning I was flying without wings, Ronan fucking Keating style. So was highly suggestible. After sex, Si? I'd have surely regretted not going back in the limo with the lads. But *before sex* Si? Different viewpoint, altogether. But as for the after sex part? I hadn't estimated for just how rocked my world would have been both at the party and then the 'after party' that we had there in her hotel room.

I, for the first time of the night, popped into Zico's booth to let him know that I was heading back to Marisol's hotel, and that I'd catch up with him down in Guadalajara at some point. I detected a wee bit of attitude from him, saying he'd not seen me all night while he was standing there chained to the fucking decks, which was fair enough, I suppose. I was too busy having a good time in as many ways as I could. I felt bad for him that he'd missed some party, like. He was all good by the time I was leaving the booth, though. Shaking his head at - probably not even believing me - me telling him I'd met a Peruvian actress. I think this was around four in the morning by then but had no longer felt the need to even acknowledge what time it was. The party was still going quite strong at the point, but what we had needed surpassed recreational activities like dancing to Zico and chatting and drinking with friends.

Before leaving, we sought out Ovidio to wish him happy birthday again and to thank him for an amazing party, which was not a lie to describe it as such. In broken but clear English, while saying goodbye to us. He looked, specifically, at me and said that he would see me 'tonight' at the Ballam. I had absolutely *no* idea what he even meant by this. I know I had possibly overindulged over the course of the night but I heard clearly what he'd said, and there was no sense to it. It took him to point towards the booth and say 'Selecao' for me to even know the *name* of the club where Zico was opening his tour at.

'Ah, nice one, amigo. Marisol's coming too. What about Veronica?'

He confirmed that his other half was coming to Guadalajara too for that evening. He wished us goodbye and told us to get some sleep as it would be night time before any of us knew it. Doing so with a knowing smile on his face that someone does with you when they know that you're away to get your Nat King.

Back at the hotel we had a much needed sleep to energise ourselves for going again in Guadalajara, well, eventually. Like that Lee Majors in The Fall Guy, I'm not the kind to kiss and tell but between you and me, the sex back at the hotel was the kind that leaves you questioning if you fell in love with the other person *during* it.

After both passing out and having a forced sleep. When we woke, we spent several hours just lying watching TV - with me left with no idea what was going on, dialog wise - and ordering room service. Was barry, like. So was the sex that we ended up back to, again. Tell you, though. Once we'd worn ourselves out , the fucking *last* thing I wanted out of life was to jump in a car and drive around seven hours - depending on traffic - to get back to being in a position of *then* going out for the night.

And to be fair to Marisol, she managed to take that problem right out of the equation, terrifyingly so. Not wanting to face a car but also aware that the time was wearing on and we'd need to be getting on our way if we wanted to be there in time for Zeek, I started to get a bit anxious about us needing to get on our way.

Picking up a grilled cheese sandwich that she'd just had delivered. The reaction of the hotel waiter when seeing who had ordered the sandwich that he was delivering was priceless. Saying how he'd probably get the sack if caught but could he have a selfie with her. Brave man, considering she was a woman and had not exactly made herself presentable to the public. Marisol, diplomatically choosing to tell him that she would seek him out when she was leaving the hotel later and get a picture with him. The way that she delivered this, she was left with putty in her hands that used to be a hotel waiter.

She told me that transport had already been arranged and that we didn't have to leave for hours yet, and that we could lay there and recover from the party, *both* of them.

'Buttt Guadalajara is like, fucking *hours* away and Zeek goes on, as an open to close set, at eleven, I think,'

I said hesitantly, unsure of when exactly he started because until around forty eight hours ago I hadn't even planned to *be* at it. I won't judge myself for the mistake I'd made, because I reckon most cunts would've too. I had made the leap by already 'assuming' which mode of transport we were taking.

She flashed me that amazing smile, but with a wee bit of cheekiness on the side before telling me that, aye, Guadalajara *was* fucking hours away but that it was a *lot* quicker, if you went by helicopter! Finishing off the last of her grilled cheese and wiping her mouth with the napkin on the plate, she told me that she knew someone who would fly us down the coast and that she would figure out her own transport the next day after Zico's set while I was telling her that it was Mexico City up next for him - and me - and that she was welcome to extend her trip. She had told me over the night that filming was on a month's break and she now had some valuable down time with the normal schedule dominating her time so this was her letting loose while she had the chance.

So the good news was that the seven hour journey time had now been cut down to two. Undoubtedly, the *bad* news was that it was because it was by helicopter. I'd never been in one before but my overriding opinion of them is that they crash, a lot. Or maybe it's just because you always hear when one crashes? Anyway, in my opinion, cunts went down in them all the time. I was going to say 'rich cunts' who go down in them but the mode of transport such as a helicopter isn't one that you'd normally find someone popping down to the dole office in.

Hours later, we found ourselves ready for the night and down by some kind of a marina that had a helicopter pad near the end of it. I was fucking bricking it, not going to lie to you. Marisol could tell by the face she pulled while taking my hand and squeezing it like some mum to her kid who's frightened by something.

Once I'd managed to get past my insane fear of ending up in a mangled piece of burning metal, I quite enjoyed it. The view of the Pacific from up there was ridiculous, and normally I'm the cunt that misses half of these sights because I'm blethering some shite to someone or, even more of a possibility, sitting napping.

One thing that we hadn't really spoken about over the night had been me and Zico's friendship so - with our headphones on - we sat and passed the time with me sharing some stories of him and me from over the years and gave her a little tutorial into the DJ that she was flying towards Guadalajara in a helicopter to dance to across the night.

We flew in the direction of Guadalajara with what could only have been a top, top night on the cards. Although a *very* high bar had been set, because I couldn't recall a more unbelievable twenty four hours - plus - than the one I'd just spent. From getting picked up at airport by a limo with free drink and drugs inside it all the way to me being in the back of a helicopter with some foxy forty something Latin American TV star.

And to think, I could've been still back in Las Vegas with that torn faced boot of an ex girlfriend and bamming up the blackjack dealers and players at the tables.

Masterful gambit, sir. I thought to myself. Knowing that by flying from Nevada to Jalisco - and what had followed - had been the equivalent of having, quite literally, blackjack, with a twenty one.

The lights of the vast Guadalajara landscape suddenly started coming into view. It's brightness sort of reflecting against the sky as part of its light pollution process but by how brightly lit the sky was, it gave you an idea of the size of the place. Seeing it come into view

Seeing the city coming into view, it gave thought to getting a chance to - along with this diamond of a girl - party in downtown Guadalajara. The night before had been a departure from what I was used to, but I'd had the time of my fucking life. More of a ball than Zoe, like. But tonight? Well that was more my favoured arena, a dark sweaty club with Zico not dumbing down for the crowd in front of him, which he had undoubtedly done the night before but with good cause and in a way that allowed him to keep his dignity over.

Aye, the night before was one that would forever rank as one of the best nights of my life but that's the thing with 'best nights of your life,' you never know when and where they'll happen, which means that, technically, any time you go out could be one of *those* nights.

And that's *exactly* how I went into Zico's opener, that night.

As we confirmed my name plus one to the doorman - although going by his reaction to seeing Marisol in front of him, I reckon he'd have let us both in, regardless - and him unhooking the obligatory velvet rope to let us in with a mini brightly lit arched tunnel to walk through before entering the main club, I squeezed Marisol's hand and told her.

'You let me see a bit of your world, last night. Now let me show you a little bit of mine.'

Now what's the Spanish for MDMA? I thought to myself before laughing at how much of a complete fanny I could be at times. The *Spanish* for it is MDMA, Si, mate, I told myself.

Now let's go and find some, my follow up thought as we entered an already filling up room, filled by filthy beats from a Zico stood playing in a lowered down booth that was so close to the crowd that those at the front would've been able to lean on the edge and watch him.

I decided to take Marisol up to meet him before things started to unravel. Better to do these introductions when the night is yet young and faces are at their freshest, as well as minds.

Zico's approving look to me - when he knew Marisol wasn't looking - was enough validation for me, not that I needed it. We said we'd check back in later while he looked behind me and said there was more than enough room for the two of us to stay and hang back there. Marisol, used to that kind of treatment was excited to take up Zico's offer - I was still new to this celeb stuff and hadn't grasped what Zico had done immediately. That a night out in a busy club for someone like

Marisol would've been a nightmare, with constant people wanting to speak to her or have a photo taken - so we stayed there all night and danced while still close enough to the crowd to feel like we were there in amongst it.

When I had told Zeek that I needed to go looking for some mandy and how I hadn't a clue if you could even *get it* in Mexico, so good the ching was. He just told me to sit tight. Calling over someone from the club who went away and returned back ten minutes later, with a bag of - approximately - a couple of grams of MDMA crystals. Telling me that when he'd arrived before his set, someone from the club had been there to welcome him and show the set up that they had for him and while doing so, the boy had whispered to him that if he needed any gear over the night then he just needed to say. This boy telling Zico all of the different stuff available and when I'd mentioned mandy, he remembered that he had included this in his list.

What a man, Zico. And, also, the boy from the club who rustled it up for the lads, and Marisol. Who couldn't keep her hands off me, once it hit us. All part of ze plan, though.

Some mandy across the night, dancing away to my best mate on his - so fucking proud of the boy, like - Latin America tour opener with my new - not sure what to describe Marisol as - friend.

That was the plan, and then when Zico finished which was either four or five in the morning, away back to the hotel room - which at that point in the night I hadn't remembered that I had not even *booked*. This through my unexpected arrival in Guadalajara, *exactly* as Zico was leaving. This made worse with me then not returning back to his hotel along with him the next day, but that's another story although, once again, the presence of Marisol during this was not a disadvantage - for some sex, some sleep and then, when we woke, me and Marisol would start to work out what would then follow for the two of us

Chapter 8

Lee

Well Stevie's opening night of his tour of some of the coolest countries on the planet to visit? A complete revelation. A tour de force, a bloody tour de force. There was a mini riot outside through those without tickets trying to get into the already sold out club. Some without tickets got in while - with the gaff already at bursting point - others *with* tickets were denied. It's unfortunate, but it happens, and will again. Still, the mini riot, apparently, made the local news, which can never be bad for bidness, you know?

I'd seen Stevie's mate, Si, across the night, behind the booth with the girl he'd come away from the Flores birthday party with. I couldn't deny, she was an absolute sort. But with *him* it was a case of beauty and the fucking beast, you know? I was still trying to deal with the night before at the birthday party so the last thing I was concerned about was skirt. I was there on a purely professional basis, ish. Mainly I just wanted to be there on the opening night. Noticing that the journalist and photographer from the magazine were impressed by the fervent crowd that had packed out Ballam for DJ Selecao. Luke, snapping away with his camera anytime you looked in his direction.

Seeing Simon had brought about a chilling memory. One from the night before and one that I had managed to let slip from over the night of the birthday. But seeing him there, behind the decks, I saw that face again. Looking around that mansion door at me, while I was stood there in a more than compromising position. This was something that I was going to have to bring up with him - for my sanity, if anything - at some point, if he planned to tag along on this tour with Stevie.

But it wasn't what he thought he'd seen, although, paradoxically, was *exactly* what he thought he'd seen. Fuck, what he *had* seen?! But allow me to explain. I had taken some Mexican hottie from the party - who had ground herself up against my thigh more than enough times to let me know how she was feeling about this new friendship of mine and hers. Of course, the copious sniff that we were engaging in leading up to then had only expedited things.

As you do at house parties, you look for a spare bedroom that no one's using. And I found us - I forget her name as I never saw much of her after we left the bedroom again. Possibly Luisa but if I had a gun to my head I wouldn't have been certain - one. I didn't discriminate on *which* bedroom. I just needed to find *a* bedroom for us, which I did. Looking back, now. Yeah, it wasn't exactly small. The bed was so large that when you lay down on it you were made to feel like a midget. There were museum like framed pictures on every wall and some kind of a Roman theme to the ceiling and pillars. A large en suite bathroom with one of those rainforest style showers, with room for two. Whose bedroom it was, that really did not matter to me and horny state. What *did* matter, though was that whoever the bedroom belonged to, that they weren't there at the same time as I was.

So when me and - let's call her - Luisa made ourselves at home inside there. She'd wasted no time in getting naked and lying across that massive bed. I did something similar - while standing to the side of the bed - before joining her. After a few minutes of kissing, bodies lying pressed against each other, rolling around a bed that you couldn't fall off if you bloody well tried. Before we went any further, I stopped and told her to wait a moment. Wanting to fish out some of the gear that I had from earlier, with some depraved thoughts of sniffing it right off that juicy behind of hers. I jumped off the bed and went looking for my trousers.

When I found them, lying in a heap on the floor what seemed like a good six metres away from the actual bed, inside this indoor arena of a bedroom, I fished out the plastic baggie I had and - spur of the moment stuff - tipped a little of it out onto the chest of drawers in front of me and made it disappear almost as soon as it had appeared.

Dealing with the sudden rush from the sniff and how hard I already was through lying on the bed with this Mexican sort, I was stood there with what I'd heard Zico refer to in the past as 'a right stane on.' Then I looked at the table, beside the chest of drawers, and saw her. Some horrific looking old woman. Face like a pit-bull eating a bag of Haribo sour jelly sweeties. Sitting there, proud, but, also, miserable as fuck.

'Aww, cheer up you ugly old hag. You want some cock, yeah? Fuck, you are ugly though. Who the fuck would be desperate enough to slip you an end? Not when they've got someone as SO FUCKING HOT as this Mexicano beauty over on the bed?'

I said, looking at the photo. Hearing the girl on the bed giggle at this. I felt like I now had a pass. An actual sign of encouragement that I should continue. Gripping that hard cock, I continued playing to the apparent watching gallery. I continued talking towards the mystery woman in the photo. Taking my cock and smacking it around the picture frame, so much so that I only stopped when I had completely knocked the frame off its stand and sending it falling back, with her *still* looking, - mocking, even - back at me. I had stood there and slapped my cock around a photo of some old woman and, while thinking that my actions were somewhat appropriate of the moment that I was in - and fuck's sake, how I feel like a politician who has been caught as part of an undercover sting involving a fake sheikh and a tabloid - but once I'd come through the other end of this coke fuelled horny moment, I looked up, suddenly aware that someone else was watching, in that sixth sense way that people can show that they have on occasion.

You wouldn't have wanted anyone - apart from the woman in the picture or any of the Flores family who it would appear would be related to her - apart from Simon to be looking around the door at my performance. But the cards that were dealt were that he had to be the one who saw some of that performance from me.

This minor setback did not in any way stop me from going back over to the bed and joining my friend from the party and giving her a good two minutes of her life. When it dawned on her, after five minutes or so, that I'd had no desire to keep the kettle boiling - so to speak - she got dressed in a hurry and stormed out in a right strop, calling me a Puta Madre, which my hours spent learning Spanish had not been called upon in understanding what it was that she was trying to convey.

But, yeah. That was a topic that I would be forced to revisit with Simon at a later date, while hoping that, in the mean time, he'd have kept things to himself. Admittedly, I hadn't covered myself in too much glory since landing in Guadaljara. And it wasn't even as if the incident that Simon had stumbled across had been the end of it. But enough about that, for now.

Back to the Ballam nightclub, which I had been told was loosely based on the name of a mythical Mayan warrior where the name itself had required a little tweaking before it would be marketable, with the owners settling on a way to *pronounce* the name of the warrior, while spelling it in a different way. Which led to the name 'Ballam.'

There had been *many* moments over the over the more than thirty years I'd had the boy in my stable that I had been left proud of Stevie. His first Ibiza residency, - early in the night set of course, but still a massive achievement for him, and my negotiating skills as a manager - first time playing Creamfields, and then all of the other festivals that followed after him almost taking the roof of the tent off. One of those occasions where Creamfields security had to resort to a one out one in strategy. When he was nominated for a Grammy? That one went without saying. Like I said, many times the boy had left me marvelling at where he'd seen his career go. And watching this capacity filled club staying there until lights on at ten to five in the morning, I couldn't have been *more* proud of him.

Myself, and how the rest of my morning went. No, I very much was not proud of myself. When I woke up, I could see that it was a hotel room, that much was clear enough. There's only two types of habitable rooms in this world and one is a hotel room and the other, an actual house bedroom. And as much as hotel's try, they haven't quite nailed the look of something other than a hotel. But this wasn't *my* hotel room. I had spent enough time inside my room that first day, following that whole unpleasantness back at the cantina, and my first meeting with Don Flores.

As I began to come to, so did various memories from across the night. Well, morning, to be accurate. I remembered the part about me not going back to the hotel after Stevie's set with the rest. Instead, jumping in a taxi and asking the driver to 'take me to the women.' I had no recollection of the drive, for how long it took *or* what I'd even paid for it. I wasn't that smashed though, not after the night before where the recovery turnaround time simply hadn't been long enough to get over things before going and doing it all over again. So why was my memory so hazy from what had only been a series of hours before? The sun was starting to come up for the day. I remembered that.

Then the woman with the big hair popped into my head. The one who'd reminded me of Amy Winehouse. When I lay there on the bed trying to force the memories to return to me, it hurt my head a little. Fuck, it was so patchy, though. Flashes coming back to me but like a half completed jigsaw puzzle. The woman with the tall hair and then several missing scenes before her then popping back into my mind again, giving me a blow job. So where was she *now?* And which hotel was I lying in bed in? The hotel part, specifically, had completely escaped me.

Lying there confused as hell, I then realised that I was bursting for a pee and most likely had been since waking, but this had been superseded by my state of confusion of what had taken place. Despite feeling like I was so wiped that actually peeing the bed had felt like a viable option. I went to force myself up and out of it to go to the bathroom. Mind over matter, Lee my son, I told myself, trying to engage brain with body.

And it was when I went to get up out of bed that I felt something digging into my wrist, and me unable to move out of the bed any further. What the fuck is going on, I thought while turning to look at my wrist that seemed to be stuck to something. That's when I saw the handcuff around it, and the other half around the bed post.

'Awww FUCK. Not *again*,'

I shouted out loud there inside the room. Unfortunately, for me, the use of the word 'again' was not by mistake. The memories of a trip to Bangkok in the mid nineties flooding back to me. Now realising that despite my recollections of things being sketchy at best, I could *now* see just what had taken place. There was a bottle of beer on the bedside table that I could not recall asking for or drinking, but was sure that I had, which had more than likely been my undoing.

Almost as if prompted by the sight of the handcuff around me. The memory of the woman telling me that she had a hotel that she used and that we should go there. I had literally taken a taxi to seek out a woman exactly like this, so *of course* I'd been in favour of this suggestion.

And due to how out of it I was upon waking. My thought process was only able to function at a limited capacity. While I thought of one thing, this did not necessarily mean that I would then link that to something else notable of the same subject.

So, lying there handcuffed to a bed, naked. My initial thought was of how I was now going to have to get someone from the hotel to help me get out of this predicament. Who would they call to assist. Police? The bloody fire brigade? Back in Bangkok, they had called a local locksmith to come out and free me from the handcuff in what *had* to have went down as the single most humiliating thing to ever happen to me, and in what was a *fiercely* competitive field.

It took me a few moments even to register that if I'd been handcuffed to a bed by a prostitute that I'd never met until that night and, truth be told, if you'd put six women with tall hair in an identity parade I'd have toiled when it came to pointing her out, then this would mean that my shit was gone. I didn't know this for sure as my trousers were way out of reach. Clearly I'd been a man in a hurry when entering the room as my trousers appeared to be across the room, near to the inside of the room door. But it was taken as granted that my stuff was gone. Otherwise what would've been the point in handcuffing a punter to a bed and - going by how my head was feeling - *also* drugging them, so that they don't give you any problems while you're relieving them of their belongings?

What a way to wake for the day. The absolute fucking *last* thing that I'd wanted to do was reach over and grab the room phone to tell reception that I needed some assistance. Now that I was thinking a bit more clearer, I hadn't ruled out that the hotel, itself, was even in on this thing, with the prostitutes using their hotel for business. In the end, I really didn't have a choice. And I was fucked if I was just going to lie there all day and hope that the woman of the night hadn't been smart enough to stick a do not disturb sign over the outside handle and that room service would come to my rescue.

I covered myself up with some of the sheets and - while almost cutting my hand off through reaching across the other side of the bed - just about managed to grab enough of the corner of the room phone to drag it towards me and onto the bed. Dialling zero on the keypad to speak to someone down in reception and tell them that I had been robbed in the night. Wishing I hadn't actually used the term 'robbed' because for all I knew, that would've meant an automatic call to the local police, who would've been able to see for themselves that I had prompted the trouble I'd landed in simply by going looking for sex. Because it went without saying that I wouldn't have been the first 'gringo' that the Guadalajara police would have found handcuffed to a hotel bed in the city centre.

And call the police was *exactly* what the hotel did, which - by default - allowed me to have *another* most humiliating day of my life all over again. First of all, someone from the hotel came up, following my phone call. You could tell that she wanted to laugh, while putting on the front of being apologetic that this had happened in their hotel. She told me that the police would be able to help get me out of the cuff around my wrist. I asked her if there was any way where I'd be able to get out of it *without* the police being involved, which I'm sure she understood my reasons for wishing to know this. But no dice.

She stood there, saying that she needed to call for two reasons. One being that as part of their hotel policy to try and ensure as little crimes possible are committed under their roof, they report any incident of a serious nature. Which, I suppose, always left them with the higher ground to stand on when something less than legal went down inside their establishment. Her other reason for calling them was as simple as her not having an idea who else could possibly come and free me from the handcuff. I'd thought fire brigade but with how small that piece of metal was wrapped around my wrist I wasn't too sure about wanting to take my chances with having one of them standing there with that machine they use to cut their way into cars. One little slip while doing it and they'd have been able to finish what Don Flores had started, back in the kitchen of that city centre cantina.

While she was stood in the room with me. I asked the hotel assistant if she could pick my trousers up and throw them onto the bed for me. I felt a little dirty about this, watching her bending down to pick them up, with my boxer shorts also lying there in quite close proximity.

I think it was to do with the fact that she'd known that I was lying there on the bed naked that she followed the letter of the law and picked my trousers up for me and then literally *threw* them across the room and onto the bed for me. Unless she had completely overlooked the whole point of things. I was fucking *handcuffed* to the bed. It wasn't as if the naked man was going to make a grab for her and have his way.

When I got hold of my trousers - with the hotel assistant telling me that when they arrived she would send them up to the room but for me to not hold my breath as it may take *hours* before they actually turned up - I got the confirmation that the prostitute had turned me right over. Like Rakim, when going through my pockets and coming up with nothing other than lint. From nowhere, I had got the memory of leaving my wallet in my hotel room, my *real* hotel room. Leaving for the night at the Ballam with enough money in my pocket to see me comfortably through the night. So there was at least that, and that I wouldn't need to go through the whole process of calling my bank and credit card company to get my cards cancelled and - even worse - now have the complete pain in the bloody arse of being in Mexico - and not returning to Britain for a couple of weeks - and not having any means of getting money out. My phone was gone, though. Naturally. And this was not good. A phone being something that I, quite literally, could not survive without and a scenario that would lose me money every day where I didn't have one in my possession. Fortunately I still had a second one back in my bag at the hotel. Back in the day it was a case of me always having a spare battery for my phone but when technology moved us onto phones with fixed batteries, well *that* moved me onto a second phone. The only other win was that she wouldn't have managed to get herself into the thing. And they called me paranoid when I said I didn't want a phone with fingerprint reader as well?

The police did *not* make things easy for me. Taking the piss right out of me and laughing. Either not allowing for the fact that I could speak Spanish or simply not giving a flying. Using some kind of a skeleton key on me which popped the lock within a few seconds of the copper wiggling it around inside the lock. I'm not sure that they'd thought the subject of asking me for a bribe - once I'd been released and they'd started to talk about how I shouldn't have put myself in such a situation - quite through, though. *How* could I pay them a bribe when I'd been fucking robbed? Them not taking too kindly to the sight of me grabbing my trousers and pulling the empty pockets out. I'd have *happily* given them a few shekels in thanks for helping me get out of the predicament that I was in. But you cannot give someone what you do not have.

I tried to work this situation to my advantage, figuring that if they wanted a bribe out of me then they'd might have been so inclined as to *drive* me back to the hotel, and save me the taxi fare but their reaction to this told me that the bonus received as payment of the bribe would've been undone by the hassle to take me to the hotel, which in its way told me that the two hotels were not exactly close to one another.

Absolutely *none* of this, I'd needed. I mean, who *would* need to be waking up in the morning in a strange hotel, handcuffed to a bed, having been robbed by a prostitute? Obviously, no one. But *especially* not me, not that day. While it was the day after Stevie's opener, with him now left to - for the first time since arriving, at least - see a bit of Guadalajara, before flying out late that night to Mexico City, ahead of his festival appearance the following night. I had other plans for my day, and night. And this had *seriously* set me back. When I *should've* been waking up in my own hotel bed, having breakfast and then going to collect the car rental that I'd arranged and getting on the road to Acapulco. I now had to get myself *back* to my hotel to get showered and changed, grab my cards and find an outlet in Guadalajara that I could get myself an iPhone, because - and you can call it OCD if you will - having just the one phone is a case of tempting fate for me. Then *back* to the hotel to get it all synced up and ready for using. It was just the worse day for this to have happened. As always with Mexico. When you want to go from A to B, it's *never* bloody half an hour away. The drive from the Guadalajara capital city of Jalisco to Acapulco taking something along the lines of nine hours. I needed to be on the road as soon as possible.

In amongst all of what had been going on. I'd neglected to tell Stevie that I would be bailing out from things for a while, and that I would catch up with him later on, although had said to him that while I would be there for the tour I *did* have other plans for over the three weeks. One of these things - and my reason for making the nine hour trip down the coast - was to try and secure the services of an American DJ, - Kenny Korff - who I'd been keeping my eye on and had known that he was on the cusp of breaking through in a big way. In truth, he *should've* broken through by this point - as he'd been on the come up for more than a year - but his party animal slash frat boy reputation which at times had landed him in trouble had been enough to hold him back. It was a scenario that rung a few bells with me, even if Stevie wouldn't have known what a 'frat boy' was if one walked up to him with a can of lager and pierced the bottom of it and told Zico to *chug chug chug*.

When I'd been in attendance at the electronic music convention in Texas - in the days ahead of travelling to Mexico - I'd heard a little birdie chirping that Korff had sacked his manager after a big bust up at an afters, following his set at a Vegas casino. I guess completely sparking him out with a bottle of champagne could be classed as 'sacked,' anyway?

With the correct guidance from someone who knew the industry inside fucking out. I knew that it would be the skies the limit for the American DJ, which would equal something similar to my bank balance. Looking up his upcoming schedule from my hotel room in Dallas I knew that it had been a slice of fate that would place him and me in Mexico at the exact same time, so had gone ahead and booked the rental car - one of those deals that you can collect in one place and, if required, drop off in a completely different city - with the idea of attending his appearance in a resort that had always been popular but had now appeared to be moving with the times and offering something a bit more modern to the kinds of clientele that were now visiting the place.

Go and hit him with the old Lee Isaac charm. Tell him how I would make him a super star in Europe, if the American's weren't interested in valuing what they had in their hands. Knowing full well that he was going to be stellar on *both* sides of the Atlantic. I do my homework and *always* know what

I'm getting myself into. There had been certain deejays across the years but, doing the due diligence, they'd clearly been not worth getting into bed with, despite the money that would've been made off their backs. Kenny Korff, didn't quite fall into that category, but I also knew it wouldn't be easy to sign him.

When you're dealing with someone who appears to be arrogant, ignorant, childish and violent, then they're clearly never going to give you an easy ride. And, since I was going to be cold calling him, at the venue, I'd had no idea just how he would receive a stranger like me when the time came to introduce myself.

But it was a risk I'd been willing to take. the fact that I would drive nine hours to even see him, that alone highlighted just how special I thought that he was going to become.

There had been no sign of Stevie - back at the hotel when I popped in to shower and grab my cards - and I was happy for that to be the case. Didn't much feel like answering any questions about where I'd disappeared to, having turned down the opportunity of the free ride back, courtesy of the club. I figured that I would send Stevie a WhatsApp - after I'd got myself on the road and out of Guadalajara - just to keep him in the loop. Limiting things to telling him that I was away on business and that I wouldn't be flying to Mexico City with him but that I'd meet him there, ahead of his festival appearance. Something that, despite my best intentions, I would not manage to stick to.

I saw no upside in telling him *where* I was off to and *why*. Not because of him being jealous of me trying to sign Korff, not when I had approximately forty deejays on my books and Stevie being but one of this larger stable. Loose lips sink ships, as they say and I'd saw no benefit in telling him who I was hoping to sign to the agency. Not when the DJ *himself* didn't even know that I was on my way to accost him. Never underestimate the element of surprise with these such matters. I'd have been surprised if I'd been the only talent agency who'd been looking at Kenny Korff so what if a rival of mine had come into the knowledge that I was travelling across Mexico, specifically to meet with the American DJ? And if *they* were quicker to Acapulco than I was? These kind of people will never have such intel if you've not shared them with anyone. As long as Stevie knew that he would see me in Mexico City, that was all he'd need to know.

Finally getting my hands on an iPhone - not from an official Apple Store but from a small shop where you could by anything from a smart phone to a weed grinder to a six pack of beer. I had to slum it with an iPhone four but in that moment, as long as I could get my hands on a phone which could sync with my laptop and have this new one in an 'as you were' format and allow me to make phone calls, send WhatsApp messages and read emails then, for now, that would be more than enough and *far* better than having to go with just the one.

Still no sign of Stevie on my return back from the shop with the phone or when I finally left the hotel room. I wasn't sure if he was still sleeping or was out doing something, possibly with Simon? If out and about, I hoped that he would've fared better with Guadalajara than I'd managed.

As long as he's on that flight to Mexico City at half eleven tonight, whatever he's up to. I thought, putting on my managerial head. He had a slot playing at this yearly festival in the country's capital. One of those multi stage insanely large affairs. I'd bagged him a spot in the A.N.T.S curated tent. The musical collective which had completely taken Ibiza by storm the year before were now branching out. It was almost a badge of honour to get on their bill, so it had been a big thing for him. While his tour had been arranged as an 'open to close' strictly personal series of appearances, which would take place in, purposely, small clubs. But the chance to make the appearance at the '*El dia de la danza*' festival, which translated to Day of the Dance.

With no plans on returning, I checked out of the hotel, on my way through reception to get in the taxi which was there to take me to the car rental place.

On getting in the car - a fucking tiny one litre *Chevrolet Spark*, following a mix up with the company who had already rented out the Ford Mustang, with soft top, that I had booked from my Texas hotel room - I plugged in the sat nav and felt like I'd been stabbed when I saw the five hundred and forty three miles it was telling me to reach my destination. I wasn't a complete idiot, even if I had a tendency to fuck around and find out. I had looked, first of all, and found that the average flight from Jalisco to the state of Guerro involved one connection, with the combined travel time coming out about twelve hours. So had managed to convince myself of the merits of romance that a relatively shorter road trip in the Mexican sun, in some luxury convertible car would be, and how it felt a much better option to go with. But now I had the navigation telling me over five hundred miles and a journey time of around nine and a half hours, with a rocked head through the - likely - Rohypnol I'd had dispensed to me, in a car that I reckon a Lambretta could've beaten in a race.

Before pulling out of the car lot. I checked again that I had everything. My case already put into the boot of the car, almost struggling to get in, such a limited space there was. Phone, - plural - wallet, cigarettes, lighter and sniff. All there.

And thank the bloody lord for that cocaine. With the kind of journey that I had ahead of me, I was going to be *needing* it, in spades.

Chapter 9

Myles

I went out for a walk. To take a look at the city. Combining this with trying to process what the previous forty eight hours had been like since arriving on the assignment I'd been presented with right out of the blue while lying on that Goa beach. Obviously Daniel Garnier-Colston had already anticipated some kind of drama over in Mexico - and for the rest of the tour - but he could *never* have imagined how it would've all started off. Neither me or Luke. And *had we* then I'm not sure if we'd have been so quick as to board our flight to Guadalajara. That incident, alone. The one involving a private military unit stopping us and ordering the group out of the car? *That* had been the moment where I had realised that this wasn't going to be just your by the numbers assignment that the international features correspondent - aka, me - from One's & Two's Magazine would've normally found themselves despatched to cover. For 'normally,' read *ever*. That kind of stuff was for *war* journalists and I sure as fuck was not paid enough for such capers.

I had left Garnier-Colston swivelling in his chair - during his call, looking for an update on how things had been going, while jokingly asking me if the DJ I'd been sent to cover had lost the place yet - while offering him a teaser of how a trip to an off the books appearance of Selecao had gone, involving a menacing check point on route to the party.

'No, but I almost fucking did,'

I replied back to him. There was no way that I could have even come close to covering the previous couple of days over the few minutes that we spoke for so I kept things basic. Yeah, mentioning that we'd been to an appearance *before* his tour had even opened, and how it had been like nothing I'd ever attended in my career, before offering a brief description of the *official* opening night. Inevitably, Daniel only wanted to probe further about the party *before* the tour opened but - from my position of strength, knowing that what I would have to put down in writing, it would blow him away while providing him with the level of sensationalism that he had sent me there *precisely* to secure - I just teased him a little by saying that all would be revealed in good time but not to worry because the content that I had was going to do some *serious numbers* for the website. I hated myself straight away for engaging in such speak, which appealed to him much more than it did me.

'Intriguing,'

he replied, while beginning to suck his own dick by asking me whose idea it was to send me out to Mexico to cover such a story, and how it had been a piece of genius on his part. He left things by reminding me that my flight - later that night - for Mexico City was for half eleven. Booked onto the same flight as Selecao. Due to how late in the day my assignment had been given to me, it had been a case of take what you can get, when it came to the flights to take us around Latin America on the tour. Having Selecao's itinerary opened up to the magazine, by Isaac, our admin had tried to match my flights with his but this had only been possible for some of them, with the others either seeing me arriving in the designated city hours before him or on the other side of him getting there.

I said a goodbye while telling him that he would have my first article emailed over within a couple of days to which he said he was more than looking forward to. Asking one final question to me.

'When I receive it, am I going to need to run it past our lawyers, before it goes live?'

I just laughed at this and replied something along the lines of.

'If the answer to that was no, what even would've been the point of *sending* me here?'

'Good man,'

Garnier-Colston laughed while hanging up.

I was knocked out by the architecture around the city, walking around, and was glad that I'd taken the chance to see a bit of the place before leaving it later on that day. I couldn't help but get myself lost amongst its sheer beauty. That whole colonial architecture that left you in no doubt of the history that the city was steeped in that you could almost feel as much as see. I'd always been a bit of a sucker for cities such as the capital of Jalisco state. The type of environment that blended the old world charms that it had with a pulse that made the place feel alive in a kind of sensory overload way. One of those cities that always feel like they are just teetering on the edge of some form of chaos. Naples one of the best examples of this I could give but not only there. Some of the others of note to me, Marseille, Istanbul and Buenos Aires. Obviously, the *original* plan had been for to have a good walk around the previous couple of days. Something that was placed out of my reach when finding myself hundreds of miles *away* from the city on day one and then day two, sleeping my way through the daylight hours, as a consequence of day one.

This was as close to a day off that I was ever going to get, so I took off from the hotel for a while. Luke saying that he was fine there chilling in the hotel, when I'd asked him if he wanted to get out and about for a swatch. I hadn't seen Selecao since the car had dropped us off at the hotel earlier at around six in the morning, nor his manager, or the guy, part of this mini entourage - Simon - who had come up to Sinaloa with us. The same person who had issued Luke and me with his worldly advice, back in Mazatlan, that - amongst the company that we were in - we shouldn't have been too quick to disclose what our chosen field was where we earned a crust in. Yeah, I was happy to fly solo for a few hours and avoid having the distraction of needing to engage in conversation with anyone for a while.

On the surface of things, Selecao had come across as a decent and chilled guy, even if I'd been left with the suspicion that he'd been holding back a little, when around me and Luke. Possibly playing things low key while around those that he didn't know and that, possibly, when in his comfort zone would've been a completely different beast altogether. Looking at it from his perspective, if two members of the music press that I didn't know from Adam suddenly started hanging around me, with their remit being to write about my goings on. I'm not so sure if *I* would be comfortable enough to show them who I really was, mostly out of concern for the things that they would go on to write about me.

Clearly, though, there had been way too many stories linked to the DJ over the years for him to have ever been a choir boy. But, equally, spending a bit of time in his company and - *crucially* - even during those moments where various drugs have been consumed, he had never morphed into some arrogant arsehole, in danger of disappearing up his own backside. And I had met *plenty* of those types. Most who hadn't even been in the business a quarter of the time that Selecao had, while possessing even *less* than a quarter of his talent at deejaying, producing and gathering a decent sized - and musically knowledgable - following.

But from what I'd witnessed, the guy had been a bit of an enigma. His general reputation in the music press had been of a narco affiliated party animal. Living a life of wild nights with almost endless debauchery. But I had come away with the early impression that this wasn't the *whole* picture to him. Well, as I said, from what *he* had showed me across those early couple of days following our arrival in Guadaljara. While the assignment was to cover him - and the events that would surely follow him - *specifically* for the madness that would surely engulf him on the tour. But I had found that the madness hadn't been just centred on Selecao himself but, instead, *everything* that swirled around him. Although, in those early couple of days, 'everything' pretty much translated to the one person.

It had been undeniable that - in the early days of the tour - the *real* chaos magnet had been his manager and agent, Lee Isaac. Already someone with a bit of a reputation - justifiably gained - in the industry from over his years repping for a list of deejays longer than your arm. A fast talking cocky Cockney who was as good at providing events and clubs with big name deejays as he was at getting into trouble, or at least inviting it in. I had seen both sides to the man. One minute he would have his professional head on, with things strictly business, the next sitting with his nose in a bag of cocaine that would get you ten years in prison if caught in possession with and the *next* standing shaking hands and joking with Mexican cartel bosses.

At this party, Luke and I had witnessed many attendees who had appeared to be with apparent cartel links. Just the general vibe you got over how someone was dressed, carried themselves and - most importantly of all - how people *acted* around them. Some serious looking people out of what had, in a general sense, been a beautifully fantastic and eclectic mix of a crowd. The pair of us - a little overawed by things, so different to what we'd have ever classed as our comfort zone, when covering a story - had stuck together like glue for the majority of the night, having the occasional friendly exchange of a few words with others along with a few drinks and other recreational activities that, to be fair, were no different to pretty much any other assignment that we'd have ever been sent on. Although, admittedly, it had never before been so widely available and in such quantities as the 'hospitality' had been inside that Mazatlan mansion.

While Luke had been denied entry with his camera - something, he'd told me had left him feeling naked - he *had* managed to carefully sneak a few pictures with his phone of Selecao playing, along with some crowd shots and various other scenes from across the night, such as the mariachi band - where someone had reliably informed me that this style of music had originated in Jalisco. That and tequila - playing a special gig, to an adoring crowd. The no photos rule had all seemed to have been a little on the hypocritical side as the locals in attendance barely had their phones in their pockets!

The difference, though, between a Mexican - known to the birthday boy - taking a picture with their phone to remember their great night and a strange gringo carrying a professional camera around his neck is one that would be seen as notable. All a little CIA'ish, although surely the Mexicans wouldn't have thought that a secretive group such as the Central Intelligence Agency would just walk up to a narco party with a camera around their neck?! Standing inside the large floor of the mansion, I'd heard rumours of an extravagant piñata that had been stuffed full of all kinds of drugs but, sadly, by the time we'd been told of it, all evidence of the busted up donkey had been snapped up by the revellers before we could get any photos from the scene of the crime.

It had been a bit of an eye opener all round and I had lost count of the amount of times that either me or Luke were discreetly nudging each other, trying to draw the other's attention towards something or someone. The two of us barely able to believe the 'material' that we were being blessed with, in terms of the story that we'd been flown in to cover. The subject of our assignment, standing inside a DJ booth that most super-club's could only have *dreamed* of having. Behind the decks, playing a house music journey to a crowd that - in part - looked like they'd have been more at home line dancing.

But that really was only one element to it all. The behaviour of Isaac - who had become progressively more high as well as annoying and obnoxious - across the night had not shown him to be in a good light. Long gone had been the slick and smooth talking DJ manager who had greeted us on our arrival at the hotel. Instead, it was a broken man with sunglasses permanently around his head that travelled back in the stretch limo, such had been his excesses that had now caught up with him from over the night and subsequent morning. Not that I could've described myself or Luke as 'fresh faced,' when it came to leaving the party ourselves. But *our* conduct at the party - compared to Isaac's - had been almost night and day. In a way. It was refreshing to have someone else be the one who 'went too far' and, in doing so, would automatically take the spotlight away from you, and allow your own actions to go a lot more under the radar.

The part that had really stuck out for Selecao's manager though was, how extroverted he had been at the party. Speaking to everyone as if he was old friends with them all.

Not shy in making his presence felt in any way. This only showing what kind of a person that we were talking about, and the unflinching confidence mixed with arrogance that must've flowed through them because - if what Simon had told me, at the party, had been the truth - considering how they had come to the attention of this mafia boss, the day before, you'd have thought that he'd have either swerved the party completely and just sent his DJ or, at the least, attended but sat in a corner and tried to attract as little attention as possible.

I'd questioned the behaviour of Isaac, though. And whether he was going to have the tendency to get even worse, as the tour progressed. It would've been excellent viewing, while having ringside seats for the circus performance, had I not been *that* close - for comfort - to the actual show. Obviously, it had been in his interest for me and Luke to have been kept out of the loop, over *why* we were all heading in a limo to a birthday party in Sinaloa. But Simon had spilled the beans to us both, while at the party. That Selecao had had absolutely nothing to do with - or no say - in him appearing there and, in fact, it had all been a bit on the reactionary side, to save his manager. Even the next night, after the end of Selecao's tour opener. Something that - compared to the night before - had actually *felt* like work. Luke with his camera - unlike the previous night, having been told by a man in military uniform that he wasn't allowed in with it - snapping club scenes of both Selecao and the local crowd who had packed the small club to see him.

Yeah, Selecao - and his friends - were all kind of 'merry' by the time he'd played his final song. This, as you'd expect from *any* DJ, when playing an extended open to close set, and at the end of the night, with the lights on and the club now starting to empty out, minus those who had stuck around hoping to get a picture with Selecao. Something that he stayed there and posed for until every one of his fans had got their picture, handshake and kiss. But out of everyone, and with the sun now getting ready to come up for the day, Isaac had decided that he wasn't going back to the hotel with the rest of us, in the people carrier that the club had arranged for us. Where he was off to, though? Well that had been *anyone's* guess, but it was clearly strange behaviour for that time of the morning and I couldn't see any other reason for him parting company with us than to go and do some shady shit.

From a journalistic point of view. It excited me, massively. The prospect of us *still* having to visit cities such as Medellin and Bogota. How much further would Isaac begin to unravel, and just what impact this would, in turn, have on his touring DJ. Never mind the fact that his DJ was *perfectly* capable of - and had done, many times publicly before - unravelling all by himself, with absolutely no need for assistance.

I stopped at a street vendor and bought myself a mango spiralled onto a stick, the mango sprinkled with chilli powder. A weird combination but the public queuing up in front of me were all asking for one so I followed suit. This was just outside the magnificent Guadaljara Cathedral. The one with the two towered spires reaching up into the sky. It was moments like this which could help me forget the craziness in life, and there had been an *extra* dose of that over recent days. Those kind of moments where you just blend into the city you're wandering around in. The street sounds like dogs barking, street vendors hawking for trade, police sirens in the distance and children laughing and screaming while playing. And in your own way, even if just asking a vendor for a piece of fruit, you contribute to the noises yourself.

The semi tranquility and normality had been welcome because we had Selecao's second, and final, Mexican date - at the Mexican festival institution that was *El dia de la Danza* incoming. An event that I'd found myself excited to be attending. Whether it was in a work capacity or not, and not discounting Selecao and his appearance as part of the A.N.T.S curated tent, which was sure to register on the special scale. With deejays - also scheduled to play - who I'd wanted to see such as Masters at Work, Ricardo Villa Lobos, Derrick Carter and Hawtin, it was most certainly going to be a business with pleasure kind of an affair - still to come and then once that had been and gone, it would be time to submit my first 'tour updated' for the website.

In reality, with the ammunition that I'd been given to write with from inside those first two days *alone*, I could've knocked it up and had it submitted to Garnier-Colston already. But with my remit to 'check in' with a run down of every country we visited - with my much larger article on the tour, in general, something that would follow, when it came to our printed magazine - then it would've only been fair to Selecao - and his lunatic of a manager - to cover his tour fully.

Speaking of *fair*, though. I had already been left with concerns that quite possibly DJ Selecao - or his manager - may not have been left feeling like they'd been treated fairly, once my first tour update was to hit the internet. Because, while I hadn't even began to write my first entry, no matter *what* took place in Mexico City. It would *really* have to go some to replace the words I was more than willing to use up, on the subject of our first day there, and the unscheduled trip to Sinaloa.

Yeah, from what I'd seen. While more guarded talking to me or Luke, compared to when speaking to Lee Isaac, or his mate. Stevie Duncan hadn't been *so* guarded, when it came to getting stuck into the contraband that had been placed in the limo for us, but you won't find me judging there. I'd been *desperate* to try that gear, having had an educated guess that it was going to blow my head off, and once Isaac had got on it, it wasn't long until we were *all* getting stuck in. Like Selecao had said to me and Luke - in what felt like some kind of a semi justification to us while he was no doubt, going to take it regardless - a House Music DJ taking drugs was hardly the stuff of an exclusive story. Especially when some of his escapades had been more than documented over the years.

In what had been one of his more candid moments on that long journey to Sinaloa - although this was more to do with someone having just taken a bump of primo sniff and more a case of being willing to talk than genuinely taking the steps towards being *open* with me - he had sat and told me that while he had been deejaying since the early nineties and, yeah, had taken a *lot* drugs in the process, with him just having turned forty, he was someone who now more 'picked their battles,' when it came to his moments of excess. Citing the main reason for this slowing down that he had seen too many friends and associates be lost to the scene through their addictions to either the uppers - when partying - or the downers, to get *over* the partying.

Admitting that his good friend and frequent collaborator on tracks that they'd brought out over the years - Dundee producer, Archie Sinclair - and the crippling anxiety attacks which have seen him unable to perform live in years was a wake up call for him.

'I'm not sitting here saying that it has made me change my ways overnight and leave the narcotics alone because, well, look at me?'

He'd joked while sitting clearly looking every inch the person who had just sniffed up some as close to pure as you could get without killing someone cocaine, while holding a pungent smelling joint in one had and a glass of Dom P in the other. Before continuing.

'But at the same time, what's happened to some of the boys on the DJ circuit, and some of them *proper* legends in the game, too, it kind of gave me a bit of a wake up call. Ken? Made me realise that none of us are superhuman. Aye, you maybe *feel* that way when you're up on stage behind the decks and you've got thousands of adoring fans looking at you while they dance, or as is now starting to happen, holding their phones up, as much as they're dancing.'

(It was a fair point, about the phones. And something that was now beginning to be a conversation amongst people in the scene)

'But you're *not* superhuman, none of us are. Taking too much gear can *make* you feel that you are, though. But you ken how it all goes, eh? What goes up, must come down. And that down part has been a bit of a hefty landing for some, mate, eh? Saying that, though, Myles. When I say that I pick my battles these days, it would've been a little unrealistic to send me to this part of the world and me not being on anything *other* than a war footing. I limit myself to partying only during special occasions, and try telling me anything more special than your first headline tour of Mexico and South America.'

He giggled away, making it clear that as much as this tour was going to be work, and hard tiring work it would be, that he'd intended to enjoy himself along the way. The way he'd said this, offering a glimpse into the DJ - of the reputation earned - that I'd been sent there to cover.

On the whole - and from what he'd been willing to show who he was - he had come across as a genuinely likeable guy. But the assignment that I'd been sent off on did not include any room for sentiment. I hadn't come to Mexico to make friends. I had come to capture a story. And put in my position, what would *you* have done when you found yourself covering a well known international DJ - with documented links to a Latin America drug cartel, proxied through his father - who ends up playing for a drug lord's son's twenty first birthday party, in a notorious part of the world and synonymous with narcotics, such as Sinaloa? Talk about being presented with an open goal and an opportunity that, to not take, would've cast serious doubts on my credentials as a serious journalist.

The night at the cartel birthday party was the kind of luck that a journalist can go their whole career and never come close to being at. And what? I was just to skim right over it and pretend that my experience on this assignment began on Selecao's first night of his tour, inside the Guadalajara city centre club?

I may not have been proud about it, as I worked for an electronic music magazine and not a tabloid but when the time arrived, and it would, I was going to have absolutely *no* hesitation in burning both DJ Selecao - and his manager - when it came to telling the public what had been going on *behind* the scenes of his tour. In the world of 'clicks for engagement' that we now lived in being the key to success. You couldn't have wished for better than to link a DJ, like Selecao, with a Sinaloan narco's party for an eye catching headline. And I'd been prepared to weaponise and embellish that content to the fucking *hilt.*

I had stumbled accidentally across a story that went *way* past just reporting on what happened inside the confines of a nightclub or festival, mentioning some tracks played by the DJ while reviewing their performance on the night and how receptive the crowd had been. The tour had only ticked off one date from its schedule but already the *real* story looked like it was taking place *away* from the clubs and festivals. And with how the story was beginning to shape up it was beginning to leave me thinking that by the time this tour was over. As a journalist, my name was going to be known a lot further than just within the electronic music magazine sector.

Chapter 10

Bring me the head of Lee Isaac

The black Escalade SUV breezed its way through the bustling, colourful and vibrant afternoon Mazatlan streets. Protected by one GMC Yukon Denali in front and one - matching - behind. The watching public, or those not preoccupied by their own stuff, at least, were left in no doubt that whoever was being transported inside the middle car was *someone*. The tinted windows giving them no more confirmation other than this. The mystery passenger, sitting in the back of the SUV on his own, one Enrique Emilano Garcia Flores. Otherwise known to those in the state - and beyond - of Sinaloa as 'El Hombrecito' and someone all too recognisable. *Recognisable* possibly being an understatement. One of the most well known and regarded faces in the entire region, in fact.

Sitting there motionless. His fixed stare burning into the rear of his driver's headrest. In doing so, missing the coastal city - *his* city - passing by on the outside of the Escalade. The rhythmic and almost sedating hum of the engine was at complete odds with the storm brewing inside of him. The two things could not have been so stark. The man, tasked with running operations in this area of the state had been awake for over twenty four hours now, and the events from over the previous day on his hastily arranged trip to the Sinaloan capital Culiacan were weighing heavily on his mind.

The reason for this abrupt trip? The arrest of one of the cartel's highest ranking lieutenants, Hernan Avilla. Apprehended in a cross country agency operation between the Fuerzas Especiales - F.E.S - and the Yankees from the D.E.A, executed by the Mexican military. Quite literally caught with his pants down. Sitting on the toilet in one of the many safe houses that he would stay in on a rotational basis. This had been an undeniable devastating blow dealt to the organisation, and the kind of setback that posed the risk of having much wider reaching consequences for their entire operation. Despite what the TV shows and movies would've liked to project, criminals broke under pressure, all of the time. Even the most loyal of figures, such as Avilla. And if there was one thing that the Yankees were good at, once they had gotten their hands on a person of their interest. It was *breaking* people. And if he broke under pressure, if he spoke, there would be blood and tears to follow, and not just his own.

Flores subconsciously clenched his jaw, the tension seemingly working its way up from his seated rigid posture. But it wasn't just the subject of Avilla's arrest which was gnawing away at him, though. This wasn't the first crisis that the Sinaloa Cartel had found thrown their way over the years and would not be the last, for that matter. Yes, Don Flores had dealt with such crises before, and survived worse than a foot soldier being detained.

What was also playing on his mind, no doubt exacerbated by his lack of sleep, as the SUV sped it's way on route to his estate, and was responsible for the knot in his stomach was that he had permitted his son, Ovidio, to host his landmark twenty first birthday party, in the absence of his father. Due to being twenty one once himself. The idea of the birthday party alone had unsettled Flores, but he had given Ovidio his word. And to a man like Enrique Emilano Garcia Flores. Without his word, a man was not even a man at all.

'It will be small, papa.'

Ovidio had assured him.

'Just a few close friends. Nothing too crazy.'

By the time Flores was leaving his estate, on route to Culiacan, and just as all of the guests were beginning to arrive, it had already become clear to him that this had not turned out to be strictly true.

Flores had believed him, or perhaps he had *wanted* to believe him. When all had been said and done. Ovidio was his son, his *only* son, and despite Flores' reputation - which went before him, always - and his hardened exterior, he was *still* a father and someone who had wanted to extend some trust to his young adult of a son.

The Escalade pulled up to the grand wooden doors that were akin to the kind that would've protected a medieval castle hundreds of years before, towering iron bars that separated, as well as *protected*, his fortress of solitude from the outside world. With the SUV at a stop, he sat there, still, for a moment. His eyes surveying the mansion in front of him. The towering columns, sprawling gardens and immaculate landscaping. As a building, it was a symbol of everything that he had built, while beginning at nothing.

As a young boy, Flores had grown up in his Culiacan barrio with a dirty face, empty pockets but full of dreams. The barrio had been the extent of his world and, in fact, the only *part* of the world that he had ever seen. Those dangerous streets - where the life expectancy suffered a serious drop off from your average town or city - a playground for a poor kid with no future. But while young Flores had no money, what he lacked in capital he more than made up for in ruthless ambition.

The days of robbing from soft drinks lorries, along with his best friend Javi. Pocketing any cash relieved from the drinks company driver while selling the stolen refreshments at cost price to the residents of the barrio. Those early days when he was seen as some sort of a Robin Hood figure, when his name carried respect, if not the power that would normally go alongside.

Now, however. He was one of the most feared and respected figures in the whole of Sinaloa, his power stretching far beyond his Mazatlan base. With politicians, police and military, all on his payroll. But, as he'd found over the years, power came with the requirement for responsibility, discipline and respect.

'Open the gate,'

He said quietly to his driver. Almost as if he was in possession of the facts in advance that once inside the grounds of the estate, his voice was going to need to be raised, and that, until then, he may as well enjoy this moment of calmness.

The gate squeaked open, with the SUV rolling in at a snail's pace on into the courtyard style driveway with its centrepiece, the fountain placed in the middle. From the outside at a distance, the mansion had looked pristine, as it always did and as it had looked the day before when he'd left for Culiacan. But this had been nothing other than some kind of illusion of calm and order. As soon as he stepped out of the car, though, his senses told him otherwise. His eyes catching the glint of a discarded beer bottle, clashing with the sun above. The beer bottle left lying in one of his flowerbeds, with several of the Bougainvilleas that had been standing proud only the day before now flattened with the evidence of footprints left behind in their wake. The flowerbeds that, along with many of the other flowers spread across his grounds, he would enjoy the peace and tranquility of tending to, when taking time out from the intense world that he was an integral part of.

Next, he saw a collection of roaches, from joints that had been smoked there in the courtyard, lying on the gravel. A small clear ziplock bag that was still containing some remnants of the cocaine that had once been inside it, lying a few metres away. He scowled at this while not entirely surprised. Unlike most parents who would tell their kids that they 'weren't angry, just disappointed,' Enrique Flores was *both*.

He moved towards the front door. Some of his security detail, who had been stationed overnight at the party stood near the entrance looking nervous. For someone like El Hombrecito and his ability to read people, he noticed that they were *too* nervous. One of them - Raul - stepped forward to greet his boss as Flores reached the door.

'Don Flores,'

Raul began, with a hesitant tone to him.

It only took the one cold look from Flores to freeze the following words from coming out of his bodyguard's mouth. Raul quickly re-evaluating things and stepping aside, head down staring at his dirty black leather boots.

Flores pushed open the front door to the mansion and was immediately hit by the unmistakeable smell of stale beer, sweat, and cheap cologne. What he was seeing there inside the grand main entrance to the building was worse than even he had feared, while travelling back that day. His once - and by once, just the day before - immaculate foyer looked like a disaster zone.

'So do I call F.E.M.A here or not?'

He said, self depreciatingly as he looked around at the state of the place. Paper cups and scores of empty Malverde beer bottles cluttered the floor. A half eaten Margherita pizza sat on top of his ivory chess board, several chess pieces either lying in the vicinity of the board or missing altogether and confetti littering the polished tiles as if some form of confetti bomb had gone off inside the room. The air was thick with the remnants of what had clearly been a wild night.

'Dios mio,'

He said under his breath as his eyes took in the scene in disbelief. Yes, he had, of course, *also* been twenty one, once. But all he'd been looking for - in return for letting his son take the guard rails off - had been a little piece of thanks and respect shown in return. And he was seeing *no* evidence of either.

As he made his way deeper into the house, his anger began to boil. He could feel the heat rising in his chest with every step he took and the fear of what next he would come across. He passed through the large living room, and could see that this had been an area where people had decided to make themselves at home. One of the couches had been overturned and the glass coffee table that sat in front of it had a big crack going horizontally almost all the way from left to right. The walls bearing smudges of sticky fingers and spilled drinks, some defacing the expensive art pieces that hung there and which had been purchased from a European dealer as a way to wash some of his money.

This hadn't just been a party, he thought. This had been a *violation*.

He could feel his pulse beginning to race. Barely even aware that both of his fists were now clenched. Picturing his son, laughing, drunk and high. Oblivious to the mess that both he and his guests were creating And the disrespect that he was allowing to take place. At least Enrique *hoped* that Ovidio had been oblivious to this. The implication of the alternative being much, much more grave. Flores had worked too hard, sacrificed too much in life, to see his son squander the respect that this house, and those who either lived in it or were guests, demanded.

Continuing, the destruction only worsened, despite him hoping that he had seen the worst of it. In the dining room - where no one had had any business even *being* inside there - expensive chairs were tipped over and someone had carved the letters **FTD** into the polished wood of the dining table which, if required could sit fourteen people. Flores had no clue what these letters represented and - as he carried on - he gave consideration that they may have stood for some form of small level cartel of who he hadn't heard of. Mexico being Mexico, it was not uncommon for various organised gangs to spring up only to either be eliminated at the first opportunity or transition into working for a much more known outfit. His stomach turned as he imagined the scenes from the night before and the careless disregard for his possessions and for his home. But for a man like Don Flores it wasn't just about the damage to material things. He had more money than he could have ever wished to spend. Material things could be replaced. For him, though. It was about the thought of people feeling that they could behave in such a way while on his property.

By the time he reached the grand staircase, his red mist had now descended. Knowing where his son would be, he marched up the staircase in the direction of his bedroom. Ovidio's room was at the end of the hall, the door slightly open which gave an insight into the frame of mind he'd been in when it was finally time for him to retire. Peeking through the open door, Flores could see his son lying face down on the bed, hanging halfway off it and one wrong movement away from falling out of it completely. His girlfriend, Veronica, in bed with him. Her, lying to the side with her back to the bedroom door, on top of the covers, naked. This had been enough to stop Flores for a moment, thinking of the embarrassment that was about to be caused, when he appeared and served as some form of crude alarm clock to them both.

But no, fuck that and *fuck them*, Flores thought, having taken a moment of pause and found that nothing had changed. Not bothering to knock. He pushed the door open with such force that it slammed against the wall. This, enough to jolt Ovidio awake who did indeed make that one wrong move, sending himself falling onto the floor. Veronica, screaming at the sight of Enrique standing there in the bedroom beside them, quickly grabbing the bedsheets and pulling them up to her chin. Ovidio, in panic mode and in the kind of moment that you wouldn't wish on anyone to have as their first waking moment, scrambled to his feet and quickly grabbed his pair of CK boxers shorts from up off the ground and got himself into them.

'Papa,'

Ovidio croaked as he now sat down on the edge of the bed. His quick movements upon waking had completely betrayed how fragile his mind and body were, following his birthday bash. And now he was looking every inch like someone who had just celebrated a milestone birthday, and had probably only *stopped* celebrating a few hours before.

Flores didn't speak at first. His eyes scanning the room. More empty bottles of beer, one used condom on the floor and another lying on his bedside table. Clothes strewn across the bedroom floor. The smell of beer, sex and cigarettes made Flores nauseous. It was a disgrace. The anger that Enrique had been keeping at a containable level now had nowhere else to go other than to explode.

'What the fuck is this, you little pendejo?'

He barked at his son. Every single syllable like a stab wound to Ovidio. Now that he'd been given a proper chance to study his son, he could see that he was still very much under

188

the influence from the party and hadn't yet had the required quota of hours to sober up. Groggily, the best that Ovidio could muster was,

'It was my twenty first, papa. We cleaned up a little before going to bed, didn't we V?'

He turned around to his girlfriend for some backup but she appeared to be doing all that she could to *avoid* looking in the direction of her boyfriend's father, while she was left in such a compromising and embarrassing position.

His excuse was barely out of his mouth when he was finding his dad's slap colliding with the side of his jaw. The force of it sending him back onto the bed and the back of his head crashing down onto Veronica's legs under the sheets. Because there are slaps, and then there are slaps. And you really did not want to be on the receiving end of one from Don Flores when provoked in such a way. Paradoxically, this one act from father to son sobered Ovidio up in ways that another six hours of unbroken sleep could not have wished to achieve.

'*A little?* This is how you show respect for me, for our house? You fucking spoiled junior narcos, or whatever you call yourselves? You do nothing but take take take, while behaving like *this?*'

Flores growled at his son who was making an attempt to sit himself back up again. Veronica was crying through fear and had appeared frozen to the spot and in no way in a position of helping Ovidio with back up.

Ovidio groaned in pain, rubbing his red cheek where the force from his dad's slap still burned. Sitting back up, he met his dad's scowl again, the fear in that moment written all over his face. Yeah, he'd annoyed his father hundreds of times, if not thousands. But what kid *hasn't?* But this was a whole new level of anger, and one that he hadn't seen in person but knew of through the stories and narco corridos sang about his father. He was scared, and had every right to be.

'Papa, I didn't mean …'

'Didn't mean to what? Turn my house into a pigsty? To invite 'friends' who would trash everything that I've worked for?'

Ovidio, struggling, got to his feet and showed that he was a little unsteady on them. Flores couldn't decide if this was through still being drunk or if his son was still reeling from the slap that he'd just taken.

'I'll clean it. I'll clean it all. I'll fix everything and whatever needs replaced I'll pay for, I swear, papa.'

Ovidio stood there making promises that he could not deliver. Well, some of them, anyway. The coffee table, for example. That had been shipped from Europe more than ten years before and the chances of them still being in existence would've been zero, at best. These hollow promises only served to enrage Don Flores further.

Stood there, he could feel him shaping up with his right hand ready for a second slap, holding his hand down at waist level but preparing himself. He, nothing more than, wanted to unleash the fury that had built up inside of him from the moment he had arrived back, but he managed to restrain himself. Only just. Taking a step back from Ovidio, his chest almost hyperventilating with his efforts at containing his anger.

'Oh you'll fucking fix everything, have no doubt about that,'

Don Flores replied to his son before letting rip, unable to bite his tongue.

'You just don't get it, though, do you? You've been given absolutely *everything* in life, and this is how you repay me? I started with nothing, Ovidio. I *earned* this house and this life through my own hard work and ambition .. and *you?'*

Flores pointed a shaking with anger finger at him.

'You take it *all* for granted.'

His son stood there, still rubbing at his face while gazing downwards, unable to look at his father. In this moment he looked exactly like a child who had been scolded by their parent over some form of misbehaviour, *not* the man that he had just become.

'Now you're going to get your pitiful fucking ass downstairs. Clean up *every single inch of* this mess. Every inch. Every beer bottle, every half smoked joint and empty cocaine bag. And if I see even one single stray tossed roach when I come back down after I've had a sleep, you better have skipped the country and even then, as you well know, I'll *still* have someone find you.'

Ovidio, quickly throwing on the clothes he'd worn for the party in his hurry, nodded as he stumbled past Enrique towards the door. Seeming to remember all about his girlfriend who was still there in bed. Turning around and telling her that he would see her downstairs, which Enrique took as his code speak for asking his girlfriend to help him with the cleaning up while not daring to come out and ask in front of his father.

On Ovidio bringing Veronica into the conversation, Enrique told her that he would give her the privacy that she needed to get herself ready.

But, leaving his son's bedroom, if Flores had thought that this was going to be the worst part of his return to the mansion, that afternoon, he was in for a nasty as well as unexpected surprise.

After being up all night and then coming home to what he had, and the outburst that inevitably followed this, he needed the sanctuary of his bedroom, where he hoped that he would calm down to an adequate level that would be enough for him to hopefully pass out on that outlandishly large bed of his.

Without thinking, he left the bedroom and marched down the hall towards his master bedroom, which made the average 'master bedroom' feel like a storage cupboard. He needed to see it, needed to reassure himself that, at least, one part of the house had remained as untouched. When he pushed the door open, he froze.

The room was an absolute shambles. His bed, which was *always* meticulously made, lay in a state of disarray. The sheets twisted and hanging off one side of the bed. Only half of the eight pillows were still in their natural home, the rest thrown indiscriminately around on the floor. The cocaine that was still scattered over the chest of drawers. The rage that had, for the first time since surfacing, only began to subside now coming on strong inside of him as part of some second wave. He swore with no cohesion to it, almost as if he had Tourette's as he took a few steps closer to the bed. His hand reaching out to touch the sheets that he was sure people had been touching - possibly - only hours earlier.

And that was when he noticed the series of white stains. A random series of small blobs next to a much larger one. On the red velvet sheets, a blind man could almost have seen them.

'You fucking filthy puta madres.'

He shouted out loud, now fully raged up. But this was more than rage or anger. This was something that went way, way deeper. *This* was the ultimate in a violation. A violation of the personal kind. Turning back around to see if there were any other signs of destruction in the room, his eyes were attracted by the series of pictures that he had sitting on a table. Specifically the one with his long since departed mother's picture. A beautiful hand carved wooden frame which held a black and white portrait of her. It was one of his constants, the picture, and no matter how his life had changed over the years the one thing that *always* reminded him of his past, of who he was and who had helped him *become* who he was and where he'd come from.

The picture had been moved. Flores didn't have obsessive compulsive disorder, although he had never been checked to see if he had it or not either. Things like the positioning of a simple picture frame to him were important, and he knew if one was ever out of position. The frame with his mother, Isabella, in it, though? This hadn't just been nudged a little or knocked by accident and put back again. Far from it.

It had been moved, that much was clear. But it was worse than that. The frame was smudged with both fingerprints and a kind of fluid hardened coating around her face in the photo. He didn't want to but felt like he *had* to, when he brought the picture up to meet his nose. When he smelled the cum that was staining the glass of the frame, had it been any picture other than the one he was holding he would've, without question, thrown it against the wall.

He felt a strange cold chill going down his back, while in the red zone, anger wise. It was a confusing mix of emotions for him to deal with. His hands trembled as he looked at the picture and the signs of how it had been abused. How the memory of his mother had been abused.

'*Who the fuck did this?*'

He said, placing the frame carefully down and in the position on the table that he was comfortable with it sitting, then walking towards the en suite bathroom to wet a towel and come back to clean the glass. You probably haven't seen an angry man if you haven't seen a Mexican narco boss having to clean someone's cum stain from off a cherished picture of their dead mother.

After cleaning his mother's picture, which out of everything this had been deemed as the most important thing to be taken care of, he turned sharply to the corner of the room. Zooming in on the discreet security camera. It would've been naive at best for a man of his standing to *not* have wall to wall security on his property, but this had been to ensure that his family would be safe. Now, though. The cameras would serve a different purpose for him.

It only took him five minutes at best for him to pull up the recordings from the day before. Heart beating faster with anticipation as he hit the fast forward button to take things up to the hours of the party, His eyes scanning the screen for signs of anyone going near his room. Then he saw him. The unmistakable features of the gringo, Lee Isaac, alongside some girl.

Isaac had been in his room. Isaac had used his bed. And *Isaac* had dared to touch his mother's photograph, and explicitly so.

Don Flores had never wanted to kill someone more in his life - and he had killed *many* - than when he sat there, looking at Isaac's embarrassing performance. No one should have to watch another man stand there and masturbate in front of their mother's picture, laughing and joking while taking his cock and smacking it against the glass of the picture frame. While he hadn't fully stood there and ejaculated on the frame, he'd clearly been 'excited' enough to have left a stain on the glass. Saying disrespectful things to Flores' dear Isabella Carmen, while laughing at her. Even knocking the frame so hard with his penis that it knocked the frame down. But witness all of this, Don Flores did. And this was not a conflicting scenario that he was now presented with.

Lee Isaac had to *die*.

'Your death is going to be *especially* slow and painful,'

Don Flores muttered while shaking his head as he watched Isaac finally leave his mother's photo alone and turning to the girl on the bed to have sex with her for a remarkably short period of time and it had appeared that he had spent more time acting the monkey in front of the picture than he had with his partner. Not only had Don Flores been left to wipe off Isaac's cum from off the picture frame but it was now confirmed that he had pulled out at the point of ejaculation, and it had all gone over his satin sheets.

With the way that this was impacting Flores' breathing, he feared that he was going to pass out with sheer rage. Grabbing a glass and pouring what must've been the equivalent of four whiskies in one to calm his nerves. No matter how much he tried, he couldn't shift the arrogant coke fuelled smirk of the English DJ manager while he stood there stroking his cock in front of his mother.

Ironically, the gringo had come close to losing an arm at the hands of Flores only the day before this. Flores had decided to show him mercy and give him a second chance and was as much of the *last* person he would've ever thought disrespect him in such a way, barely twenty four hours after *initially* disrespecting Flores, which had kick started the whole chain of events which now brought matters to El Hombrecito contemplating which way he was going to end the life of Lee Isaac. That he was considering having his legs tied to one jeep and his arms to another and for each driver to go off in the opposite direction, a window into how darkly his mind was responding to this all.

Still with trembling hands although now helped by the soothing hit from the whisky, he pulled up the name of one of his chief enforcers. The call answered on its third ring, as tended to be the case when the jefe's name showed up on their phone.

Flores, with a voice that was as steady as it was laced with menace done away with any pleasantries by telling the voice on the other end of the phone.

'Find Isaac, the gringo from yesterday. He's in Guadalajara now but will be moving onto Mexico City soon, as part of a music tour. Fortunately, he's the one man in the world who I want to find, and he has left a tour schedule including dates and times for me to *look* for him. Take Jorge with you and find this fucking gringo pendejo before he leaves Jalisco and bring him back to Mazatlan.'

'Si, jefe.'

His man replied without hesitation. Flores telling him the name of the hotel where Isaac had been collected from in Guadalajara, in addition to the Mexico City festival that the gringo had shared with Enrique, when they had been making small talk before he had left for Culiacan.

Yes, there *was* the element of how much blatant disrespect that the Englishman had shown, but for Flores, what he had watched take place inside his bedroom at the party. This was now a matter of *principle*. For someone with the standing and mentality of an Enrique Emilano Garcia Flores. If you enjoy their hospitality - and repay them with - by masturbating to their mother's photograph and have sex in their bed. Then they will die for their actions. It really was that simple. Lee Isaac hadn't crossed a line, he had shot his cum right *over* it. And it was a line that could never, ever be uncrossed. And now? El Hombrecito was going to show him what *real* consequences looked and felt like.

'That puta is going to *wish* I'd cut his fucking arm off yesterday,'

Don Flores thought with some kind of consolation while he began reluctantly stripping his bed.

Chapter 11

Zico

I leaned back on one of what was one of your standard uncomfortable back breaking plastic seats at Guadalajara airport, staring up at the blinking departures board. Fuck, how I hated airports. It had only been that brilliant Twitter account - Complaining Deejays - and their retweeting of any tweets from a DJ that showed them, well, moaning, which had stopped me from ever having a wee vent about the places online.

Maybe I was biased, what with me being in the industry and that, but I didn't see the problem with some cunt having a wee moan about the transport when they're working? Like, someone saying how shit the traffic was getting themselves back home after their day's work, good. A DJ pissed off because his airline have cancelled their flight at the last minute, bad? Bit hypocritical, like. Airports though? Fucking questions would probably be getting asked of you if you actually *enjoyed* being in one. Lots, and lots of annoying as fuck cunts. The going through security part, and how wide some of those security bods can be. The people - who I never fail to be behind - who act like they've never been inside one in their life and end up slowing you down because of their own idiocy. And then, obviously, the fact that when you set foot inside of an airport the prices of literally anything that you would find outside of it triple under a matter of principle, and because the cunts know you've got no other choice. Aye, not a fan and can safely say that I'd felt that way before moving into the kind of career that meant I would never manage to go even seven days without having to be inside the fuckers. Some are better than others but that's not saying much. Not when they're all shite!

Mexico City was just a couple hours away and the next stop on the tour, but all I could think about was the silence in my phone's notifications. Where the fuck was Lee? My manager had vanished, and apart from a cryptic WhatsApp that he'd sent - telling me that he had checked out the hotel early and was away to another part of the country on business, and would catch up with me in Mexico City - I didn't have a clue what he was up to. But knowing him, it was probably some shady as fuck shit. Not that I was missing him, mind. The last forty eight hours had been bad enough with him *around*. I mean, if anything, the break was welcome. Still seemed strange, him taking off and disappearing in the way that he had, mind.

Still, and as much as he was a complete fucking head the ball. I couldn't help but wonder if he'd landed up in some serious bother, over his own conduct. Lee had a unique way of getting into trouble, and this time I had a nagging feeling that if he *was* in trouble then it might well have been a case of his luck running out and being the kind of issues that he might not come back from. I checked my phone again, half-hoping for a micro managing message, asking me if I was there for my flight, but also half-grateful for the peace. The bi-polar feelings I had, there in the terminal, were a good example of how you can have someone in life who does your absolute fucking nest in most of the time but, yet, the hint that they might be in a spot of bother and it shows you how you *really* feel towards them.

Sitting nursing a roasting hot cappuccino - which had cost me the equivalent of the deficit of a small country - I had a wee deek around the, near, empty airport terminal. It appearing that the majority of flights coming in or going out had mainly been taken care of. There's always something unsettling about an airport that quiet, especially that late at night. The feeling you have where you know all the normal people, the ones *outside* of the airport are doing normal stuff, like chilling watching telly or already in bed sleeping for the night, while you're in this brightly lit massive building, waiting to get into a metal can that can fly through the air. Si and Marisol would be joining me in the capital city the next day, and I'd feel a bit more normal then, but right there, I was in that weird space where everything felt distant and unreal. Tiredness had met with the effects from earlier on in the day and I felt a wee bit spaced while hoping the coffee would do its job. Normally I'm the first cunt to pass out on a plane and sleep for the majority of the journey but with the flight being as short as it was I knew I'd end up feeling even worse if I allowed myself a bit of kip between one city and the other. A reflective Si had texted me once I'd got myself through security. Asking me if I'd been able to *believe* what had happened to the pair of us, earlier on that day.

Because *that* was the thing, thinking back on our afternoon to early evening in the city centre. It felt like a near miracle that I was even there, sitting in the airport awaiting on boarding being called.

On getting back - to the hotel - from playing my first gig of the tour it must've been around eight in the morning when I finally got to sleep. Which I didn't even get very much of, which was no cunt's fault other than my own. Forgot to stick the *do not disturb* sign around the door handle, didn't I? Which all meant that the back of eleven I was woken by the sound of some woman singing. Thought it was in my dream, ken? It must've been loud enough to make me stir a bit and when I did I could now hear that the singing was still going, even with me awake. It was coming from the bathroom. The maid had come in and had made straight for the bathroom so hadn't clocked that I was even in the room. She fucking *shat* herself when she eventually came through and found me lying in the bed, trying to tell her that she doesn't need to do the bed today. Tried to get back to sleep but knew I was nothing but pishing into a gale force wind with that so got ready and left the room.

The only thing that I had officially scheduled for the day was to sit down with Myles and Luke and give them my thoughts on how I'd felt the opening night had gone. Spying them sitting in the lounge I managed to get that part out of the way early doors. The two of them were growing on me, even if I didn't quite trust them yet. I doubted that I ever would across the three weeks. No matter what I tried, there was no shifting the thought that anytime you opened your mouth around them that Myles might then take my words and use them. Sitting doing the *interview* with him, though? That was fine because you know where you stand. Everything you say will be taken down and used, as part of the article, which the interview is obviously going to be a part of. It's being around these types when the dictaphone is switched *off* that you need to worry about. I left them to it for the rest of the day, with us arranged for getting the same ride to the airport, later on in the night. I think that Myles was going off for a deek around the city while Luke - who had definitely been the worse off out of the pair of them during my all night long set, the pair of them *absolute* caners - wasn't looking too clever and was going to try and get some sleep for the first time since we'd all arrived back.

Si, as usual, had a special talent of pulling me into these situations. Who knows, maybe some might say that it was the other way around?

'Zico, we need to talk, pal,'

he had said to me earlier in the afternoon, when we caught up with each other for the first time since the night - and morning - before. I was surprised to see him without this Peruvian girl tethered to him. The boy had appeared *well* loved up since that narco's birthday party. Proper inseparable, so they were. Couldn't blame him, mind. She was some catch, like. My mate was absolutely punching and even he would've admitted to that. She was sound too, as well as good looking, and famous, and rich! Had to be a catch somewhere but I was fucked if I knew what it was. When he sat down to join me at the table, with me sitting going through the tweets and Instagram tags that had been sent across the night of my set, and said that we needed to talk. It didn't sound good. It never, ever does when someone says those words. Have you ever had someone say them to you and it turn out to be something good?

'What do we need to talk about, like?'

I asked, while wondering if it was something that I was going to wish hadn't been shared with me.

'The weed, Zeek. The fucking weed. We need to talk about *that* situation.'

'What do you mean?'

I asked, although already knowing the answer.

'We've only ever been approximately one metre away from a pre-roll since we got here.'

'Aye, Zeek but let's face it. With the best will in the world. It isn't the best, is it?'

Si replied, with his way of stating the obvious in the most bluntest of ways possible.

I had to admit, though. He wasn't wrong.

'Aye, you've got a bit of a point, there,'

I affirmed. This Mexican brick weed was rough. It wasn't like the gear that we got back in Amsterdam. What was our bread and butter.

'Amsterdam's fucking ruined us, mate,'

I joked as I evaluated the state of play. The one where we had never needed to put our hands in our pockets to pay for drugs since we'd got there in the country, but yet were turning our noses up at the free marijuana. He nodded in agreement, saying what he'd have done for a fat joint packed full of Jack Herer. We had standards now, which was kind of ironic, considering our past.

That's when Si had decided we were going to fix this weed problem of ours. And this was how we ended up wandering around an absolutely blistering hot Guadalajara, with the class a toxins wasting no time in leaving us by way of us two being drenched in sweat. A pair of complete messes, asking anyone and everyone where to find some 'hydro, hombre.' It was supposed to be simple, like in any other fucking city where you can't walk fifty yards without smelling someone smoking it. Aye, we'd find the right people, get some decent sweet smelling nuggets, and head back and tan it.

Of course, nothing's ever that simple. And *especially* when me and him were in close proximity of one another. When asking him what Marisol was up to he'd told me that he'd said to her that him and me hadn't spent much time since we'd arrived so he was heading out with me for the day while giving her the chance to catch up with things her side. How much of this was true, I'm not sure. But I had an idea that if he hadn't been left with the need to get his hands on a *decent* bit of grass then I probably wouldn't have seen the cunt.

After some dead-end conversations, we found a local - some guy who was trying to sell us cartons of Mexican cigarettes from right off the street - who told us about a notorious spot behind the main train station in the city.

'What you can't get behind there hasn't been invented yet,'

he said, laughing. That should've been the first clue to just call it a day, but no, Si was determined. As far as he went, the heart wanted what the heart wanted, and he wanted something decent to smoke. So did I, to be fair. Only I couldn't be arsed with any drama in procuring it. Which meant I was going to be right out of luck.

The area behind the station was shade city. Gone, all of the commuters rushing in and out of the terminal entrance. Instead, an all star team of well dodgy looking characters. The dealers did not look to install much confidence in interacting with them but, by comparison, the users who were lying and sitting around this area made the dealers look like pillars of the community. Clearly, these dealers were not used to gringos coming around looking for drugs, and possessed no English to assist in such a potential transaction. Si didn't care. He never does. He asked the first boy we saw, then onto the second, but they both had the same Mexican brick that we were trying to upgrade from. When the second dealer realised we weren't buying, and that we were wasting his time. Despite being outnumbered, he got all arsey, pushing Si back - hard in the chest - like he'd called the boy's mum a slapper.

That was around about the time when Si clocked the cunt. Just one punch, and the dealer's hitting the ground. I didn't even have time to react. My *thought* had been to step in and push the boy back, following him doing the same to Si. But with my overall lack of sleep - since arriving in Mexico - now beginning to take its toll, my movements were not the quickest. Si's was sharp as a fucking tack, apparently. My brain was still catching up to what had just happened when Si's grabbing my arm, - I then noticed a few of the locals all making their way over to us, having seen the boy go down - and we were off, like that Usain Bolt, chap.

I think the dealer must've looked to be sound, though, as no cunt really made any serious attempt at catching up with us. Which was handy, considering running was, in all honesty, asking a bit much of me. Following that, things just got silly. I was up for heading back to the hotel and just lying around by the pool. I was fucked if I was going to spend the majority of my day walking around Guadalajara looking for weed, *especially* when I was leaving for the airport towards the end of the night. Si wasn't on the same page, though. A few streets away from the train station, he spies a cannabis leaf t shirt in some tourist shop. Some of the t shirts were well mad, like. The 'I heart MILFS' one was my favourite. Si's reasoning being that if he was to wear a shirt like that, plain white with that world famous leaf on the front, then cunts would come to *him* and ask if he wanted any.

Sticking it over his other t shirt while still inside the shop, having paid the woman, he flashed me that grin - the grin that I'd seen for more than half of my life and the same one that would have you getting up to all kinds of nonsense, just because he gave you it - and said,

'Let's see where this baby gets us,'

'Well it better get us somewhere fast because I'm leaving for the airport in around eleven hours, for fuck's sake,'

I replied, starting to get a bit annoyed at myself that I was on this goose chase. Aye, so what if the weed back at the hotel wasn't as high grade as we'd been used to. At least it was fucking *weed* compared to what we were inhaling, there in the city centre, which was the pollution from the busy streets with constant cars flying past you.

I didn't outright say that him buying a t shirt was idiotic and the actions of a desperate man. I didn't because, with Si, you never rule fuck all out. We spent around another half hour walking aimlessly. Him giving off the appearance of someone who is just *waiting* on someone stopping him and doing the international sign language for having a toke. The one that makes you look more like Tommy Chong than it does actually resemble you having a draw from an actual joint.

But then the wee kid came up to us, and specifically Si. It would've been ambitious, at best, to have expected the wee man to have been able to speak English, but between him and Si, they found a way to make it work. The kid saying,

'Smoke?'

while pulling the imaginary joint up to his mouth and taking a draw. To which Si nodded his head and then - pointlessly - told him that he was looking to buy but didn't want any of that 'Mexican shite, either.'

The wee man just kind of looked clueless at this, looking at me for help which he was never going to get. After a moment, he then holds his hand out and *now* he seems to be able to speak English, although I was sure it was two carefully rehearsed words that he'd known would make sense to the English speaker.

'Finder's fee.'

This wee bastard, eh? It actually made me laugh, the hustle that he appeared to be trying to pull. But Si was all in. Sticking ten dollar's worth of mixed into his hand and telling me to do the same, which I told him to get himself to fuck! First of all, we didn't know if this kid was going to lead us to the same old same old which seemed to be the *only* weed in the fucking state and secondly, we didn't know if there even *was* any actual weed, and that the moment he got his finder's fee he'd be off.

'Tell you what, Si. *You* stick the other ten spot in and if this doesn't turn out to be bogus, and that's a pretty fucking big if, *then* I'll give you half back,'

I said this to him fully confident that I was never going to need to do it.

The kid motioned for us to follow him, and with a shrug, Si and I fell into step behind him, heading deeper into the back alleys of the city. The fact that he hadn't just ran off after Si handing him the money had at least provided a wee bit of hope. Well, hope if you weren't half considering the possibility that he was just going to lead us somewhere only for us to get ourselves robbed. This was either going to be one beauty of a story or a complete disaster. Knowing us, though, probably both.

It was down one of these back alleys in the city centre that we came to some stairs, which led you to below street level, and into some kind of basement. The door to the place was non-descript in every way possible. No door number or business sign. No signal whatsoever towards what was going on behind the black metal door with assorted graffiti scribbled on it. But then again, I suppose that was the point.

The wee kid performed this series of bangs on the door which, at the time, I'd taken as someone around ten years old being a wee dick, when it came to knocking on someone's door, but looking back I'm sure that it was some form of code. When the door opened, this guy with eyes like half shut knives and frizzy hair that was completely out of control kind of looked at the wee man and greeted him but then, turning towards me and Si, his smile dropped. This leading to him having a conversation with the kid in Spanish that showed us that he wasn't too cool about us being outside his gaff. I'd assumed him to be a dealer but for whatever reason, wasn't thrilled at some potential customers. Whatever the kid said, though, it had been enough to get us in the door. Wasn't sure if I'd wanted to be going in though, mind. Not with the 'welcome' that I'd seen, there at the door.

When we reached the inside, I saw that I'd got it all wrong. Not that there'd been anything prior to this moment to leave me thinking otherwise, mind. Instead of it being some dealer's house and us faced with an awkward transaction for which will still be this same standard grass found elsewhere. This was like a fucking *Amsterdam coffee shop!*

The place was decked out in comfy seating with soft lighting and the only off putting aspect of it being that monotonous Mexican Norteno music which the only way it had seemed to be able to avoid the accordion heavy genre on my trip had been when I'd been behind a set of decks. I wasn't ready for the surprise of a place like that being behind such a grim looking door which had had the look of some murder room being on the other side of it, or something dark like that.

You could see straight away that a lot of the locals sitting around smoking - and who had, to a man and woman, all turned around and looked at the three of us when we'd walked in - and the man behind the counter all knew the kid. Teasing him while giving the boy some loose change, like any other adult does when they see a kid they know and give them money for sweets, even though this little man was well beyond his years to be getting money to buy sweets.

I was thinking that the kid was someone who was sent out to pull in business for what looked like an underground smoking club and not a place that could advertise without grassing on themselves.

'Would you look at that. Oh glory of fucking glories,'

Si, excitedly nudged my arm and pointed at all the jars full of various different strains. One half Sativa and the other Indica. After around three hours of searching in the searing heat for what could well be have been a unicorn. Yes, it was one of the greatest sights of all time. But I only had one eye on it, because I was getting the vibe that we weren't too welcome in there. Maybe it was just me and I had an insane fear of basements that I wasn't aware of but I was getting the impression that a lot of the cunts sitting around on the sofas were talking about us.

The kid - who we'd find out to be called Nino - once again had a blether in Spanish, but with the man behind the counter, and the gatekeeper of all of those strains of green sitting on the shelves behind him. And once again, the guy did not appear to keen on what the kid was saying. Our problem was that we didn't have ride all of a clue understanding *what* the problem was. Because Nino couldn't translate and apart from saying 'gringos nada' to us the budtender didn't have it in him either.

The *gringo nada* part was clear enough. Fucking barry. We fuck about for all of those hours. Land up in a place that has twelve different strains in total, and the cunt wont sell to us because he doesn't like where we're from? Did he not know that we were Scottish? Not Americans. What the fuck have we ever done to Mexico, eh? But it actually went a bit deeper than that.

Si was in the middle of telling the boy to look past the colour of our skin and to just judge us on how sound we were when one of the locals helpfully stepped in. Telling us that this place we were in was not strictly legal but was, also, not technically *illegal* either and was an entity that kind of existed in the grey. But one rule that was strictly adhered to was that these smoking clubs were not to sell to non nationals.

Come on, for fuck's sake, man!

'So is it illegal for a non national to *smoke* it?'

I asked him, trying to get my head around this grey area law in general. He took a second to think about it, I'd imagined that it was a question he probably didn't really need to know the answer to. Eventually he said that, no. *That* was legal. Just illegal to sell it to. This seeing the organic steps which saw this absolute fucking legend of a man who asked to be called Killy agree to purchase our nugs for us, with us throwing in a wee bonus for him for his help and for explaining just what had been going on for us.

Spying a spare sofa and table sitting there. The two of us ended up over on there. Si so chuffed with what we'd discovered that he'd thrown the kid another ten before he left us there. Just showed me that I shouldn't have been so quick to have my so called street smart head on and to have assumed that the kid was was going to rip us off. Instead he had brought us to a place we couldn't have ever imagined seeing that day when leaving the hotel.

Our inventory from our splurging. For Si. Two grams of OG Kush - which showed me that he really wasn't for fucking about that afternoon - and two of Bubblegum. On my side, I'd only procured the two grams of Pineapple because, well, I was fucking *leaving* for the airport so didn't see the point in buying too much only to then have to hand it over to him. Si didn't have such a problem so would have done well to stock up to save him until the next day, which he clearly had. Aside from the different strains that were purchased. We also came away from the counter with one slice of Madeira - space - cake each. Which, as it would transpire, *completely* rendered the OG Kush, Bubblegum and Pineapple as moot.

We didn't know the danger at first. But then again, you never do with space cakes. I hadn't had any in a long time, not since Amsterdam's coffee shops had stopped selling the more stronger ones. Those ones, back in the early days rocked your world, and for hours. But they'd morphed into some sanitised mass produced effort that barely contained any THC. So it hadn't been something on my radar for a long, long time. To me, I guess I'd kind of looked down on space cakes and had felt that they were the kind of thing that you'd hear more *non* tokers talk about than you would from those who actually lived the 420 lifestyle. People who were drug free would talk about space cakes while having no concept of what they were even talking about. Which had helped me drop my guard when Si had suggested we get a slice each. Telling me that I would be nice and chilled hours later for flying to Mexico City. I mean, in a way, he wasn't wrong. Even if, unaware in doing so, he had *no fucking idea* what was coming our way.

After around an hour of sitting there savouring in the chance to enjoy a *real* smoke, I began to feel the cake starting to hit. Si admitted to the same. We continued chatting, talking about the bucket list things we were looking forward to doing across the tour. By the end of hour two, though. Things had deteriorated And we had gone downhill quicker than Franz fucking Klammer.

I hadn't even been aware that I'd come close to having passed out, and was only aware that I had when I came to again. My head back on the sofa and mouth wide open. For those first few seconds, I wasn't even sure where I was. Shit was blurry and my head was as light as a quaver. I turned to look at Si, and he was sat there sleeping but with his head forward in an impossible position for sleep but him managing it all the same. I had the scary thought that *this* was the part where the gringos would've been robbed but no, these cakes were full of some mad shit that was, quite literally, enough to knock a man out. As far as space cakes went, this pissed all over *anything* I'd ever eaten in Amsterdam. And it wasn't even close.

I'd genuinely never felt as high as this in my life. I know it doesn't make sense but it felt like my mind was sitting higher than the rest of my body, like it was floating away from the rest of me because of how little weight there was to it.

'Jesus fucking christ, what the fuck is going on with these things?'

Si just about managed to say to me. Taking a solitary toke on the half smoked joint that he'd just relit before throwing the joint back into the ashtray and saying that it could get to fuck. I sparked up my one that had been there in the ashtray right about the time I fell asleep and, just like Si, found that even the one toke from it was enough to deliver a fresh knock to the head which only served to wake up any of the effects of the cake which had rested when I'd had my involuntary pass out.

This was not just something that either of us had been able to sleep off, though. Far fucking from this. In fact, when I woke, and my mind had managed to piece everything together again. It was now even fucking *stronger* than it was, pre sleep. I'd smoked for more of my life than I hadn't. Had lived in Amsterdam for fourteen years. Forgive me if I'd had the misplaced confidence and impression that after smoking so many different strains and from all kinds of different vehicles, that I'd experienced all there was to cannabis.

And, fuck me, was my face red, there in that basement falling in and out of sleeps, like someone with narcolepsy while coming across as a proper novice. The exact same with Si. This was not some scenario where one out of the group cannot handle their intoxicants. Nah, these cakes had been made by some complete fucking radgey. Or, possibly, by someone without a recipe to go by, and who have forgotten their glasses that day.

The boy behind the counter had apparently gotten pissed off after a few hours of us sitting there sleeping, waking up sleeping and so on. Our English speaking pal, telling us that we weren't allowed to sleep, only smoke and that if we're going to keep falling asleep then we must leave. I just laughed at this while pointing towards the budtender and saying,

'Well *he* sold us this mad shit?! That's like Argos selling the IRA an alarm clock and then having an issue what happened next, eh?'

I'm sure, at least, half of it went over even the English speaking boy's head, but my point was valid nonetheless. Still, though. It didn't help my case much that while I was staging this half arsed appeal for clemency, Si was sitting snoring his head off, having fallen asleep mid speech. What chance did you have, like?

The budtender having had enough and saying that we'd have to leave. Aye, fair enough, mate. But agreeing to leave and *actually* leaving were two completely different things altogether. I swear even then I felt the cake as strong as ever and was having an internal semi panic over just *when* it was going to start to at least show some kind of signs that things were on the way down again, because this had been fucking *hours* now. I genuinely did not know that it was possible to be as out of this through a mere plant.

I - and have no choice but to - guess that while I was in the middle of speaking I had passed out again because the next thing I knew *Si* was shaking *me*, telling us that we had to leave. I could've sworn that it had only been minutes before where he was snoring and the guy behind the counter was telling us to go. Yet now *I* was the one passed out, and Si making a poor attempt at getting some life into me, while he had zero about himself. What a sorry, sorry state of affairs, like. Proper blind leading the fucking blind stuff.

Nothing more embarrassing than a hardened smoker going into a foreign environment and coming across as if they've never even *seen* cannabis before. But that was our reality. What a fucking mess for two people to get in, like. And we'd seen enough of them in our individual and collective puffs. Somehow, out of the two of us, while sitting there and trying to prepare for getting on one's feet and actually managing to climb - which would prove to be literally - those stairs back up to ground level. I managed to find a thought, and maintain it, and ask the - now angry and all out of patience - budtender just *what* it was that they'd put into the Madeira Cakes. When translated for him and the answer deciphered back to me, all became clear. Hearing that each slice had the equivalent of one point five grams of Moroccan, each slice. Factoring in for the fact that kind of hash would have completely melted and soaked every inch of the sponge of that cake.

I felt like I'd manically laughed at this intel.

'You absolute mentalists! That's too much, lads. And I say that having not gone through life saying those words, when speaking of drugs.'

I wanted to say much more to them, but didn't have it in me. Everything seemed like just so much, *too much*, of an effort. Including having a thought and transferring it into words leaving my mouth.

'One point fucking five, rocky, eh?'

I looked to Si who - for the person who was the one who had woken *me* and told me we needed to leave had now fallen asleep in the middle of gathering his things from the table. I gave him a push, feeling like the two of us were now trapped inside some recurring scene where we would forever fall asleep on each other, with no fucking sign of this space cake ever wearing off.

Eventually, we managed to get to our feet, and that should really have been taken for granted but, at the same time, I cannot overstate just what an achievement this felt when we were both in a standing position. Not that this meant we were out of the woods yet. We were not even *in* the fucking woods yet, for context.

It had seemed like some sort of progress when Si had found himself in the middle of the floor, having done some really strange monkey on its way to evolution in a fusion with Liam Gallagher's walk to get him from the sofa to where he now was. But on my side, where I'd tried to follow suit, minus the Gallagher walk, my mind had told me that I didn't have walking in me just yet, so at the last minute had grabbed onto a pillar to the side of the sofa. Holding onto it like my life depended on it while Si is holding his hand out for me to take. This state was without *any* point of reference and we were on completely uncharted ground. No 'one small steps for mankind' or fuck all, though. Not when I *couldn't* walk, at all. Understandably, the locals - sitting there just having a wee toke to themselves - were pissing themselves, which told me everything.

And this cunt? Simon Milne? Despite *everything*. The unheard of mess that these cakes had made of us. Taken us into an orbit that we never knew existed. The fact that hours later, we were struggling to - normally - exit the premises. He *still* managed to find something inside that saw him arranging the purchasing of another *two* slices of it to go. What that one slice had done to me, I didn't care what his intentions were for those extra two slices as long as they were kept away from me. It had - and continued to be - the most intense assault on my senses that I'd ever had when removing the class a factor and I reckon that had it not have been so strange, so novel then I'd have probably appreciated it a lot more, instead of having been left with a fear of when exactly this was going to wear off. Because I was due to board a flight later on and while not even really in a position to confidently put one foot in front of the other, it had felt like the jury might've been out on whether I could even *board* a flight. Because it went without saying that if the me - that was trying to leave that smoking club - had rocked up at Guadalajara airport security, the one that couldn't really walk, or hold a coherent thought or piece of speech, would not have even got to the stage of putting his belongings onto a plastic tray.

Cannabis as well, just cannabis, mind?

It took us a good fifteen minutes to even leave the place and get ourselves up those basement stairs and back onto street level. But what the fuck were we supposed to do once we got up there? Our chances hadn't looked too promising while both going through this whole charade for all the tokers - watching on with amusement - where Si had appealed for me to take his hand while I'd clung to the pillar for dear life. Unable to trust him to take care of me. Not while he couldn't walk upright and looked like the man had turned up for a limbo dancing competition.

Now while we were making an undisputed cunt of ourselves down below in the basement of the smoking club, at least that was contained. There had been only a handful of people who had got to see the show and even then we were semi protected by the - toker friendly - soft lighting inside the club. Up top and out on the street, though, we were not so shielded. Fuck was it bright, and hot. I remember having the irrational thought of that if I was to stay out in this heat for any length of time I was going to die. I didn't have an explanation for why, just that it was one hundred percent going to happen. Due to how nutted we both were, we were devoid of a plan. Well, our *plan* was to get back to the hotel, but we'd been devoid of any form of strategies on *how* to actually make this happen.

Taking things from moment to moment. We had no right to plan for anything more ambitious than this. We decided that we, at least, needed to get ourselves out of this back alley and onto one of the main streets. But the walking was far from up to scratch. I was fixed to a wall, leaning against it while trying to visualise the putting of one foot in front of the other and the swinging arms that would accompany this. Si, on his side, was walking away from the smoking club while looking like he was about to take the stage on his third consecutive night of playing Knebworth. The fact that he wasn't commenting on this peculiar way of walking had made me think that he wasn't even aware of what he was doing. Looking around at me to see that I was still outside the club, he shouted back to me,

'You want me to find a supermarket and steal a trolley to stick you in it?'

Was it really as bad as this? My mate thinking he needs to steal a trolley to get me home? Playing devil's advocate, for a moment. Let's just say that there *had* been a supermercado near to us. He'd have probably taken so long to reach it and return that my tour would've been ready to move onto fucking *Colombia*, never mind Mexico City.

'Mate, I've never been so fucking baked in my life. What the fuck are we going to do? What happens if the pair of us konk out again? We do that out here we'll be waking up in our fucking underpants, if we're lucky,'

I said to Si before the thought popped in that now we were outside of the smoking club we were no longer under their house, and their rules and regs.

'Well the first thing we need to do is get some gear into us and straighten us up a wee bit, eh? We definitely need to bring things down a notch,'

Si replied, weirdly appearing to have a similar thought to the one I'd just had.

'So get it out then, lad,'

he urged, walking back to me. Still leaning against the wall. Even with my shades on I was having to close my eyes due to the brightness but to close my eyes I was then scared that I was going to pass out in this standing position.

'I don't *have* any. I thought *you* would?'

Shit. This was a major blow to find out that while the pair of us had been surrounded in primo gear for the duration of our stay in Guadalajara. None of us had felt like we'd need to bring any out with us. I hadn't intended on taking any but now had reached an unexpected part of the day where I now *needed* it. We both did, really.

'Nah, wasn't really thinking about that when I left the room earlier. Obviously didn't know the fucking blaze that we'd be ended up left in otherwise I'd have brought every single bit I had, and the way I'm feeling just now I'm not even sure that it would've been enough to fix us, but at least would've been a start, eh?'

So ching was out. Aye, technically, we could've got it back down at the train station but I was no longer sure how to even get back there. It had felt like the walk from there - earlier - to the smoking club had been totally erased from my memory. Could barely even remember what the wee kid had looked like from those hours before. Plus, the train station could've been five minutes away and I swear it could've taken us five *hours* to get to it and for what? Some questionable ching that may or may not have even *been* cocaine. There was also the small matter of the boy that Si had decked and in the way the cakes had left us both, we couldn't be around any hostiles as we could've neither fought anyone off or ran from them. In this moment I'd believed that it would've been possible to mug us by just walking up and sticking your hands into our pockets.

'Well, look we need to do something, here, because this shit isn't easing off any. At this moment in time I'm not even sure if I'm making my flight because I have no fucking idea when this cake is going to start wearing off,'

I said, trying to mentally work out what could help, apart from any sniff. The only thing I could think of was food. That normally helped a wee bit whether you were stoned or pished. And to be fair, once I started *thinking* of food it allowed me to make some kind of connecting thoughts that, actually. I was fucking *starving*. It's mad how one second there was no such thoughts and the next it had felt like the single most important thing in the world. Once I mentioned this to Si. He, too, was all for it. But we weren't going to find much places to eat in this filthy back alley.

Eventually we managed to work out a happy medium that allowed us both to get on our way. This, by the pair of us linking arms and starting to gingerly move along the street. Weirdly, through linking arms with me, this had been enough to get Si into a full upright position. He was no longer appearing like some swaggering orangutan. Fuck knows what this must've looked like to the general public passing us? Normally when you see two people with linked arms walking in such a slow and careful way, you can clock which one is the fully fit person and which is the one being helped. This, thought must've looked a bit different. Instead of a case of the blind leading the blind this was the stoned leading the stoned. Only, *no cunt* was doing the leading.

One of the first people we passed in the back alley - while walking with linked arms - was a couple of men in their thirties, who looked us up and down while they passed us. One of them calling as 'maldito maricons' and the pair of them laughing as they walked on.

'Did he just call us fucking Americans?'

Si asked, getting all bammed up about it. Knowing the boy had insulted us but trying to work out in which way. There had been completely *no* point getting bammed up, not when your reaction times were slower than a Central American sloth.

'No, Simon. He called us faggots. He thinks we're gay,'

I said, accepting this while more concerned that the two of them were considering kicking our cunts just because we were 'flaunting our sexuality' out in public. Because you know what some Latin America countries can be like, eh? Two against two. Me and Si would *always* take you on. Didn't mean that we'd necessarily win, like. But we wouldn't back down if confronted with a situation. But not when like this. Somebody wanted to commit what they thought was going to be a hate crime against us then we were effectively rolling out the red carpet for them to do so.

On hearing this from me. Si quickly unlinked his arm from mine. I genuinely could not have given a fuck if some random 'Tapatio' from Jalisco had looked at the two of us and thought that we were gay. Not in that moment we were locked into. It was still very much a fight for to get to a better place, mentally and geographically and the thoughts of strangers who you would never see again in your life came way down my list of concerns. When Si unlinked arms I found that while I could now take steps on my own, I was fucking far from steady. And neither was he. In a weird as fuck way. The hit from the cake wasn't so far away from what it had felt like when you slipped into a K Hole. And *no cunt* can look after themselves when in one of those fucking things.

'We're here. We're queer. We're …'

I said pissing myself laughing as we linked arms again. Forgetting how the end of the slogan even went. Took us an age but we managed to get ourselves out onto the main street. Where next? A question that neither of us really knew the answer to other than find someplace to get a scran. Trying to find something suitable. This random guy came up to us and stated speaking in Spanish until realising that we couldn't understand and quickly then slid into English. Telling us - while looking around to see if anyone was listening - how much he admired that the pair of us weren't ashamed of who we were. Saying that he couldn't come out because his father would take him out to the desert and bury him alive, due to the shame that it would've brought on the family.

I, for one, couldn't be arsed explaining what the reality of things were, that we were so fucking baked that we had required each other to get from A to B. Si, who had got past being mocked in the street for his apparent sexuality, was actually quite sound with the boy, even if his advice would possibly have, in time, probably got him killed by his dad.

'Live your life for you, pal. Not for anyone else, because you can't always please others but you *can* please yourself.'

With this massive and sincere smile. The boy took Si's words and embraced them, then done the same to Si, and me. Thanking us and saying to have a good day as he continued on with his.

'See the boy and the way he looked at me, there? That was *gratitude* written all over his coupon.'

Si asked, well chuffed with the difference he'd made to this random stranger.

'Aye, lets see how much gratitude he's got for you, Si, when his dad's making him dig his own grave, out in the desert, eh?'

I replied, hoping that it would not be something that would end up *actually* taking place but sometimes you're better staying out of other people's lives, ken?

We tried asking some locals for anywhere good they knew for a scran but - looking back - I can only imagine what the two of us looked like as we attempted to navigate our way along the street. Thank fuck for the sunglasses factor, which had been able to hide our slits that were doubling up as eyes. Small mercies. I wasn't sure if it was because we looked like we were a couple of gay men, or if we were giving off heavy druggie vibes, but no cunt wanted to give us the time of day.

Walking without any form of purpose. We turned a corner - mainly since to continue to walk forward would've involved getting across a busy road which was not catering for the slow walkers of this world, never mind the ones going at *our* pace which, to be fair, was a population of *two*. Because no cunt could possibly have been walking about the city like we were. Turning the corner and off in a new direction. Down the road a bit and on the other side from us, I knew how stoned I was when I saw a place that I thought had been called 'Dirty Simon's.'

Saying as much to Si only for him - after taking a good few minutes to work out where I was pointing to and for to focus on it - to say that he was seeing the same as me! As we got closer though, it was now confirmed, unless we were having some shared hallucination. It fucking *was* called Dirty Simon's. Closer still and you could see the logo of the restaurant underneath the words. Some wee kid with dirty knees and a comedy sized sombrero on his head.

'What's the fucking chances?'

Si asked. While it was a coincidence, it wasn't *that* wild. By no means an expert, I'd thought that Simon was one of those universal names, used by lots of nationalities. Still was a bit mad, though. To stumble across it when we did. Of course, we thought it was well funnier than it really was. Like a lot of things had been once the cake had hit, and during the times that we were not asleep.

Si got out his phone and took a few pictures of the restaurant from across the road. While he did so. I clocked one of the waiters, who was standing outside having a reek to himself. He was standing watching us, and the interest that we'd been taking in his place of employment. As Si took the pictures the waiter pinged what was left of his cigarette and headed back inside.

'Here, take this, mate. Get a picture of me with the sign in the background.'

He passed me his phone and then walked over onto the middle of the road and stood there, pointing a finger deliberately up in the air towards the big 'Dirty Simon's sign. I'm not sure he'd thought this through as this was Guadalajara and there was not ever one or two seconds away from you needing to get out of the way of a car or moped, as was the case with this street that we were on. Si, though, deciding that he would just hold the traffic up where he stood, for enough time for me to take a few pictures of him. The boy in the Fiat 500 wasn't exactly the understanding type. Spending the whole time that Si stood there posing in front of the restaurant with his hand repeatedly pressed down on his car horn, while shouting some form of expletives in Si's direction.

'We good?'

He shouted over at me, looking for confirmation that I'd got the shot, before making his way onto the pavement outside of the restaurant. The Fiat driver crawling past Si and shouting abuse at him while accompanied with a middle finger with Si either obliviously or sarcastically giving him a thumbs up and saying *gracias*.

I waited on the built up traffic passing before attempting to cross the road. You knew things were all fucked up when you were congratulating yourself for managing to walk across a small road all by yourself. But I did so all the same.

'About grew a beard waiting on you crossing, Zeek,'

Si greeted me with, which then made me question just how long I'd taken. The fact I'd managed it had been a decent result for me. Never mind how long it had taken me.

'Well I guess we've found our place for a scran, eh? As long as the dirty part from its name doesn't include the kitchen then we're good,'

Si said enthusiastically while pointing towards the front door. The way I was feeling. I just wanted food, and lots of it. And didn't care *what* the name above the door was. Could've been fucking 'Hungry Hitler's' for all I'd have cared. It was, as far as my limited mind had allowed me to estimate, the only way that I could have seen us go some way to returning to being a normal functioning human being once more. Something that we hadn't been for several hours by now.

Walking inside, it wasn't the best of signs when the vast majority of tables were sitting empty and, in fact, there was only two of the tables that had diners sitting at. Two separate couples who were sat at almost opposite ends of the restaurant. A waiter - not the one who had been watching us outside - came to ask us if we'd like something to drink. Beer was one of the last things that we probably would've needed but it had been such a hot slow walk in us reaching the place so we still ordered a couple of Estrella Jalisco. So nice and cold these had been that we had both downed our bottles by the time the waiter came back to take our order for our starter and main. Thinking ahead, we asked for a couple of bottles each while also giving him the food order, which was not a short list that was given to him to write down.

Tostadas, Sopes, Queso Fundidos, Chicharron de Cerdos and some Empenadas for the two of us to share from. And that was just our *starter*. For our main meal we decided on the shared Taco Platter which consisted of beef, pork, chicken and fish tacos, and had been suggested for *six* people. I had never been so hungry in my entire puff, and the order highlighted this. I remember thinking that if after eating half of what would be coming out to our table and found myself *still* high as a kite then I would need to take the sensible decision of rearranging my flight.

'Fucking *love* Mexico, though. Barry as fuck, eh? You can have tacos for breakfast, dinner and tea and on *any* day of the week. Doesn't even have to be Tuesday or fuck all, eh?'

Si said, no doubt going through the same emotions that I was. Which was that state of mind where you were hungry anyway, and now you've placed your food order, and this having an impact on you where, somehow, you find yourself infinitely hungrier than before. Like, the knowledge that food is coming makes things worse, then better.

The beer was conflicting as fuck. It was freezing cold and tasted a-fucking-mazing when going down. But it wasn't exactly helping, as it was never going to be the ideal mix with the effects of the cake, which seemed to resurface anytime you took a toke of a joint or sip of beer. I told myself that I should slow down with it. But telling yourself that you *should* do this, while the stuff was going down so well. There was only going to be one winner. The food will help, though. It *has* to. I sat there thinking, waiting on those starters arriving.

Once they all came out and were placed carefully around our table, we both set about it as if we'd been held hostage for a year in the Middle East and had just been rescued. If anything, I thought that we'd possibly underestimated how many starters we'd need, because we made light work of all of them. It hadn't been a magical wand by any means but even just sharing those starters, I could feel a tiny difference in terms of how spaced my head was. Just tiny, mind, but was still welcomed. In that royally wasted state, I would have taken anything that would've been enough to take me away from that metal clamp around the forehead feeling, the eyes that could barely stay open and the falling asleep on tap. And the giggling at absolutely fuck all. Back out on the street, Si had started laughing at something, so hard that just his laughing had started me off, even though I'd no clue *what* had caused this. Every time we'd looked like we'd stopped, one of us would snigger, and off we would go again. By the time we'd fully stopped, and I'd asked him what had started him off, he couldn't remember, even though it had only been a few minutes before.

By the end of the starters, I noticed that one of the couples had left now. So into the food that had been there on the table nothing else had seemed to matter, or exist. There hadn't even been a word spoken between us both other than the occasional comment on how good we'd found one of the starters to be.

When it came to the main. They didn't fuck about in bringing out the platter of tacos. When I saw it arriving I felt a wee bit moist, like. This beautiful collage of colours and smells. The tacos themselves - already sitting with fillings placed inside - sat on a large wooden board accompanied by small bowls of tangy salsa, some spicy sauce made from tomatoes and chillies, this smooth green one that tasted like avocado and another one that was well decent but I didn't know what it was, kind of like a mix of lime and chipotle.

It didn't even take to the end of this platter for me to feel like I'd just had a heavy, heavy smoke, instead of the 'have I been spiked by LSD' feeling that I'd had until sitting down to eat. Thank fuck, as well! I'd have said that I was now seven out of ten stoned, which was still quite high but was not the fucking *twelve* out of ten that I'd been back at the smoking club.

As we sat scranning our way through the tacos. I noticed that the other remaining couple had now finished their meal and had squared up the bill. The waiter - the one who had been clocking us outside - offering them many thanks for their business - I'm assuming the tip had been decent - and walked them up to the entrance. Due to this catching my eye, I clocked the fact that once they had left, the waiter had flipped the open and closed sign around, then locking the door after.

This, left me thinking that maybe they were closing up for a few hours, maybe to let the staff have a wee kip before they went again for the rest of the night, like they do in Spain with some restaurants. Still, they hadn't said anything to us about it plus we *had* spent quite a bit of money by this point on food and drink so it wasn't as if we were wasting anyone's time by sitting there pushing a salad around a bowl while blethering.

Picking up a pork taco - which had been my favourite out of the four. Apparently, a true homage to Jalisco, or so the menu had said - with the slow cooked carnitas that were crispy on the edges but meltingly tender inside. Topped off with pickled red onions and guacamole. Absolute fucking best of gear, so it was. As I tucked into it, I had that feeling - you know that almost supernatural one - that I was being watched. And we were.

Three of the staff. One waiter and two men in suits were all standing watching us from a distance. I matched this through having just watched the other waiter lock the front door. They weren't outright telling us to finish our food and get to fuck, but from the way they were standing, they may as well have done so.

Because of this, we decided against a dessert, while I could have easily went a couple of different things on the menu. Finishing up the rest of the tacos and the waiter over like a rat up a drainpipe to clear our table, I asked the boy for the bill. He smiled at this and said that, as a thank you for our great custom, the proprietor had wanted to personally deal with our bill, but first wanted to join us for some traditional after dinner tequila shots. Considering the fact that the cunts drank the stuff morning noon and night, I wasn't sure of the importance of having some after you've eaten, when the chances are you probably had some *before* too.

Me and Si told the boy that we were honoured but it wasn't necessary to give us some free tequila. Fuck no, not then. Not when the food had worked absolute wonders on us. Regardless, we were told *nonsense*, and to wait on the owner coming out to see us. Moments after, we saw this man in a designer suit with open shirt collar and the kind of flute that made him look more European than Mexican. Carrying a bottle of 'Don Julio' in one hand and three stacked shot glasses in the other.

Carried such an air of confidence about him. Actually looked a wee bit like Jose Mourinho to be fair, which made me laugh considering confidence could be hardly something that The Special One would've been accused of lacking. He looked slick, confident and rich.

He placed the bottle and shot glasses down onto the table then grabbed one of the spare dining chairs at our table and turned it around back to front before sitting down to face us, placing one elbow onto the top of the chair to prop him up. Introduced himself to us as 'Fernando' while shaking both of our hands. Si, unable to help himself, said something along the lines of,

'There must be something in the air tonight, eh?'

This ABBA reference going right over the boy's head and, instead, he questioned what Si had meant by that. Simon explaining to him that it was nothing and just a wee joke, referencing a song. Fernando's face kind of lit up with this, like he had only now twigged what Si had been referencing. Telling us that he loved Phil Collins and, *especially*, that song.

Si was about to correct him until I discreetly shook my head to signal for him to just leave it, to make things easy on us all.

'So did you enjoy your food, yes?'

The owner asked while pouring out some of the Don Julio for us all. Obviously, he knew the answer to this, having seen how *much* scran we'd ordered - and consumed - over the one sitting.

'*Salud,*'

Fernando said, as the the two of us joined him in his pre tequila toast. In true Mexican fashion, no sooner had the glasses been emptied, and he was refilling them again. Me telling Fernando that this would have to be our last one, as I was fucked if I was going to see what a tequila sesh was going to be like when crossed with one point five grams of Moroccan hash that has been melted into the one small slice of cake. Fernando seemed to have listened to this but not felt like he needed to give any acknowledgment back while he filled the glasses.

'*Salud,*'

once more, as we all knocked them back and now ignoring what I'd said, ahead of the second shot, made to fill out the glasses for a third time. While he was doing so, though, the whole tone of this 'owner coming to sit with customer' was completely flipped on its head as the fixed smile he'd been sitting with dropped, when he asked,

'But why are you, *really* here, gringos?'

This kind of threw us. Hadn't that been obvious? We just looked at each other, both mute for a moment which was probably to do with it being such a weird question to ask two highly stoned boys like we were sat there. We didn't realise the seriousness to where Fernando was going with this and I think that sitting there not giving him an answer to his question only made things look worse to him. Not that we'd an idea we were doing so, mind.

Eventually, Si gave him an answer and quite a candid one at that. Telling Fernando that we had mistakenly eaten the strongest space cake that had ever been made in the history of the world and how we'd both become so hungry that we could've eaten a horse's decayed carcass in between two pish stained mattresses, hence why we'd eaten so much. Half of most of this, Fernando was going to struggle with but had seemed to have picked up enough. Sitting there looking from me to Si and back again while confidently shaking his head, not buying what had been fuck all other than the truth.

'My men have told me that you were taking pictures outside, and I think it would be fair to say that those clicking noises I hear when I make a phone call is something that you both would know of also?'

This boy was more away with it than *we* were, which had seemed unlikely to impossible for anyone else on planet earth, post cake consumption. You could tell that he'd been hitting the ching hard after just a few minutes in his company, and that he'd clearly had a fresh bump before coming over to join us. Not that me or Si could or would judge him there considering the state *we* were in. But clearly the ching was not helping him with whatever paranoia he was going through. I didn't help things though, by trying to inject a little humour into proceedings hearing him asking about his phone being under surveillance by replying that this was a matter of a need to know basis. If I hadn't been so fucking high there's no way I'd have said that to someone who, on the surface, had appeared to think that me and Si had been some undercover agents or something. Fuck me, how way off could you be, there? Si started laughing at my reply, maybe thinking that Fernando would get it too and follow him. But my jokey comment had only cemented things in the boy's head, by the looks.

'Oh, oh. So *this* is how you want to play it, yes? This is the road we travel down?'

he said, shaking his head at the two of us in disgust before getting to his feet and looking down on us and saying a sharp,

'Ok, then.'

Leaves the table and disappears through the back of the restaurant. Me and Si are just looking at each other in amazement at the exchange we've just had. Once again, remove that *fucking* cake from the equation and we'd have been thinking in a completely different way. The survival instinct wasn't there. Had it been, we'd have been looking to get ourselves out of there, locked door or fucking not. Had I the foresight of being able to understand that someone thought we'd been staking out his place and tapping his phones then I would not have been averse to the throwing of a chair through the plate glass of the restaurant front to escape.

Instead, we sat there. Si's looking back at me whispering a genuine,

'what the fuck is going on here, Zeek?'

I honestly wasn't sure if I'd got it right or not, because it hadn't been a day that had been full of clear thinking so was hesitant to tell Si my theory of what I thought was happening here as it did sound pretty out there, when I thought about it. So offered Si a non committal,

'other than this boy looking like he's been doing so much sniff that he's all para out of his nut and seems to be confusing us with someone else, fucked if I know,'

while I grabbed for the tequila bottle and poured out another for us both. Also signalling for the waiter - for the second time - and asked them for the bill but got another KB from him as he told me that 'Señor Velazquez' was in charge of my bill now. But he had fucked off and left us there, with no clue what he was away doing. Which left us sitting there, kind of trapped I suppose. We just wanted some cunt, *any* cunt, to take our money, but things are never, ever simple, eh?

As me and Si sat there, speculating on where Fernando had gone to. Si managing to find a bit of sense to look at his watch and tell me that unless we got ourselves away and find a taxi for the hotel soon then it might start to get tricky for me getting to the airport in time. To be fair, half of me - from hours back - had already factored in the very real chance that I would miss the flight, so it would have almost been looked on as a bonus if I'd actually managed to catch it.

Must've been a good ten minutes - where during this I'd said to one of the waiters that it didn't matter who was dealing with our bill and that surely we could just pay it and get on our way but the boy was giving heavy not wanting to step on the toes of his gaffer vibes, which I suppose I had to respect - before Fernando appeared again, carrying two brown envelopes.

Reaching the table and throwing one down in front of Si and one in front of me. He told us that there was ten thousand, American, in each.

'Ten thousand dollars for me to never see you inside of here or outside in the street. In fact, if I see either of you gringo fuckers *again*, the footage will be released to your bosses.'

As he said this, he asked us to turn and wave to the camera. Him waving at it while telling us to do the same.

'Do we have an understanding, agents?'

Now you'll understand when I say just what a head fuck this had been, and how it was hard to process it all in real time, when you were baked out of your fucking skull. And this showed in me and Si, when presented with this question from Fernando Velazquez, owner of Dirty Simon's restaurant and fuck knows what else 'enterprises' that would have him thinking the Federales were interested in him. We just kind of looked at the envelope in front of us and then at each other. Fuck how we were wishing that we could have a private word with each other, like how those entrepreneurs do on that Dragon's Den when they get made an offer from one of the Dragons.

'Do we have an understanding, agents?'

Fernando asserted. For someone who was freaking out about having gringo agents on his case, he wasn't in any way intimidated by it and was not shy in taking charge of this - in his mind, anyway - sit down with the enemy.

'Of course, if we do not. We can always go the Camarena way?'

I had no idea what he meant by this but the *context* of how he'd said it had managed to cut through because, obviously. If one offer was free money then you'd have had to imagine that the *other* offer might not have been such a good one.

'We have an understanding, señor,'

Si broke the silence. Having managed to concentrate enough to see what was in front of him. A pile of money and, as long as we played our cards right in the next few minutes, a clear passageway out of the restaurant and to safety. One thing was for sure, though. If we managed to blow it and let him work out that we *weren't* agents, after taking his money, then we wouldn't have been leaving the place again, and the money would be right down the swanny.

Fernando looked at Si, then to me, to make sure that I was on board too. My nod in his direction while trying to maintain some form of poker face.

'*GOOD!* Then let us drink to understandings,'

he said, joyfully before pouring out another tequila for us all while toasting,

'to Mexican and gringo alliances.'

We both did the same. Man it was so fucking batshit, all of it. But it was too late to have told him the truth and, being honest. Telling him the truth at the start hadn't helped in any way. It can be hard to persuade someone of something when they've already made their mind up, even if they're wildly wrong.

I necked the tequila and turned to Fernando and told him that he would need to excuse us as I had a flight to catch out of Guadalajara.

'Excellent, make sure you do not come back again,'

he laughed but the eyes told the story of this being truth also. There was still the issue of the bill, which had proved to be such a fucking nightmare to take care of. When I offered to pay before me and Si left, Fernando waved this away while reminding me that we were all friends here.

When we both got to our feet, he met us with a firm handshake each.

'Well it was a pleasure meeting you and I look forward to never meeting you again.'

Si telling him that they were sure they could stick to that, to Fernando's approval. He walked us to the front door and unlocked it to let us back out onto the street, the sun now long gone and the insane head splitting brightness no longer a factor on the fragile heads of the two of us. As we were leaving, Fernando whispered to us that if we intended on taking his money and then turning around and fucking him anyway then we would see just how much harder he would be able to fuck back.

'Nobody's going to be doing any fucking, Fernando amigo. Don't worry. It would be as bad for us if our bosses were to see us taking that money, but you already know that. You'll never see us again.'

Si delivered this in such a convincing and careful way, I almost fucking believed him *myself*. He shook Fernando's hand again, and so did I before he closed the door behind him again. Turning the lock before disappearing from view.

'Look, man. It's been a *weird* fucking day. So I have to ask. Did that all just happen, there?'

I asked Si as we walked slowly away from Dirty Simon's. Walking more in a stunned kind fashion than the messed up way we'd bumbled our way down the same street earlier. It clearly fucking *had*, though. There was a thick envelope shoved into my shorts pocket which had told me so. Si was still carrying the one thrown in front of him in his hand.

'I'm pretty sure it was, Agent Selecao,'

he said, taking the envelope and slapping my face with it. This bringing on a series of uncontrollable giggles. The cake letting us know that while it had decided to calm the fuck down, it was still there.

Once the laughing stopped, I took a peek at my phone - which had been completely neglected from the moment the cake had began to hit - but found nothing of note waiting for me. *Did* notice that, aye, it was starting to get a bit nervy in terms of the part where I got myself to the airport in time for my Mexico City flight.

Which brought me back to there, in the airport. I'd arrived later than I should've done but still in enough time to catch the flight. The two from the magazine had got tired waiting, assuming I'd gone AWOL with Si - which in itself wasn't too wide of the mark - and left without me. As I sat there and heard boarding beginning to be called I couldn't help but stop for pause while thinking about Guadalajara and what a fucking *real* couple of days it had been.

As I'd kind of suspected, before even leaving. Events away from the decks on this tour had eclipsed the tour opener. With my appearance at the Ballam - which had been one of my favourite gigs in a long time - relegated to an almost mere footnote of my time in the city.

And this was just city number one, out of seven, out of five countries.

I hoped that this first forty eight hours was simply me getting stuff out of my system, before getting on with the tour. Because if this was going to be sustained, from city to city. I feared that I was going to either be dead or a basket case by the time the tour reached it's final destination in Rio.

Chapter 12

Lee

Rumours of my demise have been greatly exaggerated, isn't that what they say? Although a ten - plus - hour drive in a bloody minuscule Chevrolet Spark in the unforgiving heat of the open roads of Mexico will definitely take you to the brink. And, yes, finish off lesser mere mortals than Lee motherfucking Isaac.

The car was shaking again. The tin can of - and excuse for - a vehicle I'd been stuck in for the previous ten hours on the drive from Guadalajara to Acapulco. A 1.0 Chevrolet Spark. Honestly, it sounded more like a cruel joke at this point. Fuck that rental firm. Those bastards were going to be saying hello to a one star trust pilot review the first moment that I got the chance. And I wasn't normally *that* guy, but yet while enduring *that* journey, it seemed to soothe me. Knowing how much that one star would fuck with their overall rating. The moment I hit that pothole outside some random tiny town that I couldn't pronounce if my life depended on it, I felt the tyre go. This I did not need, not out in that climate. The heat - while I went about changing the tyre - pounding on my temples like the worst hangover you could think of. And I'd had *enough* of them to measure up against, I assure you.

I pulled over at one point of the journey to stop by a stall selling fruit by the roadside. At least the fruit was good. The best mangoes I'd ever tasted—flesh so juicy and sweet that I was tempted to fill the car with them, leave the world behind, and just fuck off and live off fruit, somewhere that no one could ever find me. But that's not how it worked, was it? Not in my world, not in *anyone's*, really. But what are we without our dreams?

Back on the road again, in this quest, fuck, *crusade* to reach Acapulco. Not much choice, really. Head thumping and sweat dripping where it had felt to me like every single line, bump and gram of sniff I'd consumed since arriving in the country was all trying to escape me at once. I kept my eyes on the next turnoff, looking for anything that resembled an alternate route. The cartel roadblock earlier had been tense. A stark - but very much non required, not with my own personal experiences over recent days - reminder that this country wasn't playing by anyone's rules other than its own. If I'd thought the first one up in Sinaloa, on the way to the Flores birthday party, had been nervy, then this roadblock was way, way worse.

There was no negotiating, nor searching the car. Literally eight SUVs parked up across all four lanes and blocking the roads with some tasty looking boys stood about with automatic weapons around their necks looking bored and hoping that someone might give them a chance to use their weapons. Getting through was a no go. No one could. I could see this when my offer of payment to let me through had been laughed at, while the operative signalled with his hand in the air for me to turn around. The roadblock set up purely to cause disruption to the state, while a war was taking place nearby between two cartels. Funny but I never stopped to ask which cartel these guys blocking the road were from. According to the sat nav. There *was* an alternative route, but only if I double backed and then performed a series of elaborate turns to enable me to be, once again, travelling back in the direction of Acapulco.

The desired B-road I eventually found myself on wasn't much better, though. *Another* roadblock. Tremendous stuff and just what I was needing. Two narcos, leaning lazily against their truck, obligatory rifles on display. Partially blocking the small two lane road like this was some unofficial toll, knowing *no one* was ever going to be driving around the men with guns, blocking the road. The look they gave me as I rolled up made it crystal. Pay us, or this drive was over. In terms of entrepreneurship you had to hand it to them. Take command of a stretch of road that people are going to need to use if they want to leave the state, but a road that is in the middle of nowhere and with no police around overseeing things. I slipped them what pesos I had while fucking praying that I wasn't about to lose a *second* phone inside twenty four hours, and they let me pass, like I'd somehow earned their permission by showing them the colour of my money. The cunts.

By the time I pulled into Acapulco, I was a broken man. Completely wrecked. Exhausted, filthy and supremely pissed off, mainly at the rental firm, still. The ten plus hours doing nothing to ease that particular irritation. I wouldn't have even wanted to have driven a car like that to fucking Asda - not that I'd even be able to fit the shopping into it even if I had done - for a food shop never mind covering hundreds of miles in Mexico. A hard journey had been made infinitely challenging just through having to drive it. Chevrolet themselves? Well they should've hanged their heads in shame for even giving the thumbs up to such a car being released for mass consumption.

I handed the keys to the guy from valet parking and told him to either park the Spark somewhere out of sight where I'd never see it again or simply just take a match to it, whichever was easer. I didn't care. I never wanted to be near that fucking thing again in my life and was already considering just taking the fine that would come through not taking the car back to one of the official collection and drop off points and, instead telling them how pissed off I was with them that I hadn't got the Ford convertible I'd confirmed as booked with them, so they could then come and collect their car themselves, telling them the hotel car park that it would be sitting there in, waiting on being collected.

Walking into the hotel lobby was like stepping back into the real world again from the relative no mans land that I'd spent the majority of the journey travelling on. The instant breeze of the air conditioning flowing down onto me and travelling down the back of my neck when I walked through the automatic opening glass doors towards reception. I felt my shoulders drop, tension easing as I checked in. Acapulco had better be worth what it had taken me to get there. I wasn't just here for any DJ, though. I was here for Kenny Korff, the troubled American DJ with more attitude than talent, and the boy had talent. Talent wasn't even the problem. The problem was Korff had a reputation, one that followed him everywhere he went. He'd just gotten rid of his last manager, literally. Assaulted the guy after a bender and was now subject of a lawsuit from his - now - ex manager. But I knew that a man of my experience, I'd be able to give the boy a bit of balance and reel him in a little, while not completely putting out his flame, like I'd done with many a DJ who had come before him. The payout, in return for this, would be massive. I could already see the pound signs. And *that's* really what mattered at the end of the day.

At the club, I didn't waste any time on arrival. Bribing a bouncer, at least, a night's wage - after some bartering - just to get me into VIP. Networking is nothing without key access, and I wasn't leaving Acapulco without making my presence felt but that was never going to happen had I been stuck down in the main section of the venue, alongside the unwashed general public. Korff was mid-set, captivating the crowd with a mix that had them zeroed in on every beat. The crowd loved him, you could see it with how into it they were. Singing, word for word, and the whole club, along to some of his own self produced tracks when he would drop them into his set. Playing up to the reputation that he enjoyed. At some point during his set, he performed his signature move by piercing a hole inside a can of beer and sucking the spray from it into his mouth to the cheers and whoops from the adoring crowd. *Then* picking up a second and, once more, piercing the can enough for the spray to begin shooting out of it and turned it around on the crowd, sending the contents spraying over x amount of clubbers in close enough a range to Korff, to their absolute delight.

It had apparently been like some badge of honour, to his fans. Being sprayed by his second can. No doubt about it. Americans were different to us Brits. But I had never claimed to understand *why*, just to acknowledge the very clear differences and use that intel when it came to exploiting it for monetary gains. If a club or event is crying out for a DJ to turn up and cover the crowd in beer, which, generally, would be enough for a fight to start in the U.K, then who am I to not want to be the one in pole position who *supplies* them with said DJ?

That's when I saw Tony Harris, another British DJ agent. We'd literally just seen each other in Texas a few days ago at the Dallas Electronic Music Convention, and I knew exactly what he was doing here. We exchanged guarded pleasantries, both of us obviously aware that the other one was there after the *exact* same thing; DJ Kenny Korff.

But you'd need to rise earlier in the morning to get the better of moi, *especially* after the journey I'd had to take on in even *reaching* Acapulco. While Harris was pretending to enjoy the night, clearly strategising for sliding in and grabbing Korff for a word, before I got the chance. I was away, having a word with a guy in a suit from club security. Describing to him someone meeting the appearance of Harris who had been seen trying to sell drugs there inside the VIP area. My fabrication assisted by the fact that I'd seen him taking a couple of lines while Korff - was playing - so knew that he at least actually had *some* gear on him, even if he wasn't trying to sell it to anyone. By the time that this intelligence was acted on, it would be too late baby oh it's too late for my competitor. Took the security a few minutes before they swooped in on him but when they did it was like some form of a military operation where they are tasked with grabbing a target and extracting them. Harris was rushed out of the room, protesting his innocence, but it was no dice. Man down. I laughed at the horrible and unexpected twist to gatecrash his night, while now knowing that I had a clear path at pitching to Korff.

Korff came off stage looking like he'd just conquered the world. Dressed in an oversized NFL jersey - San Francisco I think? - although isn't *every* one of those jerseys oversized, if worn without shoulder pads? That along with a Brooklyn Nets SnapBack cap and a pair of baggy cargo trousers that looked like they could easily have been four or five sizes too big for him. So baggy it was practically impossible to know which brand of sneakers he had on. His energy was manic, and the glint in his eyes told me he was already under the influence, which wasn't of any surprise and was complete 'on brand,' if anything. I sat at the bar, biding my time. Korff, surrounded by a flurry of fans, post set, eventually made his way over for a drink. I played it cool, complimenting his set without coming off like the likely many sycophants that he would come across every day of his life. Saying what a set it had been that he'd just delivered and how he had the crowd eating out of his hand, I offered to buy him a drink. He took the bait, and we sat for a while, talking shop.

I knew the trick with Korff was to not come off like the guy in a suit, trying to talk 'boring' business in the middle of a party. That wouldn't fly with someone like him. This, fine by me because I'd always thought that my USP - for any likely DJ or producer who I wanted to attract - was that I *wasn't* an industry suit. I was someone who - had I not owned the business that I did - would have still been attending various events, as a punter and for the love of the scene. I pulled out a small baggie of gear, offering him a line. He grinned, took the offer, and sniffed it up from off his clenched fist without a second's thought. Part of this from me was purely performative and was all part of the game. Make him feel like I was one of the boys, so to speak.

Korff was surprisingly engaging, funny even. Not the loud and obnoxious frat boy of a nightmare I'd expected. It wasn't long before we were laughing over some of his more recent antics, like the well publicised time where he had caused a transatlantic flight from New York City to London to turn around because he was snorting coke off the tray table on the back of the seat in front of him and got into it with the flight attendant, who had, understandably, taken umbrage of his consuming of illegal drugs on her flight. Banned from United, sine die. Now on his final warning with American Airlines. That's Kenny Korff, though. A walking liability, but a *profitable* one. And, having always done my homework, something that I knew I was walking into with eyes wide open.

I started laying the groundwork, as part of my pitch, which had up until then been a pitch *without* any pitching. Talking about my agency, the DJs I had under my wing, many that he knew of and respected, and what I could do for *him*. I had his ear now. And before the night was through, I knew I could seal the deal.

Korff leaned into my spiel closer as the night wore on, and I could feel the shift. His walls were down. Whatever bravado he had started the night with was crumbling under the weight of the drinks and drugs. It was the perfect moment to talk business, but I played it slow. If there's one thing I'd learned, it's that coming on too strong, too fast, spooked people like Korff. This kind of man wasn't the type to be boxed in by details or contracts, not when he was on a high like this and too busy having a good time to get bogged down by things like details.

Still, he gave me an opening.

'You know, buddy? I'm playing an after-party at this other spot, in the city,'

he said, throwing back the rest of his drink and wiping his mouth with the back of his hand.

'You should come along to that with everyone. We'll talk more, yeah?'

He glanced at me with that cocky grin, like he was challenging me to keep up with him, it now being around three-ish.

'Hope it's not past your bedtime too much, though, pops?'

I laughed this off, with mock insult on my face while I delivered some cold facts for the kid.

'Please, fella, you're talking to someone who has been partying longer than you've been alive.'

He met this with an approving nod of his head while holding his arm up vertically to give me a high handshake.

Telling me he would catch up with me at the next venue, Casa del Ritmo - The House of Rhythm.

The after-party was another level of chaos. We ended up in this underground club, a lot smaller and more intimate than the venue we'd just vacated, which made sense considering the amount of money that Viento House had put up to install Korff as a resident, with his fortnightly residence. Here at Casa del Ritmo, though. Korff would've been receiving peanuts for playing, if anything at all and was clear that it had been set up as much for Korff and his entourage to continue partying than it had been as any kind of real money making exercise. With the limited capacity, brick walls and incredibly low roof, the place had felt like a return to the good old days where - in the U.K - you could have been dancing away inside a building that every other day of the week had been used as a car park or to house shipping containers. You would return from one of those events absolutely *filthy* but having had the time of your life.

Korff was buzzing, bouncing between people, everyone wanting a piece of him. I sat socialising with the occasional person or group. Social chameleon as I was, fitting in had never been an issue, whatever the environment. I chatted with a light engineer from Chicago for a while where - small world as it was - I'd found that he had worked the lights at some of the stages I had stood from the sidelines and watched one of my deejays play at. I also had a brief chat with the owner of the club, Sam Eckhart. An American entrepreneur who must've had the benefit of having been whispered a few words in his ear from someone in the know, when it came to buying property in Acapulco, *right* before the place exploded and the boom came. We swapped business cards with me saying that if I had any business in Acapulco, in connection with any of my deejays then I would be in touch to organise hiring his place. When it came to Korff, I kept my distance at first, watching him while biding my time. I wasn't here to kiss the kid's backside, just to make sure he knew who had the connections to take him further. Another way of putting it, *me*.

Finally, he pulled up a chair next to me. Him sitting to the side before I'd even known that he'd been in the vicinity

'You know,'

Korff started, voice slurred but sharp enough to cut through the haze,

'it's a crime I barely play Europe anymore.'

'True,'

I nodded, casually.

'The European scene - and your *fans* - has been missing out. All the top American deejays are there regularly. Ibiza, obviously, but the U.K and all its festivals as well as the rest of Europe. Everyone over grafting, *except* for you. It's time something was done about that.'

Korff smirked at this while saying in a self depreciating way that was *also* mixed with some apparent pride to go with.

'Well, yeah, it's a little hard to get gigs when you're banned from flying United, on thin ice with American Airlines and probable one more incident away from ending up on the no fly list!'

I shook my head, while reminding him that, undoubtedly, being on a blacklist of the two major airlines from your country that are responsible for getting people *out of* your country is a pain in the arse that you could well do without when you have an occupation that - if you are successful at it - means you're hardly going to be *off* an airplane, there *were* other ways to get from America to Europe, via other international airline companies. As much as a limited amount of choice of flights you would be presented with in such a scenario, when unable to use the two major American companies. I also let him know that for certain big events, he wouldn't have to worry about airline companies, not when he would be travelling via private jet.

'That's where I come in though, Kenny. You need someone who can deal with that kind of bullshit, smooth things over, keep the focus on your music, not your... extracurricular activities. and I mean no disrespect towards your now ex manager but it doesn't appear that he'd been up to the task of it.'

Stopping to take a bump of sniff - and then passing the baggie over to Korff - I then, without any hint of embarrassment from me, told him,

'I'm not wanting to toot my own trumpet but if you'd had me looking after you, back during that incident with United, when returning the plane back to JFK and banning you for life. I'd have got you off with a slap on the wrist.'

He leaned back, as if weighing this up, massaging his nostril to help the rest of the gear to flow freely upstream.

'You got connections like that, yeah?'

It had been nothing other than an outlandish claim, following a bump of cocaine. How the hell would *I* have managed to talk around a multi billion dollar company into letting a passenger off with causing a serious incident that had led to one of their planes - over the Atlantic Ocean - having to turn around and emergency land? But I'd said it and to now try and walk back would have done nothing other than make me look like a complete bullshitter. And I was *never* securing Korff's name on the dotted line if he'd had the merest of a whiff that I was full of it.

'More than connections. I've got a stable of deejays who play the *best* clubs and the biggest festivals around the world, and I always make sure they're exactly where they need to be, whichever continent and whatever time zone it is and I'm in. Fuck, mate. I'm only *in* Mexico right now because one of my guys, DJ Selecao, is headlining his open-to-close tour across Latin America. You've heard of him, yeah?'

Korff stopped for a second, as if he was trying to place the name before the lightbulb went on and nodded.

'Yup, I haven't ever played in the same place as him before but yup, I've heard of him. He's been doing well. Seems to be anywhere that's worth playing, he's played.'

'*Exactly*, mate. And I had a *lot* to do with that,'

I replied, taking credit for as much of my Scottish deejay's career as the man who'd played all of the records in all of those settings did himself.

I could see it sinking in with him. Korff wasn't some idiot who needed arse licking or empty promises. He needed someone who could handle his mess, and mess there *would* be. A protector and guardian who could make sure his talent wasn't overshadowed by his antics, but who had the business savvy to tread the fine line between *merging* the mythology of his antics and weaponising it into making him box office, when it came to him and his talent. I was that guy, I'd proved this time and time again with previous artists, and I had to make sure that he knew it too.

Hours passed, and as the drinks kept coming, and the cocaine intake racked up, no pun intended, I started to feel the weight of the day begin to hit me. The marathon drive, the cartel roadblocks, the flat tyre, every single uncomfortable bump in the road that the car's lack of suspension had left me vulnerable to. Everything began to catch up with me. Korff, on the other hand? Well, he was only getting more and erratic and completely MWI, as Stevie would sometimes describe for someone in such a frame of party mode. He was feeding off the energy around him, becoming louder, wilder, more reckless. The party fed him, and he was determined to be forever at the centre of attention.

At one point, he bought a round for everyone airside the afters, shouting on the microphone while muting the track he was playing for a moment, like he was some kind of rock star. The next minute, he was threatening an American music journalist who'd been pestering him all night, issuing them with the ultimatum of,

'If you don't fuck off out of my face, I'll have your legs broken.'

I took this as my cue to make a move to get myself back to the hotel. I'd done enough, by then. In every sense. I didn't need to stick around and risk my own reputation by being too close to whatever disaster Korff was going to pull next on the night. As far as the business side. I felt that I'd had him hooked. Now I just needed to let him reel *himself* in. The last thing I wanted was to come across as desperate. The party mode that he'd been in - and showed no signs of abating - though, Christ, I hope he even *remembers* our interactions from over the night. The sudden thought gripped me as I thought that when turning his pockets out the next day he might come across my business card and ask himself, who the fuck is that guy?

'See you at the *after*-after party, then?'

Korff asked, eyes gleaming with mischief after he'd done some half dance in between the crowds over to where I stood, as I finished what I had planned as my last drink of the night. Some local DJ now having replaced Korff on the decks, with his second set of the night now completed and it now being six in the morning and the American DJ now looking to take matters on to a *third* venue. A part of me feared that this would've been the case with him which meant it hadn't been a surprise to me for this to turn out to be so. Approximately twenty four hours before, I was with a prostitute who was in the process of robbing me blind. And fast forward to twenty four hours later and I was being invited to an after party, following the end for the *after* party. Thinking back, the - suspected - rohypnol had probably been a bit of a god send as I'm not sure I'd have even had any sleep in between had it not been for that.

I hesitated at Korff's invite. All forms of sense and sensibility screamed for me to call it a night. I'd done exactly what I came to do in Acapulco. But then, this was Kenny Korff. The guy who *thrived* on chaos and unbridled madness. If I bailed now, maybe he'd think that, actually, I maybe *wasn't* the kind of guy who could keep up with him. So, against all reason, I nodded back his way.

'Wouldn't miss it.'

Looking down at my watch and then back at him I mentioned the old saying that you're as well as being hung for stealing a sheep than a lamb, as a metaphor for the reality that saw it being after six in the morning so what would be the point of calling it a day, instead of going for a few hours more, since you were still up? A few hours more? I fucking *wish* it had been a few hours more. Because, in reality, it was much, much longer than this, and felt even *longer*.

The after-after party was pure and utter madness. When anyone makes the decision to go to the after - after party, they have already decided to out themselves and take matters to a place where there is nowhere to hide. It is now daytime and you are not able to hide in the dark or in the shadows. After after parties can be one of the most sad, depressing and depraved environments that you can ever have the misfortune to find yourself in, and this was no different.

We'd all ended up at some beautiful villa on the coast, the sun already starting to rise by the time we got there. Whoever owned the villa - if in attendance - had never made it clear that it had been their place, and that they were hosting everyone else. No, it just came across as a beautiful gaff that everyone had decided to descend upon. People were sprawled out, some of the crowd passed out having impromptu disco naps or lying around chatting and smoking weed on couches or out by the pool, as the morning sun began to take on a bit of heat about it. While the rest? They were all still going strong to Korff's third set of the night, in the large indoor floor space, with the above atrium that let the daylight stream through it and gave off an unmistakable resemblance with the world famous Amnesia atrium. Most of everyone indoors dancing as fervently as they'd done back at that *first* club of the night. Korff was in his absolute element. Playing some undoubted crowd pleasers, knowing that each time he dropped a big tune it would have an impact on the energy within the room. Midway through his set, while playing the extra long remix of Deep Dish's stab at Tenaglia's 'Music is the Answer. Him leaving the decks and deciding to swing from a crystal chandelier, like some kind of deranged circus act. The crowd lapping this up and cheering this on while he swung back and forward. Inevitably, it gave way, crashing down onto the dining table below, completely free from the ceiling with Korff still clinging to it as he crashed down onto the large dining table that sat underneath the chandelier, laughing like a maniac. It made me think about WWE and where they throw each other onto tables. Only that was a lot more planned than what Korff had done for everyone's entertainment.

The party didn't even stop. Not through the star DJ in attendance almost paralysing himself. Not for anything. Like the professionally unprofessional performer that Korff was. In the time that he'd began the track. He had managed to fit in the swinging on the chandelier right up to it dislodging from the ceiling and him ending up seriously winding himself, yet had *still* managed to take his place back behind the decks in time to mix out the track. He was a showman, you had to give him that.

And then there was the monkey. A small, mischievous little macaque, darting through the crowd like it fucking owned the place, while being one hundred times more sharp and switched on than any single other being in the room. At one point, it grabbed my phone, while I was racking up a much needed medicinal line for myself while starting to flag a bit, and I freaked out. Chasing it around the room - it shrieking so loud that it was competing with the sounds blaring out of the speakers strategically situated around the room, while people laughed and cheered me on as I chased after it. In reality, I was *never* catching it, even if I hadn't been indulging in drink and drugs across the night and was now suffering from sleep deprivation. I'd lost all sense of time, energy, or reason, though.

With this being what appeared to be a 'pet monkey' that was hanging around the house, and not just some random one that appears and robs you of your shit, a few others reassured me that I would get my phone back. Telling me that there was a pile of everyone's stuff up on the second floor and that the monkey had been stockpiling everything that it had stolen. Somehow, though, about half an hour later, the same monkey brought my phone *back* to me, like it had just been messing with me for fun. Not just a random phone or accessory that it had pinched from someone, but my *exact* phone. I could not believe this and was sat there trying to tell others about it while they all reacted as if this was completely normal and nothing to get that excited over. I'd thought that at the very least, I'd have had to barter with the fucking thing, like how you do with them in Gibraltar when you swap them something of use to them - like fruit - in return for the valuable phone that they're holding onto, which are of absolutely *no* use to them. I watched it, fascinated, for the next hour or so as it walked around like it owned the place. Stealing, running away only to come back with peace offerings later on.

'I've *got* to get one of these fucking things for my parties back in the U.K,'

I told one of Korff's mates, as we stood there, eyes fixed on it, watching the macaque jump from one person's head, directly onto someone *else's* about a metre away before then propelling itself upwards to climb up to the second floor of the villa.

It was about this time, with it now mid afternoon, I was *done*. Exhausted beyond belief. A thousand authors with unlimited overtime could not have found the words to describe how drained my mind, body and soul now was. The energy sapping ten hour drive, the drugs, the alcohol, it had all caught up to me. I found a spare bedroom and collapsed onto the bed in the corner, and reckon that I was out cold before my deranged head had even hit the pillow.

When I woke up, it was early evening with the sun now starting to go down, and there, tied to the bedpost with a rope, was the monkey, although as I focussed on it further, not *the* monkey. This one appearing to have a series of streaks on its tail where the previous one hadn't. It lay, sleeping soundly, looking like it had been through the *exact* same all-nighter that I had. I rubbed my eyes, overwhelmed by how fatigued I felt on waking, trying to make sense of what had happened after I'd gone off to sleep. Because as wrecked as I'd been when calling it a day, I'm *sure* I'd have noticed a monkey in the room before going to sleep? Grabbing my phone and checking it, I saw a text message waiting there from an unknown number. Opening it up, it was from Korff. Our promises over the night to swap number never quite coming to fruition, and him clearly using the card that I had popped into his hand earlier on in the night.

Bro? What a fucking night?! That's how we doooo, doe!! Was good meeting with you and now that I've seen first hand just what a crazy motherfucker you are, I can't think of anyone more suited to representing me. Get a contract put together and sent over to me and we can take it from there?

KK x

P.S. You seemed to really like the house monkey at the afters to the afters. So much that I bought you one of your own. Word of warning, though. It came freshly tranqued, so if it's not already woken up it will do soon. Apparently, they get in a bad mood when they wake up from that shit. GOOD LUCK, muchacho!

I stared at the screen, half in disbelief, half in victory. I'd done it. Somehow, despite the chaos and madness spread across the night and morning, the sheer exhaustion on my part when running on empty. Despite it all, I'd nailed down Kenny Korff.

And now, apparently, I had a monkey.

The tranquillised little creature stirred on the floor, and I knew that this day wasn't over yet. But that could wait. For now, I just needed to rest, *desperately*. Sometimes your body gives you a warning that it needs some time out from the world, and you then go and *ignore* its warnings, which brings you to the mental and physical place that I found myself in, following the three nights in a row which had been Mazatlan, Guadalajara and Acapulco. Each of the three where I had been up the whole night. No one could keep *that* run going without ending up doing themselves a mischief. And *especially* not for a man in their fifties.

When I woke, and managed to take a few minutes to see the lay of the land. I knew I was absolutely dead. Hadn't felt so tired in *years* and the mere thought of even getting up out of the bed gave me the complete fear. Unless the owners of the place, who at no point had made any attempts to wake me up and ask me to leave - going by Korff's text, him long gone by then - then I wasn't going to be moving. Fuck, I wasn't sure if I even *could've* done, had I been tasked with doing so.

Despite being in relatively close proximity to Mexico City, considering the sheer size of the country, general. In all honesty, Stevie's festival appearance could've been taking place two minutes outside of the bedroom where I lay and I'd have *still* felt it more than a bit of an effort for me to get up and go and see him. No, I was ratifying the message that my body was sending me. I had hit a wall that, for that night at least, I was never going to be able to scale. And all the ten out of ten cocaine in Mexico would not have been able to change that.

I decided to skip the festival in Mexico City and meet up with Stevie, on his next country of the tour, when he reached Medellin, Colombia. Saying to myself that I would send him a message later keeping him in the loop, but with my phone battery now sitting at a dangerously low percentage of four, I switched it off so as to have the four percent there for an emergency, if required. Possibly there would be a charger somewhere in this large villa but to even address this would mean having to get up out of bed, so was put on the back burner. I would contact Stevie as and when.

Because I wasn't moving from this spot until I'd had at least twenty four hours of sleep, owners of the property being understandable to this not withstanding.

The monkey, now starting to stir and make some muted squeaking from its mouth that was a world away from the high pitch scream that it was going to be capable of, once it got itself into gear. I was going to have to trust to use whatever street smarts that it had. Reaching down and untying the rope from around the bed leg and the other end around the chain on its neck. I trusted that once it was mobile, it would use its head and escape through the open bedroom window. And if it could've done this while not taking its anger in being shot with a tranquilliser dart out on the face of sleeping beauty, there in the bed, that would be a bonus.

As a preventive - but very smart from someone in my head state - measure, I put my phone under my pillow and sank my head back down into it and closed my eyes. The fact that I fell asleep as instantly as I did - despite waking up to the news that I had secured Korff, as well as a monkey - only illustrating just how much I badly needed it.

Chapter 13

Reuters News Agency

ISIS terror grips Amsterdam: Coordinated attacks leave Dutch capital paralysed by fear

Friday 7th November, 2014

Wout Rensch: Netherlands Correspondent

Earlier this morning, Amsterdam suffered a series of terrorist attacks across the city centre in what appears to have been a coordinated attack by newly formed terrorist group, Islamic State.

Amsterdam was plunged into terror on Friday morning after a series of coordinated attacks, claimed by terrorist organisation Islamic State (ISIS), rocked the city centre. The devastating attacks, which took place within two hours of each other, left nineteen people dead, with dozens injured, many critically. The city centre has since been placed under a heavy security lockdown which has seen an unprecedented security operation launched, the kind the city has never witnessed before in its seven hundred and thirty year history, with authorities warning residents that the worst may not be over.

The first attack, out of three, took place just after eight in the morning when Centraal Station saw two gunmen open fire on morning commuters in and around the main terminal. Passengers scrambled for cover as gunshots echoed throughout the station's main hall as scores lay dead or badly injured. Dutch anti-terrorism unit, Dienst Speciale Interventies (DSI) responding swiftly, taking out both attackers but not before seven members of the public had died with many others seriously wounded.

As gunfire erupted in the heart of the city centre, miles away in the busy de Pijp district, the second attack then began. A suicide bomber detonating a device aboard a rush hour tram, killing five people and critically injuring twenty four. The force of the blast blowing out windows in the nearby houses, bars and shops. Survivors described a scene of horror as the explosion ripped through the carriage, sending metal and debris flying.

Elsewhere in the de Pijp district, minutes later, the popular Bernie Jaansen street market, a market used by both Amsterdam residents and tourists, was targeted by a lone attacker driving a Mercedes Sprinter van driving down the centre of the busy trading point, leaving a trail of death and destruction in his wake. The attacker speeding through the crowds of shoppers, mowing multiple people down before exiting the vehicle and launching an indiscriminate stabbing spree. His rampage only brought to an end by a quick thinking fish monger from the market who rammed the attacker with his delivery van. The swift action from the vendor preventing further atrocities but not before more lives had been lost with countless others left traumatised by events.

Hospitals across the city were overwhelmed with seriously injured as emergency services worked to treat the victims.

Hours after the attack, the Islamist terrorist organisation, who only formed last year, ISIS claimed responsibility for the attack. Boasting through their online channels, and shared widely by their supporters, of their success in bringing the Dutch capital to its knees. This being their first major attack on a European nation.

Speculation has already begun that this wave of attacks may be the first of many to come. Caught by surprise, major European intelligence agencies are reportedly scrambling to assess the scale of the threat, with some international Jihadi experts warning that these attacks may be but only part of a much larger scaled plot, targeting some of Europe's major cities.

This morning's attacks, however, come hot on the heels of the controversial speech from prominent Dutch right wing politician Pieter Hoogstraat last week where the leader of the far right *Nederland Eerst* party had made inflammatory remarks, branding Muslims as terrorists, fuelling tensions between right wing Dutch nationals and immigrants across the the country.

The timing of this morning's coordinated attacks, in the wake of Hoogstraat's comments, has only served to stoke the fires of fear, as some quarters lay the blame at the door of the party leader.

By nighttime Amsterdam remained under tight security with the DSI visible in all districts of the city centre. This while the city's residents are left with the harrowing task of coming to terms with this grave tragedy. A city universally known for its tolerance and freedom now finding itself under siege and without certainty over what its future holds In the coming days.

As the early investigations on this morning's attacks take place, authorities have urged the public to remain vigilant, while security measures have been heightened nationwide.

Dutch Prime Minister, Denis Sier is scheduled to make a press conference at 9am tomorrow morning with an update from Amsterdam Chief of Police, Sieb Djkstra, scheduled for shortly afterwards at 10.30am.

Chapter 14

Flo

Why is it that sometimes you're left with the feeling that the universe is completely fucking with you? Having a good old chuckle to itself at the tailspin that it can send you into? No real explanation to this other than why I found myself on an overnight flight across the Atlantic, and one that I had not even *planned* to be on, when I'd first woken that day. In the middle seat for twelve hours, sandwiched between two of the fattest men that you could've ever imagined up in your life. And I'm talking the biggest baddest Icelandic strongmen you've ever seen. But I'll return to those bastards in due course.

Nope. When the alarm clock woke me that morning. *Zero* in the way of heading anywhere in the vicinity of Schipol Airport. But the universe had other ideas, apparently. The day before? Simple normality and just another ordinary day in, what I had come to regard as the greatest city in the world. A city, so full of diversity, that for Zico and me, it had *never* been about fitting into our new surroundings. Simply *being*. The *next* day, however? I was waking up to a Dutch capital that was going to be shocked to its foundations before its citizens - as well as the incessant stream of tourists it saw week upon week - had even eaten lunch.

It all started like any other morning. Because, that's the thing. Things are always normal, right up until they're a million miles from. I was in the kitchen, making my first coffee of the day. The streets of de Pijp district - and an area that after so many years of living there we both called home - were busy with the locals getting themselves on their way to work. The familiar sounds of both bikes and trams past outside my window. I wasn't really thinking about anything, to be honest. Who *can*, before their coffee, though? With Stevie thousands of miles away on his tour of Latin America, it was just me kicking around in the flat. The day before had been one of my scheduled days in the office, as part of the charity that me and a friend had formed after moving, - Tess who, like me, had moved to the city from outside of the Netherlands. Coming from across the border in Bruges - to help clothe the homeless. This, something I had thought of during the first winter that Stevie and myself had lived in Amsterdam for and me coming across a homeless woman late at night, when we were walking back from a meal, who was without a jacket and - as cold as that November evening had felt *with* a coat on - was rolling the dice on even *seeing* the next morning.

Me, before the night was finished, taking a walk back to gift her one of my old ones. The *beauty* of forming your own charity, well apart from that warm glow that you get inside knowing that you're doing a bit of good in the world, of course, is being able to pick and choose which hours you do, and when you do them.

Then, exactly as the kettle was making its click noise to indicate that the water inside of it wasn't going to get any hotter, this enormous boom. The timing of it was hella confusing for a moment because - impatiently waiting on the kettle - my eyes were fixed on the switch, willing it to flick itself back to the off position, and it flicking up *right* at the same moment when the boom was heard. It hadn't been loud enough to make me think that something terrible had happened, but *still* strong enough that it made me forget about finishing making the cup of coffee. Which, until then, had been the single most important thing in the world to me. Amsterdam being Amsterdam and like any major city across the world, it wasn't quiet. But like anyone else, you get used to all of the regular noises outside, not that the noise I heard had been regular.

I walked over to the window, peeking out through the blinds, and looking down onto the street, from the reactions of the public who were out and about down there, they seemed to be asking themselves the same question as I was. It's probably just construction or something, I thought, trying to tell myself something of the equivalent of what I'd have wanted to hear. There's always construction in the city, right? But to counter this, I couldn't ignore the one question I had. What kind of a construction noise sets off all of the car and house alarms on a street? The scores of intermittent alarms all going off at their own tone and speed was a collective noise which would have seriously tipped a person over the edge if they'd had to listen to it for any length of time. In fact, it had been the alarms going off - as opposed to the boom that had preceded them - which had left me with the horrible feeling that something *bad* may just have taken place, somewhere close to our flat.

Due to the extremely tight ways the traditional Amsterdam houses were built hundreds of years before, generally looking out of your window would mean that - apart from the street - you're most probably going to be staring back at a similar house, across from you. So I could not see much, but what I *could* see didn't look too hopeful. The *bewildered* look about the people down - our three floors to our place - on the street had now turned to something that looked to be a lot more of panic. People starting to run in different directions. While still those alarms were all singing off key in their own collective little choir.

Then my phone buzzed, still on silent from my night's sleep. A message from Tess.

Hey, babe. There's been a terrorist attack in Centraal Station. Just checking you're ok. Luv T xxx

Her words giving me a sinking feeling in the pit of my stomach. Amsterdam, while being a city - like any other - where you needed to have your wits about you in some parts. It had never been a place where you'd have ever linked it with terrorist attacks. Unlike London - where I'd moved from - which had been on the receiving end of practically from before I was born and ending near to when I moved to the Netherlands.

But hang on, I thought as it started to occur to me that we lived over three miles away from the city's main train station, down in Centrum. Whatever noise I'd just heard, and what was causing the scenes of panic, could not have come from Centraal Station.

I reached to switch the TV on and see what the news had in connection with and saw a reporter, live from the city centre, standing at the bottom of the Damraak - with the grand entrance to Centraal in view behind her up ahead - giving a live account of the attack. As she done so, you could see police dealing with members of the public and ushering them away from the direction of the station while police vehicles and ambulances flew past with their sirens on. Combining this with looking at Twitter - which was fast becoming the place to get your news *before* the major networks - it took me seconds before I was sitting looking at a video of two men carrying automatic rifles wandering casually through the main hall of the terminal.

'Casualties are unknown at this point.'

The reporter continued although having just seen two men with rifles walking around such a heavily populated place - and *especially* at this time of the morning - I already knew that it was going to be a miracle if no one had been harmed. I was now looking at a second video that had been taken by a member of the public and posted online which showed people running while the two men stood there laughing and spraying bullets towards them. Like Twitter tended to be, however, some videos you could've done with a warning before seeing. Like that one. Sitting there horrified and on the verge of tears at what I now knew was taking place elsewhere in the city, I heard the voice of the news presenter as he butted in on the reporter's latest update by saying that they were now receiving breaking news from 'de Pijp' district of Amsterdam that a public tram had been blown up, with the suspicion, by a suicide bomber.

Even though I was in a sitting position. The room started spinning for me. So sucked in by the TV and social media, I had almost forgotten the noise outside but now that I was listening again, I could hear that the majority of alarms had now reset themselves, but had now been replaced by multiple sirens belonging to the emergency services. There could be no doubt about it. A fucking tram had just been blown up a few streets away from our apartment.

Grabbing my cigarettes from off the table and lighting one up, when, in truth, had it been humanly possible I'd have happily smoked three or four all at once. I was unsure of what I should do and the only thing that I *was* cast iron sure of was that I needed to not be going outdoors.

Even through the much needed calming properties of my ciggie, my breath catching in my throat. I couldn't believe this was happening and wanted to just pretend that none of this was real, and that I still needed to wake up for the day. No way was this happening. Not here. Not in my city.

Only it was, and as inconceivable to me as it was in what was one fucker of a surrealistic morning, it was to become even worse. It could've only been five minutes or so from the blast that had gone off outside my door but I was now seeing tweets that had only been on Twitter for seconds now mentioning *another* incident in de Pijp. This time, at Jaansen's market. Chillingly, a place that Stevie and me would often walk down, visiting Barney's to have some of - what the proprietor boasted - the best chicken that you could find in the city. We would often have a 'dessert' by getting a tray of Dutch pancakes from Gertie's stall. These people, over the years, had become more than just street vendors and were now people that we now *knew*, as in day to day life.

There was no video or pictures to go with the tweet, which I was thankful for, but the text was saying that someone had driven a large van straight down the middle of the market, mowing down anyone it could find who hadn't got themselves to safety in time.

Now the tears came. I was frightened for all of those poor innocent people. Vendors and customers. I couldn't help but get myself in a bit of a state over this latest development. It was just that bit more personal to me. Fretting over what kind of gruesome scenes that were in such a close range to where I sat. Feared for the fate of some people that I had classed as friends. Fuck? Even though I sat there, indoors, I feared for *myself.* Whether rational or not. When two horrific incidents take place within minutes of each other, and only yards from where you are, it would be hard *not* to fear for your own safety, because the most logical thought that you will be left with is, what's next?

For being just the one TV news network. The channel I had on now didn't even know which event to *cover.* Dancing from Centraal Station up to the two separate areas in de Pijp and back again on a loop, offering further updates from on site each time they came back to the respective reporter at the scene.

The news was also coming thick and fast on Twitter, only faster. And none of it was good. Absolutely nothing. I could barely look at the still smouldering wreckage of the tram, and the market? Those poor people. I felt like my heart had broken that morning. Like every emotion brought on by what I had seen had been too much for me. It only seemed to become more grim with each tweet that I scrolled through any time I refreshed the page. When the realities of things started to become known, and how many people it was looking like had died, across the three sites, I almost had myself a fully blown panic attack.

My heart started to beat so hard and fast that I swore I could hear it, even above the constant noise of police, ambulance and fire engine sirens. I was suddenly drenched in sweat, my hair felt soaked. The room was spinning and I was increasingly starting to feel that I wasn't really there, detached from real time. Yup, it was definitely a panic attack. I tried to think of the breathing techniques that Zico had taught me, for the times over the years when my PTSD - from Ibiza in Ninety Six - had got the better of me. But, this time, it barely worked. Then again, I'd never tried that deep slow inhaling and exhaling while the world was crumbing outside, either.

When it started to pass, I came off Twitter and called Zico. It not even reaching one ring before going straight to voicemail. Of course it did. The *one* time more than ever that I needed to hear his voice on the other end of a phone, and he wasn't there. Stopping to think about it, I wasn't sure but with the time difference between Netherlands and Mexico, and that Zico had been due to fly to Mexico City, there had been the chance that I was calling him while he was still in the air. I sent a short and barely sweet text to him,

'*CALL ME BACK ASAP*'

Seeing the message not go fully through as delivered, this alone made me sure that his phone wasn't in operation at that moment in time. My fingers felt as numb as my head as I started scrolling through the many messages that had now been sent my way, from both inside Amsterdam and back in Britain from family and friends. Everyone asking if I was okay. Some were sending news links, videos of the attacks spreading across the internet. I didn't even respond other than confirm that I was ok. What else really could I have said at that moment, when I was having a challenging time processing it all. All I could think was, What am *I* supposed to do now?

The Dutch authorities at least took some options out of the question by locking down de Pijp, which I suppose had been the smart thing to do when it had just suffered from two gruesome terrorist attacks. Because who knew if there was going to be *another* attack, and where.

I found myself curled up on the sofa, as if I was trying to protect myself from something. Hadn't even realised I was doing it until I found myself in that position when I came out of whatever trance I'd been in. The phone joined to my hand, fingers numb with the dreaded iPhone 'claw hand.' Outside, the sirens were endless, a constant reminder of what had just happened. I got up and looked out and could still see people running past the apartment, some tourists who clearly didn't know where to go by the looks, and locals who had probably lived here their whole lives, but now reduced to being just as confused and scared as the city's visitors.

According to the news, the lockdown was confirmed until mid afternoon and by then the authorities would make a decision on whether to extend this further. Which was fine, because I definitely wasn't fucking going anywhere while trams were exploding and nut jobs were mowing people down on purpose with vans. Well, I wasn't going anywhere in those early hours, following the attack. But at that time, I could've just as easily imagined me never leaving the house for days. But things escalated.

Unfortunately, in major crises like Amsterdam had suffered from that morning. Rumours then spread on social media and only made things worse for anyone in the city. The three attacks had been just sickening but to then hear things like another suicide bomber blowing up himself along with a bunch of visitors to Anne Frank's house, and a lone gunman go on a spree in the busy Rembrandtplein did not help one's already fragile mental health. Neither, I would find out later, had actually taken place but had not stopped the original tweets from being shared thousands of times over before being confirmed as hoaxes.

As the news anchor sat there talking to some counter terrorism expert, speculating who was likely responsible for the attacks - some group called Islamic State, who I had never heard of - the guest was of the opinion that these attacks may well have been the entry point into what would be a bigger operation, that may now see several major European cities hit and that, following Amsterdam it would not be a surprise to see cities like London and Paris raise their terror alert statuses.

Fuck, how I'd wished that Zico had been beside me, there in the flat. Just having him there would've been enough to keep me together. But, of course, on this day of days. Naturally, my man was thousands of miles away. And sitting there thinking of the distance between us, and how I *really* needed him. Once I had the thought of joining him, I couldn't shake it again. I'd quickly considered flying back to London to mum's but what would have been the point in flying from Amsterdam to a country where there would already be a degree of nervousness about it? You never, ever saw terrorist attacks in a country like Mexico, did you? Obviously, there was no gap in the market for terrorists there when it was full of psychotic drug cartels, all killing each other to try and confirm their dominance. No terrorists, though!

It really did serve to show just how badly impacted I had been by what had happened outside that I was even *considering* joining Zico, when I'd been given the opportunity to go with him and had replied with a hard *no*. Zico more than understanding of this, when it came to the summer we met and the kidnapping I'd had at the hands of those two Colombians. Funnily enough, since then I'd developed a little bit of an allergy, when it came to - and no offence to the millions of nice ones - Colombians, and Colombia as a country. It was a place that brought me too much bad memories and, where best I could, I just tried to forget that it was even a real place. And with two of his dates taking place inside this same country. It wasn't hard to see why I hadn't been too keen.

But things had changed and I was now in the middle of something *real*, not some insane fear of a country due to the actions of two people - out of over fifty *million* - who were born there.

I couldn't stay here in Amsterdam. Not after what I'd just seen taking place inside Centraal Station, even if the gunmen were now confirmed as shot dead. Not after the explosion a street away from our home that sent a tram flying off its tracks and *definitely* not after seeing the footage of the lifeless bodies lying in Jaansen's market, possibly even a familiar face underneath the cover for all I knew. It didn't matter that they said things would be 'safer' by the afternoon. My mind was scattered. While I knew the safest place would have been indoors, the actual idea of staying in this apartment, waiting for the next bomb, or gunmen rampage, or whatever was coming next in the city did not track with all of my gut instincts. I couldn't breathe here anymore. While a decent sized floor space that our flat boasted, it felt like I had been zipped up into a suitcase.

I had to get out. But couldn't. Well, not for a while, which had still to be confirmed.

And yet, getting out meant going straight into the heart of my worst fear in a frying pan fire scenario, only I felt that it was reversed as I was already *in* the fire, which was exactly why I needed to get out of it and into the relative calm of the frying pan. If I left for Mexico and joined Zico on tour, I'd be heading right into the storm. Colombia was on the horizon after Mexico. Medellin and then Bogota. The city that had sent those evil cartel sicarios to Ibiza. A city that still haunted me, even now, and even though I had never been there in my entire life. I felt paralysed, trapped between two nightmares. Stay in Amsterdam, where everything felt like it was crumbling to shit, or go to Latin America and come face to face with a city that I'd done perfectly fine in avoiding my entire life.

I felt sick and feared that I was feeling the beginning of another panic attack. My hand shaking as I started looking up flights and my other hand, holding my cigarette, had managed to flick ash all over myself through my less than steady hand. Mexico City. If I could just get there, I'd be with Zico. He *always* knew what to do. He'd calm me down, make me feel like everything was going to be okay, like he always did. That side of Stevie , one that no one else ever saw.

Looking up flights on the app, I could see that there were three direct from Schipol for that day. While I was still in an area of the city that was under police lockdown, choosing one of the late afternoon or early evening flights seemed a little on the optimistic side that I would've got there to the airport in time. The one am flight, though? That seemed like the best option, with speculation that the lockdown would be lifted late afternoon at the worst.

I was in the middle of being taken to the KLM website to confirm my ticket when Zico's face showed up on my phone calling. That photo of him from Creamfields, in his retro Dundee United shirt from the eighties and with the biggest grin on his face looking at the crowd with one hand on the mixer and the other ushering the crowd to 'come on.' It had always been one of my favourite photos of him and, somehow, even just seeing the picture in that moment gave me my first smile of the day. KLM ticket purchase aborted, I answered his call. He'd just landed and had read my message, once his phone had reconnected.

'What's up, you ok?'

he asked, urgently. I didn't know if he had meant this in connection with the attacks - which were surely world news by now - or off the back of the shortest of text messages I'd sent. It was the second of the two.

'Have you seen the news?'

I asked him and he told me that he hadn't seen anything as he'd been in the air and that out of the notifications that were on his phone, mine had been one of them so had looked at that first and then called. I took him through the events of the morning. He didn't seem to know just how to react to all of this, which was fine considering I'd been left the same way. He just kept repeating, asking me,

'you're ok, though, aye?'

I explained physically, yeah but mentally I was fucking ruined and was bricking myself about if there was anything else still to come.

'Well, look. I know this probably isn't what you want to hear but I don't like the thought of you stuck there on your own while no cunt knows what's going on in the city. I think you need to think about flying out here to join me. No fucking Islamic nutters here. Enough Mexican ones though, mind.'

It wasn't a time for joking but sometimes that's *exactly* what is required. It made me smile that *his* reaction on hearing what had happened was to ensure that I was safe, whatever that involved.

'Would you believe that I was right in the middle of buying a ticket on KLM when you phoned?'

I told him while hearing an email notification and, seeing the small preview, could read that it was from KLM who were at the 'you wanting this ticket or not, mate?' stage of proceedings. Had he not called when he did then I'd have already completed the transaction but still stopped to ask him if this was sound with him, telling him the time of the flight and when it would be approximately landing in Mexico City.

'Well, it would help me breathe a bit better if I knew you were here rather than that madhouse of Europe. Words I never thought I'd be saying from the moral high ground of Mexico, by the way,'

he confirmed that unless he'd got his timing wrong - saying that he'd not seen Lee for days so hadn't had him chipping away at him, when it came to appearance times and so on - by the time he'd finished his set at the festival he was playing he would be able to get a car to take him up to get me at the airport and then we could head back to the hotel.

The reception where he was now in at the airport was starting to get a bit sketchy and conversation was beginning to become a bit of a problem so I hung up and sent a quick text to tell him that I'd catch him later but was now away to buy the Mexico City flight and then start to pack.

He replied back that he'd be going to his bed, once he checked into his hotel, but would leave his phone off silent for me - something that he never done at night - in case I needed to get hold of him, that I was to be careful and, finally, that he loved me.

I went back and confirmed the flight, the website showing that there had been two seats left. Well make that one, I thought to myself and making my way through to the bedroom to pack, knowing that this hadn't exactly been a plan that I'd known about in advance, and that I would now need to get all my preparation done. And still the sirens outside continued.

Packing was a mechanical affair rather than my usual well planned out and methodical strategy. Normally, you'd have me packing while already *knowing* which outfits I was going to be wearing on every night I was away. This didn't feel like a holiday or excursion, it just felt like an escape. And I think the hurried choice of clothes I shoved into the case reflected that. I picked enough garms to do a couple of weeks and barely discriminated when it came to *what* I chose.

While, like every other Amsterdam resident, the day had been spent, largely, glued to the news for the round the clock coverage. I took it as a good sign when it started to reach the point where they were now no longer providing any 'new' news, and just the stuff they'd already reported on. The lockdown of de Pijp had now been lifted, this coming around 6pm.

The text, to tell me that my taxi for Schipol was outside, popped up on my phone just after half seven. I had timed things to perfection with regards to the flight I chose against the lockdown being lifted. Would never have normally left so early for a 1am flight but it didn't take a genius to deduct that Schipol was going to be a nightmare to get from arriving to your departure gate. I ran through to the bedroom and zipped up my suitcase and stood in the middle of our apartment, looking around one last time before leaving. The sirens outside were a lot quieter now and matched up to the lack of fresh news on the TV, but they were still there. A constant reminder of the broken city that I was leaving behind. I felt a pang of guilt as the driver took my case from me and popped it into his boot. Was I abandoning my city in its time of need? One of those moments in a city where its public are the ones who pick it back up from off of its knees. Where was my sense of community? In truth, though. I could barely help myself, what the fuck was I going to be able to offer the district that I lived in?

Fight or flight, they say, don't they? Yeah, I chose the flight option. And I never chose that lightly, either. Not, considering, *where* that option would take me. You *knew* things were bad when I was choosing the flight option. As we reached the outskirts on the way to hitting the motorway for the airport I hoped with everything that I had that the city wasn't going to see anything further, and the more hours that went by, without incident, the more hope that brought.

The actual *flight*, though? When boarding and finding my seat, I found - with me in the dreaded middle seat - there to be two absolute *hulks* of men sat in the window and aisle seat. Felt like a fucking dagger to the heart when it sunk in that I was going to have to spend twelve hours sandwiched in between the two of them. The one in the aisle seat, wearing this overly baggy muscle vest, was rank with BO. This I could already smell from standing and putting my bag into the overhead locker, I cringed at how much worse this was going to be when sat next to him. To be fair, the man in the window seat helped with this, by smelling *equally* as bad as the other man, which did assist in taking my mind off the man in the aisle seat.

Before taking off it appeared apparent that the two of them were *friends*. And had booked their fucking tickets specifically with a seat in between, so as not to inconvenience the other with how much of a battle would be going on for claiming part of the other's seat with their legs and body. Nah, why do that when you can leave some mug to, in all ignorance, choose a seat where they can *both* infringe on a part of their seat, while having a *conversation* back and forward with each other and not giving one single fuck about the person in the middle.

Had this scenario taken place on any other day, or any other flight, I would surely have instigated some kind of major incident which would have seen the plane landing someplace other than Mexico City, simply through the absolute piss that these two had taken, not to mention KLM who should've had the bottle to tell the two bastards that they would need to purchase two tickets each. But, you know? If the worst thing that was going to have happened to me that day had been an unfortunate seating position on a long distance flight, then I'd have happily snatched your hand off.

Instead, I was sat there - listening to the two of them speak about which was their favourite Phil Collins and or Genesis single - with those images from the three areas that were attacked running through my mind. My deep thoughts momentarily broken when the man by the window let absolute rip. This was no fart where there would be a finger of suspicion pointed at some. Not when you heard it *before* you caught a whiff. And, Jesus Christ, so bad was the smell that, due to our seat being near the back of the plane, I overheard some other passengers talking about how they thought the toilet was maybe broken and the prospect they now had sitting next to it for another eleven hours.

I popped my eye mask on, then ear plugs in and put my head back in the seat. Praying that the plugs would be enough to take the inane chat down a few notches and that if I was lucky enough I would slip into a sleep and help remove that montage of images, from the morning, that were running through my head.

Chapter 15

Si

Aye, you might be rock and roll but are you touching down at Mexico City airport in the middle of the afternoon and having a film crew, photographers and journalists ready to catch you leaving arrivals? Thank fuck I'd dressed for the occasion, as well. Even if after my limited time - so far - in Mexico I'd found it to be pretty much on track with America, as in your designer labels - and the ones you'd find popular in Europe - did not really carry much weight with the locals. Where you could wear a fifteen hundred pound jacket for all you liked and cunts wouldn't know it from a *fifty* dollar one.

Aye, at least I looked good, while, paradoxically looking very, *very* bad.

At first, I'd just thought that the film crew and other assorted media bods had been there as standard. Simply doing that thing where they catch celebrities when they're leaving or arriving at an international airport. I think even some airports actually *employ* one, purely for that reason.

Fucking Walter Samuel in a bad mood couldn't have wiped the smile from my face at that moment, seeing those photographers snapping away and journalists near on panelling each other to get a prime spot to shout out a question towards Marisol. Proper digging each other in the ribs and that, like. One look at Marisol's coupon, though, after a couple of cunts holding dictaphones had barked questions at her - which the photographers and cameraman continued snapping and filming away - told me straight away that there was *ride all* standard about this ambush. And simply through seeing her reaction to this frenzy wiped away what had been a short lived smile from my face. Fuck only knew what they'd been *saying* to her but the smiley and happy Marisol who had stepped off the plane with me was no longer walking beside me.

Looking at me with horror and tears beginning to form in her eyes as she reached out and grabbed my hand tightly, she stuck on her oversized looking Chanel sunglasses - no doubt to hide what was now showing - and turned back to the media scrum and just kept repeating the words

'Sin commentaries,'

until the poor cunt in the suit and hat, who had been standing next to the press pack holding the iPad with the name *M Bolivar* written in bold black letters across the screen waiting on us coming through arrivals, had managed to walk us to the car waiting outside.

Marisol holding onto my hand so tight I thought she was going to crush a few bones while we had press behind, to the side and in front of us, all continuing to compete with each other when it came to shouting over top of each question asked. Well I didn't have a fucking scoob what was going on, but going by Marisol's reaction, I wasn't daft enough to think that this was just all part of the job of being a celebrity.

Once the chauffeur had opened the door for us to get into the back of the car and closed it again after us. Now protected by the severely black tinted windows in the car, she just lost it. Fucking bawling her eyes out, so she was. Shades taken off again and resting on her lap, her make up was running down her face within seconds. It's never not awkward when someone you barely know starts crying their eyes out in front of you, but I did my best. Putting my arm around her and pulling her in closer to me while, naturally, asking just what the fuck was going on.

Since bumping into her at Ovidio's party, I'd barely seen her without that trademark smile on her face. Whatever the news she'd just been given, there, moments after stepping off the Guadalajara flight, it had been the kind that had put a bomb underneath her. As we'd rushed through the airport and into the car, I'd found myself trying to guess what it had been to upset her like this. Maybe someone close to her had died?

Maybe her show had been cancelled - although this had seemed a wee bit on the unlikely side, with how popular it had been in all of the Spanish speaking countries of Latin America. In truth, though. I wouldn't have been able to guess if you'd given me a a hundred attempts, with the aid of a clairvoyant.

Marisol, waited on us getting into the back of the car before sharing our bad news with me, because it was most definitely as well as unfortunately bad for the both of us. Picking up her phone, staring at the notifications on the screen and throwing it down on to the car seat without even opening the phone up to explore further. She then opened up, only in a different way.

'What's going on, Mary Doll? Talk to me, babe,'

I asked, using the pet name that I'd used the first time she'd introduced herself to me, even if it hadn't achieved 'pet name' status at that point. Me explaining to her that her name wasn't a million miles away from Rab C Nesbitt's other half. Through her tears and sniffling, she attempted to unveil what was behind the theatrics, inside the terminal.

'It's my cloud, it's been hacked and, and someone has leaked some personal stuff online.'

She eventually got herself together enough to answer me, breaking out in tears once again, simply through saying the words out loud. It was just a glimpse but I could've sworn that I'd clocked the driver's smirk reflected back from his interior mirror. Almost like he already *knew* exactly which 'material' had been leaked. Which was one up on me, like.

Now I know me and her barely even knew each other but things had been personal in the time that we had. So I wasn't just going to be saying to her oh don't worry about it and leave it at that. Obviously I was going to be wanting to know *what* personal stuff had been leaked online. Because you can't tell some cunt - while you're in a proper state - that you've had your shit hacked and put online, without expanding. As much as I was smitten with the girl, she'd have surely had her skeletons. Fuck, I certainly did. But you need to know *what's* going on before you can help some cunt, eh? And if it turned out that whatever had been leaked was something deemed too shady for me, then she'd have been getting dropped like a fucking stone. No room for sentiment in the game of love and war, like.

I'd already sussed out that it was something bad, simply by her reaction when she'd been ambushed by the press. But now I *definitely* knew it was something fucked up when I asked her what had been leaked. And found her a wee bit hesitant when it came to giving me an answer. Aye, maybe it was to do with being embarrassed and fuck all other than that but there was no point in holding out on me when I could've probably seen for myself inside the space of one minute, simply by typing her name into Twitter.

'What has been leaked, onto social media is some pictures and a video and ...'

Her phone started ringing and when she looked at the caller she apologised while telling me that this was a call that she had to take. Part of me thought, aye that's a bit convenient, getting a call right at the exact point when she was about to tell me the juice.

I sat there while she spoke in Spanish in what was a pretty animated conversation. Fuck, how fast did she speak during it, though? And in a raised voice, as well. And to fuck with who heard what. Clearly objecting to at least half of what the caller was saying due to all the head and index finger shakes that she was performing throughout it. Again, the driver - who, once more, had one up on me, this time due to understanding what Marisol was saying on her side of the conversation - seemed quite amused by things. Who knows? Maybe the boy was just happy in his job, but I doubt that.

With how into things she was on her phone call, I leaned forward to talk to the driver. First of all trying to establish if he could speak English at all. Figuring that if you have a gig picking cunts up at international airports then you'd maybe have a wee bit of English in your locker. When it was confirmed that he *did* speak English, I whispered to him if he could tell me what was going on, when it came to Marisol's phone call. The boy just shook his head and laughed at this and told me that while, aye, he *could* tell me. With how upset - as well as angry - Marisol was, not a fucking chance was he sticking his nose into things. Paraphrasing the cunt, like.

'Who was that?'

I asked her when she hung up, appearing to be swearing at the person on the other end of the phone as the call ended. No way was I changing the subject that was there before the call, but to ignore the fact that she'd taken this call and was now angry as opposed to the upset that she's been previously would've just made me out to be a bit of a heartless prick.

'My agent, Ricardo. He is such a pendejo at times,'

she answered, well hyped up by everything before I rowed things back to before the call, telling her to start at the beginning and then we could work our way forward from there.

She lowered her voice for the next part, so as to exclude the driver from this part, which was as good as a waste of time in my opinion. She picked her phone up again for a second and as she did this I clocked the screen from the side. I'd never seen shit like this on a phone in my life, the way the notifications were coming on screen. They weren't so much popping up, like any normal cunt's phone, as streaming from top to bottom. Like the fucking Matrix screen or something. The social media notifications appearing and then being replaced by the next one so quickly that it would've been impossible to even clock who it had come from. She sighed and put it down onto her lap again before dropping it on me.

Taking my hand With an outstretched thumb that was stroking the side of it and choosing the tone that she did in addition to her general body language, I got the weirdest of feelings that this was exactly like cunt's acted when they were about to give you bad news, news that was going to directly fuck my own shit up.

'Simon, the video and photographs that have been leaked online and are now trending on social media, it's .. it's .. it's of *us*, from Mazatlan.'

She looked at me as if she was bracing herself for me beginning to freak out, so would've been surprised when all she got back was a look of indifference. Me sat there, thinking about what pictures and videos anyone could've possibly posted online from the party that showed us in a bad light. But *then* it hit me. Shit, shit, fucking *shit*. I'd forgotten about back at Marisol's hotel, when we'd had ourselves a second party, that was several levels above the birthday party, when it came to debauchery.

Now I was having vague memories of us back there in the room, both of us having just taken a couple of huge lines each - we'd worked out a perfect kind of strategy that would see us have a line or two, then fuck it out of our system, then go again and repeat those two steps - and Marisol, and I cannot overstate that enough, *Marisol*, not me, because I know cunts would automatically be assuming it was me out of the two of us who'd suggested taking pictures and videos - saying that it would be fun to take some photos and videos, just for our eyes only. Saying how much of a turn on it was for her to watch herself on video. Hey, we all have our kinks, eh? The state of mind I was in at the time, there wasn't much I *wouldn't* have been up for with this Peruvian actress I'd left the party with so taking a few videos and pictures wasn't exactly walking on the wild side.

It's not like we shot a fucking porno or anything. Fuck, I can't believe that I'd even forgotten about us doing that. I'm sure we said we would lie in bed at some point and look through what we'd taken, but we never did and then after having a sleep and trying to take on board all that had happened the day before, and that I was waking up with this tidy as fuck TV star, I was already onto what was going to be happening the day ahead. Was more like thirty second clips *from* a porno, if I remembered correctly. One thing I couldn't remember was all of what we took, I only had the hazy recollection of her giving me a gam, with me directing and telling her what to do. I'm sure there was another one where she was riding me and me on my back and filming her and at one point her saying that I wouldn't believe the smile I had on my face - which I wouldn't have fucking doubted for a second - and reached to grab the phone and flipped it around to film me as she continued doing her thing. The pictures? Fuck knows, like. As much as I tried, I couldn't remember taking any of them, so maybe she'd taken some of me?

Jesus, man. If they've posted the one of her riding me then aye, that's proper fucked up, I was sat there thinking.

'Well, say *something,'*

Marisol, said, having gone through enough torture, waiting on my response.

'I'm not even sure what to say, babe. You know? It's not every day that I find myself at the centre of a celebrity sex scandal, ken?'

She just gave me a 'you for real?' look while saying that, funnily enough, neither was she and that, as much as I might've been freaking out - mad as it might've been, though. I wasn't freaking out as much as I should've been and maybe it still hadn't sunk in yet - right now then it was worse for her because, without disrespect, *she* was the celebrity in the celebrity sex scandal. Which was fair enough, to be honest.

Because that was the thing. I hadn't seen the video and pictures yet, so had no choice but to go on and assume the absolute fucking worst, while anything less would then feel like a win. But assuming that millions of people were going to see me having sex, it just so happened to be in a part of the world that very rarely aligned with Britain. So, and this was through no experience in such matters, from my back of a fag packet thinking, as bad as this all seemed to be, I might well have managed to get away with it without one single cunt back in Scotland ever knowing about it. Had I been riding some BBC presenter or something, though? Aye, proper fucked I'd be. My mum and dad, every cunt would see it. But, here, I had been caught on camera riding some famous TV star in Latin America … that not a single person in the United Kingdom will have heard of.

Was all a bit of a paradox because while I was caught up in this scandal that - if my guesswork turned out to be correct - no one back home would be none the wiser. But, and that's a *massive* fucking but, like, while on this tour of South America and that. If I was about to become famous - assuming my face was going to be seen in at least one of the three pieces that had been leaked - then for the duration of Zico's tour, cunts *would* know, and recognise me.

Don't get me incorrect, though. If I make out that I was sitting back chilled and laughing about it, I was not. I wasn't freaking out scared to even look at the content that was online through the sheer embarrassment of seeing what millions of people, men and woman, had all been looking at and commenting on. Some things you're maybe best not to know but at the same time for your own self preservation it's a case of maybe you *should* know. Whether they knew me or not, knowing that people had been looking at personal stuff involving me in a setting like that creeped me out. Ken? Like some old boy in say, Cordoba sitting having a wank to me and Marisol's video clip? Best not to think about things like that, though. For the old sanity, ken?

'What is it that's been leaked? I don't remember all of what we even *took*?'

I asked. Marisol replying that she had been too scared to look, since the media back at the airport had broke the news to her, although she'd admitted that when her phone had reconnected to a signal, when we landed in Mexico City, moments before we exited arrivals she had seen an abnormal amount of notifications popping up and was going to wait until we got to the car before looking at them all. And also, neither did she remember all of the content that we had captured from our night. I think one of the only pluses I could think of was that this had just been a 'sex' related leak, and there hadn't been any involving drugs. So at least that was something, because the way that we were lit that night, if we were taking videos, it wouldn't have surprised me if there was a video of me taking a line from off one of her erse cheeks. It was that kind of a night, well morning. And the thought of the outside world getting a window into what went on was almost enough to have me telling the driver to pull over so I could be sick.

I know it might sound a bit silly, but one thing I love when I land in a city that I've never been to before is the taxi ride from the airport to the hotel. Where you get a chance to see what's going on outside on the journey there. Sometimes it's boring as fuck, others you see all sorts. You roll the dice. You already knew that Mexico City would've been an interesting drive from A to B. But this time around, I never even got a chance to clock the outside of the car on the way to the hotel. Obviously, this 'topic' was the dominating factor. A topic that it was clear was going to completely take over the day. Hadn't been sure what the plans were for when we arrived and caught up with Zico again but I *definitely* didn't think it would be spent fighting fires over this fucking mental scandal I was now apparently caught up in.

The reason for how angry Marisol had become, during the call with her agent, had been because he - Ricardo - had said to her that these leaks could actually turn out to be a massive opportunity for Marisol and that if carefully played it would make her even more famous and loved by people in Latin America. He had seemed *happy* that it had happened, rather than be going out his nut because a client was in the process of tanking their career. He, apparently, had shown no sympathy and was already looking like he was going to use this to his advantage, when it came to getting the most of his client, and maximising his twenty percent into the bargain.

'Is he a good agent?'

I asked, trying to simplify things for a person like me not from that world. She said that he was and had helped her career grow since signing with him so I told her that if that was the case then, chances were, the boy maybe knew what he was talking about, even if he could've shown a bit of support to his client, who was obviously in a bit of a state.

Fucking hell, though. I'd been a few positions where it was a case of damage limitation but fuck all compared to that day. I told her that first of all, she needed to get some kind of a PR style response put online for everyone to see. The type that would help gain the public's sympathy, because at the end of the day, *she* was the victim here. Me too, obviously, but I wasn't worried about my career. Was maybe worried about cunts seeing my dick, or what my cum face looks like, but at least not my career.

I offered to help her construct it, advising to post it on her active socials and then disable the notifications on her phone and just let the next few days play out. Another thing I sat and advised in what was more like a fucking war room than the back of a car stuck in traffic trying to get us to our hotel. She'd have to report it to the police. Aye, what was done was done but you can't be going and trying to ruin people's lives like that and get away with it. Who knows, maybe the cunt that hacked her cloud left some bread crumbs behind them? Something you wouldn't know if you didn't at least have a wee deek, eh? Another mortifying experience that she would go on to have - at the hotel - when a couple of detectives came by to take her statement.

And *before* they arrived, though. That was when the two of us had to pull the trigger and face our fears by looking on Twitter to see *what* had been leaked. Because there's not much point in filing a report with the coppers if you don't give them the full information.

Jesus, man. We were all over the fucking place. So many Twitter accounts having pinched the content from the original tweet and passing it off as their own original content. Some had thousands of retweets, others - thankfully - barely any. Such was my strategy of assuming the worst, I was then not left disappointed when, aye, we were sitting on the hotel bed watching the video of Marisol grinding herself down onto me, my shaky camera work focusing on her, moving up until the camera was just focused on her, then back down again. I definitely wasn't going to be in with a shout for an academy award for 'best cameraman' come Oscars season. You could hear my voice, doing a wee bit of dirty talk, and that, before taking the camera back up again. That was when she snatched it off me and turned it around. Fucking *knew* that would be the video that got posted. Fuck's sake, like. How fucked up it is to be looking at yourself having sex, ON FUCKING TWITTER.

This is a new low, I thought to myself. That was until I clocked one of the pictures. Absolute fuck all memory of this but one of the pictures had me standing posing with each arm up flexing my muscles with this big stupid grin while down below I'm holding up a bathroom towel with my erection. Why did they have to do me bad like this, though? I wasn't the fucking celebrity, eh? The other picture was more bad for the pair of us as was of Marisol grabbing my dick, with her open mouth near it. It was content that I'd wanted to just pretend wasn't in existence but we'd been left with no choice but to see it and confirm that it was.

There was so much to unpack that day. Every time you thought that you'd covered every angle, something else would then pop into your head. Like her cloud. The fact it had been hacked had dominated things, but she hadn't even went into it, or thought to change the password on it. But I suppose by then, the horse had bolted and was well gone. What good would any of that be when the person who hacked in has already probably taken copies of all of the incriminating videos and pictures? And who's to say they wouldn't just hack into it again anyway, even with a new password. She went in all the same and I saw that we'd taken around a dozen pictures and half a dozen videos. I think under any other circumstance we'd have just lay there on the bed, got comfy and watched them, but not that day. Marisol's instinctive action to seeing them all in her photos on there was to delete every picture and video. I'd assumed the hacker would've already had copies but this was not something that she needed to hear. If she felt better in knowing that they had been deleted then why get in the way of that?

The statement that we crafted - in her name - was one that I'd told her would have to be the kind that appealed to your fellow human being, as in we all feel and suffer from the same emotions, no matter if you're a celebrity or if you are someone who lives in a favella.

Yesterday I suffered from an invasion of my privacy, and in the most personal of ways. My privacy that has now become the property of the public. Am I ashamed or embarrassed by what many of you have now seen? No I am not. Because I am human, like every one of you. What I AM is truly heartbroken over this violation I have suffered from, not as Marisol Bolivar the TV actress but as a regular person who deserves to live their life without being subjected to such intrusions. I pity the person responsible for what they did to me. I hope and pray for them that they manage to find something in their life that fills them with enough joy that stops them from being more interested in other peoples lives with intentions of causing pain and suffering. While my heart is broken today it will not stop me from living my life and being the Marisol that friends, family and fans have always known.

Love, M xx

She'd told me that for some incident like this, it's always clear that the celebrity had never even written it never mind post it online. Both jobs handed over to someone on their online admin team. Looking back at what we'd collaborated on writing down, she said that whatever Ricardo would've come up with - something that at this point he hadn't even thought of - it wouldn't have come close to what we'd ended up with.

Clearly it was too many characters for Twitter so she wrote it out on a note, took a screen shot and posted it to her socials with a cute short caption that said 'when you wish you hadn't got out of bed today.'

She did as told and switched off her social media notifications. I couldn't help but have a fly look on my own phone, when she popped to the bathroom. Saying that she'd cried so much her eyes were a mess and was going to fix them up. Her post with our statement had gone nuts. The retweets were in their thousands by then, loads of quote tweets. Of course, I couldn't *understand* any of what cunts were saying. I spied a lot of love hearts at the end of a comment - clicking on a few of the profiles they were from woman who looked normal and, not some creepy men, like I'd been on the look out for - so had to take that as a positive. Even if you can't understand the words on Twitter, the use of emojis normally at least let you know which angle the person is coming from. I was looking for some containing the laughter emoji, and there were some so I had to take them as some trolls latching onto something juicy to get trolled up about but there were more positive looking emojis in the comments than negative.

Obviously, there would've been thousands of tweets on there in connection with us, away from Marisol's tweet, but those were best not thought about. I'd already seen a tweet with my picture and it being from some Mexican entertainment account that looked like they were always tweeting some celebrity gossip. Because the tweet had just my picture, I went to the trouble of copying the Spanish and translating it online.

Marisol Bolivar's new man, and he's Scottish! See what's under his kilt.

The link below providing the gateway to what I'd already seen enough and didn't care for any more repeats. Fucking hell, again. The butt of some tired worldwide held fascination for what a Scotsman has under his kilt, as if being born in Scotland makes a male genetically different to any other male. It's our fucking *cock and balls* that's under our kilts. Just get past it. Aye, though. Back in the car, I was all chill about it but was now seeing what it was like when the machine got turned on and then couldn't be turned off again, while it gathered and gathered pace.

Marisol ended up saying that she wanted to de-stress so was going to take a bath. She asked me if I wanted to share it with her but, to be honest, the only way I'm going to lie in a bath with someone is if there's going to be sex either during or after it, and sex was never happening that afternoon, so I told her that after the shock of everything, I thought she should have a nice long deep bath all to herself, with no one taking up space. I picked up the complimentary bottle of bubble bath from the side of the bath and poured half of it into the water and shook it up enough to have bubbles all over. Saying that I was going down to Zico's room and that I'd probably be back before the bubbles were gone.

Zico's coupon when he let me in and I came right out with it. To fuck with any pleasantries and how was the flight or how's the hotel been, mate?

'You will *not* fucking believe what I've got myself roped into since I saw you yesterday, Zeek.'

'I forget, refresh my memory. Wasn't it just yesterday, actually round about exactly twenty four hours ago right now, that we were in that smoking club, and the unpleasantness that followed. How the fuck have you managed to get roped into anything other than staying in your hotel room last night and then coming to the airport today for your flight?'

'Well, first of all, it's not even my fault. I'm a victim in all of this, here,'

I said, sounding *totally* like someone who was guilty and already trying to get ahead of things with their first lie. Zico, understandably, gave me a raised eyebrow that would've given Roger Moore a run for his money.

'No, honestly.'

Which is what cunts *always* say, when they're not being honest. The boy believed me though when I told him the whole story, minus showing him the evidence on Twitter, as you'd normally do when telling your mate a story, that was linked with the social media platform. I didn't want to show him any of it and he didn't need to, or *want* to, to cover all angles. Knowing that this would not be something that I would make up - make up? You couldn't fucking *dream* it up - he just shook his head while not bothering to hide the wee smile he had on his face. Roles reversed? I'd have been the exact same with him.

'You were always building up to being part of a sex scandal, mate. Congrats for finally achieving it,'

He said, patting me on the shoulder.

'Now, mind, Zeek. That intel is like level fucking *five*, which means you're the only cunt with a high enough clearance to ever hear about it. So if anyone, from the west, knows about it then I'll have no choice but to assume that *you've* fucking told them.'

He said something about how I already knew he'd keep his mouth shut but that wasn't I worried about the millions of people in Latin America who *would* see me.

'Aye, mate. Very fucking much so. But what can you do? A good scenario would be to find out *who* leaked our stuff, and knock the absolute fuck out of them. But for now, I'm just going to do what I've always done, mate. Doesn't matter if it's being outnumbered five to one at a train station or having millions of people looking and talking about you. You just stick out your chest and get your head up. Marisol's well in a tailspin but I'm working on her. She'll get there. You have to remember, this is a proper catholic set of countries so I'm not sure if that makes things worse for her.'

'Bit of a nightmare to get into with someone you only met a few days ago, eh? I'd ask what the fuck were you doing taking photos and videos with someone the first night that you met them but then again, this was *you* operating on a day and night without ever having to stuck your hand in your pocket to pay for any drink or drugs. Plus, I saw you, fleetingly, at the birthday party. And you looked like you were loving life, so I'm sure that continued after you left.'

Saying that I better get back up and - with a bit of gallows humour, which always gets you through - make sure that she hadn't slit her wrists in the bath. Zeek asked if we were still going to El Dia de la Danza festival. Me telling him one hundred percent I would but that I was going to have a major task in talking Marisol around to go out in public the same day people had been watching her having sex, but that I'd manage it. We arranged to have a few drinks downstairs before getting the car to the festival site and I headed back up to our hotel room.

Before leaving, Zico gave me *his* news, about Flo. Fucking hell, what a twenty four hours we'd all had, collectively. I'd been so wrapped up in things with my own shit to worry about such trivial things like what was going on in the world. While Zico had level five clearance, I was also not naive enough to know that his level five access pretty much meant that Flo had access to it, but that stuff's a bit of a given with someone and their wife, of they've got a trusting relationship. Fuck knows what she was going to be thinking, flying in from a city under attack and finding me internet famous in Latin America, for all the worst reasons.

Marisol wasn't long out of the bath and was still wrapped up in a towel when I came back. Once again, under any other circumstances - in terms of how we'd been together since this 'thing' had started between us, the towel would've been on the floor before the lock in the hotel room door would've been activated but, instead, I walked up to her, gently grabbed each side of her face and held her there and gave her a wee kiss and told her that it would all be fine, and that in a few days everyone would be taking about someone else.

I steered things in the direction of us going to the festival that night and got a categorical no, but still managed to persuade her otherwise. I swear, I could be a fucking life coach, the way I can provide confidence to someone and turn their whole thought process around. I admitted that, aye, even though I wasn't the celebrity out of the two of us, that hadn't stopped all of those people from seeing me all the same, so I would be recognised at the festival, even if not as much as her. Admitted that the easiest thing to do would have been for us to just stay there in the hotel room but then what? Do we travel to Medellin next and stay in *that* hotel room?

'We're the victims in this, babe and we need to remember that,'

I said to her while giving her my opinion of what a proper 'get it right up you' to the hacker and those who've trolled us over that day if we were to choose to go out in public and be seen having a good time, rather than be forced to hide away from the world.

'If we do that then *they* win. And I can't have that.'

There was no fucking way on earth that she was going to be able to resist this impassioned plea.

I pulled out my phone and - took a chance by trusting the emojis in the comments - showed her the responses to her statement, and all the love and support that he fans appeared to be showing her.

'If we're seen out at the festival tonight, showing two people with no fucks given. *We* win.'

I'd seen her face change as I'd gone through all of my reasons for us to go out and stick two fingers up at any of the haters, and by the time I'd finished she was nodding her head and saying,

'Si, Simon. Let us fuck them all,'

It was a wee bit of an unfortunate turn of translation but I got what she was saying. I don't think I'd ever carefully deliberated on what to wear that night, with the novel feeling of already knowing that a lot of people would be looking my way. Deluded, I chose a nice sky blue Stone Island shirt, thinking that while wearing something like this in this part of the world meant absolutely fuck all it *might* give me the opportunity of being in with a shout with some free gear if I could be 'papped' while wearing their gear. Aye, as if they'd want to be associated with the boy from the leaked sex clips as well? Marisol looked ridiculous, as always. Tidy wee matching top and hot pants set up with some corked heels which my initial thought had been who wears footwear like that to a festival before remembering that I wasn't in fucking Britain.

We met up with Zico downstairs, already sitting with a beer and his record box, something that over the years had become a *whole* lot smaller than it used to be. The fact that a lot of his music was on a fucking flash drive was something that, still, fried my brain. By the looks of things he was onto his third beer so either had been suffering from some pre gig nerves or was just thirsty. He wasn't one for nerves, to be fair, and even if he'd had any over the years, that had always been remedied. There had been, of course, that one sorry incident, when I gave him ketamine which I'd thought was cocaine, on his first appearance at Amnesia, which we were eventually able to laugh about even if it hadn't exactly been overnight.

He got up and gave Marisol the obligatory air kiss on either side, which he'd had the impression he had to do anytime he saw her because so many people had done that with him at the party and he'd carried it on from there. When she sat down and he'd got us both drinks he wasted no time in addressing the elephant in the room. Marisol already with a bit of a complex, even just from sitting outdoors at a hotel.

'I just want to say, Marisol, that I'm so sorry for what happened to you but just wanted you to know that I haven't looked at the video and pictures and never will. This isn't like some 'boy's club' stuff with pals. Trust me, the *last* thing I want to see is my best friends penis. Some things you see, can never be erased.'

To try and inject a wee bit of lightness to this moment, although I could see that she appreciated what he'd said to her, I stood up at the table and unzipped the zip of my shorts and pretended to get my cock out. Marisol theatrically screaming 'nooooo' while reaching over and putting her hand over my unzipped crotch.

Right as I was standing there, the two from the music magazine appeared, turning the corner looking to find Zico and join him. What a sight to turn around and find, though. Because it must've looked like I really *was* in the process of whipping the fucking thing out.

'Alright, lads. You're just in time to see Simon, here, getting his cock out. Ok, Luke. Cameras ready prepare to flash, ya cunt.'

The two of them just seemed to shake their heads, laughing. That Myles with a look about him that suggested 'here we go again.' And he wasn't that far away, if that had been the case. Due to the world that they were in, they hadn't come across anything involving me or Marisol, so we would, obviously, keep that to ourselves. Marisol not even on their radar. They were there to cover Zico, and his tour. Why would any readers want to know about the deejays mate?

As we sat waiting on the car arriving. Marisol sat and looked at me and Zico had said that we were some pair, when together and that in whatever shape or form, things hadn't been dull since she'd met me.

'I've known this boy here since nineteen ninety, the stories that we could tell you. *Plus,* we're just coming to the end of the first country on the list. Still got Colombia, Argentina, Peru and Brazil to come, if you can go the distance that is?'

I teased Marisol. Noticing that Zico's attention had been diverted by the cameraman, Marisol replied back to me In the most sexiest of fucking ways while sporting her first proper grin of the day

'You know *exactly* how much distance I can go, don't you?'

She confirmed what, by then I'd already assumed, that she would see for herself when she tagged along in Colombia. Zico telling her that by the end of the night she would have some female company, with his other half flying over from Amsterdam. Me telling her that Flo and her would get on like a house on fire, while leaving out the part where Flo would be potentially arriving as damaged goods and bearing the mental scars that can sometimes come from terrorist attacks, *especially* when fucking *trams* are blowing up around your pad. She was coming to be with the right people, though. And who knows? Maybe being around talk of narco birthday parties and leaked sex content involving me and someone famous it might've been enough to take her mind off the atrocities that Zico had told me that had taken place in the city that I lived in. My flat, having moved to the Jordaan district, was nowhere near any of the attacks but that wasn't really the point. When you feel like you belong somewhere then you feel it when harm comes to it. But, without being selfish here, the fact that I was all over Latin America social media felt more impacting than the terrorist attacks had been. Marisol seemed pleased to hear that there was going to be company that would be the same sex as her. Because tagging along with me and Zico for the best part of three weeks might've been a bit much for her. Being in *each other's* company for any extensive amount of time can be a bit much for me and him at times, so any bystander tethered to us would've been caught in the crossfire, eventually. That was something I'd also predicted to Zico would happen to Myles and Luke. Their mental states by the end of the tour was going to be shot to pieces, as would the rest of us.

When Marisol popped to the bathroom, Zico had a private word by saying to me that I must've been doing something right for her to not have ditched my radge erse by Guadaljara at the most but fair play to me, she was a cracking girl. Which she undoubtedly was. In fact, if I was to wind up as part of a viral sex scandal then I couldn't think of a better partner to go through it with.

We had time for one more quick drink while Zico sat, quite hyped, speculating about how good this festival was going to be to play, and that the A.N.T.S tent that he was playing was going to be a bit special. This was going to be the one and only 'big' appearance on his tour, which had been slotted in when Lee had been given the call that they'd requested Zico as part of their curated tent at the much bigger festival. Talking of Lee, where the fuck *was* he? It went out of my head before asking Zeek but unless I'd just kept missing him then I hadn't seen his agent since we'd left the club in Guadalajara. Maybe the way he'd started off life in Mexico had been something that could not continue, and the place had eaten him up? I'd still not seen him since I'd saw what he'd done upstairs in one of the bedrooms at the party, when he was standing wanking in front of a picture. He was definitely hearing about that, whenever I actually saw him again. Because while I forgot a lot of that night - including which videos had been taken back at the hotel - *that* was not one of things. I only hoped that I would remember all of it, even if it wasn't really the kind of memory that you'd have chosen to retain, normally. With the way the tour had been since minute one though I don't think *any* of our minds were in the most mint of conditions though so simple things like remembering things from one minute to the other were not as simple as they'd be in regular life. The one where you *do not* take class a drugs - and lots of them - every day without any pause.

Mind you, though. I'd rather than he wasn't around, than being around, for me to have a few digs at him while asking just what the fuck he'd been up to when I'd burst in on him, because that shit wasn't normal. Where's the justice, though? Fucking me and Marisol end up trending on Twitter with what we were up to when social media would've fucking *melted down* if it had been given access to Lee, and what he was up to that same night. At least ours was fucking normal and in no way weird and questionable. Ok, maybe the erection and towel thing was semi weird, I'll admit that.

Just like back in Guadalajara, Zico had been given access to whichever drugs he requested, so would take care of me and Marisol, when it came to some mandy when reaching the backstage area of the festival. Because if there was one night where two people would want, fuck, *need* to just have a wee dab of those dirty looking crystals and forget the madness of what the day had provided, then this night would be it.

The driver arrived, walking over to the tables by the pool - most of them now full with people sat drinking - looking unsure of himself and us clocking him before he'd clocked us. Zico telling him we'd be out in a minute as he downed the last of his beer.

Dead paranoid about going out - despite my self assured exterior - in public, to somewhere that wasn't exactly going to be filled with a few hundred people, I trusted in the process. Which was that enough MDMA would leave me without any fucks to give out, when it came to anyone looking our way. Fuck, I'd already started to get used to people looking our way, *anyway.* So not much would be different, there. Obviously, you couldn't stop the thought process that involved you knowing that *they've* seen you fucking someone. But once again, that's where the mandy comes in.

'Mon then, Mizz Bolivar. Let's go and face our public,'

I said to Marisol as I took her hand - while there were a few murmurs going on around all of the surrounding tables, a few people taking a picture of us - in a show of that it wasn't just her going through this, and that it was the two of us, and that we'd get each other through it. It had been one of the, actually *the* most, surreal days of my life, and I'd had a few of them, like, and yet I still couldn't fully comprehend what something like that must be for a celebrity, when it happens to them.

As we walked towards the car, Myles and Luke were beside us, and then Zico rushing to catch us up, having quickly popped to the toilet before leaving. Must've looked like a shit remake of Reservoir Dogs, all of us walking to the car.

We all had work to do, to be fair. Zico? His, obvious. Same with the journalist and photographer out of our quartet who set off for the festival site. Me and Mary Doll, though? Ours was a lot more of a 'recreational' nature, but yet, one with more commitment than any of the other three put together. *Our remit was to* take *loads* of fucking crystals, dance until the sun came up, and show any of the watching Mexicans, and general media that picked up on the fresh Marisol Bolivar tweets coming out of the festival, - complete with man from the video, - that we'd had a fucking shitload of, well, shite, come our way *all* of that day, and yet by night we were out dancing and joined to each other in that sensual MDMA way you find yourself with your partner, when you're both out and *on it*.

Aye, what had been, initially, planned as nothing other than another night out on the tour was now a case of proving a point and saying a massive 'get it fucking right up you' to anyone that needed it said their way. Nothing screams 'I don't give a fuck' more than being photographed at five in the morning, shades on, dancing with a TV actress at a festival, and the same woman that half of Latin America has been looking at the two of you having sex in a Sinaloa hotel room all day long.

Marisol would go on to find out that she would have a one hundred percent ratio of anyone who spoke to her over the night giving her unwavering and complete support while some of the more cocky and confident of other girls who spoke to her would chance by telling her how hot she looked in the pictures and video. This delivered in a way that fell on the right side of appropriate with Marisol. The amount of Mexican men who, out of earshot of Marisol, while she was busy talking to someone else, through broken English - because they already fucking knew, because of me talking in the video - pretty much patting me on the back and saying shit like, and paraphrasing,

'go on my son,'

but, like with the girls talking to Marisol, I wasn't daft enough to not know that honest words spoken during an MDMA or pills session can be greatly exaggerated. You could literally meet someone you hate, but while rolling on MDMA, and have a cordial conversation with them. But, anyway. It was nice to feel 'accepted' on the night, because had there been any negative stuff in our direction, like cunts laughing at us or anything, then I'd been of no doubt that Marisol would've been for heading straight back to the hotel, regardless of how close it had been to when we'd arrived. She was understandably fragile, not unlike myself. But once those crystals hit, the pair of us managed to make an almost superhero transformation.

I never thought that when I woke up that morning by the end of the day I would be engaging in some kind of an accidental public relations exercise. I'd have asked you what a public relations exercise even involved and why *I'd* be a part of one. And as far as our 'work' task, we *more* than pulled it off.

And probably worked harder than Zico, Myles or Luke while we did so.

Chapter 16

Zico

El Dia de la Danza? What. A. Fucking. *Gaff*. What a set up, and what a night. Sometimes I shake my head and wonder just how the fuck I managed to get myself into the kind of a position where I get fucking *paid* to do this for a living. Over the years I had played at some two bob festivals that had clearly been put on by a bunch of charlatans but had also seen things from the *opposite* end of the spectrum, where no expense had been spared, when it came to the sheer scale of the show that was being put on, and El Dia de la Danza most definitely fell towards the latter side of things. I don't think I ever did find out how many tents and main stages there'd actually been, dotted around the place. With the time I spent there - mixing business with pleasure - it would not have been technically possible to have seen the whole site.

When we'd arrived I headed for the A.N.T.S tent, just so I could dump my stuff that would be needed when it was time for my set, which wouldn't be for a while yet and would allow me time for having a look around the place. The tent I was playing in looked incredible from the inside. That massive fucking ant which was clinging to the roof of the tent, which stretched almost the whole length of the enclosed above? One look at that and you already knew that there would be several cunts in the crowd over the night who may have had their struggles with such an insect above their head, being lit up in all kinds of colours from the lighting system. Could think of *many* other things that I'd have preferred to see above me when I was out of my nut than that fucking thing, as undoubtedly cool as it was.

While briefly backstage, the DJ who was currently playing for the crowd noticed me storing my record box and gave me a smile, nod and then pulled me in for a quick friendly hug and a few raised words back and forward with each other. It was the Dutch DJ, Ferry van't Schip and an absolute diamond of a boy from Rotterdam who I'd been on the same bill as many a time over the years and - due to us living in relative close proximity to each other - had enjoyed a few drinks together when one was in the other's city.

'Eating out the palm of your fucking hand, Ferry, lad,'

I said to him as I looked out across the thousands that had packed the tent out and by the amounts of moving that you could see the crowd doing, appeared to be receptive to the tracks he'd been hitting them with.

'As always, my brother,'

he replied in his typical arrogant sounding way that, when you got to know him, wasn't actually him being arrogant at all and, in fact, was just being Dutch. Not wanting to get in the way of his work, we left it at that. Just a few words while saying to each other that we'd catch up properly, once I'd had my set. Something that we wouldn't end up doing but when you're playing something as large scale as a festival like that you can make all the plans in the world that you'd like but that doesn't necessarily mean that you'll actually *achieve* them.

There was another DJ - Englishman, Mikey P, owner of the Palm Tree record label - sandwiched in between Ferry and myself so with a bit of free time on my hands I chose to have a look around the gaff. A lot of the times, I'd have probably just chilled backstage, talking with a few people and doing a bit of socialising, until it was time for my set but with there no guarantees that I'd ever be at this festival again - with my booking only being a last minute one, which had shown that my name hadn't exactly been at the forefront of the organiser's minds, when planning their event - I fancied taking a wee look around.

Walking around the site, I couldn't help but be impressed by the sheer scale of everything. This festival was fucking massive and on a level that I hadn't considered when booked to play, and the energy all around was infectious. It was impressive how well it all ran. I've played at some dodgy setups before, but El Dia de la Danza had the same polish and professionalism I'd seen in your more top-tier events across Europe and the States. But what made it special, as it had appeared while I walked around, was the people. There was just something about the Mexican crowd, like they reminded me of what crowds were like back in the U.K at the start of the nineties. Most people back home wouldn't have ever entertained the thought that Mexican's could have all been like this in the one place, because most of the time Mexicans were too busy killing each other to party collectively in such a way, that's what we're always told, right? But these cunts knew how to have a proper party, no fucking doubt. The vibe that they were bringing, and in whichever tent you chose to pop your head into, almost made me want to sack off my appearance, get a couple of ectos down me and just join them for the rest of the night.

Not that I'd ever thought that it had ever been required in a festival, because cunts were there to dance, not go on the waltzers or winning a fucking goldfish in a ring toss game, the actual fairground section of the site would've put Alton fucking Towers to shame. I mean, there was a fucking *rollercoaster* that had been constructed, for context. As I walked through the fairground, on my way to check out another tent, I got a text from Santiago - one of the Colombians that I'd got talking to at Ovidio's birthday and who we'd arrange to catch up when I got to Bogota for my tour date - telling me that he'd been listening to a few of my sets on Soundcloud, following my all night set in Sinaloa and was hyped for the Bogota leg of the tour. This part of the text, while I was of no doubt being true, only appeared to be the entry point into the *real* reason that he was messaging me. The text explaining that one of Santiago's mates - Freddy - had travelled from Bogota to Mexico City for the festival and Santiago had told him that he needed to go and see me play, which he said he would. What Santi was asking me in the text was if I would play a specific tune in my set, for Freddy. His favourite song, apparently. Armand van Helden's 'You Don't Know Me.' A fucking barry tune and an undoubted classic. But not one that had been part of my planned set and, actually, one that I couldn't even remember when I'd last played out. It *was* about fifteen years old, though, to be fair and I think that by this point in time the *only* cunt that you were ever likely to hear it being played on the regular would've been if you were seeing van Helden himself.

Asking a DJ to play a specific song, as part of their set? Big fucking no no, as far as my take on that was. I wasn't a fucking jukebox that you could just stick a sheriff's badge into and select what you wanted to hear, eh? Generally, someone asking me to play a tune, which would more often come *during* a set, did not produce a favourable response from me. But, there's always an exception to the rule, always. And with Santiago having been quite a sound and likeable boy, he *also* had been someone who was responsible for being in control of a part of Bogota, and I knew that you didn't get to do something like that without being a bit of a boy, or someone with heavy connects to call on. I felt that with Colombia still to come, why risk any avoidable issues with anyone? So diplomatically, I told Santi I'd include it for his man Freddy, and to tell him that that I'd be playing it just for him.

Santiago texting back his appreciation of this and reminding me that when I reached Bogota, him and Jhonny were going to be treating me like I was a head of state visiting the city, and wishing me well for my set that night. With this taken care of, I started walking again, trying to get through the fairground. As I was navigating through the series of rides and food vans - Food vans, another thing that had never made sense to me, inside a house music gathering kind of setting. Having a taco in the middle of the night at a festival, a concept that I would not have managed to get my head around so would not even bother. - when I saw this poor soul, clearly having went too early with whatever drugs they'd been taking that night, which couldn't have been good for them, when the festival didn't end until six in the morning.

He was walking, with no real strategy to it, sometimes walking directly to the left, other times in the figure of eight, head permanently staring down at the ground as he paced around. Due to the fucked up multi directional way he was walking, despite lots of moving, he didn't ever really get anywhere, in terms of leaving the area that he'd found himself in.

I felt a bit sorry for the boy, because we've all been in some funny states in our time, so went over to see if I could help him out. Sometimes, it just takes a word or two, even from a stranger, to set someone back on the straight and narrow. Well, with this boy, maybe not so much the straight part, but my sentiment still stands.

'Needing some help there, pal?'

I asked, instinctively, forgetting that I wasn't in an English speaking country so this, straight away, might've been wasted on him. He looked up for a second and stared straight at me for a second with a proper distant look on his coupon before fixing his stare right back to the ground again, while telling me - in that cockney accent - that he needed to find his passport as the people at the desk weren't going to let him board his flight. As I'd experienced time and time again over the years, this planet of ours is pretty fucking small. Doing nothing but minding my own business having a wee pre set stroll around a festival thousands of miles from Europe, I'd bumped into one of my oldest mates from the House Music scene, Perry Stokes. Although going by the fucking nick of the boy, there was a high chance that, out of the two of us, I was the only one who even knew who he was, right there. Because when you're at a festival, and think that you're in an airport departure lounge, waiting to board a plane? That can never be considered as a sign of things going all swimmingly for someone.

Me and Stokesy had known each other for over ten years. Friends for life following that first time we played on the same bill in London at Fabric. The two of us ending up at an afters that took around forty eight hours to come to an end. Missed a fucking flight to Lisbon because of that cunt, Stokesy, that particular time. Anytime we were in the same city we'd hook up and go out. Thankfully, such is the unpredictable life of a DJ, those occasions were few and far between, for our collective sanity. Playing at the same nights with the boy was always nothing less than a joy. The following that he had and the energy they would show, something that would have the deejays feeding off of.

He hadn't recognised me, another signal for how wrecked he was. Due to the scale of the festival, and how many differently curated tents there were, I didn't even know that Perry was playing. I grabbed hold of his arm and tried to slow him down from this obsession he had, looking for his passport.

'It's Zico, Perry, mate. DJ Selecao. You know me, ya mad bastard, we've literally played at the same event twenty times together, some of them back to back, and by the way, you're not in a fucking airport!'

He seemed to twig, looking back up from the floor again and to me. Reacting like he'd just thought of something.

'Fuck's sake, mate. I think I might've had a little bit of a moment there. I'm *not* at the airport, am I?'

No, alright Zico, how you doing, pal? What's the chances of you and me bumping into each other in this part of the world? Of all the people to see I see you? Fucking nada in the way of those usual kind of things you'll find yourself saying to someone in such a scenario. But there was *fuck all* usual about Perry, that night. Just because he'd had the revelation that he wasn't about to board a plane, that did not mean that the boy was suddenly all good again. He'd done too much, way too much, ketamine. The signs were clear on that. It was hard to have a conversation with him. Sometimes you would get some sense out of him, other times he'd say something that was completely unrelated to what any of us had been talking about.

Asking him how his set had gone down, while saying the crowd had looked well up for things, he replied by asking me if he was meant to be playing? The first mistake that I'd made had been to see the state that he was in, and make the assumption that this was *post* gig. And now he's asking *me* if he's scheduled to play?

'Well, I'm assuming that you haven't flown over from London because you had a spare date in your diary so fancied going to a Mexican festival, eh?'

I joked with him while fishing out the festival itinerary I'd been given when I arrived, along with my laminated 'DJs and performers access' pass. The itinerary which had given you a map of the site and all of the set times for each specific tent. Having to move us nearer to one of the rides for me to be able to read the tiny print on the sheet of paper. Scanning the page looking for Perry's name. I eventually found it. Soon as I saw it, I immediately looked at my watch.

'Perry, you're on in twenty minutes, you absolute fucking maniac.'

I broke the news to him while already safe in the knowledge that the boy wasn't playing *any* fucking set in twenty minutes time. Truth be told, had I not stumbled across him, his set time would've come and gone and he'd have probably been *still* there looking for his passport.

Now I didn't need to do what I went on to do for the boy, and in this ego centric business that I was part of there were hundreds who *wouldn't* have, but knowing that he was in a bad spot, and was going to miss his set, not get paid and disappoint anyone who'd been excited to see him, I knew that I still had time before my set was due to start. So, looking at the site map and working out where his tent was situated, I took him by the arm - second time in two days where I'd have been seen walking with linked arms with another man. Cunts would be starting to talk, eh? - and led him off towards the tent.

Agreeing for him to spring a *surprise* on the crowd by announcing a B2B set with me, which we had done on many an occasion when playing the same club. His appearance behind the decks, purely for a cosmetic factor, because he sure as fuck wasn't doing any deejaying. Knowing the state he was in, I figured that at least an hour into his set or so he'd maybe have found himself in a bit better condition, and that I could duck out and leave him to it. There standing taking all of the applause while probably barely even able to remember getting behind the decks at the start of his set. For that first hour, though? I just told him to stand there and pretend to move and twist various non impacting knobs on the fader and give off the impression that he was looking tracks up on his MacBook. I have absolutely no idea what set he'd planned to play for the crowd that night, but they seemed to lap up the one that I chose for them. Leaving things with *Crack House* by Kevin Andrews and Jason Chance and the crowd cheering when they heard the beat kick in, I whispered to Perry - who was now beginning to resemble something close to his old self - that he was on his own for the rest of the set, and that he was now due me one *massive* favour.

'You fucking saved my life you beautiful jock cunt,'

he smiled and grabbed both sides of my face and kissed me on the forehead, some random photographer creeping in from the side and capturing this. Telling me that he'd give me a call tomorrow, wishing me a good set over in my tent and then he put his game face on and turned round to the decks again to have a bash at at least earning his performance fee for the night.

On my way towards the A.N.T.S tent, walking through the scores of festival goers, excited and chattering away in that enthusiastic way that only class a drugs can bring, I was passing what was only one of the two main stages to the site. Near to the side of it I was barely paying attention of what was going on up on the stage when I heard the familiar Scandinavian tones of two friends who I had not seen in years.

'We've been Lucas and Hugo from the Swedish Party Collective and you have been fuuuuuccccckkkkking awesome. Thank you for dancing with us. We love you Mexico City.'

I smiled as I thought of the first time I'd met Lucas and Hugo, back at that festival on the outskirts of Amsterdam, in that disused prison, and the calamitous night that followed, when the three of us got back to the city centre, following the festival end. The night where we ended up in what was pretty much a whore house. Some boys, them, like. I still had enough time so, hearing them saying thank you at the end of their set, decided to pop up backstage to say a quick hello to the both of them. I think it had maybe been Ibiza I'd last seen the two of them, maybe ten years tops. So who knew when I might seen them again. Of course, things like them splitting up for over five years before getting back again didn't help.

Flashing my pass to the hulk of a security man blocking the door for backstage, I passed him and made straight for Lucas and Hugo, who were standing for a few photos from the press. Hugo noticing me mid photographs and pointing over to me with a big smile on his face while nudging Lucas. This annoying some of the photographers who had been shouting for them to look towards the camera. Once they were done they both came over to me for a series of hugs. Hugo asking me if I'd been watching their set and me telling them that, no, and, actually, I'd just had to perform a set on behalf of another DJ who'd found themselves a little under the weather.

'Away to do my set in the A.N.T.S tent now, lads. Fire over if you've got time,'

I said but, in reality, knew the demand that the two of them would be in, now that their set was over. Such was the level of stardom that the pair enjoyed. It had felt like a death in the family to a lot of people when the two of them split to do their own thing so you can well have imagined how much publicity - and money generated through gigs - their reformation had received.

'Hey, it's a *sign* that we're all here in Mexico City at once. You should come out with Lucas and I, after the festival. We know a place.'

Hugo said, with a bit of cheek behind his grin.

I just laughed back at this suggestion, telling Hugo that I *knew* the kind of places that they'd end up in, and that my other half was literally in the air right this minute, flying into Mexico City to join up with me on my tour so in the interests of *staying* with my woman of eighteen years, maybe, just maybe I should probably decline his invitation. We were saying our goodbyes almost as quickly as the hellos that had been shared with each other but it had been brilliant to see those two lunatics, even if it had only been for a few minutes. Such was the life.

Eventually, I made my way back to the A.N.T.S tent with my set due to begin in around ten minutes so I really needed to be getting myself up and hanging around the decks, waiting on the handover to take place with Mikey. Getting myself backstage, though, I spotted Ovidio Flores and Veronica, his girlfriend. Both standing talking with Si and Marisol. They were meant to come from Mazatlan to the opening night of my tour in Guadalajara, at Club Ballam but apparently, Ovidio's dad - Don Flores, a man whose seriousness had been well documented - had returned from his overnight trip to Culiacán and when clocking the mess left at his mansion after the birthday party. Instead of partying in Guadalajara, the two of them had spent the night cleaning up the mansion. Ovidio admitting that the optics of him and Veronica going out to party would not have sat well with his father, so he'd had to skip Guadalajara. Telling the four of them that I needed to go and earn a living, I left them to it and headed off in the direction of the side of the decks, Mikey P on what would be the last song of his set.

While it played out and I stood there to get myself ready for a smooth transition from his last track into my first one, the two of us stood and gave each other a hug and shared a quick friendly word. I'd always felt that handover hug was like the deejay world equivalent of when two bus drivers wave to each other when they pass on the road. But was always down for it, unless it happened to be a complete dickhead who I'd already fallen out with over the years, which would occasionally happen due to some deejays on the circuit believing their own hype. Mikey leaving, saying he was off to see a bit of the festival and that maybe he'd see me later on at some point before giving me one last fist bump and gathering his stuff. Leaving me to it. When putting my set together for the festival I'd already decided on *Pick Me Up* by DFK and Toris Badic to open matters with. Thinking that the Latin style horns on the track would see things go off with the crowd and provide an explosive start, and see things keep step from there. The couple of nights before, especially with it being an open to close set, I had taken the crowd on a journey, as the hours passed. But that stuff always worked more in a club setting. For a festival, though? Just hit them with banger after banger and no cunt's going to be complaining about what you've delivered for them.

The sea of dancing bodies, to this opener from me, almost left me hypnotised, stood there behind the decks but looking *past* them. The amount of glow sticks I could see moving in the air, there must've been thousands of them. Girls on their boyfriend's shoulders dancing away while more visible from their high vantage point. The lights reflecting back off that giant fucking ant that was sitting precariously above them. The crowd - eight to ten thousand, I'd have reckoned - was a blur of permanently moving and raised hands, bobbing heads, and two steps, them seeming to be packed into there like sardines but just about managing to make it work. The high-tech lighting system strobed across their faces, transforming them into flashes of light and shadow, creating a surreal, almost hypnotic scene.

Managing to pull myself out of just staring at them. I put my hands up into the air and gave them all a wee round of applause, because they fucking deserved it. This wasn't a group of people who had come to stand around and chat to their mates or fuck about on their phones. I pointed out to the crowd and heard the cheer come back in my direction. Turning around for a second I clocked the *DJ Selecao* in massive letters on the electronic screen at the back of the stage. Just for a nano second, I took this in. The thousands there in front of me. My fucking *name* up on that big screen. Sometimes you'd find yourself having that 'is this shit really happening?' thought no matter how long you'd been playing for. I got it there in Mexico City but you can't go dwelling on that stuff. Not when you're in the middle of playing. I got Santiago's mate's song out the way early doors, mainly because I knew that if I got carried away and right into my set I'd have most probably forgotten to even play it. Not wanting to to make a cunt out of Santiago - who I was sure would've already told his mate that he'd fixed things for me playing the van Helden track - I stuck to my word.

Predictably, the crowd went wild for it. Wherever you play it, the crowd does, and always will.

The set seemed to fly by and I was into the second hour before I'd even realised it. Once again, with it being a festival, I stuck to more tried and trusted tunes, rather than testing the crowd with any hot off the press tracks. Playing a lot of twenty thirteen tracks alongside the occasional oldie, ken? The vibe that night, though? I was left with the impression that the crowd was in such a mood that I could've barely missed with whatever I selected. When *That Organ* by Pete Gelderblom was playing, the MC who to be fair to him pretty much kept his trap shut for the majority of my set must've shouted for the crowd to put their hands up - at the piano - and they did as told. The lighting engineer, ingeniously switching the main lights of the tent on for this, capturing everyone there in the brightness and showing all of those hands in the air. It was a special, special sight and for those seconds, actually seeing just how *many* people were actually there in the tent left me with a pleasant chill going up my spine.

On the night, I was wearing the latest Mexico mens fitba team top, which a fan had brought for me, back at the Guadalajara tour opener, which I had thought had been well thoughtful, like. Actually made sure that him and his two pals could come up for the rest of the show when he'd passed it up to me in the booth, indicating that it was for me. I'd told the boy that he should look out for pictures or videos of me in Mexico City, because I'd have it on. To go with this, though - mid set - as I was playing *Strictly Funk* from Groovebox and Phunk Investigation someone threw a Mexican flag up onto the stage at the decks. Because I wasn't looking for it coming I about shit myself when it flew into me. Once I clocked it, though. I wasted no time in holding it up above my head, like some Olympian who'd just secured a medal at track and field. I didn't think about it - or know it - at the time but the image of me in the fitba top holding up the Mexican flag would be come quite an iconic picture and help gain a whole new group of followers, who were listening to my sets but who hadn't heard of me, initially, until seeing the photograph.

I bowed out with the complete fucking banger that was *Mercy*, the Boddika's VIP mix. Sharing the same hugs and handshakes with Paulie Naar - the German DJ and producer who was now up next for a two hour stint at keeping this tent going - that me and Mikey P had done two hours before, I made sure to acknowledge the crowd before departing. I don't want to sound like fucking Bruce Forsyth but they were absolutely brilliant, I'd buzzed off *them* buzzing off me and were so much better than your usual crowd.

The first person to greet me - when I returned to the back of the stage area - was Juan Valbuena, one of the onsite bods from A.N.T.S. Juan with a massive smile on his face - no doubt chuffed with the party that they'd came to Mexico and, evidently, put on - saying how much he'd loved my set, and commenting on the reaction of the crowd to it. He stood there and told me that their brand was only in the early stages of the world domination they intended on achieving but that I could look forward to a lot more bookings for future events, both back in their native home of Ibiza and for their international events. Slapping me on the shoulder once again he told me that they'd be in touch with Lee in due course but, apart from that, offering his thanks again for me coming to play for them and wishing me a good rest of the night.

Aye, get in touch with Lee all you want, I thought to myself. Doesn't mean to say that you're going to get *hold* of the cunt. I considered my - by now - absent without leave agent. The last time I'd heard from him had been the day after my appearance at Club Ballam. Hadn't told me where he'd fucked off to, just that he had business to attend to, and that he wouldn't be flying from Guadaljara to Mexico City with me, and that he'd meet me there. Which he didn't do. I wasn't his keeper by any fucking stretch and nor would I have wanted to be, not for that head case. A well connected and extremely good at his job head case, granted. I'd still tried him, though. Couple of calls that didn't even ring before going straight through to voicemail. So had just got on with things. But, obviously, couldn't help but be left a wee bit curious what he was up to, and where he was. Because this was Lee, he could've been dead - easily, by the way - by now or sitting in some jail cell somewhere.

Making my way over to join Si, Marisol and our new pals from Mazatlan. Ovidio and Veronica grooving away to the first track from the German DJ while Si and Marisol stood posing for a photo with some other woman standing in between them. Before I reached them I felt a tap on my shoulder. Turning around I found a couple of men in suits standing there. Initial thought was that they were Feds, like. You don't see many cunts wearing suits are festivals, ken? Looking down, though, I clocked that one was carrying a suitcase, which removed any thought of them being police, even if it wasn't any less weirder to see.

The two of them all smiles as they introduced themselves with names that I had forgotten the moment they'd been said to me as I had someone shouting to me from the side which offered a bit of a distraction and me feeling that it probably wasn't important to ask them again. Explaining to me, it wasn't even myself that they were looking for, but Lee. The taller out of the two of them telling me that they were looking to do business with him and how they had been meant to meet with the man from London back at the hotel in Guadalajara, but that when they'd got there they'd found out that he'd checked out of his room a day early.

'Why would he do this?'

The smaller one asked, with a confused look on his face.

'Because he's Lee Isaac, pal.'

As much of an answer as I could give him, because there was no way you'd have been able to get me to explain the intricacies of the mind of my agent. I told them that Lee had been meant to travel to Mexico City with me but, instead, had disappeared, telling me in a text that he was away off on business and that he would re-connect with me in the capital. Me turning around to survey the room for them as a show of telling them that he hadn't followed through with this, and that I hadn't seen him since arriving myself. With nothing to hide - not that I needed to do this, anyway - I showed them the last text message that he'd sent me. The two of them carefully reading the text, and I'm sure, and then the follow up ones I had sent him, looking to see where the fuck he was at.

I asked the pair of them if they had business cards they could give me to pass onto my agent for as and when I finally saw him again, or if they had any message that they wanted me to pass on for them. The pair of them just shook their heads and thanked me for my time. Saying that they would catch up with Lee at a later date. I watched them for a second as they walked away. Literally now leaving the place, having had confirmation that Lee wasn't there. With him always in negotiations over one thing or another I shook this off and went over to join the group.

Si was dancing behind Marisol with his arms around her. The both of them two stepping in unison. Massive smiles on their coupons which were part MDMA assisted and part completely organic. You wouldn't have guessed that they had started their day off with the news that they'd become a trending topic on social media, due to the riding that they'd been doing, with how they were there at the festival, looking like two people without a care in the world, which they absolutely fucking *must've* done. Because there's no way that you just shrug off a wee setback like half of the world seeing you having sex. At least for one night, though. They were having a top night, and fair play to them for it. Could've been easier for them to just both get holed up in the hotel room and avoid all of those eyes on them and I'd have understood if Si and her hadn't come with me.

As we stood around, having a few drinks and a laugh. Me speaking to the occasional new person for a wee word or two, and that. I couldn't help but have a wee ironic laugh to myself, as I clocked all of the people who wanted to stop and speak to Si. It wasn't a competition or fuck all. But despite the fact that I had just freshly delivered one of the best sets that the

El Dia de la Danza festival would see across its three days, there were more people backstage wanting to speak to Si - the deejays mate - than me, the actual fucking *DJ*.

All of that hard work, spent honing my craft both in my bedroom each day and when starting out playing. All of those years of touring the globe. The constant flights, the hardly ever sleeping in your own bed for more than three consecutive nights. The hard work put in to build myself a following of fans in this part of the world, such as touring with Citizen Caner. And for what? For my mate to race past me in the space of hours, becoming internationally famous, and for what? For getting his fucking *hole*. You couldn't make it up, like.

Knowing that I would need to start getting the car organised to take me up to the airport to collect Flo, I asked Si and Marisol if they needed a lift, all be it with a diversion to the airport before hotel, but Si replied that they were having too good a night so were going to stay until the end of the festival at six and get their own way back. Marisol - who you really would not have thought had been a famous star who had just been subject to personal stuff leaking online, the way she was that night - saying to me that she was looking forward to meeting my other half and that the four of us should have brunch after we'd all had a sleep.

I didn't bother even trying, when it came to offering Myles and Luke a lift back. With me away to pick up my girlfriend and someone who was surely going to be in a bit of an emotional state, they had no business being witness to any of that. Neither were to be seen when I left the backstage area to walk to the car. The last time I had seen any of them on the night had been when I had clocked Myles taking a couple of photos of me during my set. I'd quickly asked him why the *journalist* was the one taking the *photos*. Him telling me something to do with his partner having taken some mushrooms and things having not gone too well and that Luke was currently hiding out in someone's tent that Myles had paid them for letting Luke sit in it.

I left the El Dia de la Danza grounds, with multiple beats and bass lines all competing against each other off in the distance hoping that it would not be the last time I would visit the place. Thinking that, on principle, if the A.N.T.S team were to be invited back again, then so would I, with how successful it had gone.

Meeting up with Flo at the airport was as emotional as I'd anticipated. She'd called - when I was in the car - to let me know that she'd landed and was waiting with everyone else to go through passport control. Me telling her that I was on route but it was a good forty five minutes away so if she got through arrivals first just to sit tight and wait but if not I'd come in and kick around waiting on her coming through the doors.

The usual way it can be at your typical international airport. Despite being three quarters of an hour away. By the time she'd got through passport control and then finally collecting her case from the baggage carousel, I was stood on the other side waiting on her. Spying my other half straight away walking in a matching two piece of soft pink fleeced bottoms and hoodie along with a pair of Ugg boots on her feet, lazily pulling her case behind her. She had her hood pulled up around her head, looking absolutely shattered as she started to look around to see if I'd arrived yet.

When she clocked me, her face lit up and she quickened her pace. But when she reached me and instinctively gave me the biggest and tightest hug she'd ever done in all of the years we'd been together, she just burst out crying. Like it had all been waiting to come out. And when it did it wasn't going to be minimal.

'I was so fucking scared, babe. Dead bodies lying two streets away from our flat, suicide bombers, gunmen and psycho lorry drivers,'

she managed to say in between her sobs and uncontrolled breathing. And this was from a ballsy girl from South London who had never not been from anything other than the *real* world. Someone who the vast majority of the time - on seeing a potential argument brewing between us - where

I'd ended up sacking it altogether, knowing how sharp as a tack with a machine gun rate of delivering words she had. But everyone has their breaking point. Keeping my arms clenched around her, while empathising how I couldn't have even begun to imagine how scared she must've been by it all going off around our flat, but that she'd done the correct thing by heading to Mexico, and that she already knew that I'd take care of her now.

We headed back to the hotel where, in terms of sleep, Flo endured a tough night, which pretty much meant so did I. When she *did* sleep she was restless during it and literally could not lay there in the one position for any length of time. At one point I was woken by her screams and her sitting upright in bed.

This had reminded me of how she used to be, following her experience in Ibiza with the two Colombian sicarios, La Cobra and El Jugador. Sleep for her, for the next few years, had *also* been tough with her waking up after having dreamed about having that plastic shopping bag held over her head again. It had been a long as well as scary day for the girl and you couldn't have blamed her being left like that by the end of it.

It was horrible to see your other half left like this - and I already know that there would have been *thousands* back in Amsterdam left traumatised in the same way as Flo - but the only consolation I could take in that moment was knowing that she was nowhere near Europe and any mad bastard terrorists and that she'd be safe from any harm now.

Right?

Chapter 17

Zico

It was written all over Flo's coupon when I first introduced her to Marisol, when we met them for the brunch that Si's Peruvian woman had suggested the night before. She didn't *need* to say 'so how the fuck did you pull this off then, Si?' because her face said it for him.

Mainly as a way of trying to make sure events in Amsterdam weren't allowed to be dwelled on, I'd been keeping Flo up to speed with all of what had been going on, since I'd arrived and, inevitably, I arrived at the part about how this TV star that Si had met at the party that I'd only had to fucking *play* because of my agent being a complete liability, had only had her cloud hacked, and some incriminating pictures and videos of her and Si had surfaced online. It had been the first genuine laugh I'd seen from Flo, hearing about this. Laughing first, on account of this happening to one of her friends - but someone *like* Si - and then having the secondary sympathetic thought, in the direction of 'poor Marisol' and how mortifying it must all be for her, with millions of people knowing her.

'Marisol, meet Flo. Flo, Marisol,'

I said, officially, even if it wouldn't have been too much of a task for them to have worked this out for themselves.

'Flohhhhhhh, it is so good to meet you, *and* have some female company!'

Marisol said, quickly getting to her feet and giving Flo a cuddle in the kind of way that only two women - who are relative strangers - could've given each other. I could tell by my other half's reaction to this first impression for me to see that the smile she had for Marisol was a genuine one and not the product of some kind of a forced tolerance. They stood there engaging in some excited small talk before eventually taking their seats at the table beside both of their men.

'What is Flo short for, can I ask you? Florence?'

Marisol asked, admitting that this was a new name for her. Apparently 'Flo's' a bit thin on the ground in South America. Flo replying back that it was short for *Floella*, while letting her know that Floella wasn't even her name anyway. This always made me smile when I thought about because, funnily enough, where *I* was from, you weren't exactly always bumping into people with that name either, as different as Fife, Scotland was from Lima, Peru. My only point of reference for this name, in fact, being the children's TV presenter - Floella Benjamin - who I had loved when I was a kid, as part of the Play School presenting team.

Despite her truly hellish experience, the day before, and a hard, hard night for her. You would not have known by Flo's face or her behaviour. Sat there appearing as her same old self. Interesting, engaging and funny as she sat poking fun at Si in a light hearted way which showed Marisol that the two of them had known each other for years, and possessed the ability to have a dig at each other without things ever being taken the wrong way.

The two girls - now in a bit of a more natural environment instead of an introduction where, let's face it, I don't think *anyone* is ever truly themselves while they stand there and just try their best to act normal and not say something stupid that will be attached to the first impression that other person will take away with them of you - looking like they were getting on with each other and definitely not short on things to talk about.

While Si was sitting and telling me about an incident that had happened during my set, behind the stage in the VIP area, where a guy had taken a champagne bucket across the napper from his girl, or possibly *ex* now. Apparently he'd been sitting there on one of the sofas with a girl, drinking champagne and doing a bit of heavy petting when this other woman appeared and had started going batshit at him. This producing the girl on the sofa standing up to say her piece and getting pushed back onto the sofa in one breath and, in the other, the boy's finding the woman - the one going radge - picking up the empty champagne bucket and her swinging it by the handle and giving him a cut underneath an eye. The security dragging her away - still screaming the place down - at this while the boy sat there a bit sheepish while the *other* girl - beside him on the sofa standing up - was now, also, giving him grief. Lucky she never used the fucking champagne bottle, eh? Small mercies.

As he told me this, I was hearing bits and bobs of what the two girls were talking about. Marisol saying something about that she was planning on going out clothes shopping for the day - something she *always* did when in Mexico City, due to the amount of amazing boutiques and streets that the capital city boasted - and how she'd love it if Flo came out with her for the day for a girls day out.

'We buy some nice clothes for our wardrobes, have a nice lunch and some fine wine and get to know each other more?'

Marisol asked Flo, flashing her that deep and genuine smile of hers that shouldn't have been anywhere near the face of a woman who, only the day before, had found out that millions of people had been watching her having sex, and were now all talking about her, and her personal life in the most intrusive of ways.

With the two of us - back up in the room - already discussing plans for the day which involved nothing more than my desire to look for a record shop, which I'd been told about the night before from another DJ at the festival, and for me to treat everyone to a meal at night, to mark the end of the Mexico leg of the tour. Flo accepted the offer straight away while Si joked to the table that this was going to cost me and him by the time the two of them returned. This, purely for show considering I'd have bet all of my own DJ earnings on Marisol having more money in the bank than my mate. Aye, he'd been wise - as well as lucky - with money over the years so wasn't exactly short of a bob or two but out of the two of them, he wasn't the TV star, recognised all over the continent.

I could see what Marisol - possibly already after discussions with Si - was trying to do, when it came to Flo. And I couldn't help admire her for it, while it showed what kind of a person Si had hooked up with. No cunt, and I mean *no one,* would've blamed her if she'd wanted to concentrate on her own shit that day, which she'd have surely had plenty of. Fight fires and try to win any PR wars that were potentially brewing. Instead, though. I could see that she was more interested in taking Flo's mind off from thinking about the obvious. It said a lot about someone's personality when they'd have been willing to put a relative stranger - and what needs they they might've had - before you would yourself. *Especially* for someone like Marisol.

As I sat there, drinking my coffee, and watched Flo talking to both of Si and Marisol, I had a wee bit of a moment of reflection. Where had the time went? I asked myself. Flo, who was every bit as beautiful as the night I'd first met her, inside Space in Ibiza. The same night where I'd mistaken the hat that she was wearing for a table - Yes, I was absolutely busted that night, I admit - and had tried to place a bottle of San Miguel on top of her head. While Si? He's sitting beside his fucking *TV Star* girlfriend?! And the *reason* that we're all at the one table, because I'd just wrapped up the first part of a Latin America tour in Mexico City and now preparing to move on to *Bogota.*

What had happened to those two teenage radgeys who had become pals with each other on a football special train to Aberdeen, back in Nineteen Ninety? Two boys whose only real interests back then were trying to find some clobber that no cunt else had, two points for Dundee United every Saturday and a good old scrap before and after the match? The differences in the Zico and Si of Nineteen Ninety and Twenty Fourteen were there for all to see and about the only constant from then to present day was our unshakeable ability to land ourselves in trouble. Aye, all grown up after those twenty four years of being mates but as a clear indicator of how the more things changed they would stay the same. I was sitting questioning if my agent had landed up somewhere dead while

Si was in the middle of a *very* public sex scandal that had left him recognised by the average Latin American in the street.

Speaking of that agent of mine, as we sat there having brunch that comprised of Chilaqueles for Flo, Tacos de Barbacoa for moi, Huevos Rancheros for Marisol that once he'd seen the delicious looking fried eggs on tortillas Si ended up asking for a plate of, alongside the Molletes that he'd already ordered. I clocked those two men who had been looking for him, back at the festival. I seen them but without them noticing me. Thought I was *seeing* things at first because I'd almost forgotten all about the wee word I'd had with them, when they were looking for Lee. I found myself thinking of whether I'd told them which hotel I was at, and where Lee *should've* been too, but as far as I'd been able to remember. It had been a short conversation and I'd shown them his text, which had confirmed he'd been somewhere else. There wouldn't have been much point in telling them which hotel I was at, not when Lee hadn't even seen the *inside* of the fucking place. Hadn't even seen Mexico City itself, for all I'd known on my side.

Funny how the cold light of day can throw up an alternative to what you think you saw, when things were much more darker. Because, due to the pair of them being dressed in suits and with one of them looking extra professional carrying a suitcase, I had built them up in my mind to be something quite apart from the two of them, there kicking around the hotel. Suits replaced by jeans and polo shirts. One of them, his arms completely covered in tattoos, one on his face as well, which was too far for me to clock what it was. Some on his neck, too. Give me a bit of credit, though. It was dark and I'd just come off stage after one of the greatest sets of my life and was buzzing to fuck. Add the few beers and lines I'd had before my set and, aye. I probably was never going to be the most perceptive of people.

I watched them take a seat, together, on one of the sofas in the massive reception area that my - the five star Gran Palacio Mexicano - hotel had. With the bright lights above that reflected down onto the white marbled floors, I'd found the whole area *well* too bright for my liking. Almost developed a migraine just through the process of getting myself checked in. Good luck to you if you're going to sit there, I thought. And better luck if you're going to think Lee Isaac is going to stroll right in any minute now, too. Maybe it had just been a coincidence, though? Them in the city on business and ending up in the same hotel as me? But I didn't believe in *those* kind of coincidences. End of the day, they weren't looking for me, had they been then they'd had the chance the night before. I saw no reason to reacquaint myself with them again. It was hard not to think of *why* they were looking for Lee, though. Of course, if the cunt had been willing to answer his fucking phone or reply to a text message then I might've been able to ask him.

As Marisol sat there telling Flo about a clothes shop called 'Couture Celeste' which enjoyed the privilege of various designer pieces that no other shop in Mexico - or further south - got access to, and that all of the big Latin American stars shopped there. A shop where you couldn't just walk in at your leisure and that to gain entry would require an advance time slot having been confirmed, something Marisol had done when she'd known that she was going to the capital city with Si.

While Marisol told us about the place she was too into her description of the shop to clock Si getting a text, picking up his phone to look at it and his face completely draining of life before he put it back down again, but I did. After the girls had left the table to go and get ready, I asked him about it. Because he'd been on good form - for someone operating on *zero* sleep after the festival, and who was going to spend the afternoon finally getting some sleep - as he sat there. Laughing, joking and full of the patter. But whatever the fuck he'd seen on his screen, it had been enough to drain him of all of those good vibes.

The message had been from his - now very much - ex woman, Greta. Still there in Las Vegas on Si's dollar. Rather than just give me the headlines, he turned his phone around and pushed it over to me to read what was on screen.

*Well you didn't waste any fucking time getting over me.
BASTARD. Yeah, I saw what you've been up to on Twitter and
I am going to take GREAT pleasure in telling everyone back in
Amsterdam about it. EVERYONE is going to know that you,
Simon, are the type of man to jump out of one bed and into the
other and you will do well to ever get another woman in the
whole city again in your life after I'm through. Fuck you, very
much. G*

How the fuck did she find out? I asked a very gutted
looking Si. He'd already told me that despite how viral
everything had been he'd had the idea that no cunt in Europe
would be any the wiser about it. Well that was his theory blown
right sky fucking high.

'I don't know, Zeek. She's well into her gossip columns
and all of that shite, eh? Maybe because of it being a sex
scandal, the fact that it's a high Latin profile celebrity has
managed to seep through into the western media's cycle? She's
into all of that reality show nonsense as well so while she
wouldn't be able to tell you the name of the president of the
United States she *could* tell you the goings on of some cunt that
you've never heard of before in your puff who is living inside a
house until the public vote them out. Probably the *worst* person
I could've pissed off, given what was then going to turn out to
happen to me.'

I don't think he'd have ever expected to get to the day
after the pictures and video being leaked and everything all
back to normal. That day was going to take a long fucking time
arriving, as far as I could see. But he couldn't have expected a
bad situation being taken and then turned into like something
fucking nuclear level.

'How the fuck am I going to be able to show my face
back in Amsterdam, once she's made sure everyone in our
circle of pals will have watched me riding Marisol? Proper
fucked now, me, eh?'

I told him that, considering what had just been going on
in Amsterdam, she might've found that a lot of people were
more interested in how many people had been killed and

injured, and how they were going to recover as a city, than they would've been to see him shagging a TV star, even if I didn't really fully believe that myself. Because it's not as if someone couldn't have done both? I also reminded him that we still had around a week and a half before the subject of even going back to Amsterdam had to be a thing, and that a week and a half was a long time. Him replying to this that while that, aye, would be a long time. Pictures and videos that go online are *forever*. Which he wasn't wrong about there, like.

I knew he'd be sorted again, once he'd had a sleep. See things a bit more clearer and logically because while, aye, Greta *was* going to make sure everyone we knew in Amsterdam would find out about what Si had been up to. The part about him ditching her in Las Vegas and then shagging someone the next day kind of rubber stamped some retribution being sent his way at some point. Some would call it almost instant karma. But it wouldn't have been the end of the world for the boy. Easy for me to say that, though, mind. Hey, if he was smart, he'd be able to *capitalise* on his new found fame and once you get yourself a wee reputation for yourself, before you know it you're riding a *different* celebrity then another. Party invites clogging up your fucking letterbox. Like that Callum Best boy was for a wee while, ken?

As we were starting to wrap things up. The day ahead - separately - would see Si going to his scratcher and me off hunting for a record shop that a local DJ had told me about, when we were having a blether backstage after my set. A shop called Bajo Circuito. Thank fuck I'd written a note on my phone when he told me because there wouldn't have been a hope in hell of me remembering it by the next day. He'd said that it was the best electronic music record shop in the whole of Mexico and that it was a 'crate diggers paradise.' And you can't be telling me stuff like that and then just expect me to forget about it and move on with my life. If I was to ever lose the buzz of digging through random crates of records in even more random cities then I would sincerely hope that I would do the decent thing and retire from the industry.

We were in the middle of squaring up brunch when Myles and Luke came trudging past. The absolute *nick* of the pair of them, though? I think, possibly through the need to try and maintain the image of professionalism on this assignment even though both of them were fucking kidding themselves if the thought that they'd pulled that off so far on the tour. They tried to avoid me and Si, but once we'd clocked them both, doing an afternoon walk of shame of sorts, there was no way they *weren't* being pulled up by us.

'Afternoon, lads. Enjoy the festival, aye?'

I asked and immediately got the memory flash of Myles taking photos, and something about Luke being completely twisted, lying in some random's tent, scared to come out. Through what looked like a combination of exhaustion and drugs, Myles just laughed at this while popping an imaginary gun to his head and pulling the trigger. Luke, though. He looked like he just didn't want to be standing there. Not sure where he *did* but it definitely didn't look to be standing outside in the shade by the outdoor restaurant.

'How the fuck are you just getting back now, though? I was there to the death and I got back about back of eight,'

Si asked Myles. Myles really the only outlet for any kind of a conversation with them, something that was obvious from the moment that they both stopped to chat. The both of them a state in every way. Neither looking the most sane, although Myles being made to look more switched on than a German rocket scientist, simply by standing beside his mate. Their clothes, absolutely filthy and reeking. Considering this hadn't been your U.K festival, where you're covered in head to toe in most of the time, you'd have really had to go some to end up as dirty looking as them two.

'Yeah, mate. Things ended up going a bit sideways, didn't they?'

Myles replied in a very croaky and lazily delivered Mancunian accent. He went on to explain to us that the reason that they were only getting back from the festival now was that they'd been there until the end, and the owner of the tent had returned and politely - and then the second time around *not so politely* - asked Luke to leave his tent. When they'd eventually left the tented village that the festival had for those staying for the three nights. Luke had wanted to go to the bathroom. But once he'd got inside of there, he didn't want to *leave* again. My thoughts on this was that you'd have left his sorry fucking erse behind by that point. You'd looked after him for hours and now, festival ended, you can't even *leave* because the cunt is too scared to depart the toilet cubicle. I could see why Myles hadn't, though. If Luke was to end up doing himself a mischief, while on a story assignment, it might've then exposed Myles' extra curricular activities, while covering the story.

'So, you've been hanging around the festival all this time, trying to get this radgey to leave the fucking cubical, aye?'

I laughed, Si too as we both imagined the scene. I hadn't taken mushrooms since I'd been a teenager and could barely · remember what they'd even been like, but knew that they hadn't left me in a position like Luke. And that had been the best part of an Irn Bru bottle's worth of them that I'd drank. Christ? How many did that mad bastard take? Because looking at him, he was well out of sorts and by my estimation, purely on his body language and inability to look at me or Si, the boy was *still* tripping.

'Oh, god no. I managed to get him out after around three quarters of an hour,'

Myles said, laughably in a way which tried to make that forty five minutes seem like it had only been a couple of minutes he'd been trying. Because forty five minutes to get your pal out of a toilet cubicle is *still* pretty fucking excessive, no matter which way you look at it.

Apparently, these two fiends had negotiated with a soft drinks delivery driver to take them back into the city. Myles sorting this out when they saw him making an early morning delivery to the festival site, no doubt as part of stock for the Saturday ahead. Unfortunately for these two music magazine space cadets, however, Myles' Spanish hadn't been as good as he'd possibly thought because by the time the driver was reaching over to wake them up to tell them that they'd arrived, they were nowhere fucking *near* Mexico City. Myles hadn't been joking when he"d said that things had went a bit sideways, almost eighty *miles* to the side, to be close to exact.

'Obviously, we're not from round here, mate? So when the driver told us we'd arrived. We got out, he fucked off in his lorry and it took around fifteen minutes of walking around to find out that we were in a place called Chiautempan ... *two and a half fucking hours* drive to Mexico City. No public transport so we've had to pay for a taxi that I already know my editor is never going to pay for, when I submit it for expenses,'

Myles said, almost in tears over the cost of the taxi, because it doesn't matter where you are in the world, no matter what rate you've managed to negotiate for yourself. A two and a half hour taxi ride is a two and a half hour taxi ride. End of.

'Are you sure that you two aren't just a couple of caners who killed the *real* cunts from One's & Two's Magazine and are fuck all other than just *posing* as journalists and cameramen, just so you get access to the fucking rave?'

I asked, which, as far as I was concerned - and I now had three separate events to now fairly judge them by - was as equal to a joke as it was a valid question.

Si left with the two them, saying he would get them up. Me reminding them about the dinner I was treating to everyone later on, and that I'd text them the details later. Leaving me there to get myself together and head out for an afternoon of crate digging, a few beers and what would officially be the last of the - many - tacos of the trip.

Considering the near non stop circus that it had been since arriving in Guadalajara I was really looking forward to just going out and having a bit of normality to myself. There hadn't been too much of that in supply throughout Mexico and with Colombia up next, I already knew *that* country did not owe me one single promise of normality.

So, while I had the chance, I grabbed it with both arms. With a record bag over my shoulder and back, a joint in my mouth and a smile holding onto it, I headed off into the city centre looking for Bajo Circuito to get myself some vinyl.

It's the little things, sometimes.

Chapter 18

Donde esta, Señor Isaac?

Lee Isaac leaned against the bar at his chosen beachfront club, *still* in Acapulco, having finally managed to brave leaving the villa that he had been holed up in for more than a day, following the after-after party with the object of his - business related - desires, DJ Kenny Korff. A much needed quick shower and - just as much required - change of clothes later and against all logic was stood there, propping things up at *Tiki Towers*. Fresh Moncler short sleeved buttoned up white linen shirt, Gucci chinos with white branded sneakers from the same Italian designer to match. Glass of whisky in hand, the vibrant pulse of electronic music thrumming in his chest, the two top up bumps of cocaine that he had just taken in the privacy of the bathroom making him feel like a million dollars in this environment, *his* environment. Where over the years he had effortlessly combined his business with his pleasure.

The neon lights flickered, casting a kaleidoscope of colours across the sand and beyond, over onto the water. But it all felt like a blur, having laid off any substances or intoxicants for a day, the first taste of - some of - his vices hit him strong. He had come to Mexico as a man with purposes. To look after his DJ who was on tour in the kind of environment that set off all kinds of alarm bells, when it came to the thought of *DJ Selecao* left to himself, in such a rich - for trouble - playground. Isaac had also, however, come to this particular part of the world to sign a promising, if challenging, American DJ to his roster. But the intoxicating atmosphere of alcohol, drugs, women and generally burning the candle at both ends had chewed him up and spat him out, and he found himself lost in a haze of partying. Hey, at least I managed *one* of them, he thinks to himself. Now in the knowledge that Kenny Korff was ready to get into bed with Ragamuffin Talent in what he felt would be a mutually rewarding agreement for both of them. Thanks to Isaac, Korff would *finally* crack Europe and thanks to Korff, Isaac would find himself *financially compensated* out of it.

He hadn't told Zico, his already established internationally regarded, and loved, DJ where he was going. Isaac's protective - although some would have said paranoid - instincts warned him that sharing his plans could - and with his luck at times - *would* hex the deal he was hoping to strike with Korff. Zico, in Isaac's opinion, had a knack for spilling secrets, *especially* when he was in the party spirit, a state of mind that his DJ had been in from the moment he had got into the back of that cartel supplied limousine, tasked with taking them all to Sinaloa, and found the free cocaine and weed, and this time, Lee had been determined to keep the potential signing of the troublesome American under wraps.

But as the sun dipped below the horizon, casting a golden glow over the ocean, Lee felt the gravity of his life choices niggling away at him. Days of relentless partying had left him feeling like a ghost, disconnected from reality. The metaphorical brick wall encountered, and shit out of luck, when it came to any 'metaphorical' ladders lying around. While he had been full of nothing other than good intentions when telling himself that he would travel from Acapulco to Mexico City, rejoining Zico before, now back on track, moving on to the next leg of the tour in Bogota, for the first of two dates in the Colombia. It was *never* going to happen. He knew that his main reason for being in the country was more than two hundred miles away in the capital city, but lying there in that strange bed, the exhaustion clawed away at him. He felt more drained than an outdoor swimming pool in the winter.

He *needed* one or two days to recover, to give himself a complete reset and a firmware upgrade before facing the whirlwind of the tour again, because he was too long in the tooth not to know that the tour would not slow down on *his* account. With the kind of cities which lay ahead, it he was indeed to rejoin his DJ again, such as Medellin, Buenos Aires and Rio de Janeiro he knew that things weren't going to be quiet, but he made a commitment to himself that he was going to try and slow things down a little, just so that he could make it to the end of the tour. Thinking of the time when the actor John Travolta announced his quite considerable weight loss to the world. The *secret?* He had kept eating what he had always done, only he had *halved* his portions. If Travolta could do it with food, then why couldn't I do it with drugs and alcohol? Isaac had thought.

During this time of recovery, calling or texting Zico felt like an afterthought, overshadowed by his own *stuff* that he had going on. His iPhone battery being wiped out for almost twenty four hours, again, did not help matters, when it came to communication with the outside world. Well, did not help anyone trying to contact *him.* Isaac's phone, in fact, could have sat at a full one hundred percent battery and he would not have been contacting anyone. For that time, anyway. The man had become a ghost. Leaving the world behind, for a while at least. Going off the grid and incommunicado in the hope that it would stave off the looming sanity that his partying had been beckoning.

Back in Mexico City, Zico, despite not exactly been left pacing the floor back and forward beside himself, was already growing slightly worried for the man who he'd enjoyed a love hate relationship with over the years. He would *always* be grateful for the assistance that Isaac had been to him over the years but that did not mean to say that being a DJ for Lee Isaac was an easy thing to do. The last he had heard, his agent was somewhere on business, but he hadn't shown up for the next gig, as had been his original plan. Zico's mind raced with possibilities. What if Lee had gotten himself into trouble? Very fucking likely, Zico thought of that possibility. Away from Isaac's own personal talent for getting on the wrong sides of the wrong type of people. The electronic music scene was rife with potential dangers, especially when dealing with the organised gangs that could smell a hustle and outlet to make money better than a bloodhound could find a human being, and Zico couldn't shake the feeling that something was amiss. That, for a person like his agent, who was practically *glued* to his phone all of his waking hours and notoriously carried a back up, to always be available? It left Zico fearing the worst, telling himself to wait until getting to Colombia to see if Isaac would come in from the cold. Either way, he would know by Colombia.

. . .

Meanwhile, in Mazatlan, the city's Sinaloa Cartel affiliated boss, Don Enrique Flores, was fuming. Having made the grim discovery of Isaac's disrespectful antics, particularly how the manager had sullied a picture of his mother during a drunken and cocaine fuelled escapade in his bedroom. The offence cut deep. To use the bed of the man known as "Don" for such vile purposes was a declaration of war in itself but to soil the memory of his dead mother was tantamount to signing a suicide note, and Flores was not one to let such insults go unanswered. He had his own pride to answer to, never mind a reputation that would require upheld.

Luis and Jorge, two of a much larger team of enforcers loyal to Flores, stood before him, their expressions hardened as they patiently awaited orders, keeping silent until spoken to. Luis, the younger of the two with a 'curtains' style middle parting hair style and a calculating glint in his eye, had a reputation for being quick on his feet and as wise to the streets as such an occupation demanded. Jorge, a muscular brute adorned with tattoos that told a thousand stories, stood by, ready to act on their jefe's word, which they had already assumed would be like any other from Flores, to unleash the worst and most twisted violence, at his behest, at a moment's notice. But they were both wrong, on this occasion.

'Find him,'

Flores commanded, his voice cold and unwavering, coming across as someone who is deliberately speaking in the cold and controlled manner they are because they know the alternative will be for them to be *hot* and completely out of control.

'Bring him back to me.'

The men nodded, understanding the gravity of their task. To them, it would have been far easier to have just found him and killed him. But to hear their Don request to have Isaac found and brought back to Sinaloa. This meant that no matter what, they could not harm Isaac, which would, naturally, make their orders harder to carry out. But if Don Flores had requested the gringo be brought back to be put on his knees in front of their jefe then that would *have* to be the only outcome. Working for the cartel, it allowed them to enjoy the level of wages that they could not have dreamed of, by working in honest employment but one of the prices of this was that you were only ever one bad mistake away from losing favour with your boss, and there was only ever one outcome if you wound up there. Mexican cartel bosses did not take too kindly to failure, and Enrique Emilano Garcia Flores was no different in that aspect.

As they departed Mazatlan, Flores' mind raced with thoughts of vengeance, he had been unable to shift the thought of a naked Isaac standing masturbating in front of the picture of his mother. It had *consumed* him. He had already - unintentionally - gathered information about Isaac, who during some small talk with each other had mentioned the tour that his DJ was in Latin America for. This making Isaac a predictable target. Just follow the tour dates. It really was that simple. If only *everyone* I wanted to find left a series of dates and locations for me, Flores thought. But little did the cartel boss know, Isaac had veered off course, diverting from the path he had expected him to take, or where Jorge and Luis were headed to.

Upon arriving in Guadalajara the two sicarios - who had been given the location of where the Flores hired limousine had picked up Isaac to bring him and the DJ to his son's birthday party - made their way to the hotel. The hotel where they expected to find Lee Isaac was bustling with activity. Guests coming and going while others were either trying to check in or check out. Used to how they were received, the pair strode confidently up to the reception, if you had been sitting watching them from one of the two sofas to the side of the long reception desk, you would have noticed that there was just something a little different to them, compared to any of the other hotel guests. They had that look of danger to them which any self respecting cartel enforcer *should* be looking to have about them.

'Where is Lee Isaac?'

Luis asked, not in the slightest concerned about making up a story in an attempt to get her to provide information on Isaac, like his room number in the hotel. He was used to asking a question and getting an answer, his tone - towards her - firm but polite. The receptionist, a young woman who appeared to be trying to take care of three different things at once and achieving none, looked up from her computer, immediately wide eyed at the intimidating sight of Luis and Jorge standing looming over her.

'Uh, he checked out earlier today,'

she replied, after having them wait a few minutes while she checked the guest information on her database. Looking up, glancing nervously between the two men while worrying how this news was going to go down with them.

She found this with Jorge, leaning over the counter with a menacing intensity, visibly annoyed that the one destination they had for Isaac was now confirmed as a bust.

'Checked out? Do you know where he was headed?'

'I'm sorry, I don't, I wasn't here when he handed back his key,'

she stammered, shaking her head. She could see the line forming behind the two intimidating 'customers' that she was attending to. But the mounting line of people was the least of her worries while she had a Jorge and Luis stood there in front of her.

The two sicarios turned to each other and exchanged a frustrated look. Just drive to the hotel - like they discussed in the car on the drive along the coast - and that would be as far as they'd have to go, even if they may have had to wait around for a number of hours. This was *not* how the night was supposed to go. They had anticipated finding Isaac *relatively* easily and delivering him back to Flores without incident. Instead, they were now chasing shadows. They didn't know it at the time but they were now looking for a ghost. To Isaac's extremely good fortune, he had left 'on business' at the *exact* optimum time for him to get away before the people sent specifically to kidnap him arrived on the scene. Something that Isaac, while incredibly fortunate, was completely in oblivion of. Flores had resisted calling him directly, knowing the anger that he was filled with he could not have trusted him to remain calm, and try to reel Isaac in through proposed friendship. He wanted Isaac to be caught with his pants down and to have given him a warning that his was in trouble with the cartel would have likely spooked him enough into going into hiding, possibly ending his own South American tour prematurely and going back to the U.K. A scenario that Flores had considered and already vowed not to have left Isaac as 'safe.'

After reporting back to Flores, they sat in the car and hesitantly relayed the disappointing news to him.

'He'd already checked out of the hotel before we arrived, Don Flores,'

Luis explained, his voice steady despite the rising tension in the car. It hadn't been hard for him or Jorge to notice just how badly their jefe wanted this man, and they were now having to tell him that, for now anyway, they had drawn a blank.

'Looking at the tour dates. We think that he might've left for Mexico City ahead of schedule.'

'Oh fucking *fuck fuck fuck*!'

Flores slammed banged fist on the table, sending papers scattering and his glass of scotch leaving its surface for a portion of a second before landing safely back again, without a drop spilled. Flores glad that he had put the call on loud speaker and had placed the phone down, knowing that he would have more than likely have thrown it against the wall when he'd heard what Luis had told him. Flores had been a habitual 'phone wrecker' and would sometimes go through more than one in a day, depending on how smooth - or not - his life was going at the time.

'Do *not* let this fucking gringo puta madre slip through our fingers. Get to the festival venue. He *has* to be there, surely?'

Luis and Jorge drove through the night on the over three hundred mile journey to Mexico City. Determined to receive the kind of thanks, and goodwill, that they'd get for successfully carrying out their mission, fuelling their every move. Sharing the driving, they strategised on how to play things when they reached the capital. Upon arriving backstage at the festival where DJ Selecao was performing, they donned their best business faces, as well as attire. With the kind of event they were at being so high profile and with thousands of people around, they elected to bribe their way backstage, as opposed to their usual intimidatory means. They approached Zico, who having waited to the side of the stage on his performance ending, and introduced themselves as potential investors, interested in the electronic music scene and that they were hoping to, specifically, do business with Lee Isaac, with him being such a fountain of knowledge about the industry and someone with a wide network of connection. These were just words to the two of them, and completely believable to the Scottish DJ.

Zico eyed them warily, not used to coming across businessmen in such a setting, but curiosity piqued.

'Have you heard from Lee, aye?'

he asked, concerned but with an added element of hope lacing his voice. The pair of businessmen shook their heads at this while Jorge lied to the DJ by saying that they had already been told by acquaintances of Isaac that he would've been at the festival, hence their appearance there looking for him

Zico's brow furrowed, he'd hoped, at least for a few seconds, that the key to the disappearance of his agent was going to be right there in front of him.

'He's not been in touch with me for days, now, like. He told me that he would catch up with me here in Mexico City, and as you can see, he's not here,'

Zico lifted his arm out wide and moved it around the room, inviting the two Mexicans to take a look for themselves.

'Can you help us?' Jorge asked, the pressure palpable. 'We're trying to track him down To talk some business before he leaves the country. It's on a subject that will stand to make him a lot of money.'

With a sigh, Zico flashed them a non committed look.

'The boy won't answer his phone or reply to any messages, here, look.'

He opened up his messages, revealing to Jorge and Luis the distinct lack of replies from Isaac. The truth was now sinking in for the two Sinaloan enforcers, Lee Isaac had gone off the grid. The *reason* for being in Mexico was standing right there in front of them and if *he* didn't know where Isaac was then they had a problem. Neither of them had been left with any reason to doubt the intelligence that the Scotsman had given them, or lack of, so to speak. They literally done this kind of a thing for a living, and knew when they were being lied to or dealing with someone who was giving them less than the full story, and they didn't detect this from the DJ. He'd been friendly and helpful, as much as he could on his side, while looking if *they* had answers for him.

In a last-ditch effort, after napping for a few hours in the car, after leaving the festival, the next morning the two enforcers decided to visit the hotel where they believed Isaac was staying, this was not a confirmed destination but it was something that Flores had managed to pluck from his mind when thinking of when he was chatting to Isaac about his Mexico stay, his Guadalajara hotel being one of the best the city could boast and Flores had been interested in where in Mexico City he was staying, and if it would be a place that he had heard of. After bribing a hotel receptionist who hadn't been so susceptible to intimidation, they discovered to their disbelief that he had never checked in at all.

'Back to Flores,'

Luis grumbled, his frustration boiling over at the realisation that it looked like they had blown any chance of finding their target. They had failed in their mission, and the consequences of this loomed large for them.

When they reported to Don Flores, he did not take the news well, as would have been easy to predict.

'So, you pair of *fucking clowns* are telling me that he's disappeared? One job. One fucking job.'

Jorge held the phone away from his ear due to the volume that was screaming out of it. Telling Luis without speaking that it wasn't going well

'Yes, boss. The trail has gone cold, even the DJ does not know where his own agent is. He's been missing for days, now,'

Jorge replied, his voice nice and steady despite the tension there in the car as him and Luis both imagined the scene along the coast, in Flores' mansion. He had demanded that the gringo be brought before him, and they were now nowhere near forward, but if the tour dates had actually meant to mean something - because they hadn't for Mexico City - then the window on Mexico was closing fast.

'Medellin,'

Flores spat, the name like burning coals on his lips.

'I can't let him leave Mexico. I want eyes on the airport. I want to know if he shows his face. We have to assume that Colombia will be the next place he's headed. But he's not going to make it. We will not let this go unpunished.'

If he had been honest with himself, he would've admitted that it was now needles in a haystack territory. With limited manpower, it would've been impossible to fully monitor the airport, and that was even on the basis that Isaac would *be* flying out of Aeropuerto Benito Juarez, which had hardly been a given considering he hadn't checked into his hotel room in the city or attended the festival there, which had been his reason for even visiting.

But while there was, at least, a chance of Isaac and his compatriots still being in Mexico, there would be no giving up on things from Flores. No admitting defeat. This was not going to be a matter of win some lose some for the Sinaloan boss. The narco corridos that had been written by musicians over how ruthless Don Flores was did not tell the story of a man who would let this matter pass.

As the enforcers left, Flores' mind raced with possibilities. Killing Isaac - because the moment that the Englishman left Mexican territory he would no longer be able to be brought back to Mazatlan - in Colombia would be far more complicated than was anticipated, when sending for him to be brought to Sinaloa. The logistics of crossing borders and engaging with local authorities, as well as the criminal gangs who kept the *real* order in the country would require careful planning. There was no point to killing Isaac in a city like Bogota or Medellin and then it coming back to bite everyone on the behind, with it coming onto the radar of the police or gangs, who would not take kindly to Sinaloans engaging in warfare in their backyard. Which would've been fair as the thought of Colombians murdering people in Sinaloa was not something that the local gangs would stand for either. But, regardless of this, he was unwilling to let his chance for retribution slip away. Anytime he thought of that revolting image of Isaac he knew that he would go to the ends of the earth to make sure that the gringo received *exactly* what he deserved.

He issued no other instructions to his two enforcers, other than to watch the airport. Advising that he would update them the next day with further instructions. But, due to anticipating a much quicker completion to things than had turned out was sat there asking what the chances were that even one - never mind *two* - of them was in possession of their passports. Which meant they'd have had no chance of reaching Colombia, from there in Mexico City. Unless Flores could pull off some magic, then things would possibly need to wait until Bogota. Medellin had been a city which had been a problem in the past for him and he, now that he was taking a moment to think things through somewhat more rationally, was reevaluating things, feeling that creating fresh, and potential long term problems with Medellin would not have been worth the short term joy experienced through the killing of the gringo.

Still, Flores was like a dog with a bone, when it came to the subject. The weight of his deep disrespect felt hung heavy in the air as he contemplated his next move, having now dismissed his two men. A next move which would begin with a few phone calls being made to what little friends he had in the city of Medellin, just in case there *might've* been a way around things.

Because for a man with the reach of the Sinaloan, there generally always *was* some sort of way around things.

Chapter 19

Flo

Yeah, Si's Marisol was a breath of fresh air. I liked her within the first five seconds of meeting her and bloody *loved* her five *hours* later, when she was, single handed, springing me from a Mexico City police cell. See, it's this kind of shit that I had wanted to *stay* in the Netherlands to *avoid*. But, regardless, there I was.

Without even coming close to saying so, it'd been clear to me that this suggestion of hers for us to go out for the day on a girls trip had all been part of the woolly mammoth that had been in the room, regarding what had taken place the day before back home in Dam. It had actually been *me* who eventually brought it up because Si and Marisol were going to great pains to speak about something *other* than Amsterdam's terrorist attacks.

Considering the stuff that Zico had told me that Marisol, herself, had been going through in the more present of times, I was touched that she was trying to think of someone else in such a horrible time. So, of course, I wouldn't have dreamed of knocking this gesture, and friendliest of welcomes to Mexico, back. Plus, I'd thought that it would've been the perfect activity to help take my mind away from the day before. Because there's not much that can take centre stage in a woman's mind, when it comes to clothes shopping. It was *exactly* what I needed. Some semi-normality introduced to things, because the day before had been anything *but.*

Marisol, herself, was an absolute breath of fresh air. The type of woman that I could not have ever imagined up Si getting together with. I'd barely been able to tolerate any of Si's - short term - women that he'd been with over the years we'd all lived in Amsterdam, let alone be *friends* with but the

Peruvian TV star was nothing like them. Like, *at all.* She really appeared to have it all. Not a single redeeming quality missing. She was pretty in the kind of way that would've had people - when seeing her together with Si - questioning if Si was a billionaire or had a massive dick, or both. And I mean no disrespect to Si when I say that. Because he had his own charm about him with a look that, depending on your way of looking at the world, could either be someone sitting in a cell in D wing of a prison or, alternatively, walking down the cat walk for Balenciaga. You just had to work out which way you saw him as and then get on with it.

Aside from the looks, though. I'd quickly found her to be as beautiful inside as she was out, which is *always* the more important of the two. Because there really is no point in god gifting you with the stunning actress Latin looks that she had if it meant that she was going to be nothing but an up herself conceited and intolerable cow. Which she wasn't anywhere even close to. She was engaging with everyone, despite being around three friends whose primary language was not hers. She was funny, enthusiastic and infectious. I could see *exactly* why Si had appeared to be completely smitten with her. Not that you'd have ever got him to *confirm* that verbally. But with the way he looked at her, he didn't need to. If he'd even had the remotest of clues that he was giving it away so much he'd have probably tried to temper it. But that kind of stuff when it happens to you is just the greatest thing to enter your life and neither can you try to dampen that feeling, or *should.* I was happy for him, even if there was the conversation that the two of them might've needed to have by the end of the tour, if Si hadn't managed to drive her around the bend by then. Yeah, she was *everything.* Face of a model and a literal perfect body. Shapes in the places that people would - and *do* - pay thousands to achieve. Such a stylish and fashionable dresser too. The type of person who while head to toe in designer labels it was in that don't need to try too hard understated way where you could only tell the worth of what she was wearing if you knew about fashion yourself.

I probably knew more about the life of an average soap star, because you could've called it a telenovela if you wanted but at the end of the day, we'd have classed her as a soap opera star. Because of this, I knew just how hard work it was for them and that the show practically *owned* them. She had confirmed this to me when telling her how everyone from the show was on their summer break before shooting resumed, and that once it did it would be six day weeks for longer than - while on her holidays - she even wanted to think about.

No one could say that she wasn't making things count during her break. Not when she'd hooked up with Si and was touring around with him and Zico, and all of the variables for what could take place across such a scenario and setting.

When we stepped out for the day it didn't take long for me to get a taste of what it's like to spend a day in the life of an internationally well known TV star. The taxi driver, picking us up at the hotel to take us into the city centre, when recognising her getting into the back with me, serenading Marisol with - what she told me once he'd finished - the theme tune to her show, *Disputa en la Familia*.

Marisol, who you couldn't have blamed her if she'd thought to herself that her day out hadn't even started and our driver was singing to her, offering him a friendly compliment about the good voice that he had while giving him a round of applause.

'Palonca, Avenida Presidente Masaryk, señor,'

Marisol requested as he turned around and pulled the car out of the collection and drop off point outside the main reception to our hotel.

Without being able to understand ninety percent of it, it had been quite clear that the driver hadn't brought up the big news that the region had all been reading and watching in relation to her. Neither did most of the rest of the public who would walk up to her when we were in the city strolling around. Yeah, she had *multiple* people approaching her, looking for a quick friendly word or a selfie. I could already see just how much this attention would've driven me crackers, had it been myself who had to deal with this on a daily basis. Marisol, though, she just continued smiling and with that engaging way of hers, and exchanging a few words with everyone who had wanted to talk. Sending them on their ways, almost floating with their day having been made, possibly *week* or even beyond that. When Zico had told me that Si had met a TV star. Obviously, my first opinion on this was that Zico was taking the piss and trying to make me laugh, following the fucked up state that I arrived to him in. But when he assured me that this was no joke, and told me her name. I had a little social media search for her. And when I found that her IG had more than three million followers, and her Twitter account in quite a healthy state as well, I could see how big she was. Which, obviously, made the fact that Simon had pulled her all the *more* outlandish.

I suppose with the law of averages, and with how big news her sex leak had been, and how nasty some people can be through having zero of a life themselves, it was really only going to be a matter of time before we stumbled across someone who *wasn't* so nice as all of the people - mainly other women - who had approached her for a picture or quick chat. Even before Marisol had reacted, I could already tell by the leery way he looked at her and with a smile that was clearly for his own personal means, that the man did not mean well.

Dressed more suited for the beach with shorts and random print t shirt with a pair of flip flops on his feet - think Pulp Fiction when Vincent and Jules need to borrow Tarantino's clothes - than he was for walking around the busy and bustling Ciudad de Mexico. He had seen us walking his way and was already staring at Marisol with that look on his face. I think I'd seen him before she did, with her never really getting much in the way of precious seconds before someone, even just in the passing, would say hello to her.

The happy exterior that she'd carried with her since hitting the street was sucked from her in a second by one sentence from the man. I had only known the girl a matter of hours but the hurt face that she was left with made my heart break for her. I hadn't seen her with anything *other* than a smile on her face, which made it all the more hard to see in that moment when it had been wiped clean from her by this greasy haired and filthy stubble looking man with the creepy smile on his face and even creepier eyes, which did not show someone to be smiling in any conceivably authentic way.

She regained her composure after a second, she would tell me later that this was the first time that she'd had to hear something of this nature, in person, from anyone, since her scandal had dropped. Wisely, she'd stayed away from social media so didn't know what the trolls were saying about it all, which they most definitely *would* have been doing.

Like a machine gun, she rattled of a selection of Spanish at the guy, who seemed shocked that she was defending herself in this way. This wasn't how this was meant to go down, you could almost see it on his face while he took the abuse being sent his way and, going by the short sentence he'd said to her and what she replied back with, finding that she had a lot more to say about him than he'd for her.

A couple of other members of the public stood to watch, and offer support. Before the guy knew it, not only did he have Marisol letting rip at him, but now various members of the public. He started to continue walking down the street, but not without being chased by a couple of random angry women in their twenties who, with one on either side of him, were giving him it really tight in the ears. He was making arm gestures to try and get them gone but neither wanted to know about it.

The damage had been done, though. Once it had all passed, Marisol had been left with tears in her eyes and a wobbly voice while she tried to tell me what had just happened. Apparently the man had said something to the effect of if she had wanted to make more videos and take pictures she should do them with him. Boasting to her she she would *love* his cock. Ugh, what an absolute creep. One hundred percent one of those that sends unsolicited dick pictures to strangers online while deluding themselves into thinking that it is ever going to get them anywhere. Well, presuming he'd been able to even afford a data plan for his phone, which, looking at him, was not something that you'd have been quick to presume. If someone looks like they can't afford soap, as well as deodorant, then quite possibly they won't have a phone contract at the top of their priorities.

As we walked towards the street that she'd told us we were going to, back at the hotel, she completely opened up to me. In that kind of way that two woman who have only just met can do with each other that two men in the same position could never have done. I got the impression some of it she hadn't even shared with Si yet. Telling me that while she had decided to elect to stick her head in the sand and just try to avoid everything, with Si and the tour the perfect distraction for things, that this did not mean that it wasn't all happening.

Saying that she was being dragged back and forward between her family - who were *very* religious - and how she had brought the shame and unwanted attention to them and then the more money orientated and driven people like her manager and bosses at the telenovela. That *they* were doing nothing other than rubbing their hands at the attention she would get, and what that would mean for things like viewing figures for the show. Her manager was already on the offensive and trying to organise some chat show appearances for her to maximise what she - and by extension, *he* - could get out of this scandal. And in between all of those, sat the general public. All of those millions of people who had watched her and Si having sex. She cried while she shared just how humiliated she was by it. Telling me how, for someone like her, she'd had to deal with living her life in public in most ways but that *because* of this she didn't have much in the way of secrets she could ever protect. If she was stepping out with a man, then everyone knew about it. And it was *because* of this that the public already knew that the videos and pictures, now online and the property of the public, were of her and a man that she only had just met at the birthday party she'd attended and had not built up a long enough lasting relationship for the content that had been leaked to leave her looking like anything other than a bit of a slut. Her words.

She had wanted to do anything *but* walk around the Mexican capital that day. Stricken by the fear that she would end up in an exchange with someone like she'd now just experienced. On the plus side, she had admitted that a lot of the others who had stopped us on our walk had offered her some words of support on things. But as always, though, when you're fragile as she clearly was. You could have a hundred people offer support but all it can take would be for that *one* person who doesn't to stick out much, much higher than everyone else's opinion.

When we turned onto Avenida Presidente Masaryk, there was no requirement from Marisol to tell me that we had reached our destination, and the street she had told me all about when we were eating brunch. The street, itself, was happy to accommodate this. Stacked against any of the others ones that we'd walked down since getting out of the taxi, seeing shops, literally one after the other - on either side of the street - dedicated to the biggest of the Italian and French designers confirmed for you that you'd reached your destination.

The first thing I noticed were the storefronts, all gleaming glass and shining marble and exuding wealth and in a country where this was not the first impression that you were ever left with, as beautiful and charming as I'd already found it to be. Gucci's sleek, black façade stood tall across the road from us, its gold lettering almost daring me to cross the road like some mermaid's siren while my bank balance was telling me, don't you fucking dare. We passed Chanel next, with display windows immaculate. Mannequins assembled to pose like they've stepped right off a runway in Paris at fashion week. The fashion is understated yet impossible to ignore. Each piece draped with care, with delicate lace, rich tweed, and the finest softest of leather, practically *begging* to be touched.

Further on down the street, we passed Hermès. The iconic orange box displayed in the window caught my eye, and

I imagined what it must feel like to be the kind of woman who didn't even need to think *twice* about walking in and choosing one of their handbags, each worth more than most Mexican's annual wage. The thought - as much of a nice lifestyle I had myself while not being close to *that* kind of level - something that I couldn't comprehend but, given the chance, would've had no problem in *trying* to. Zico, having already promised me a *Birkin 30* for my birthday that time, after receiving a bumper payout as part of his once a week residency at Pacha in Ibiza. Well, dependent on when they would issue one to him from his place on the waiting list. I had laughed so much when he had come home moaning about 'how fucking elitist' it all had been and how he'd found that it hadn't even been a case of him being able to just pop to their shop and pay a deposit, and how they had refused to deal with him, due to him not having any *previous* purchase history with the label.

'How am I meant to have any purchase history with you if you won't sell me something?'

He'd asked them, scratching his head. I know him all too well, though. In a mark of how much he loved me, instead of telling them to shove their handbags up their arses, like he'd have *wanted* to do. Instead, he stood there and *convinced* them to put him on the list for the bag. In what is something he absolutely *hates* having to do and, in fact, generally *refuses* to. He hit them with the do you know who I am? Picking out some carefully selected videos on YouTube where he was playing to thousands in Ibiza and back in the U.K to show them and once this had been done, suddenly they were then more than happy to take his business.

Further down the street, Couture Celeste loomed large, but inviting. When Marisol had told me about how she had booked a shopping time slot in some kind of an exclusive shop that was not welcome to the general public, I had imagined a small personal and pokey space. The actual reality of it was quite different. It was *more* than just a shop. It felt like a symbol of status here, or something in that area. With its brass accents and expansive windows that offered the promises of treasures inside. The kind of treasures people collect, not because they need them, but because they can *afford* them.

Stopping outside for a moment, waiting on someone coming to unlock the door, following Marisol ringing their bell. When the women opened the door, there was none of the confirming names and time slots, when they saw Marisol standing there. I had already assumed that the assistants inside the shop - when seeing their schedule for the day - would've all been fully aware that they had a star visiting them. As soon as she looked at Marisol - and then me purely in a secondary capacity - it was a case of 'holas' and 'bienvenidas' as the door was opened fully and us ushered in. Marisol hadn't been joking. The shop was completely empty, apart from staff, all looking like they'd been given carte blanch to choose any outfit from inside the stock. I'd never seen such well dressed shop assistants in my life. All beautiful too in a way that made it obvious that if you were less than a nine out of a ten then you wouldn't even get past the interview stage for a position inside the store, ethically correct or not.

Everyone was super friendly to us, which I suppose should be the bare minimum from staff in a shop where, taking commission into account, one or two purchases from your shopper could really make a difference to your pay packet. I hadn't come to *buy*, so tagged along with Marisol wherever she chose to go in the shop.

She picked out a beautiful scarlet red Valentino dress for herself, telling me that, coincidentally, while Zico was in Lima for his one Peru date, she had a film premier that she'd been scheduled to go to and that this dress looked perfect for the event. Asking if I would give her my opinion on it, which of course I'd be happy to, she popped into one of the dressing rooms to try it on. Waiting on her, the staff tried to make conversation with me, possibly hoping that it wasn't just Marisol who was there to spend but once all three of the girls standing around found that I couldn't speak Spanish and they couldn't speak English, they kind of just gave up again.

The only sound in the shop was the music that was playing from the radio. Which, as it would then turn out, I was wishing that there hadn't been. Or if anything, they had some non threatening generic 'store music,' rather than an actual radio station. Marisol appeared from out of the dressing room and looked absolutely fucking *stunning* in it. Standing watching as she gave me a three sixty, asking what I thought. I could already visualise her stood on a red carpet, turning back and forward to please the demanding, rude and shouty paparazzi, barking instructions at her.

'Yes, as your friend and confidant I would advise that you buy this dress straight away without delay,'

I said with a smile on my face, confirming just how good she looked in it. It's easy, I guess, to tell someone to buy Valentino, when you're not the one who is paying for it. I didn't even know what the dress she was modelling even *cost*.

While she was still outside in the dress, one of the assistants came up to her with a jacket and pair of jeans that she had asked them for in a size not currently on display where they exchanged a few words before Marisol headed back in the direction of the changing rooms.

No sooner was she out of sight when, out of the speakers situated inside the shop's ceiling, produced a round of gunfire, that sounded like a machine gun firing at someone. While it had only been the intro to some Mexican rap song, by the time I had *realised* this, it was too late to pull myself back. My reaction on hearing the sound of it, was to think instantly of all of the Centraal Station videos I'd watched across the day before. Linking both to the one thing, I just lost it for a bit. The panic on hearing the gunfire superseded anything else that was going on, right there. Rational or not. Panic attacks or PTSD don't care for *where* you are and how you'd prefer to carry yourself, when it decides to descend on you.

My heart started beating in the way that it had done back in Amsterdam, once I'd known how serious things were outside of the flat. Due to the Mexican heat, I was hardly overdressed but yet *still* felt like I had ended up covered in sweat inside a matter of having one single thought pattern. The fact that the air conditioning inside of the shop being the equivalent of the North bloody Pole not counting for anything inside that moment. Once I heard the gunfire. All I wanted to do was get out of there. Even when I was leaving the shop, in a hurry, I could now hear the rapper on the track while a few solitary - more like shotguns now - bullets were being fired in the background in time to the Cuban style hook. Not that this mattered in any way to me. Such was my panic that I didn't stop to ask any of the staff to let me out. Taking care of unlocking it myself before hitting the street. Closing the door behind me and hearing the latch close behind me, locking me out.

'Come on, babe. It was just a song. Pull it together.'

I told myself, as I looked around the street, while I found it was *Zico's* voice who was telling me this in my head, bending over trying to catch my breath. Possibly some kind of a coping mechanism because it hadn't been intended. As I looked around the street, with everyone just strolling past the shops and, more importantly, not looking anything close to people who had heard someone firing off rounds of bullets, it offered more assurance that I had flipped out over nothing other than the beginning of a song. Peeking through the window of Couture Celeste the staff were *also* not showing signs of any gunmen running around inside and, in fact, the only thing that had appeared to disturb them was the scene they'd just been treated to, by me. The one where a customer had, and completely out of nowhere, had just upped and ran from their shop. I'm sure one had initially thought I'd stolen something as they followed behind me until I left but - I assumed - through noticing that once I left I didn't go anywhere, they didn't pursue me outside to the street.

Happy that there hadn't been any gunfire but still left to now calm myself down, I saw no point in ringing the bell to get back into the shop and join Marisol. I was a little embarrassed by what I'd just done so was feeling like the very opposite of where I wanted to be was stood inside a shop where moments before I'd ran out of in a way that I don't think anyone could have expected, never mind me. I decided to stay outside and get some fresh air while feeling that a few tokes on one of the two joints that I'd taken from Zico before going out for the day would've helped. I fished one from out of my sunglasses case - where I'd stored to keep them from being crushed - and sparked it up without hesitation.

In one of those impeccable of timings examples. I had only taken two long draws from it, standing outside nervously shaking while trying to compose myself, before two police officers were soon walking in my direction. The worst part, for me, had been the fact that while they had been walking up my side of the street, I had been standing there smoking the joint, looking in the *opposite* direction of them. So much so that when I turned around and finally realised that they were approaching, I was left with no way of ditching or hiding it from them. Any unusual movement in front of them was already going to get their attention, while the pungent smell would already have done.

They were already looking at me. One pointing towards me while saying something to his partner. The best I could come up with was to try and cup the joint and hold it to the side of me, with the plan being that as they were level with me I would then start to move the cupped joint towards the back of me and continually hiding it from them, as they passed me.

They never passed me, though. Instead, coming to a stop when they reached where I stood. The older one, - stocky, with a thick moustache and sharp, no-nonsense eyes that seemed to assess me for any threat posed. Carrying himself with authority. His hands constantly resting near his belt, where his handcuffs and radio dangled - immediately started talking directly to me with a pissed off look on his face. The obligatory fast paced Spanish which I couldn't understand, although I *did* understand the 'marijuana' part. Which really was all I needed to know. As he was saying this to me, the other one, a much younger officer who looked like he was fresh from police academy was already on the other side of me, his grip around my wrist, having spied the joint I'd been making an attempt at hiding. The young boy all smiles and proud of himself as he lifted my hand up to show the other one what I was concealing.

The older one just comedy tutted at this while shaking his head, almost in disappointment but most definitely mock rather than authentic. The cuffs were around my wrists and the older one talking into his radio before I'd fully taken any of this on board. I had a dizzy spell while straining to keep standing upright, instead of just collapsing on the pavement. If I had been arrested, which the cuffs were a little bit of a giveaway, there then I wasn't sure if they had read me my rights although that would've been a lot more clear if I'd been able to understand what they had *said* to me, since they'd stopped to talk to me.

I wasn't sure if it was just paranoia on my part but I'd been given the impression that they'd been left *extra* pleased by the fact that it hadn't just been some local having a crafty little puff they'd caught. Almost like, being a tourist, of sorts, I had been a level or two above this, in terms of a scalp for them both. I got it. Coppers back in the U.K would be the same, if they thought holiday makers were looking at a place like Britain that they could just go and feel like they could do as they pleased. Amsterdam was not one of those cities where I could give this same example of, yeah a *lot* of Amsterdammers absolutely hated that out of towners would come visit and walk around stoned, but that, obviously, was not helped by the easily available weed in such a liberal city as there. So was not exactly apples to apples with anywhere else.

I was trying to tell them that it had just been a couple of tokes on a joint and was trying to explain that I had been in Amsterdam the day before and that I'd just had a panic attack and for them to ask the staff of Couture Celeste, alongside my friend, Marisol Bolivar, who was in the middle of getting changed.

The old one just shook his head and told me 'no ingles' while the younger one standing to my other side clearly *could* as he just laughed while telling me, 'sure, you're friends with Marisol Bolivar. What else? Married to Rafael Marquez?'

whoever he was when he was at home. It was quite evident, though. Neither were in the mood to just shrug all of this off and just go about their day and let me go about mine. Obviously, had I stopped for a second and thought about things, I wouldn't have sparked it up, not there. While smoking in public has always been something I'd done. You had to know where and when you should or shouldn't do it. The richest street in the whole of Mexico City? Yeah, in hindsight, not the best place to engage in anything illegal, not when there's sure to be a higher police presence, simply on account of the price tags on some - most - of the items on sale along the one street. From two thousand dollar Valentino dress to a two *million* dollars Rolex. Even so? While I was in no position to argue my case. Considering this was taking place in a city where it was possible to buy a gram of cocaine for the price of a good coffee in Europe, I'd felt like maybe this was all a little *extra*, for nothing more than a few tokes from a joint?

I think it was, also, due to where I'd been apprehended that it had taken a matter of one to two minutes tops - stood there on the street in cuffs - before a police car came crawling down the busy street. The young officer wasting no time in pushing me into the back of the Nissan - of some shape or form - while the old one exchanged some words with the two officers sat in the front. The bang on the roof from the young officer the signal that I was now in place and ready for transporting.

Just as the car was driving away, I turned around to see Marisol coming rushing out the shop. Due to being handcuffed I couldn't bang on the windows or anything like that but through craning my neck around, we managed to lock eyes enough for her to watch me inside the car going down the road. Just as her and the shop was disappearing from view, I saw her rushing back into Couture Celeste again. Despite how fucked up this was. I was just happy to know that she'd *seen* it. Because at least I had someone who could get a message to Zico, to help get me back *out* again.

Marisol had other ideas, though.

On arrival at the station, which had seemed a good ten miles away from where I'd been picked up. I was escorted through the entrance and brought to what I'd assumed was some front desk where they would book in the arrested. The air thick with the smell of urine and disinfectant, my wrists aching from the too-tight cuffs, skin beginning to break on my right hand with the left sure to follow if they didn't remove them and soon. The room was without windows so required fluorescent lights which buzzed overhead, casting a harsh glow over the grimy, worn-out counter. Behind the desk, a bored-looking officer glanced up lazily, muttering something to the officer who had brought me in. Whatever it was that they were saying was well over my head although I *did* manage to catch the word 'English' being mentioned. Once they'd finished speaking, it appeared that plans had now changed and I was told to sit on one of the benches close to the desk. Just when I thought I was getting out of those fucking handcuffs too, I sat pissed off wondering what was going on.

After being made to wait on an English speaking officer to arrive to deal with me, I was helped up from the bench - well, *grabbed* really - and shoved forward towards the desk, facing a tired-looking woman in uniform who motioned for me to empty my pockets. The process was mechanical. My phone, handbag, even the loose change I had in my pockets was dumped onto the counter. Laces removed from my trainers. She scribbled down notes, glancing up occasionally at me, then rattled off a series of questions. My name, where I was from, if I knew why I was being arrested. My responses felt like they echoed into some cold and indifferent vacuum. As she handed me a form to sign, I couldn't help but think that none of this was actually taking place and that I was going to wake up on the plane with my eye mask providing nothing but darkness while the sounds of the plane were muted from my earplugs. This wasn't supposed to happen. Fuck? I'd flown almost six thousand miles for *protection*. Not this.

'Follow me,'

one officer barked, grabbing me roughly by the arm, handcuffs now removed. The walk to the cells was short and noisy - as we passed other cells - but felt eternal. While we walked, I asked about my one phone call and the officer just laughed at this while telling me that I must've watched a lot of movies. Every step further into the station felt like a step deeper from any hope of getting out. The rusty steel cell door clanged open, and the smell hit me. Sour, dank, like mildew and overpowering BO - from a cell that I was not surprised to see minus windows or air con - mixed together in the damp air.

The cell was small, barely large enough for the iron bunk that was bolted to the wall. There was a filthy toilet in the corner with zero in the way of privacy, just sitting there, mocking me. I glanced around at the other women already crammed in, some with hard expressions, others just as concerned as I was. I took a seat on the cold, hard bench, pulling my knees up to my chest, trying to make myself smaller. Almost like if I'd been able to do this effectively then no one else inside the cell would even be able to notice me.

As I was pushed into the cramped, filthy cell, and left there to look after myself. I was told that I'd be called when they were ready for me. I immediately felt the weight of all the eyes on me. The small room was packed with women of various ages, all of them Mexican, their faces a mix of hardened resolve and exhaustion. This, not exactly helping me to blend in. While my brown skin was closer to most inside the cell, my English accent marked me as an outsider.

A few women - who from body language looked to either already be friends or had forged an alliance while stuck inside the cell - began speaking to me in Spanish, their voices, as well as facial expressions, with the undertones of curiosity and suspicion. I struggled to follow their rapid-fire words, trying to piece together fragments out of any of the Spanish I'd picked up over the years, while wishing all my summers spent in Ibiza had been in a place that hadn't spoken as much English as it had. I caught the word 'gringa' tossed around a couple of times. A term that stung, not just for its directness and that I was being singled out by others in the cell, but for how it underscored my difference, my *foreignness* to them. Some of them stood around laughed, not cruelly, as such but more dismissively, clearly amused by my confusion and inability to respond. Like I was stupid in their eyes.

One woman, tall with a hard stare and a face like a Rottweiler, muttered something in broken English that made my stomach twist. It sounded like she was accusing me of thinking I was better than them, and the others chuckled darkly, a sound that raised the tension in the room. I'd done nothing to earn this accusation other than be stuck in the same cell as them, with no way to communicate. Surely they'd have seen that as the reason rather than to judge me as the aloof type? Maybe it was the clothes I was wearing that also added to this? The majority of them had been dressed like shit but for all I had known, maybe the majority of them hadn't had exactly full wardrobes in the first place, which I'd have totally respected. But, at the same time, just because I had nice looking clothes on that were made by world famous designer fashion houses, this did not make it my fault that they *never*.

I'd never been scared of any other woman, regardless of how tough or unhinged they looked to be. Growing up where I'd done in South London you had to be able to look after yourself. Be that verbally or physically and I had always found that, If deployed correctly. Any threat could be effectively dealt with by a few carefully chosen words, to let the other person know what they were dealing with. This setting, though? Well, this was completely different and a *long* way away from London Town, plus when you're looking to get *out* of a police cell, sometimes it might be better for you if you weren't to commit *further* crimes while detained. Sometimes you just have to cut your cloth accordingly, and that was *one* of those examples.

I tried to keep my head down, staying quiet, but that only drew more attention. Someone shoved me slightly as they moved past, muttering something in their own language about me, and I stumbled, quickly regaining my balance before I fell.

The space was too small to find a corner to hide in and too cramped to avoid brushing against the others, never mind the smell of anyone in there that you were remotely close to. A smell that I too would no doubt end up succumbing to - if left in there long enough - in what felt like a greenhouse, because there's only so much deodorant can stand up to. They never show a commercial actor for Nivea, while showing how good the product is and what it can resist, shoved into a baking hot Mexican police cell, do they? The atmosphere inside there felt saturated in mistrust from every direction, pressing down on me from all sides.

As the hours dragged on, the majority of cell mates still stuck in there ignored me, lost in their own worries or attention diverted by someone new being introduced to the group. Others occasionally glanced my way, unsure what to make of the English woman who had looked like the obligatory fish out of water. My nerves were completely frayed. Every sound, the clinking of keys, the scuffle of feet and scream and shout from other nearby cells made me flinch, afraid that things were about to get worse.

Time felt like it was crawling, and every moment in that cell made me feel more disconnected from myself, while having to deal with the incessant thoughts, and the roads that those individual thoughts would end up travelling down. I couldn't understand the vast majority of what was being said, and, of course, no one inside there with me were the kind to help. I felt so utterly alone, despite being surrounded by people. I wondered if Zico now knew about what had happened and what he was doing on the subject and where he now was. Generally, if he ran into bother when away for work, which wasn't exactly a rare thing to happen while away, Lee would've been his first phone call but with him going missing in action. Zico would have to work it out for himself but I assumed that he would make a start by trying to find a lawyer to get me sprung.

How long was I going to even be here and what likely punishment was there going to be for me, though? The two main questions running through my mind. Those then producing the follow secondary questions such as was this going to prove to be a problem when trying to fly from Mexico to Colombia with a criminal record, because I knew certain countries would literally black ball you from entering their borders if you held one. Not that it really mattered but that realisation now had me thinking that I would no longer be able to travel to America again. Meh, I'd seen enough of it by then and had I never went back again I'm sure I'd have been able to live my life, quite comfortably, without being too cut up about it.

Should I have offered a bribe to the original officers? This had been my first trip to Latin America so I hadn't been sure of the 'etiquette' but had been to enough countries where the offer of some money to any law enforcement would've been enough to remedy - and remove - *all* of your problems. Fuck? Me and Zico had experienced this first hand when enjoying a summer holiday in Bali. This happening when we'd had our hotel grass us - pun intended - up to the local police for smoking weed on our room's balcony. Zico literally opening his pockets and offering the contents to the officers who had attended the scene. The two officers happy to split the approximately seventy five pounds worth of the local currency between them. But if this approach *didn't* go down in the way you'd have hoped? *Then* you've got a charge for attempted bribery being slapped onto your existing charge sheet. It's a bit of a balance to strike when offering a copper a bribe and if you get it wrong then the punishment will be even *worse* for you.

The hours crawled by, my body sore from the uncomfortable positions I'd found myself trying to get by while inside the cell. The lights too bright to rest, the constant noise just as preventative. My thoughts swirled, what if they *didn't* let me go? What if they charged me, but didn't let me go? One of these stupid, not to mention completely disproportionate, punishments that you hear about like seven days in jail, or something like that? The idea of being stuck here, in a foreign country, for God knows how long, made my chest tighten with irrational panic. I could hear the others muttering in Spanish, some shouting occasionally, but I couldn't make out most of it and had stopped trying hours before. I felt isolated, like I didn't belong there but had no way out.

After what felt like a lifetime, the metal clang of the cell door echoed through the corridor. I looked up, expecting to be possibly called for my interview, *hoping* that this would be the case, so that it may see me closer to being released. On the *other* side of the scale, though. Maybe even a transfer to a more secure facility. But instead, and in an almost anti climatic way but one which I was more than happy to accept, the officer simply said,

'You're free to go.'

For a moment, I couldn't process it. I blinked, my mouth dry, as I slowly stood, moving toward the door as if in a daze. As I reached the cell door I looked around and caught the envious looks from some of my now ex cell mates. The looks on the ones who had been the most hostile towards me for my stay almost made it worth *being* arrested, just to see. Well, almost, yeah? Free, though? Just like that? I didn't ask questions, even if it hadn't made any sense. Gift horses and mouths, gift horses and mouths I kept over playing in my head as I walked with him. Because why the hell would the police go to the trouble of arresting someone, transporting them to the cop shop and going through the whole process of booking them into the policing system? I stepped out, the tension in my muscles releasing all at once. I was escorted back to the front desk, and when emerging into the main reception, that's where I saw Marisol.

Standing with that trademark smile, posing for photographs with some of the officers and planting kisses on the cheeks of a few who had been brazen enough to ask, turning them into puddles there on the station floor. Leaving them blushing and smiling bashfully at someone famous having just given them a peck. She was in the middle of having another picture taken when she spied me walking through with the officer, to retrieve my belongings. Giving me a quick wave with a massive smile forming on her face before mouthing to me that everything was fine.

As she would go onto explain to me, once we'd left the front doors of the station. Police officers in Latin America were not averse to playing by their *own* set of rules, when it came to enforcing the rule of law, and she had been sure that if she'd travelled to the station to speak up for me, it would've been enough to be the difference between me being charged or released without any repercussion. Thank god for Marisol's TV star status and *also* for the corrupt Mexican police officer. The kind who would be happy to make a decision on which punishment to issue someone with *purely* down to who they knew. Marisol had told the desk officer that I'd been a guest of hers and had flown all the way from Europe for a trip to see her. Asking them what kind of a welcome would I have found it to be in my first trip to Latin America, with this treatment I'd been subjected to?

Apparently, while she was pleading for my release. Two other officers had passed by and, noticing who it was, stopped to ask if she would take a photo with them and she'd replied that she would take all the photos they liked, *if* her friend was released. This had been enough for one of the officers - I'm not sure if of a higher rank or what not - to tell the one behind the desk to arrange for my release.

'You look like you've had a bit of an experience, I think you need some wine. Actually, not *some*. A *lot*!'

Marisol said as we made our way towards the taxi that she'd had drive her out to the station and asked to wait outside for her with the car on the meter while she tried to get me freed. This being the *third* station that she had tried in a row, when looking to find where I'd been carted off to.

'You know what, Marisol. What I *really* need is a big fat fucking joint but, erm, … you know? I think I may just hang off on that until later on,'

I laughed, poking a bit of fun at myself, now that I was in a place where I could comfortably do so.

'But, yeah, babe. Wine is something I *definitely* could do with,'

I confirmed to Marisol while telling her that we should find a bar somewhere that I could buy her a glass or two. After what she had just done for me, if ever anyone had done something to deserve having a drink bought for them, it was the telenovela actress Marisol Bolivar.

Although, from that afternoon, onwards. To me, she would just be plain 'Marisol.'

Chapter 20

Lee

Not quite fully rested and recovered - it would've taken a couple of *months* for that, not two days - but as convalesced as much as I was ever going to get the chance to have, I was in a *much* better position for travelling to Medellin to join up with my boy, Zico. Following an unplanned and extended two days in Acapulco I had gotten the rest that I'd so sorely required. I thought going loco down in Acapulco was just the name of a Four Tops song. I was grossly wrong, however.

Was *it* a rude awakening, when returning back to the real world and checking my hundreds of missed calls, emails and text messages, though. As if an agent and DJ agency manager of my standing could've ever *not* taken a bit of time out without finding that it would come with such a cost. As tiring as it was to see how much work related stuff that I needed to be catching, I knew that, at least, I hadn't been left with much of a choice.

Talking of awakenings? In what was more surprising than it was ever close to being rude, I woke up, after what must've been the best part of twenty four hours of near unbroken sleep, I woke to the sound of the monkey, that had been 'gifted' to me by Kenny Korff sitting on the bed beside me, eating an orange. Another three sat there on the bed beside it, ready for consumption as and when.

With it sat there eating the orange and no longer tied to the bed with rope, with the bedroom window still in the open position or had been while I was in the process of passing out, it had obviously been out and about, getting itself some provisions. But, shit? The little fucker came *back!*

'What have you been up to, you little bugger?'

I said to it, lying on my side looking straight at it. The monkey sitting with its back to the bed headboard facing the TV, which was on but with no volume to go with the picture. I'm not sure if it was *actually* watching the football match that was on the TV but with how surreally bizarre things had been inside that house with the *other* monkey, I was not writing off *any* possibility with this one and as far as I'd been able to recall it hadn't been *me* who had switched the telly on.

Alerting the macaque to me being awake, it kind of just casually turned, still holding the orange, and looked at me. Seeing me staring back at it, it reached over to one of the spare oranges and kind of semi rolled it across the bed towards me. Talk about melting someone's heart? I didn't know that animals possessed such an ability, to share food with another animal or human. It was about the only thing that animals have - alongside their insatiable feelings towards fucking - in their world after all. But seeing that I was awake, it wanted to share its spoils with me. I was deeply, deeply touched by this. I'd gone to sleep praying the thing didn't scratch my eyes out through some post tranquilliser rage, but, instead, I found something quite the opposite. So touched by this, in fact, that I made the spontaneous decision to take the monkey *with* me to Colombia.

With Mexico to Colombia being straight road, I'll just extend my car hire, although, naturally, look to trade that fucking Spark up for something much, much higher on the car food chain.

Ok, this thought was pretty short lived when I discovered that it was around two thousand miles to Medellin. And *that* wasn't even the problem, although while taking a moment to not fool myself, it really was but yet was *not* my reason for going back to the original plan of leaving the macaque and flying Acapulco to Medellin, with the most ironic of connections in Mexico City. *Exactly* where I had meant to have been flying out from.

I sat, while this monkey moved onto its next orange. The state it was leaving the bed linen in was not going to reflect well on me and to my hosts who had been most understanding when it had came to letting a complete stranger sleep off their impending psychosis in one of their rooms for more than a day, following an afters. Looking at my phone and trying to establish the logistics of getting myself to Colombia I found out about this thing called the Darien Gap. This kind of roadless no man's land that forms between Panama and Colombia. A region that was infamous for containing a dense rainforest, numerous swamps and mountainous terrain.

So the monkey had to be left. It was probably for the best. If I'd been so quick to change my mind to take it with me, just because it had offered me an orange. I didn't even fucking *like* oranges. What would things have been like if me and it had spent some length of time together and had bonded? The pain in the arse that it would've been trying to get it shipped from Rio, on the last leg of the tour, back to Blighty? Yeah, best just rip the plaster off early doors with something like that, before it goes too far. I was sad to say goodbye to the little man, when I got myself together to leave. The look it gave me when I was leaving the room as it continued to sit on the bed eating its fruit, once again, melted me.

Despite this being a large villa that had to have cost somewhere in the region of a couple of mill, the sense of security was pretty much non existent. When leaving I couldn't find anyone, no matter where I looked. Hoping to say a thank you for all of the hospitality - and the patience - shown to me since I'd decided to to leave, following the afters, but couldn't find anyone kicking around inside, or outside, so just left by the front door and the same one that I'd reckoned anyone could've just walked in from off the street and taken whatever they liked from the place.

Just about the one thing that I had managed to take care of before withdrawing myself from the world had been to call the hotel and extend my stay there, even if it had been a complete waste of money even *booking* myself in for a stay. The entire sum of the time spent *in* the room amounting to an hour, tops, when I'd arrived in Acapulco, following the all day drive.

Leaving the villa, I headed there, back to the hotel, to freshen up before going out for the night.

Checking my calendar to make sure I was up to speed with things, it was the following night from when Zico had played El Dia de la Danza in Mexico City. While back in the hotel showering I found myself wondering how it had all gone. I hadn't managed to find it within myself to begin checking the flurry of messages that were waiting on me so did not know of any potential good or bad news waiting to be discovered. There generally always *was* a mix of both that I would be hit with across the day, in some capacity, and the key was always to aim for more of the good than bad, pragmatically speaking, of course.

Zico but one of a cast of many who I would need to sit down and address, once I'd got myself changed and found a nice environment to sit down and enjoy a few relaxing drinks while facing up to all of what was waiting there for me. The absolute *top* of my priorities before tackling anything else, once I'd found the beachfront tiki bar that I had felt would make a good 'operations room,' was to make sure I got myself booked on a flight out of Acapulco the next day. I'd already overstayed and had I not got my arse into gear then the fear was I'd *still* be there when Korff rolled into town for his next appearance at his residency and had I still been there for this then who was to say that history would not end up repeating itself. But anyway, above all else. I owed it to Zico for me to be there in Colombia for him. Especially when I had already let him down with my no show in Mexico City which was the biggest date out of all of his tour. El Dia de la Danza had also been an ideal opportunity for networking but this was something that I would just have to accept I'd missed out on. You can't have it all, though, can you?

After a few drinks and having extinguished a few fires that needed putting out that I had judged more important than the missed calls and texts from my Scottish DJ, I finally got in touch with Zico.

'At least I know one out of the two hasn't happened then.'

How he responded to seeing my name flash up onto his phone. I could hear lots of chattering in the background which only got less audible by him walking away from it.

'And what would the other thing out of the two be then?'

I asked, curious as to what he was talking about.

'Well, after a few days I thought that you were either dead or in jail. So at least I know you're not dead. So which prison are you in?'

He asked before cryptically mentioning something to do with how I wouldn't have been the first person in the group to end up in a Mexican cell. *This* worried me. What the hell had been going on in my absence. My request for him to elaborate was met with a chilled reaction from him. Laughing while telling me that it was cool and that it had just been a wee misunderstanding. And I could hardly be the hypocrite by demanding further information, when I hadn't been prepared to give him the more finer details of why I had gone missing from the tour. When he asked me *where* I'd been since taking off from Guadalajara I simplified things by maintaining that I had been away on business, which was true, wasn't it? He didn't need to know the rest and I didn't owe him a thing in terms of offering him an explanation. I didn't think it would ever be good for business to have any of your clients knowing just how close you were to insanity from too much of too much. You need faith and trust and if I can be brutally honest had the roles been reversed I don't think *I'd* have been left with too much in the way of 'belief' if I'd known that the man who I trusted my career in was someone who had put partying before professionalism.

'Yeah, things kind of overran but that's all my business here taken care of now,'

I said. Which was kind of the truth at least. Zico asking where 'here' was. Me keeping things vague by telling him that I was still in Mexico. I asked him how the festival had went the night before but he - apparently now having moved back in the direction of the same voices I'd heard at the start of the call, this time I had heard the unmistakable Dundonian accent belonging to Simon - told me that he would catch up on all of that stuff later with me. Sounding weary of what had only been the shortest of phone calls. I could tell that he'd been relieved to hear my voice on the other end of the phone but, following that, was now irritated and annoyed with me. Hey, it's good to feel wanted, though!

Letting me know that I had called nearer to the end of the dinner that he'd taken everyone out for, before ending the call, he asked when I would be meeting up with him again. I confirmed that while I wouldn't be making the late morning flight out of Mexico City that we were all booked on that I would be arriving into Medellin later on that night.

'Think you can go around twelve hours in that madhouse without me looking out for you and having some cartel wanting to murder you?'

I asked, genuinely.

My compassion thrown back in my face with Zico laughing down the line at me while informing me that I was 'fucking at it,' and 'in fuck all of a position to be coming away with that kind of patter.'

I was in the middle of replying to this while he was already hanging up without a goodbye. His tone on the call had been the equivalent of when a child goes missing and, after a series of worrying days for its parents, it is finally found. And what follows is a short period of relief and thanks to the gods that their kid has been found safe and sound. But what *follows* this short period is the anger and arse kicking phase. Clearly, he'd been happy to see me safe but was then going through the secondary emotions of being pissed off at me for whatever worry that I'd put him through, while under the radar.

I ordered another whisky, collecting it from the bar on the way back from a couple of small-ish bumps in the bathroom, and went back to the piles that were sitting in my to do list waiting to be taken care of. How was it even possible to have so much to attend to, after only a couple of days off the grid, I thought before the follow up rush, brought on by the gear, reminded me that it was because I was one of the world's biggest DJ agents and talent providers, that's *why*. The day that I *didn't* have my phone drained simply through the amount of calls, emails and SMS messages would be the day that I should've started to worry.

I, of course would need to re-connect with Zico to find out about how El Dia de la Danza had gone for him but my general impression had been that the Mexican leg of the tour had been a success. Yeah, it hadn't been without a few bumps in the road, of course, but tell me a tour that involves musicians that *doesn't* encounter a few problems along the way?

I thought of the positives that we could all leave Mexico with, as we moved onto Medellin. Even by missing out on Mexico City, I'd already taken it as a given that Zico's stock would've risen further in the country. The rammed Ballam for the opening night of the tour proved that there had been an appetite for him to come to Mexico, and I was sure that he'd have smashed it at the festival, because one thing that I trusted him with my life was that whatever nonsense was taking place in his personal life, he never skipped a beat when finding himself behind a set of Pioneers and facing a crowd. *Another* positive, even if more of a personal nature, had been that I'd secured Kenny Korff's willingness to join Ragamuffin. The phone call already having been made to back home, requesting that I had a contract for him to sign drawn up and emailed to me for quality checking - before being officially sent to him - to me by the next day. Also personal, and not linked to my DJ agency or the tour, was me being able to leave the country with all of my limbs intact. Sure, I'd had those early teething problems with Don Flores - from Sinaloa - that, had the gods not been looking down on me that day in the back kitchen of that cantina, could've seen matters taking the darkest of turns for me.

Once this had all been ironed out, however, I had found the man to be nothing other than a gentleman who had offered the warmest and most generous of welcomes to me, back there in Jalisco. Ideally, as Zico's tour progressed, I wouldn't be coming into contact with any *more* Latin America cartel affiliated figures but if I *was* to then I'd have sincerely hoped that they'd been of the kind of calibre as the diamond geezer that señor Enrique Emilano Garcia Flores undoubtedly was.

Thinking of that scary morning with him and his sicarios and then the unbelievable birthday party for his son that followed the next day. It was almost funny to me how things could turn out. I didn't know if I would ever be back in Jalisco with any of my deejays but already knew that, if so, I could've called Don Flores up any time. Yeah, I may have been an obnoxious dick with zero in the way of respect - respect being *everything* to him, something I wasn't long in finding out - in the beginning towards him but it was something that, I'm sure, we'd have now been both able to laugh about.

The give and take that we'd ended up engaging in - he *gave* by sparing me from losing a limb while he *took* the peace offering put to him by me in supplying a last minute DJ for him - had left us on a nice and friendly equal footing.

Which is all you really could hope for, when dealing with a colourfully dangerous character like the Don Flores' of this world.

Chapter 21

Zico

'To my friends, new and old, acquaintances, absent friends, wherever the fuck *he* is, and our music industry hangers on, looking at you two, lads.'

I stood up at the end of the meal to say a few words, and looked specifically at Myles and Luke, winking towards them. I wasn't quite ready to bracket them in alongside 'friends' and was not sure if I ever *would*. We'd been out for the meal that I'd promised everyone I would take them for, to mark the end of the Mexican leg of the tour. Me, well Flo, actually, - once she'd got back and de-stressed from the lively afternoon she'd had - who I trusted with that kind of stuff. Choosing a steakhouse called *Lalo!* which was upscale but with a casual and chilled attitude to it and somewhere that I'd recognised would've made the perfect setting for our collective.

I'd had more than my quota of bottles of Modello Especial across the meal, and thought a speech to thank everyone that had spent all or part of the Mexico leg with me would be appropriate. And so, thinking I was at some comedy roast or something to that effect, stood up and offered everyone some parting words as we all prepared for switching countries the next day. I was normally the *last* person that you'd find standing up to give speeches, as well. One to one and I could talk your fucking lugs off you but to a group of people? Throat clams up and, despite having spoken English for four decades, finding that I can't think of a single word from the dictionary which I can remember.

But, there, at the meal. The copious beers which had been arriving at such a rate it'd felt like they'd been placed on a conveyer belt. Like if they'd fucked off the cuddly toy, on that Generation Game show they used to have on the TV when I was a bairn, and replaced it with bottles of Modello. With that warm buzz from the lager and looking around the table and seeing my woman next to me as well as my best mate from way, way back, and his - unlikely - new woman. Them and the two from the mag who, aye, I didn't look on *as* fondly as the rest but who had proved, up until then, not to have been the pains in the Richard Gere that I had feared they'd be. Thinking they'd be hovering over my shoulder all of the time when the reality had been that half of the time they were nowhere to be seen, away trying to come down from their night.

All of that, alongside the success of the two nights of the tour. Reflecting on how Mexico had gone, I had to be chuffed with how things had turned out. Even the extra curricular stuff, away from the professional side to me being there. Aye, it hadn't been particularly beige but it had been done in a way that I'd never really come close to getting *myself* into any bother, while, remarkably pretty much every one in my inner circle *had*. Lee, Si, Marisol and Flo had all had some kind of trouble to contend with while the most worrying part of the whole Mexico trip personally - alongside all of the potential banana skins waiting on me to slip on across Guadalajara, Sinaloa and Mexico City - had been my consumption of a solitary slice of space cake.

Hey, life wasn't *normally* like that so I wasn't exactly for kicking this concept out of bed, while hoping that my streak would continue on to Medellin. Even if there was no fucking chance you'd have caught me holding my breath on that subject.

'Mexico, though, man, eh? I don't even know where to start? What a fucking gaff and a half its been, and I think I speak for us *all*, there, eh? First of all, I raise my glass to the one person missing tonight. Now it's been a few days without any contact from him and anyone's guess is as good as mine when it comes to his present location but while he *was* here all he did was nothing but sniff beak, about get bits of him chopped off by organised, sophisticated and psychopathic criminals and volunteering me for a fourteen hour round trip to do a free of charge birthday party gig for a junior narco, so maybe the longer he stays away the better, eh? Nah, in all seriousness, though. I hope that the boy Lee turns up alive and well, *especially* since I'm too lazy to have to go to the trouble of finding a new agent for myself.

Si, a last-minute dot com attendee, who I'd already taken for granted as having lost all of his money in Vegas, hasn't wasted any time in announcing his presence to the locals. Where to even start with the boy, eh? Only here hours, and he's relieved a narco of their Rolex - legitimately, mind - and around an hour *after* that, he's pulling famous soap opera stars into kidney-shaped swimming pools. The same boy whose sweet tooth was enough to have me and him bricking it that we'd ended up with permanent brain damage, thanks to the strongest space cakes known to man. From being mistaken for a D.E.A or C.I.A agent to being part of a celebrity sex scandal. And, by the way, when it comes to you and Marisol... For a man with a coupon like Davie Dodds, I still don't know how you pulled it off, but well played, indeed. On the whole, though, your conduct since getting here has ensured that *whatever* I've been getting up to has mostly gone undetected due to you taking centre stage, and I thank you for that... even if it wasn't intended on your part. I knew that when you contacted me out of the blue to let me know you'd arrived in Guadalajara that things were never going to be dull, which, so far, has been *exactly* how it's turned out. Please, Si, never change, my man. Fucking love you, mate.

And Marisol? You've been an absolute ray of sunshine, which is appropriate considering the second half of your name. Your parents must've had the gift of foresight, eh? On a tour like this, it can be well draining and heavy stressful, but any time we see that infectious smile or hear that wee Speedy Gonzales voice of yours, it can't help but lift the mood. Si is quite rightly smitten with you, and he can sit there pulling all the fake nonplussed faces he wants right now, but it won't change that fact into fiction. See, there we go. I knew he wouldn't be able to hold that face for more than a few seconds, eh? And now, while you clearly have the ability to make my best mate smile and - though he'll never admit it - leave him like some love-struck teenager, that's not the limit of your talents. When it comes to springing people out of jail cells, you're as good as Johnny fucking Cochrane, and a hell of a lot cheaper too! You've gone through so much shit these past few days, but you've taken it all in your stride like a total legend, and I just wanted you to know that you're part of the family now. If you ever need *anything*, we've got your back. You've made my best mate happy, and you've gotten my other half and absolute love of my life out of a police cell with all charges dropped. *And* without even trying, you've given my tour more exposure than a trillion posters stuck up across Latin America ever could have. I owe you big time, senora!

Flo? You weren't even meant to be sitting here tonight, and while I couldn't be happier that you are, I just wish it had been under better circumstances. The main thing is, though, that you're safe and sound, even if you weren't exactly thinking that earlier today when you were doing your whole Prisoner Cell Block H thing. Only *you* could get yourself lifted by the police and slung in the cells on your first afternoon of exploring Mexico. Actually, let me revise that, possibly Si as well. Only, if you were to remove the 'possibly' part. Once again, though, massive thanks to Marisol for getting you out, and thanks to the Mexico City police for being so two-bit that they'd be so cavalier about enforcing the law. I'm really glad that you're here, though, babe. You've shared in so many of my victories over the years, and it's only right you should be here for this career breakthrough of a tour. Now that you *are* here, though, if you could try a wee bit harder - from here to Rio - to behave yourself and not make any more mischief, that would be just great. Si and I have a monopoly to keep up, mind!

And to our two Nigels from One's and Two's Magazine, Myles and Luke. The two of you, well, apparently, here to cover the story of my open to close tour of Latin America but, if we're being honest here, you've spent *more time* covering yourself getting absolutely twisted on ching and mushies than you have my tour and I've seen a lot of caners between Sinaloa and Mexico City on this trip but you two are *unrivalled.* Just joking, boys. It's been a pleasure having you here and I'm already looking forward to reading your first tour update that'll be going online soon. Hope you're not going to be sticking the knife in too deep, eh, and mind, now. If you *do,* me and Si, there, will shove your MacBook, Myles, up your hoop and your Nikon, Luke, will be going down your throat like you're performing some circus act.

Right, I think I've blethered enough Modello prompted pish for one night. Please join me in celebrating surviving Mexico and all it has thrown at us! Tomorrow, we leave for Medellin, to keep the madness going. New city, new crowds, and God, Buddha, and their mate Allah only knows what new *problems.* Bring it on, eh? I wouldn't have it any other way. I've never *known* any other way. Cheers, ya fuckers. SALUD!'

Chapter 22

You've got to meet the deadlines if you want to make the headlines

When Myles Lomas sat down in his hotel room in the early hours of the morning to put the finishing touches to his first update from the DJ Selecao Latin America tour. He sat there, trying to pretend to himself that it was with some guilty conscious that he was feeling hanging over him, but it was only that. Pretence.

As each day had passed, since he, alongside the freelance photographer Luke Clifton, had arrived in Mexico he had kept a journal of his account of matters. He had not been left short for topics to write on. As a journalist, he could barely believe his luck and, for the first time in his long and - distinctly - blemished career, he was left in the position of having to *shave* words from off the finished draft, so that he could meet the deadline and the maximum word requirement for his submission. Something resembling War and Peace, which he'd felt he could *easily* have done with the material accessible to him to work with, was not what the readers wanted nowadays, apparently. Not in this age of reading something short and punchy but yet due to the click bait factor of it, underwhelming, before continuing to scroll on. Regardless of current trends for how people used their smart phones, he felt that his editor was making a mistake in cutting his legs off while he was in a position to *sprint* the one hundred metres in record time, when it came to running with this story that he'd been assigned to cover. But Lomas would just have to work with the words that he had available to him.

How should he relay to the One's and Two's Magazine online readers to the goings on in Mexico, though? Because if there was one thing that he was not short on, it was angles and options on how to frame things. He'd sat - when beginning the piece - musing to himself. Because while his assignment to cover the tour of Selecao - spanning Mexico, Colombia, Argentina, Peru and Brazil - there was covering the story and then there was *covering the story*. And regardless of the ruffled feathers and blowback that would be the result of his commentary. If only a *quarter* of the story had actually involved Selecao's work *inside* the clubs and festivals of Guadalajara and Mexico City then he'd have been failing in his remit as journalist if he was to completely disregard the other three quarters of the events that had taken place.

He tried to convince himself that he was sat there at his laptop with something resembling a guilty conscience, through what he was going to put down in writing - and for the millions of readers that the magazine could boast on a global scale to see - and had put this down to some form of loyalty towards the Scottish DJ. But had that actually been the case, either through loyalty or that inbuilt sense that someone is left with when they're about to do something that their inner self is already telling them is wrong. Well, it hadn't been anywhere strong enough to stop him from going ahead and doing it. To highlight how *firm* he had been, when putting his name to the work. He hadn't travelled thousands of miles to make friends or crony up to the star DJ that he had been tasked with following around for a series of weeks. Had he wanted to make friends, he laughed to himself while crossing the t's and dotting the i's on his piece, he wouldn't have become a journalist.

Mexican Madness; Opening and closing with DJ Selecao

Myles Lomas @Lomas1s2s

When American writer Hunter S Thompson jumped into that Chevrolet Impala alongside his attorney, Dr Gonzo, with the destination, Las Vegas, Nevada. People thought that this would be the pinnacle and the very elite of drug addled adventures but if the legendary writer was still alive today there is no doubt that he would have no choice but to concede that the Scottish DJ with the exotic South American sounding name, DJ Selecao, and his small entourage, in their short time on tour, have eclipsed the two drug fiends of writer and attorney - in search of the American dream - on every level.

The reason for this comparison between the two events, and events they most certainly were and are, with one of them currently taking place and around a quarter into it? For Hunter S Thompson, acclaimed master of his craft who was not averse to a hell raising drug fuelled adventure or ten, we have his kindred spirit reincarnated in the form of the DJ from Scotland who, over the years, has honed his craft, won the respect of his peers but has, without question, 'enjoyed' himself in the process. As for Dr Gonzo, the erratic and unpredictable narcotic addicted support system? He has been met with a worthy adversary in Selecao's agent, Lee Isaac. The every bit as eccentric and, frankly, batshit assistant to their main attraction of a client. Conductor of chaos, only, with more drugs on Isaac's part. A man who, assumably, watched Scarface and saw Al Pacino's 'Tony Montana's' character's cocaine consumption and saw it as a challenge.

It had taken only a few hours in their company - while both DJ and agent sat sniffing cocaine in the back of a stretch limousine, supplied to ferry them to an impromptu and secretive off the books set, for Selecao, at the twenty first birthday party for a prominent Sinaloan junior narco - for me to see just what box office this upcoming tour of Latin America was about to go on to be. And as the time spent following them around Mexico - on the first stop of the three week tour - had gone over those five days, as I followed them from set to set, piggybacking on the backs of this Mexican madness across Mazatlan - in - Sinaloa, Guadalajara and Mexico City? Box office? Absolute cinema.

While sent by One's and Two's to cover this Latin American tour it was with firmly at the front of mind the backstory of the Grammy nominated DJ, and his connection to this part of the world, and the likelihood that this was not just going to be a by the numbers House Music DJ tour. Something that the early days of the tour, while still in its first country out of five planned, confirmed to me.

Selecao, a DJ, already with links to the now defunct Bogota Cartel and now finding himself getting friendly with not so much the Mexican equivalent but Waitrose - from the Sinaloa contingent - to the Bogota Cartel's Tesco. This magnetism between Duncan senior / Duncan junior and Latin American drug cartels very much apparent in a like father like son fashion. But I digress. Let me take you back to day one of the festivities.

Following touching down at Guadalajara International Airport and our subsequent arrival at our hotel. It had taken all of five minutes in the company of Selecao - and agent - for us to learn that the itinerary that had been sent to me from the Ragamuffin Talent Agency - ahead us travelling - had been slightly tweaked. And by 'tweaked' I mean that a round trip of fourteen hours to Mazatlan, Sinaloa had been pencilled in for the day, preceding Selecao's tour opener back at base in Guadalajara, at Club Ballam. Sandwiched in between those fourteen hours? An off the books all night long set from the Scot, playing for a junior narco, Ovidio Flores - son of the notorious Sinaloan boss, Don Enrique Flores - on the night of his twenty first birthday, at his party on the grounds of his family home in Mazatlan.

This hastily arranged amendment to Selecao's tour schedule, a product of his agent's own indiscretions which had allegedly taken place before his headlining DJ had even arrived from his Amsterdam home. His agent of more than twenty years, Lee Isaac, coming within inches of losing a limb after offending one Don Enrique Flores and the none other than a high-ranking member of the infamous Sinaloa Cartel, in a Guadalajara cantina. Let's just say, being cheeky with narcos is a bad move in general but especially when it almost costs you an arm. Something that the slick and smooth talking Londoner was not privy to. Selecao's agent's alleged quick thinking (or panicked bribing) enough to have saved, quite literally, his limb. But this came with a trade off. Meaning Selecao having to haul himself on a fourteen hour round trip along the coast from Guadalajara - and the state of Jalisco - to Mazatlan, Sinaloa, to play an exclusive - and extended - set for Ovidio, the son of one of the most powerful men in the state. Talk about gig of the year, right? Selecao more used to playing out for scantily clad girls more fit for a day at the beach and men sporting the latest in western designer fashion, finding himself in the surreal position of spinning Latino House house tracks for a crowd filled with, apparent, Mexican narcos dressed in stetsons, expensive silk suits, and custom-made cowboy boots.

The image of hardened cartel members grooving to house tracks - and some of the major tunes from across the past couple of summers which had done some serious damage on the dance floors of the super clubs in Ibiza - you can imagine was so out of place that even I had to do a double-take. But what's truly shocking? These guys were loving it and, in parts, resembled the energy and enthusiasm of late eighties early nineties United Kingdom, when the House Music scene exploded on the island. The juxtaposition of the music and the crowd really was a 'you had to be there to believe it' moment and the image of everyone dancing on the makeshift dance floor - which was in actual fact the sprawling lawn that made up part of the grounds of the Flores mansion - while DJ Selecao stood behind the decks doing bumps of cocaine with a member of a mariachi band - who were also performing at the party - will take some shifting. It was as if the tension melted away, and suddenly, it was just Selecao and the music. Because, naturally, the vibe was enhanced by the copious amounts of gratis cocaine available at every turn. From the moment we stepped into our stretch limo in Guadalajara - where enough white powder was passed around to numb a small army, the party didn't stop. At Don Flores' vast mansion in Sinaloa, it seemed like no one could sit down without finding another line waiting for them, or silver bowls that were overflowing with the stuff. Selecao, ever the professional, powered through until six the next morning, keeping the crowd moving like it was any other VIP gig, even though this one carried the weight of his father's history hanging over him. A true night to remember, or maybe one you'd rather forget, depending on your viewpoint.

Of course, this isn't the first time DJ Selecao's name has been linked to the world of cartels. Let's not forget, Selecao's father was once a well-known operative for the Bogotá cartel in Colombia, until he was caught and jailed by the American authorities. Although Selecao has spent years carefully crafting his identity as one of the world's top house DJs, trying to distance himself from his father's dark legacy, it seems that trouble always finds him. Every time there's a hint of cartel involvement, lazy sensationalist journalists can't help but connect the dots, dragging his past back into the spotlight. And I make no apologies for, myself, too, going down that route.

Meanwhile, Simon Milne, Selecao's best friend, longtime party partner and part of his entourage in Mexico, was making his own headlines at the birthday party by getting close to Mexican telenovela star Marisol Bolivar, who plays a central role in Disputa en la Familia, a show popular throughout Latin America. The two spotted getting friendly and dancing close together to Selecao, stirring gossip not just because of Marisol's celebrity status but through Milne's lack of fame.

Hearing it second hand but confirmed by Milne himself, he had mistakenly pulled her into Flores' swimming pool earlier in the night and romance seemed to bloom from there. A true story of 'how we met' should they ever look to bring Mr & Mrs back to British TV screens!

I'd be remiss not to mention how, despite being a 21st birthday party we were all attending, just how tight security was. Miles away from the mansion our limo had to undergo some form of roadside military checkpoint, simply for guests on their way to the party. And then, upon arrival at the Flores mansion, my photographer Luke Clifton was forced to surrender his camera to a couple of men - decked out in military fatigues - who looked more suited for serving their country in a war rather than crowd control for a birthday party. A necessary evil when you're partying with the cartel, I suppose. But being the resourceful man that he is, this did not deter our Luke from secretly snapping a few covert snaps from across the evening with his iPhone for your viewing pleasure.

Through how late in the morning Selecao's Sinaloan birthday party set had ended, coupled with the seven hour road trip back to Guadalajara. Day one and day two did not exactly have much in the way of a definitive line separating the two and it had felt like everyone had barely enjoyed a few hours of R & R before we found ourselves at the impressive Club Ballam for the official opening night of Selecao's tour. Selecao taking his place behind the decks for his all night long set at the iconic Guadalajara city centre venue for his - sold out months in advance - performance. Ballam, a sweat box of a venue where the beats are known to be as intense as the heat is inside. Selecao taking his fans on a musical journey that involved something like a three hour long upwards trajectory before levelling out. And the party just doesn't stop. As the sun began to rise over the city, the blackout blinds behind Selecao's DJ booth were lifted, letting in streams of natural light through the large plate glass windows that boast incredible views of the city, as the crowd kept dancing through the morning. The energy was electric, the vibe unbeatable. It was the perfect start to what was supposed to have been the Scottish DJ's 'first' performance in Mexico.

Following the final track being spun, literally hundreds of clubbers congregated towards the front of the dance floor, pleading for a selfie with Selecao. The Scot, buzzing in every sense of the word, to his credit didn't leave the stage until every single one of his fans had gone away happy. If there had been any doubts held over the merits of Selecao having a tour scheduled on the other side of the world from where he generally plied his trade then those would've been extinguished the moment that capacity crowd - and their highly positive reception towards the Scot visiting their part of the world - had been witnessed in action. From a professional standpoint, it couldn't help but bode well for the rest of the tour that lay ahead.

But almost from the word go, on us linking up with Selecao and his group, I had been given the impression that professionalism and this operation were not two things that immediately went hand in hand.

By day three, and the much needed down time day that everyone were now requiring, due to the excesses of the previous forty eight hours. Agent, Isaac, had disappeared. The last he had been seen was on leaving Club Ballam with the rest of the entourage, but refusing the offer of transport back to the hotel with everyone else. Given that only two days previous to this he had come close to finding out just how brutal and dangerous some from this part of the world can be. Isaac now going missing was something that gave cause for concern, mostly for Selecao even if he had been quoted later that day as saying 'hopefully the c*nt goes missing permanently to give me a rest.' The total sum of what Selecao knew of things was the ambiguous text message that he'd received saying that he'd had to leave on business and would re-connect with his DJ in Mexico City but declining any invitation from Selecao - either by text messages or phone calls - to expand on what business he was away conducting, and where.

Day four of the tour and it was, once more, time to be on the move again. This time from Guadalajara to Mexico City, ahead of Selecao's appearance at the Mexican festival institution, El dia de la Danza. However, before his flight that had been scheduled for later on in the evening. Selecao - along with Milne - had an extreme case of biting off more than they could chew, by way of some space cakes, procured from an illegal city centre smoking den. According to Selecao, while we sat waiting on our Mexico City flight being called, he, along with Milne had been left fearing if the high that they were suffering from was going to be permanent. Fortunately for the Scot, he had managed to pull things together enough to leave him in a position where he could function enough to get himself to the airport in time for his flight.

Day five, and bringing you, the reader, completely up to speed, and the day where Selecao would deliver a tour de force of a performance for A.N.T.S at El dia de la Danza, was a day of revelation after revelation. The Spanish speaking world waking to the news that - overnight - some 'highly personal media content,' involving Marisol Bolivar, had been leaked onto social media through a series of sensitive pictures and video involving her and Milne, presumably taken at some point following their meeting at the Ovidio Flores birthday party. This resulting in their intimate moments being seen by millions. Suddenly, Milne, - a self confessed ex soccer hooligan - purely in Mexico to party with his DJ friend, found himself at the centre of a celebrity sex scandal, thrust into the spotlight despite being your average man in the street. The chaos surrounding this incident only adding an additional layer of intrigue to the unfolding drama of the tour, overshadowing Selecao's performances and putting Milne's face - as well as *pixelated body - in headlines across the tabloids and on all the celebrity websites.*

As for Lee Isaac? Despite his assurances to his DJ that he would be back with the tour by his performance at El dia de la Danza, he was, in fact, a no show with a visibly worried Selecao having no choice but to give up trying to contact his agent, following numerous calls going straight to voicemail. Selecao voicing his concern to the group that he had the feeling that his agent was either 'dead or in jail,' and with no possibilities for anything in between.

With this preying on his mind, you'd have almost given a pass to the Scottish DJ had he delivered an off key performance, as part of the A.N.T.S curated tent at Mexico's largest festival, not that he'd have needed one.

The anticipation was palpable as Selecao took to the A.N.T.S stage, electrifying thousands of partygoers with his unique sound. I stood in the big top, there along with thousands of ecstatic partygoers, and it was clear why this festival has earned its reputation as a cornerstone of the Mexican electronic music scene. The energy was like a firecracker manufacturing plant following a targeted Molotov cocktail assault — pulsating beats coursed through the crowd as Selecao controlled the decks, effortlessly guiding everyone through a journey of sound.

What struck me was the sheer vibrancy of the atmosphere, especially considering the swirling tensions surrounding Selecao's entourage over the last few days. You'd never know from the way he commanded the stage, seamlessly blending old tracks with new and pushing the crowd to keep dancing without pause until he'd played his last track. The unity among the festival-goers was undeniable. Their reaction to Selecao dropping the classic Armand van Helden track, 'You Don't Know Me' was enough to almost take the roof off the big top. It was all about the music and losing themselves in that moment, and oh my, the Mexican crowd were not shy in doing so. This was the culmination of his Mexican adventure, and, as he took the crowd's adulation at the end of his two hour set, it felt like a fitting grand finale to all of the chaos that preceded it.

This performance felt bigger than just another festival set. It was a declaration. Selecao carving out his own identity, stepping out of the shadows cast by his father's notorious past. And with the tour now moving on to Colombia, a country with deeper ties to that legacy, this performance took on even more weight. People watching, waiting to see how he'll navigate what's to come, and this performance proved that Selecao's got what it takes to rise above it all.

With Colombia the next stop on the tour, and it being virtually impossible to ignore the shadow of Selecao's father. His dad's history with the Bogotá cartel from the nineties still haunting the DJ, and as the tour moves into Medellin, followed by the final Colombia date in Bogota, the media can't help but speculate with these upcoming dates sure to stir up some old ghosts for the Scot. Will Selecao face extra scrutiny from local authorities? Or will this be his chance to hammer the final nail in the metaphorical coffin, leave the past behind and continue building his musical legacy?

It's an open question whether Selecao can ever escape the baggage that comes with the last name of Duncan. This tour is meant to be about music, but, as always, this particular DJ's past seems to trail behind him wherever he goes.

What else will this rollercoaster of a tour bring? Stay tuned, boppers, as I'll be following the action - on stage and off - for One's and Two's Magazine.

Words. Myles Lomas.

Photos. Luke Clifton.

Unfortunately for, Lomas. While he'd been fully in pursuit of capturing the story, and, more specifically, too concerned with performing a hit piece on DJ Selecao and his entourage. Focusing with laser precision on others, as he graphically - and as Zico would tell the journalist later, *too* graphically - brought to life the events of his time spent with the Scottish DJ and his group, he had completely overlooked one crucial element to life in Mexico.

If a narco has told you to do something - such as hand over your camera - then first of all, you do it but, also, always assume that there is a reason behind this. To anyone other than a self centred journalist, thinking of nothing other than 'the story,' it would be patently obvious that if someone has went to the trouble of making sure that you don't take pictures, then going ahead and doing so anyway? Maybe they would then quit while ahead, instead of putting them online, with a platform of an electronic music magazine and its millions of readers across the globe.

In a move that would haunt him, as well as his photographer, Clifton. By his sheer *need* to prove to the world that DJ Selecao had *actually* played for a narco on his twenty first birthday - rather than this becoming some urban myth of a rumour - and his inclusion of the photographs from this night, that he had included attached to the email along with his final draft sent back to London for I.T to add to the website for that day. With the time difference between Mexico City and London he had left things late but had managed to have it submitted with forty five minutes to spare.

From the moment that Myles Lomas had pressed send on the email to Garnier-Colston, barely able to keep his eyes open by then after what had been six re-reads for any errors and now readying himself a few much needed hours of sleep, ahead of travelling to the airport later that morning, he had now set in motion a chain of events that would begin in Washington D.C at the U.S State Department and wind its way right back to him in a way that would show Lomas that while he was there to cover a story, he had now *become* the story.

Chapter 23

Zico

Honestly, man. Is there anything worse than waking to a pile of missed calls and text messages? Because you already ken that it's not going to be for a good reason. Not a fucking chance, like. All very much like when I woke up to go for our flight to Medellin. Something like fifty seven missed calls. Without returning any calls or even listening to the tonnes of voicemails that had been left, as I scrolled down the list of missed callers it was a mix of pretty much every DJ I'd ever become pals with over the years and had swapped numbers with and a few of the people I knew from outside the industry. Pals, acquaintances and well wishers, like. I finally took the time, hours later, to sit down and listen to all of the messages that had been left from them, alongside two requests from investigative journalists - one Mexican the other a Sherman - for an interview and an agent from the *fucking D.E.A*, asking if I wouldn't mind a wee blether with him, in relation to the article that had been circulated around the agency.

Bit of a 'candid' article on your tour and no mistake, fella! Glad you're having a good time though, you mad bastard. Love AJ x

The first text message, along with three crying laughing emojis, that I opened - from Archie Johnson, a DJ from Newcastle who was, weirdly, barely heard of in England but had made quite a name for himself playing in Vegas and Miami and someone I'd become pals with when there for Miami Music Week - which confused me for a moment, with my head not exactly too clever after all of the beers at the meal, with more following back at the hotel.

I hadn't *done* an article, I sat there confused as I read the next unopened text down from Archie's. This one a bit longer than the last.

Remember that afters we were at, when you poured your heart out to me over just how much the whole cartel thing annoyed you? I could be wrong here but maybe if you didn't do things like PLAY FOR FUCKING CARTELS then you may be in with a chance of shaking the tag off!! See you when you get back to Dam, IF you get back to Dam, that is :)

Frenkie back in Amsterdam with his usual Dutch blunt sarcasm. He did have a point, to be fair. *Now* I got it. I hadn't told anyone outside my inner circle about the trip to Sinaloa. But from one text message to another people from America to the Netherlands now knew.

And that could only really mean one thing. And it wasn't hard to confirm. Amongst all of the notifications was one from Twitter, where I'd been tagged into a tweet from One's and Two's account. A tweet where they were linking their followers to Myles' first tour update. Considering he'd clearly written about Ovidio's party in some shape or form - judging by Frenkie's words - what else had he written? I hesitantly clicked on the link to take me to the website, and the article.

An absolute fucking car crash of a piece. If it was a fitba player, it would've been Terry Hurlock. If it was a food it would've be a poisoned blowfish cut the wrong way and if it had been a car it would've been anything with four wheels, with some fucking Mad Max style spiked bull bars on the front of it. This Lomas cunto had completely went in on things with studs up. Straight red, like. One of those reds that gets you a six match ban, too.

I felt stabbed in the back by the boy. Across the trip, we'd had our wee chats about topics that he'd occasionally bring up, and when answering it was generally with one eye on the fact that what I said may have then ended up forming part of his article. So he fucking *knew* full well my feelings, about the tired old played out playbook that journalists over the years had worked from. Gave the boy my inner most feelings - in that flying on ching way you can find yourself - about how hard I'd grafted over the years and, in fact had my first Ibiza residency four years before the news of my dad broke, but that those years of honing my craft, playing in some of the greatest clubs in the world and gaining the respect of my peers alongside building a large, loyal and knowledgable following had in some way felt like for fuck all, due to the repetitive use of this outdated trope of having to link me to a Colombian cartel, even if it is, at times, just one line in an article when referring to myself. The same trope that Myles had elected to go with. And he'd have done so fully in the knowledge that it was the one thing that would piss me off.

Well they can take themselves away to fuck if they think I'll be retweeting that, I thought to myself as I put the phone back down, already knowing that all of those missed calls were going to have been as a result of them having read the article. The bastard had went full fucking tabloid, like, and I could see how it had captured a few imaginations when reading it. Because half of those missed callers and texters I hadn't heard from in a couple of years and yet, coincidentally, they all get in touch with me inside the same period of six hours or so?

With Flo still snoozing and in a way that she hadn't come close to on her first night I didn't want to wake her but time was not something that we exactly had in spades. We'd done most of our packing the night before when we'd got back from the restaurant but had both been half pished and sacked it, saying we'd do it in the morning. Well it fucking *was* the next morning, now, and we still needed to pack before vacating the room. Once we'd taken care of that, *then* I'd be going looking for that cunt Myles.

I found him sitting down outside at a table leading to the large hotel swimming pool. Him and Luke, sitting there with a coffee on the table and their suitcases on the ground. Lomas with his head in his MacBook while Luke was sitting staring into space. With the photographer miles away and his journalist with his back to me, I was on him before he even realised what was going on. Taking a second to look over his shoulder as he took a sip of coffee with one hand and stroked his index finger in a downwards motion on the laptop's trackpad. The irony of - with what I was about to do - what looked like him scrolling through all the comments on his Twitter account that were in response to his article going live.

Reaching over his right shoulder with the stealth of Solid Snake, I snatched his MacBook with the skills of one of the finest thieves Barcelona's La Rambla could boast. Grabbing the top of his screen and lifting it up into the air. Was one of those wafer thin ones, as well. Piece of piss yoinking it up and off the table. I started to run in the direction of the pool. Hearing the hurried scraping of metal against concrete, I took this as Lomas - and his delayed reaction time - getting up to come after me.

'What the fuck do you think you're doing?'

He came only as far as he thought safe. With me standing on the edge of the pool, too risky for him to make a grab for it. What if he fucked things and I ended up going into the water, along with his laptop? He reminded me of the police, when they're dealing with someone threatening to jump. Nice and cautious, ken?

'I should ask you the same question.'

His face seemed to get it, although it shouldn't have taken that long for the penny to drop for the cunt. The moment he knew it had gone on the internet should've been the moment that he would then have had to be on notice for whatever reaction he was going to receive from me. Because there was *always* going to be one. And it was never going to be one with a congratulatory tone.

'That article was a fucking disgrace. I thought you were a respected music journalist, not some basic cunt that writes for the Bizarre column in The Sun'

'Ah, come on, mate. I'm just doing my job, surely you get that?'

He appealed with that choice of words which never, ever goes down well. Fucking be a man and own your own shite, eh? Always smacks of fucking war time nazis who've been caught and now justifying their actions by saying that they were just following their orders. By this point there was a bit of a crowd milling around, watching the two of us. I imagined the whole point of them watching was to see if the MacBook would go in the water or if things would break out amicably. That all depended on Myles, though, and the boy failed miserably on all counts.

'*All* the stuff that you could've focussed on, considering we're here *because* of a tour. Club Ballam barely got a mention and, my A.N.T.S tent performance? What? three para-fucking-graphs? You're taking the fucking piss, pal. The entire article probably had a quarter, tops, that actually *covered* the tour'

Now that I had him in my sights while venting about the article, the anger from up in the hotel room had resurfaced, only, unlike in the room, I was in no mood to contain it.

'No, mate. *You're* taking the fucking piss if you think I'm going to fly thousands of miles across the world to cover a story and people like you and your head-case of an agent provide me with so much content that I don't even know what to do with. I'm not here to kiss your arse and write up puff pieces, mate.'

'I'm not fucking *asking* you to write puff pieces. If negative press was something that I couldn't handle I'd have had to retire back in two thousand when my dad was lifted. Just don't be snide about your stuff, eh? I don't mind a tough one footed challenge from a journalist but not you and your over the top of the ball shite.'

'I'll write what I *want* to write, like any other self respecting journalist. Like how you'd react if someone requested a song. Same rules applies to my profession.'

'Self respecting journalist? Possibly I was too invested in matters but I wasn't sure anyone who would put their name to that sensationalistic pish could've ever claimed to be 'self respecting.'

We continued this back and forth.

Flo, Si and Marisol had now joined the watching crowd. Si pissing himself laughing, Marisol too. Flo? She was tapping at her watch to me when I looked over. A signal that either I should wrap up this performance or, possibly, that the taxi - for the airport - had arrived, possibly the two.

'Self respecting? Aye, ok, then. You might've once been but now you're no better than any of those other clickbait chasing wankers.'

This seemed to sting. Almost as if the comment had left him feeling seen, because he *was* a respected electronic music journalist. When I'd been told that he would be on the tour with me I had already heard of him and had read lots of his articles over the years. That monstrosity of a tour update, though, was a departure from what I'd have expected from him. He took a second before recovering again, but I saw it and he must've known that too.

'Come on now, mate. This is just getting silly now and you're starting to make an arse of yourself.'

'Aye, and you did earlier today when your piece went on the internet for every cunt to read and laugh at your work.'

'Just stop it, Zico. It's not like you're going to throw my MacBook in the pool anyway.'

He took one step closer to me, sneering at the end of his sentence. Well it was the sneer that fucking did it. This cunt had went on record and, apart from drudging up all of that stuff to do with me and my father, had told the world about me and my agent's drugs consumption and now completely blown Si's chances of keeping his leaked pictures under the radar. Fucking opposite for Si, actually. Now there'd be *thousands* of people who hadn't ever fucking heard of Marisol Bolivar or, indeed, Simon Milne who would now be looking them both up. Visualising the first time of me seeing him, post article reading, I had imagined him to be apologetic, at the least. But here he was, sneering while telling me what I was or wasn't going to do.

'Whoops.'

I let go of the laptop. The MacBook making a satisfying cracking noise as it smacked the side of the swimming pool before rebounding off the concrete and into the water.

'You fucking dickh.....'

He went to make a lunge for me and I'll never know if it was to push me into the pool behind his now fucked MacBook or if he was going to try and give me a dig. Si - always with that sixth sense when violence is about to kick off - running up from behind and with two firm hands pushing the fully dressed Lomas flying past me and into the pool. Him making an instinctive - but frantic - attempt to grab me, any part that was there and me casually taking one step to the left and watching him go into the water.

Throwing the MacBook into the pool would end up being an act that would go on to cost me the best part of two bags of sand, but at the time felt well worth it. It was only once I'd calmed down later on in the day that the 'buyer's remorse' started to kick in.

Lomas, thrashing around, was screaming all types of shit at me while me and Si stood looking down into the pool laughing at him. We weren't the only ones, either. Flo, almost crying walked over with Marisol - Luke had remained in his seat like the wet wipe I'd expected - while tapping her watch. It really *was* the taxi for the airport. But by the looks of the nick of Lomas, he wouldn't be getting it.

'I'd get changed pronto if I was you. You've got a plane to Medellin and we wouldn't want you to miss your chance to cover your story, eh?'

The parting words from me as we headed back to collect our luggage and head off to the airport. Before fetching the cases, I stopped to tell Luke that I didn't have a problem with him, and that it wasn't as if he'd written the words and, in fact, the pictures he'd taken of me and which had made the article were absolutely brand new and that if he wanted to still come to the airport in our car then he was welcome to. The boy just said thanks for the compliment and no worries but he probably should stick there with his man, while he got dried up and changed and that they'd get another taxi sorted.

By the time we all met up in the airport, - this being one of the only flights where every single one of us were flying on the same plane, well, minus Lee who had called me towards the end of the meal the night before. Fucking hell, he was alive! He told me that he would see me in Medellin but, then again, he'd said that about Mexico City, but at least it was proof of life, eh? While the man might've done my nut in a high percentage of the time, it's not like I'd have ever wished death on him. It was a relief to hear his voice. Lee being Lee simply passing off his MIA episode like he'd been only away to the shop for a pint of milk, packet of skins and bag of Nik Naks - all gathering in the hectic and - very - noisy departure lounge, with near constant announcements at a pitch that would make a dog turn its head, by then, things had chilled a bit. Me and Myles were no longer at each other's throats, which was good for any potential relationship and the airport police patrolling around the terminal.

He sat there, a wee bit to the side of the group, sitting looking at his phone. Well it's not as if he was going to be watching fucking Netflix on his MacBook, eh? I walked over and took one of the available seats to either side of him, sitting to his right. Without saying a word, I pulled out my phone and went into my photo gallery and selected a video I'd taken from earlier on in the trip, on the road up to Mazatlan for Ovidio's party. It was a general video taken showing everyone chinged out their nuts I'd taken for a laugh but when looking back at it days later I'd found that it had captured Myles in the back of the limo, taking a huge bump of gear while then going onto telling a story about a famous American DJ - Harvey Vossler - and his predilection for under age girls, that he would have brought to his villa in Ibiza when he would be there for his frequent appearances across the summer season.

Making a grab for my phone while calling me a cunt, I kept my phone out of reach while just laughing, asking him if he thought that even if he *had* managed to grab it and quickly delete the video, did he really think that it would've been this video of him erased from existence?

'You're not that naive, surely?'

I mocked him as I put my phone away again into my pocket.

'Now listen to me for a minute. That video, there, just happened to be a happy coincidence, that I should capture you in such a compromising position, getting fired into gear while saying what could well be life ruining libellous comments on one of the biggest deejays on the scene. When I was told that you'd be tagging along on the tour I wasn't sure if you could be trusted when being brought into my group. You *are* a journalist after all, eh? Looks like I was right, though. Like I said earlier to you, I'm not looking for puff pieces that lick lovingly around my ring but don't go being a dick either. Play the ball, not the man, ken? As long as you stop pretending you work for a tabloid then no cunt will see the video, especially your boss, Harvey Vossler or social media. Imagine the can of worms you would open with the Vossler accusations? That cunt rakes in half a million per remix. You better have proof behind what you said otherwise the Sherman will be having your fucking *house.* Now I may have, while the red mist was down over what I had read on your shitey website that you can barely read because of the fucking pop ups, emailed someone a copy of the video, just in case my phone was to suffer some unfortunate accident such as being stolen or damaged, can't be too careful, like. But nobody needs to be seeing the video, Myles, pal. That's all going to be on you. Stop with the son of a cartel operative tiresome shite, please, and maybe try to highlight what's happening when I'm on stage or in the booth? It was like reading the transcript of an edgy version of Eastenders, that thing you wrote. I ken it's *all* factual, like, because you were stepping into my world and when it's more than just myself then you're going to find that no one's going to change their behaviour around you because you're a journalist, but you didn't have to fucking *write it!'*

Fair play to him, given everything that had happened that day between us, he had a wee smile at the end of this.

'Fucking hell, I wished I'd showed you the video to begin with and it would've saved all of this sorry episode. Have you any fucking idea how much attention, unwanted, it's brought me. I've had cunts like journalists from the Washington

Times - Manny Ruiz, the narco journalist who had spoken to me over the course of a series of phone calls, as part of an article he was writing on my dad, following him his trial and his incarceration in his Colorado supermax jail - and agents from the D.E.A wanting me to give them intel on Don fucking Flores. Could well do without all of that, mate. This tour's fucking hard enough work as it is and I don't need you making it even harder. And you know one of the *best* fucking parts of all? You're telling the world about my cocaine consumption, and, actually, how the fuck did you hear about the space cakes, anyway? Anyway, forget that. You're telling cunts about me taking drugs, and I have taken them, I'm not denying that, but *you've* probably taken more, you fucking hypocrite.'

I'd spoken for so long, I wasn't sure what out of it all he'd been able to retain enough to provide me with some kind of a response.

'Pfffft you give a video of me taking gear too much credibility. No one, absolutely zilch, are interested in a journalist who most barely even know what they look like, taking some gear and chatting shit,'

He said, looking like this had provided himself with a bit of confidence, following all of the threats, either implied or blatant, I'd sat there and issued him with. I wouldn't have classed them as threats, more a case of showing someone that you had leverage. Nothing wrong with that. Just like two nuclear power nations and how both knowing the other has them produces the leverage that they both hold against each other.

'I know two people who would be interested in the video. One would be your gaffer at the magazine, who would probably fire your erse through panic if Harvey Vossler was to ever see the video and link you the the magazine. I don't think I need to tell you the *other* person, eh?'

He replied something piss poor involving me being a grass.

'Grass? Mate? You've literally told the whole of the House Music world - *and* my mum who always likes to read any articles about me so thanks for that, you massive cunt, - that I stood behind the decks doing cocaine with a guitarist from that mariachi band. And you call *me* a grass. Fucking gies peace, man. Anyway, good talk, man. Good talk.'

I condescendingly patted him on the shoulder once I'd stood up and walked back over to Flo. Thank fuck for the video because can you imagine how much he'd have gone for me in his *next* article, having the ammunition of me throwing his shit into the pool. Instead, I was going to be pretty much bulletproof from the boy.

On the other side of that penny, though. I wasn't exactly bullet proof from some of the things that he'd written in the piece. While, aye, I hadn't taken kindly to all of the references that he'd trotted out, it didn't change the fact that they, at least, were true. And some of the points he'd raised. He now had me thinking about. While he was laying it all out in a sensational way, the facts were none the less valid. I *did* have that stigma of me and Colombia, and now that was *exactly* where I was headed to. Aye, I'd had my run ins as well as a very close degrees of separation from a billion dollar cartel from its capital, and that it had over the years, reduced my otherwise fun filled and quite ballsy and outgoing other half to a nervous wreck through her rare bouts of PTSD, but the Colombia that we were heading to was a completely different place to the murderous radgehouse of a place that it was, back in the Nineties. When it was nicknamed 'Locombia.' I'd had a fleeting look at Medellin - when on tour with Caner - and had found the place friendly, colourful, full of good vibes and with ridiculously good food. I was looking forward to seeing it again.

I'd even talked Flo around - well, around up to three quarters compared to the zero that I'd started off having to work with - when it had come to the country. Showing her various websites and trip advisor reviews, confirming that her preconception of the place was now an outdated one.

While the Myles Lomas' of the music industry may have been waiting impatiently on drama of some description taking place while I was in the country that my father had infamously made a living from. I went there with more of a pro active and positive attitude.

Mexico had gone, relatively, like a dream and, let's face it, it could have gone a *lot* worse. With it being the first leg of the tour, there was a feeling of things now only beginning to warm up and Guadalajara and Mexico City had merely got things started.

Now let's go and confront some ghosts, I thought to myself, sarcastically, as I looked across at Lomas while the Medellin flight began to call for boarding.

Chapter 24

A winning combo-nation

In Colombia, the 'combos' system - in the barrio - was a way of life for the locals and a new world of order that had been born out of the desolation of the 'super cartels.' The highly, but ruthless, organised criminal groups who would often see their bosses fare a respectively high place on the Forbes annual 'Rich List.' Regularly taking their spots beside the billionaire owners / shareholders of internationally recognised brands such as Shell, Maersk, Exxon and Nestle. The groups, such as Medellin and Cali Cartel's, finding themselves broken up, with most of their networks left either dead or extradited to the United States to face justice, as part of the cross country alliance between America and Colombia. Both countries, fighting together to prevent both the manufacturing - in addition to the violence and corruption which forever went hand in hand with the drug - of cocaine inside the South American country, and the knock on effect of the widespread crime and the drug's devastating impact on the American public, once the Colombian produced powder would make it safely onto American soil.

But, when it came to how crime was *now* organised in the various large cities spread across one of the biggest counties in South America, there were no hard and firm rules to how combos were meant to operate, and would often differ from one city to the next.

While Medellin, one of if not *the* most violently affected city by the rise of the cartels in the eighties, and the inner city gangs it had in its hundreds, had a 'combos culture,' which saw the gangs viewed as *more* than just a gang, and were seen as a living breathing part of the city's pulse. Seen by outsiders as just your standard dangerous criminal outfit but to the local who dwelled in the barrios, they were viewed in an entirely different way. Almost seen as a form of shadowy authority, bringing order to a community who had long since given up on protection from law enforcement, from all that the city could throw at them.

Bogotá's combos, however, did not operate in the same way as Medellin. No cohesive hierarchy there, no unspoken order held by a single, unseen hand. Instead, the city's criminal underworld was a network of loose, shifting allegiances, where gangs exist as if on borrowed time, as transient and volatile as the city itself. Territory lines blur and shift with each passing week, and loyalties are bought or betrayed for the highest bidder. It was almost as if each neighbourhood held its own small kingdom, loyal only to its own. That is, until something *better* came along.

Some say these street-level gangs form the veins of the city, constantly changing shape as they pump Bogotá's criminal life through its most dangerous barrios. Ciudad Bolívar, with its sprawling hillsides and hard edges; Usme, home to the newly initiated and desperate; Bosa, where violence rises as steadily as the rent. Here, small gangs take on big risks. Seizing control of a block or two, shaking down local businesses for dues, recruiting the young and the disillusioned. The names generally don't last and with the life expectancy not very expectant. Instead, they're like whispers, barely remembered by the time law enforcement or rival groups have moved in.

Unlike Medellín's tight-knit neighbourhoods, Bogotá's population would churn daily with new arrivals. People coming to escape poverty in the countryside - or from further afield, mostly Venezuela - or to disappear into the city's vastness, leaving behind one life to build another. Here, combos aren't guardians or enforcers. They're opportunists, scavengers in a world of moving parts. For the larger organisations, Los Rastrojos, Las Águilas Negras, even the Clan del Golfo, they are disposable partners, convenient tools for shifting product or collecting debt. They get called in when needed and discarded when things get hot.

And then there are the bosses. Unlike the infamous dons of Medellín who had the loyalty of an entire neighbourhood to call - or *lean* - upon, Bogotá's bosses ran a tighter ship, knowing that every ally that they would have today could be a rival tomorrow.

In the capital city's underworld, the old rules - from the days of the Ramirez Brothers' Bogota Cartel - had faded, but the weight of family names remained. Santiago Martinez and Jhonny Lozano, both in their early twenties, were already combo bosses. The two having joined as kids and both engaged in their share of getting their hands dirty, which saw them individually rise through the ranks to where they now found themselves. Statuses they'd earned not just by their own hard work and grit they had put in over the years but by the infamous legacies that trailed them. Both their grandfathers had been notorious sicarios for the once-powerful Bogotá Cartel, names still spoken with respect in the city's roughest circles. Their fathers, not exactly the shy retiring types either and, in fact, both now inside the notorious and inhumanely overcrowded 'La Modelo Penitentiary' for their extensive lists of crimes committed over the years, and eventually caught for. That history - and coming from the family name that they both had - gave Santiago and Jhonny an edge, and in Bogotá's fractured criminal order, the respect their names commanded meant as much as their turf.

Jhonny Lozano - leader, despite his young years, of the 'La Furia' combo - held his blocks in Bosa with a quiet intensity, the kind of authority that his men followed without question. He led with a quiet ruthlessness, keeping his grip tight and his plans close. Those who crossed him quickly learned that Jhonny's control wasn't to be tested. He held Bosa like a fortress, his reputation built on his unyielding presence.

Santiago Martinez - from Los Diablos Rojos - was made differently to his friend, Lozano. Martinez controlled Usme through his own personal blend of charm and street smarts, a natural at making alliances where Jhonny drew lines. In his neighborhood, they called him Cobrita, little cobra. A nickname that was a direct 'hand me down' as result of his father and grandfather's street names that they had gone by while the youngest Martinez was still in diapers. While Jhonny ruled with a tension that aligned with his fearsome - and at times, unhinged - reputation, Santiago's power was in his adaptability, his skill at reading people and smoothing over trouble, fittingly a trait that his grandfather - La Cobra - had been long known for, alongside the amount of bodies that he had left in a horizontal position while doing Eddy and German Ramirez's bidding.

Tonight, Lozano was calling in a favour. His combo had been hit, a targeted attack from another local leader - Angel Mendoza, leader of Bogotá's chapter of 'Los Paisas,' a combo that had originated out of Medellin and expanded to the capital, bringing a similar structure towards their business. Involved in extortion, micro trafficking and targeted violence, and someone who revelled in the name that those referred to him, Angel de la Muerte, the Angel of Death - with whom tensions had been simmering for weeks. On the other end of the phone, Santiago could hear the urgency in Jhonny's voice, a tone he rarely used.

'Santi,'

Jhonny said, voice low, every word weighed.

'I need a favor. Guitars, if you can spare any, and *lots* of them.'

For a moment, Santiago was silent, letting the weight of the request settle. Favours like this between combo bosses didn't come lightly, even for two friends. Each knew that a debt like this could shift everything between them, even a bond built over years and rooted in a shared family history. But Santiago Martinez was more than just another leader; he was Jhonny's oldest friend, the only one who understood the peculiar weight of their linked past.

Finally, Santiago's voice came through the line, calm and steady.

'Mendoza?'

'Who else? This day has been coming for a while, but arrives when I have a shipment in transit, and may not arrive for another two weeks, and by then it may be too late. This fucking cops, busting my safe house last week. Bastards. On his fucking payroll, because it cannot be coincidence that the majority of my guns are busted right before Mendoza makes a move on our turf.'

Lozano confirmed back.

Martinez took a moment to respond before setting the terms with his long time friend. The fact that there were even terms to be there *to* set, an indication of the friendship that existed between both the young men.

'I can help with Beretta 92's, Colt M1911's and some MAC-10's but, Jhonny. Whatever happens between you and Mendoza, you did *not* receive the guns from Los Diablos Rojos. Plus, any weapons that you take, you *keep* and you replace, ok?'

Santiago Martinez laid down the ground rules, if he was to help Lozano. While he had no problems in helping out a friend, he did not want to do this at any personal cost to himself, or his combo. This was not his - or any of his Diablo's - fight. It was *La Furia's*. But if Angel Mendoza was to find out that he - and his gang - were being targeted with arms that Martinez had *supplied*, then this would have been just as bad as one of Santiago's men pulling the trigger. Life in the Bogota barrios was intense enough for him and his Red Devil group without going to war with the not inconsiderable might of the Los Paisas.

Lozano's problems with Mendoza had began three weeks before when one of La Furia's soldiers - Cholo C - had been found dead inside Mendoza's Ciudad Bolivar turf with two bullets in his chest. The story put out by Mendoza that Cholo must have been selling on the wrong turf, and had faced the consequences as a result. Something that Lozano's soldiers would not have hesitated to do, had the roles been reversed, if they had found any of Los Paisas dealing in *their* turf. But 'Cobrita' knew this wasn't the whole story, not even close. Cholo C had worked for the combo for two years and Jhonny knew that the kid was too smart to commit the sin of dealing outside his designated area. It was one of the things which made the system of multiple combos all living next to each other work without daily murders. Everyone knew their place and, unless ordered to or provided with a pass, without exception stuck to it.

Jhonny Lozano's guess? That Cholo C had been grabbed from La Furia turf and driven back to Los Paisas and murdered. But it was not something that he could prove. He hadn't looked at it as such at the time but now with the benefit of hindsight, he could now see that this was a test from Mendoza. See what kind of a reaction that he would get out of La Furia, if he had one of their soldiers killed.

While he chose to diplomatically not respond to Cholo C's murder, he done so through gritted teeth. He knew his man had not earned the death that Los Paisas had dealt him but to go out and start a war with another combo, based on nothing other than his own intuition, would mean that business would fall off a cliff. Because warring combos is not good for *anyone's* business. Well, unless you were a policeman looking for over time, that was. You can't sell drugs when your turf is crawling with law enforcement and you can't start a war with another combo without inviting the police *into* your turf. You could see the bind that Lozano was placed in.

Following Cholo C's death, things had seemed to have passed. While no response from Lozano, there were no follow up attacks from Mendoza. So much so that Lozano was left relaxed enough to go out of the country - along with Santiago - to a birthday party in Mazatlan, Sinaloa. A birthday party for a Mexican junior narco, who they had became friends with via Instagram and a night where Santi and him ended up partying with the rich and famous and for one night, at least, were able to forget about the pressures and demands of heading up a Colombian criminal organisation.

This departure from everyday life was brought crashing down to earth on their return to Bogota when Jhonny found that while they were in the air a car, filled with Los Paisas, had shot up a whole street of shops and bars that paid La Furia every month for the privilege of *not* having their property or business harmed in any way.

Now Lozano's *would* act. He had no other choice. Had to show all of those small business owners what would happen to someone who would have the audacity to do such a thing and he had to show Mendoza, from Lozano's *own* personal standpoint, just how hard La Furia would defend themselves. In the kind of shock and awe way that would put down a marker and let any other combo see what would happen to them if they tried it on with his boys. He had wanted to react to Cholo C's killing, but didn't have enough evidence to back things up other than Mendoza's denials while not exactly expressing any remorse over Cholo's death either. But now, things were fully legitimate. And Lozano - like the elder Lozano's - was not scared of a single thing, living or dead. It didn't matter who you were. If you left him feeling cornered then best be prepared for what comes back at you.

Knowing that Santiago had his back, with the guns, left him a lot more chilled than he'd been when making the call to his friend. You can't go to - or defend yourself from - war without weaponry and - thanks to the recent police bust on a safe house his combo used which, at the time of the bust, contained half a key of cocaine, ten thousand dollars and enough guns to kit out a Sudanese militia - with barely anything in the 'guitar' - the slang that they often used for a gun - department, it had left him worryingly vulnerable against any future attacks from Los Paisas.

Santiago leaving all things gun related at the agreement to his terms and for Jhonny to send someone over to one of the Los Diablos Rojos' safe houses in the evening to pick up the gear.

'And anyway, fuck Mendoza and all his puta madre motherfuckers, I hope you've not forgotten that we have some *serious* partying to come, when our amigo, Selecao rocks Club Nocturno?'

Santiago said, excitedly, as he looked ahead to the visit of the Scottish DJ with the Portuguese sounding name, Selecao.

'I was texting him today and he was at the airport, getting ready to fly to Medellin,' Santiago continued. Selecao was someone who they had both met when in Sinaloa at the birthday party. He had been the DJ for the party and had got speaking to him and Santiago, when they had taken a break from the party and stood in the cool night air in the courtyard of the mansion that was holding the party. Jhonny *was* quite high that night but could remember that while Selecao was the man's stage name his name that he told him and Santi to call him was, for a Scot, even weirder. *Zico*, as in the name of the famous Flamenco and Brazil footballer.

They had found the Scot to be interesting and funny, while the three of them shared cocaine around and stood smoking on pure marijuana joints. They had all got into their own private conversation - sharing stories about their own particular parts of the world and wondering at each other through the major differences - that the DJ had spent the majority of his break standing talking with them, ending with him having to rush back to make it to the DJ booth, when it came to supplying the party with its music.

By then, as an example of how much the three had hit it off, for being strangers to begin with, they had already made arrangements to catch up with each other after the two Colombians discovering that one of his tour dates - across South America - would be on their home turf of Bogota. It would have been an insult to the DJ from Scotland if Jhonny and Santiago could not be there for his performance. So as he rushed off, never to be seen again for the rest of the night, plans had already been hatched for them coming to Club Nocturno, when the Selecao played his all night long set. 'Zico' telling them both that their names would be on the guest list for when they arrived at the venue. Numbers were swapped, enthusiastic parting embraces shared and everyone all went about their night.

'We need to give him a really warm welcome when he gets to Bogota. Make sure he leaves the city with the best of impressions,'

Santiago said, while looking for acknowledgment from Jhonny. Neither of them had heard of the DJ until they'd met him at the party and did not yet fully know of the level of his fame, while they stood and spoke to him but since returning to Colombia, Santi had been listening to some of the DJ's previous sets from events he'd played at. Lozano, as much as he had enjoyed Zico's music at the party, wasn't in as much of a mood for listening to music, while returning to find the news of the attack from Mendoza and his men.

Confirming to Santi that, yes, they should roll out the red carpet for their new friend. That he would not need for any drugs for the duration of his stay, same with women. Santi suggested that they give him a tour of the areas around all of the connected combos but Jhonny not slow in displaying his hesitance to agreeing to this idea from Santi, not when in his current predicament with Mendoza.

'Ok, I need to go. Ten missed calls in the time we've spoken for,'

Santiago told Jhonny, bringing an end to the call. All business conducted. Guns agreed on, as well as the partying. Jhonny laughed at the missed calls while reminding Santi that this was the life they they'd chosen. Himself having missed some calls, also. Whoever they were, they weren't more important than him securing some small arms for his - soon to go to war - army.

'Remember, don't send anyone for the guitars until after seven,'

Santiago reminded Jhonny, hanging up without the need for any affirmation. Lozano felt like he could now breathe again. The tight chest he'd had for most of the day now gone. That relentless ball of stress that had been bouncing around the inside of him like a pinball, now replaced with a calming sense of security. He couldn't have cared less about taking on someone like Mendoza but he *could* if he had to do it without firepower. But this was not going to be that scenario. So all was well with him.

Much like Santi, when elevated to the position of combo boss, apart from make - and receive - an enormous amount of phone calls, there's not much else to the job, because everyone else does it *for* them. This business model that would see the money coming upstream to the waiting Santiago and Jhonny Lozano. With the guns problem put to bed, Cobrita decided to make a joint and kick back for a while, satisfied that he had solved a massive problem for him, and the rest of his men.

A joint, lying in a horizontal position with his eyes closed listening to some loud music, to escape things for a while.

'Fuck, yeah,'

Jhonny though to himself as he reached for his box that contained all of the key elements towards manufacturing himself a joint. His - outdoor grown - marijuana along with papers and roach clip. He quickly put it together, despite taking another two phone calls from lookouts who were doing nothing other than reporting in to confirm that things were clear, and went looking on his phone for what music to listen to, and have connected to his Bang & Olufsen bluetooth speaker.

While initially thinking of some rap, and who to pick out of Eminem and Tupac, he found himself having second thoughts on the genre, with what him and Santi had just been speaking of. He'd had Santiago telling him how good some of these Selecao mixes were but Jhonny hadn't yet dived in himself. So with his unlit joint sat there in the ashtray, he went online looking for 'DJ Selecao,' to find some of his performances that he could choose one from to lie there on the sofa, kick back and listen to.

Yes, he found the mixes. But that wasn't *all* that he found, linked to this new friend of theirs, when using his performance name on the search engine. Thinking that he would be able to find the most recent uploads of Zico's mixes online by filtering the search to the previous month, he selected these parameters and watched the screen refresh. Once the updated webpage had settled with the new links displaying, the top result was for a English speaking website which had only posted this entry earlier that day. Clicking on it - before translating the page, with his English not at the level where he could comfortably read a piece of text and be able to take it in, he could see that this was some kind of an update from his time in Mexico. One of the pictures near the top of the page, before he even began reading the article, was clearly taken from Ovidio Flores' house. The picture of a group of people sitting chatting by the large pool that Jhonny had almost fallen into later on in the night when he hadn't been so good on his feet.

There was also a picture of Zico when behind the decks in the middle of the mix, and others from his two Mexican tour dates. From some of the pictures Jhonny could see that thousands of people had been there all dancing to him. Lozano, immediately beginning to think that he had possibly not understood how big this DJ had actually been, when being introduced to him in Sinaloa.

Sparking up his joint and with a big smile on his face - thinking of both the birthday party *and* ahead to Club Nocturno - he began reading the article. By the time he reached the end, the smile was gone. Left now with more questions than answers, Lozano was now searching his new friend's name again, but with a few tweaks to things. Because, according to this music journalist, - Myles Lomas - Zico and Bogota had a past, and that it involved the now long gone Bogota Cartel.

After reading around half a dozen articles on him, some found on English speaking websites, the other on Spanish ones, through relation to a Colombian story. Everything had changed inside the time that he'd sat there reading. His joint barely touched, just sitting there in the ashtray, forgotten about by him while he sat there horrified as he began to learn why Zico was linked to Bogota. He read as many articles as he did because he didn't want them to be true. No way was the world small enough for this to even be remotely possible, he had told himself after reading that first article, and putting it all together.

Back in nineteen ninety six - when Jhonny was a mere toddler - his grandfather had died in Spain, while there on enforcer duties for cartel bosses, Eddy and German Ramirez. So was *Santi's* grandfather. Two flew there from Colombia to the island of Ibiza, but only Gilberto Martinez returned. La Cobra, as he was known, returned from the Balearic Islands, breaking the news that their target - a gringo who had turned rat against the Bogota Cartel - had had Jorge Lozano killed by the private security he had protecting him, while there on the island.

The gringo's name, Peter Duncan. A name that he would *never* forget and, as far as the Lozano family, a man viewed less favourably than the Anti-Christ. To them, having lost Jorge, Duncan *was* the Anti-Christ. The Scotsman having sold out his bosses in Bogota by stealing a computer disc which had on it all of the cartel's information - including full list of police, politicians and media on the payroll, trafficking routes and key information of where the cartel's money was stored - was never seen in Bogota ever again until he was eventually arrested but from Jhonny's father downwards. What they'd have given to have had one chance of getting hold of him, and squaring things for the murder of their father and grandfather, and even to this day, almost twenty years on from his death, the slightest of mentions of the name Peter Duncan, still enough to send the Lozano faithful into a meltdown.

And as Jhonny sat there, in disbelief, he was now seeing that this DJ from Scotland was the *son* of the man who had been responsible for the death of Jorge 'El Jugador' Lozano.

This changed *everything* for Jhonny. Yes, he had enjoyed the company of the Scot, and had felt him a genuine and warm person who had been easy to get along with.

But this went deeper than a three quarters of an hour chance meeting at a party. The Lozanos had not been offered the opportunity to avenge the death of Jorge. And it was because of this that the family had never really found the closure that they so clearly needed, to allow them to move on.

Jhonny Lozano now had the chance to do this for his family. While missing out on Duncan, himself, his son would have to be the next best thing.

He picked up the joint again and lit it, still shaking his head over his discovery and the realisation that every now and then the universe throws something at you that you can't quite believe but are also left with the feeling that it was all somehow *meant* to happen.

He took a heavy draw from his joint while he replayed Santi's words from their phone call, about how he wanted to ensure that the Scot would be given the warmest of welcomes to Bogota.

'Oh, it's going to be 'warm for him,' that I can guarantee,'

Jhonny said out loud as a malevolent smile began to form on his face. The combo boss from Bosa then taking another deep drag on his joint, with his mind beginning to float away with thoughts of just how proud he was about to make the memory of his abuelo, his padre, and the rest of the Lozano familia.

Also by Johnny Proctor

The Zico trilogy

Ninety

A great portrait of a seminal time for youth culture in the U.K. A nostalgic must read for those who experienced it and an exciting and intriguing read for those that didn't' Dean Cavanagh - Award winning screenwriter.

Meet Zico. 16 years old in 1990 Scotland. Still at school and preparing himself for entering the big bad world while already finding himself on the wrong side of the tracks. A teenager who, despite his young years, is already no stranger to the bad in life. A member of the notorious Dundee Utility Crew who wreak havoc across the country every Saturday on match day.

Then along comes a girl, Acid House and Ecstasy gatecrashing into his life showing him that there other paths that can be chosen. When you're on a pre set course of self destruction however. Sometimes changing direction isn't so easy. Ninety is a tale of what can happen when a teenager grows up faster than they should ever have to while finding themselves pulled into a dangerous turn of events that threatens their very own existence.

Set against the backdrop of a pivotal and defining period of time for the British working class youth when terrace culture and Acid House collided. Infectiously changing lives and attitudes along the way.

Ninety Six

Ninety Six - The second instalment of the Zico trilogy.

Six years on and following events from 'Ninety' ... When Stevie "Zico" Duncan bags a residency at one of Ibiza's most legendary clubs, marking the rising star that he is becoming in the House Music scene. Life could not appear more perfect. Zico and perfect, however, have rarely ever went together.

Set during the summer of Euro 96. Three months on an island of sun, sea and sand as well as the Ibiza nightlife and everything that comes with it. What could possibly go wrong? It's coming home but will Zico?

Noughty

Bringing a close to the most crucial and important decade of all.

Noughty - The third book from Johnny Proctor. Following the events of the infamous summer of Ninety Six in Ibiza. Three years on the effects are still being felt inside the world of Stevie 'Zico' Duncan and those closest to him. Now having relocated to Amsterdam it's all change for the soccer casual turned house deejay however, as Zico soon begins to find. The more that things change the more they seem to stay the same. Noughty signals the end of the 90's trilogy of books which celebrated the decade that changed the face, and attitudes, of UK youth culture and beyond.

Muirhouse

Living in the 'Naughty North' of Edinburgh, for some, can be difficult. For the Carson family, however? Life's never dull.

You'll give them that.

'Muirhouse' by Johnny Proctor is a story of the fortunes of Joe 'Strings' Carson.

Midfield general for infamous amateur football team 'Muirhouse Violet' on a Sunday and petty criminal every other day of the week. Above all, though. Strings is a family man and, like any self respecting husband and father, will do whatever it takes to protect his household.

A commitment and loyalty that he's about to find being put to the ultimate test.

El Corazon Valiente; The ballad of Peter Duncan

El Corazon Valiente ; The ballad of Peter Duncan. A Zico trilogy origins story.Picking up where Noughty left off. El Corazon Valiente offers a look at how life is for Peter Duncan following events in Amsterdam, 2000. Finally find out how Stevie Duncan's father - through his own charm, ruthlessness and sense of self preservation - went from small Scottish town chancer to a vital component of a well known Colombian cartel. And how it all came crashing down around him.

The Onion Ring

Rule number one in the drug game is to always pay your debts; but what happens when you can't?

Just how far would you go to find redemption? Something that best friends and business partners Drummond, Hammy and Hummel are faced with when their business experiences some "technical difficulties."

Leaving them to find out just how far they will go.

Keyboard Warrior

Be careful who you troll, it might be Norman Fulton on the receiving end of your words. And by then, it'll be too late.

Keyboard Warrior, follows Nora - Ninety & Noughty - ten years into his dramatic escape from prison and, seemingly, a reformed character, under his new alias, Matthijs de Groot.

But with people, like Nora.

Is someone ever really reformed?

Sun, sea & sh*thousing

When the players of Muirhouse Violet (Muirhouse by Johnny Proctor) are invited to play in Europe for the first time in their history. Upon landing on the island of Mallorca, it doesn't take the team long to find out that there is far more drama to be had off the pitch than on.

But, being Muirhouse Violet, they wouldn't have it any other way.

flame-throwing lunatic: volume 1 - the ching is dead

Sometimes, you don't know what you've got until it's gone. Something that the city of Edinburgh discovers, when it loses its underworld custodian, plunging the city into a war zone.

But out of the mess, emerges a self imposed saviour, and, one, from the most unlikely of sources.

The only question being, what is their real motivation, and what is the city going to be left looking like by the time they're done.

flame-throwing lunatic: volume 2 - long live the ching

The follow up - and second part - to 2023's volume one and launching you straight into where things left off.

Corrupt N.C.A. detective, Marcus Gilchrist playing puppeteer to the Edinburgh underworld, directly impacting on Alan

411

'Fordy' Dixon and Boabby 'BBW' Walker and their quality of living, for some 'living' may be a case of borrowed time.

Meanwhile, the reformed James 'Clem' Clemison - a now ex stick up man - finds that while he may well have been done with the stick up game, the stick up game is not done with him.

Available through Paninaro Publishing, Apple Books, Kindle, Amazon, Waterstones and other book stores.

Printed in Great Britain
by Amazon

61927084R10234